PLAYING FOR KEEPS

PLAY
with me

B E C K A   M A C K

Visit my website at www.beckamack.com

Line art: Simply Extra Jordanary

Hockey player art: SVGForYouFromMe

Cover design: Ever After Cover Design, www.everaftercoverdesign.com

Editor: Paisley McNab, www.perfectlywrite.ca

Second edition.

ISBN 978-1-7781330-5-3

To everyone who has ever felt ready to fold themselves in half to fit somebody else's idea of who they should be...

Don't dull your shine for anyone.
The right people will want to bask in your sunshine, not steal it. Until then, soak it all in.

You, exactly as you are, are enough.

Playlist

PLAY WITH ME - BECKA MACK

|◄ ► ►|

SOMEDAY - OneRepublic	♥	3:08
PHOTOGRAPH - Ed Sheeran	♥	4:19
CARRY ME AWAY - John Mayer	♥	2:39
LATE NIGHT TALKING - Harry Styles	♥	2:58
BUTTERFLIES - Abe Parker	♥	3:04
THE ONE YOU NEED - Brett Eldredge	♥	4:05
COLLIDE - Ed Sheeran	♥	3:30
SIDE BY SIDE - Jon Foreman & Madison Cunningham	♥	4:13
DRESS - Taylor Swift	♥	3:50
CINEMA (ACOUSTIC) - Gary Go	♥	3:09
RECOVERY - James Arthur	♥	4:38
FALL INTO ME (ACOUSTIC) - Forest Blakk	♥	3:56
YOU SHOULD PROBABLY LEAVE - Chris Stapleton	♥	3:33
FEELS LIKE - Gracie Abrams	♥	2:32
GONE TOO SOON - Andrew Jannakos	♥	2:49
TREACHEROUS (TAYLOR'S VERSION) - Taylor Swift	♥	4:03
FALLING LIKE THE STARS - James Arthur	♥	3:33
I GUESS I'M IN LOVE - Clinton Kane	♥	3:24
MISSING PIECE - Vance Joy	♥	3:37
LEAVE YOU ALONE - Kane Brown	♥	3:34
BIBLICAL - Calum Scott	♥	3:50
CLARITY - Vance Joy	♥	3:47
DIDN'T SEE IT COMING - My Brothers And I	♥	4:31
MY PERSON (WEDDING VERSION) - Spencer Crandall	♥	3:05

ONE
STAND DOWN, SOLDIER

Garrett

"I FUCKIN' told you."

Holding my hand out, I curl my fingers into my palm three times, the worldwide symbol for *pay up, bitch*.

Adam Lockwood, one of my best buds and teammates, drops his head back with a groan, halfway to a growl, like he can't believe this is happening.

I can't believe this is happening.

To be clear, the unbelievable part is that Adam had faith in the groom.

Standing, he reaches into his back pocket for his wallet, then drops back to his seat, grumbling as he sorts through a wad of bills. He slaps a hundred in my waiting palm, and another in Emmett's, our teammate.

Adam's glare lifts to Carter, our team captain, the groom, and the man currently fumbling for words in front of all two-hundred-plus of his guests.

He just accidentally outed his brand-new bride as pregnant.

"I had faith in you, Carter," Adam grumbles. He throws his arms overhead when Cara and Jennie start making grabby hands for their share of the winnings. "Oh come on!"

See, Adam's a great guy. Best guy I know, really. He has unending faith in everyone. On occasion, his faith is…a little misplaced. Like right now, in that man up there.

Because Carter Beckett is good at two things: playing hockey and loving on his new wife, Olivia. Something he's terrible at? Keeping secrets.

"I owe Olivia too," Adam mutters. "Even she bet Carter would blow it. Am I the only one who believed in him?"

A collective *yes* rings around the table that has Adam dragging both hands down his face, but it's when Holly, Carter and Jennie's mom, sticks her hand over his shoulder that I think he might actually cry.

"I've lost six hundred bucks in two minutes because that guy can't keep his mouth shut for one damn night."

Holly tucks her winnings away. "I love my son, but Carter likes attention and has zero filter. He gets it from his father. Wouldn't blame Olivia if she makes him sleep on the couch tonight."

As if on cue, the teensy bride storms by, Carter hot on her heels.

"You're not getting *any* of this tonight," Olivia bites out, pausing to circle a hand around her bottom half. "*None* of it."

Carter's gasp leaves him slack jawed, and he chases after her. "*Ollie!* It was an accident! You can't cut off access! You can't!"

"I knew this was gonna be the most entertaining wedding I've ever been to." I stab at the chocolate cake Adam hasn't finished yet, stuffing a hunk in my mouth. There are crushed Oreos in the fudge filling. It's amazing. "Caw-ta n' Aw-wie could hab der own TV show."

"You know what would help with that?" Jennie's perfectly shaped brows lift as she aims a pointed glance at my mouth. "Fucking swallowing before you speak."

I stop chewing, and when our eyes lock, my ears burn. Jennie's a Beckett, that's for sure. An unfiltered smart-ass like her older brother, with his same dimples and irritating smirk. But where Carter's eyes are a deep green, hers are a soft, cool blue, with almost the faintest hint of violet.

Pretty.

Or whatever.

I swallow, setting my fork down and clearing my throat as the alcohol in me forms a response I'd normally be too afraid to say. "If you want some, all you have to do is ask, Baby Beckett."

"I'm not a baby," she shoots back, pinning her arms across her chest. It pushes a set of perfect, glowing tits together, ramping up the whole *fuck me* vibe she's rocking in her shimmery cranberry dress.

I erase the thought as quickly as it forms. Sometimes I worry Carter has supersonic hearing when it comes to his sister, and can, like…hear my thoughts or some shit. I've seen him fight enough on the ice to know I don't want to be on the receiving end of his wrath. I like my face the way it is; I don't need it rearranged.

Adam pulls his plate away when I go in for another bite. "*My* cake." He ignores my pout, and before I can complain that I already ate two slices and he's not finishing his, he presents it to Jennie. "You want it?"

My jaw drops with a gasp.

"Garrett, honey." Holly squeezes my shoulders. "Where's your date?"

Heat claws up my neck and into my face, right up to the tips of my ears. "I didn't bring one," I mumble. I had some options, but I'd prefer not to give anyone the wrong idea. I think weddings are kinda special.

"Why not? You're such a handsome man, sweetheart."

I scratch my hair, dropping my gaze to my empty plate. "Thanks, Mrs. Beckett." My eyes narrow on Jennie as she snorts. "Where's *your* date, Baby Beckett?"

"I'm not dating anyone, and have no desire to be."

Holly sighs, sinking down beside me. "Honestly, Jennie, I just solved the problem that I affectionately call *my son*. Please don't turn into him." She twists my way, eyes bright. "Hey, if you're not dating anyone, and she's not dating any—"

Cara and Emmett fold over the table at the same time, howling with laughter and effectively ending Holly's words.

"No," Cara chokes out, swiping at the fucking *tears* free-falling down her cheeks. "Holy shit. Can you imagine? Holly, we *like* Garrett. We don't want him to die."

"What about you, Adam?" Holly smiles at him. "You're so sweet. Carter couldn't possibly ever want to kill you."

Jennie flings her arms in the air. "Mom! Can you stop trying to pimp me out? And I don't wanna date any of these losers." She pats Adam's hand. "Sorry, Adam. You're not a loser." There's a quirk in the corner of her mouth as she looks me over, gaze lingering on my collarbone where my tie is loosened, buttons popped. Her eyes flit to mine, and a playful —*evil*—glint shines in them as she neglects to include me on her *not a loser* list.

What's meant to be a scowl winds up being me staring a little too long, gaze tracing the rosy hue painted over her sharp cheekbones, the way her chestnut hair curls away from her face and drapes over her slender shoulders.

She's so hot, it's unreal. All I can seem to think about when she's in the room is how it would feel to get her alone in a closet, or bend her over the table and—

I keel forward with a grunt, clutching my throbbing knee under the table, glare set on Adam. "What the fuck? What was that for?"

His voice is low and scary. "You know exactly what the hell that was for. Why don't you take a fucking picture? It'll last longer."

Well, fuck. What's the point of having eyes if I can't use them to appreciate a smoking hot woman? That's what I wanna know.

Except Adam is right (he usually is). I have zero intention of fucking around with one of my best bud's little sisters, so I keep my eyes to myself for the rest of the night.

Okay, I don't, but I try *really hard*; swear it.

Somehow, I wind up standing by the bar with my metaphorical balls in my hand, watching Jennie do her thing on the dance floor. Thick waves cascade down the golden glow of her curved spine, and I follow the line of her backless dress down to her stellar, round ass as it bounces back and forth with the music. She's got a teensy waist and a wide set of hips, the kind I wanna wrap my fingers around and—

"Just ask her to dance."

"What?" I look at Emmett, then back to Jennie, and ask again, "What?"

"Looks like you wanna dance with her."

"What? No." *Am I yelling?*

"Why are you yelling?"

"I'm not yelling." *I'm yelling.*

Emmett cocks a brow, downs his beer, and shoves me toward the girls on the dance floor. His wife wastes no time yanking me into her, using me to spin herself.

"C'mon, Gare-Bear." Cara pouts at me as Emmett's arms circle her, bringing her into his chest. "Shake your ass, baby."

"I don't—my ass doesn't—I can't—"

"My God." Jennie looks me over with disdain as her hips move. "You have no rhythm, Andersen, do you?"

She rolls her eyes when I blink wordlessly at her, then links her fingers through mine and tugs me across the space. Our bodies collide with an *oomph* that seems to heat me from the inside out, and when she turns around and settles her ass an inch from my cock, I think I might pass the fuck out.

Her warm hands slide over mine, guiding them to her hips as they sway in tune with the music, and Emmett winks at me as if I'm not currently short-circuiting.

"Move your damn hips," Jennie growls.

"I don't...I don't know how."

Slanted eyes glare from over her shoulder, softening when my face flushes. Jennie sighs quietly. "Just move with me, Garrett. It's not that hard. How the hell do you get so many women?"

"It's been slow lately," I blurt thoughtlessly, then slam my jaw shut. Then open it again, for some fucking reason. "I haven't gotten so many...I mean, there was this girl last week in Pittsburgh that I almost..." I clear my throat, registering the way Jennie's body has stilled below my hands. "I'll stop talking about my sex life now."

"Sounds like a lack of a sex life to me, big guy."

Fucking tell me about it. Emmett and Cara got married this summer, and Carter's basically been married to Olivia in his head since they met last year, even though she kept him offside for a while. Adam's still in a shitty place from finding out his long-term girlfriend cheated on him months ago, but he's infinitely better off without her.

That means the first month and a half of our hockey season has seen me getting drunk postgame with my hockey buds only, followed by repeated sausage fests back at the hotels, fueled by junk food, Xbox, and listening to my pussy-whipped roommates have borderline phone sex with their wives. Things have been bone-dry on my end.

That has to be the only reason I'm currently considering taking my captain's little sister into the bathroom, hoisting her onto the vanity, and seeing what color her panties are.

Aside from being totally and completely off limits, Jennie also scares the living shit out of me. She's bold, confident, and sassy *as fuck*. My eyes rarely leave her when she's in the room. Except when she looks my way. Or when Carter does.

Like right now, at the exact moment my hands glide over his sister's hips, up to the dip in her waist, gripping it tightly. *Fucking tighter* when his eyes land on mine.

"Garrett," Jennie whimpers. "That hurts."

"Garrett." Carter's hard voice sends a shiver of terror up my spine, and he aims a pointed glare at my hands.

"*Ah!*" I kinda-sorta shriek, shoving Jennie away from me. "I'm not touching her," I toss over my shoulder as I scurry off the floor, leaving Jennie standing there alone, unimpressed, and nearly as scary as Carter looks, even though he's twirling both his beautiful bride and his golden retriever around the dance floor at the same time.

I slink down the hallway, lean against the wall, and scrub my hands over my tired face. "I need to get laid."

"I can help you out with that."

A pretty redhead stops in front of me, pulling a napkin and tube of lipstick from her purse. She presses the napkin to my chest and scrawls over it.

Am I impressed by how easy that was or do I just wanna go home and devour a box of Pop-Tarts? I'm not sure, but when Jennie saunters down the hallway, my blood pressure spikes.

The redhead tucks her phone number into my chest pocket and presses a whispered, "Call me" against my cheek, and Jennie's disgusted scowl is so terrifying I can't look away.

With an eye roll, she turns and heads for the bathroom, and my feet chase after her.

"Wait, Jennie! I wasn't gonna—I'm not—I wasn't—"

"I don't care, Garrett. Chase all the skirts you want. Maybe just not one that came with one of your defensemen."

"What?" I look to the redhead, catching her wink before she disappears. "No, but I-I-I…" I hang my head, rubbing the back of my neck as my ears burn. "I wasn't gonna do anything."

"But things have been so slow for you," Jennie murmurs, smirking. She digs a wipe out of her tiny gold clutch and tosses it at me before shoving the bathroom door open with her hip. "You've got lipstick on your cheek, big guy."

Somehow, I manage to miss the lipstick kiss, and Adam ends up cleaning my face for me, inciting coos and snickers from all the girls. By the time Carter and Olivia climb into their limo at the end of the night, my buzz is gone, my arms are permanently pinned across my chest, and every word out of my mouth is a grumble. Even the dog panting at my feet can't cheer me up right now.

I don't want to know what kind of shit Carter had to pull to have Dublin at the reception, but I'm not surprised. The man can talk his way into and out of everything. Plus, as it turns out, golden retrievers look dapper as fuck in a pup tux.

"Come here, Dubs!" Jennie calls, clapping her thighs. "You're comin' home with your favorite auntie! Yes, you are, my handsome boy!"

"You're his only auntie."

She pins her arms across her chest, luring my gaze to her spectacular cleavage for the umpteenth time tonight, then to the pop of her left hip, which she swings out, dress sweeping open at the thigh-high slit, showing me a phenomenal set of toned legs. "Shut up, you twat."

"We should call you sunshine," I grumble under my breath. "'Cause of your sunny disposition. Always so fucking nice and happy."

Man, this liquid courage is really fucking me over tonight.

Blue eyes narrow. "Get in the fucking car, *Gare-Bear*."

"Yes, ma'am."

I slide into the back of the limo waiting to take a handful of us home, and take a seat next to Hank as everyone else piles in behind me.

Hank is eighty-four years young, one of Carter and Jennie's best friends, kinda like a pseudo-grandpa, and cool as hell. He used to be Dublin's dad, which is probably why Dublin leaps across me, nailing me in the nuts, and sprawls out on his lap.

"Motherfucker," I grunt, gripping my junk.

He chuckles. "You're really taking a beating tonight." His sigh is soft and happy. "Such a beautiful wedding. Olivia was stunning tonight."

Cara snickers as she runs her fingers through Emmett's hair from her spot on his lap. I suspect it's because Hank is blind, and has been since the age of fifteen, but he never fails to pump a woman's ego.

Sighing, I sink back in my seat and close my eyes, drowning out the discussion about Carter's colossal pregnancy announcement oopsie. Adam's still upset he lost so much money, and Holly's making a name list for her first grandbaby. Carter and Olivia have decided not to find out the sex. Olivia says she doesn't want to spend her pregnancy telling Carter they aren't naming the baby Carter Jr. if it's a boy, but I think it's because Carter's terrified it's a girl. With him, sometimes denial is the best medicine.

When we pull up out front of Holly and Jennie's house, Dublin's asleep on his back in my lap, nose buried in my suit jacket, and Cara's tongue is halfway down Emmett's throat. All I hear is Dublin's soft snores and—I think—saliva being swapped, with the occasional break for Emmett to whisper all the ways he's gonna nail his wife tonight.

I leap out the door the moment it opens. "I'll help Hank get in."

Adam flings himself onto the sidewalk. "Me too."

With Hank settled in the spare bedroom, Holly starts stuffing treats into our hands the second we make our way into the kitchen.

"I've already started my Christmas baking." She shoves a bag filled with some sort of chocolate peanut butter ball-shaped version of heaven back into the freezer. "It's only November, so that's an issue." She plants a kiss on our cheeks before heading down the hall. "This mama needs to head to bed before she wakes up and realizes this was all a dream, that I didn't manage to marry off my son to a wonderful woman who's willing to tolerate him for the rest of his life."

Adam nudges my shoulder and grabs a fistful of his junk. "Gotta take a quick leak." He halts, gaze sliding to Jennie. Clearing his throat, he slowly releases himself, cheeks pink. "I mean, uh...I gotta use the... the bathroom." With a look that feels suspiciously like a warning, he leaves me and Jennie in the kitchen.

The woman promptly ignores me, turning her back on me and pouring herself a glass of water.

"Uh..." I scratch my head, searching for a way to ease this awkward tension. "So, the weather is...nice?"

She snorts into her water, pulls another glass from the cupboard, fills it, spins, and shoves it into my surprised hands.

I blink down at her. "Thanks?"

"Mhmm," she murmurs, and I watch the way her ass swings back and forth as she starts down the hallway, one arm reaching back, trying to snag that zipper that starts just above the swell of that banging peach.

Trying, and failing.

With a heavy sigh, she pauses, head down, fingers tapping on the door frame. Turning, she finds me exactly where I shouldn't be: standing there gawking at her.

"Can you please help me with my zipper? It's stuck." She twirls, giving me her backside, and I'm frozen in place.

"Uh, yeah. Totally. I'm good at zippering." *I'm good at zippering? Holy fuck, you dipshit. Shut up.*

"Might have to put your water down."

"What?" I look down at the glass I'm gripping and chuckle. Why does it sound so hoarse? How old am I? Twenty-six, or twelve? "Oh. Yeah." I drain the glass quickly, set it down, and drag my sweaty palms down my legs.

Christ, this dress. This back. *This fucking ass.* It should be illegal. It's *definitely* illegal for me to have my hands this close to it, I'll tell you that much. If Carter could see me right now, I'd never play hockey again. I'd be missing at least one necessary limb.

I don't know how to approach this. The zipper's right there, at the top of that curve, and…should I just…go in? Yeah, I'll just go in. I reach for the zipper, then hesitate. "Um, I'll just…" Cocking my head to the side, I examine that dainty golden tab. "I'll, uh—"

"For fuck's sake, Garrett, it's not that big a deal. I must have snagged it earlier. Just give it a good tug."

"Right. Okay. Yeah. A good…tug."

Taking the teensy zipper head between fingers that are way too big for this, I grip her hip in my other hand, thumb pressing into her warm skin. Her back arches slightly and my breath gets lost somewhere in my chest at the way she clears her throat, the low, raspy sound making my third leg twitch, and even more so when she steps back into me, closer, like she *wants* her ass to get well acquainted with my junk.

Oh God, what is she doing? No. No, no, no. She's gonna wake him up.

Jennie gathers her hair in her fist, sweeping it in slow motion over her slender shoulder. Dusty blue eyes peer at me from beneath thick, dark lashes, and my gaze tracks her tongue as it glides over her lower lip.

Oh fuck. Yup. He's awake.

Not now, Lieutenant Johnson. Stand down, soldier!

"Garrett."

My head snaps, gaze locking with Adam's piercing one. I look back at Jennie's ass—*zipper*—and give it a swift tug, freeing the material, then hightail it the fuck out of the house, slamming the door behind me, body sagging with a heavy sigh as I keel over, gripping my knees.

Whew. That was a close one.

Adam shakes his head, his demand low. "Find someone else. Literally *anybody* else."

Right. Yes. That's absolutely what I need to do. Jennie's off-limits. Plus, I barely know her. I don't need to fuck up any friendships or my hockey season—or any precious limbs—to get laid. I've got plenty of options.

That's what I'm still telling myself a half hour later when I'm waiting in the lobby of my condo, sighing as I repeatedly hammer the call button for the elevator.

"Mr. Andersen," a sultry voice whispers from behind me. Emily, one of my neighbors, sidles up next to me. She tosses her dirty blonde hair over her shoulder, highlighting the slight shimmer that decorates her cheekbones as she smirks at me with those cherry red lips I've devoured here and there. "Don't you look handsome tonight."

The elevator opens and I sweep her inside, noting her glittery dress, mile-long legs, and black heels.

"Best friend's wedding," I explain. "And what about you? You're looking fantastic tonight."

"I always look this good and you know it." She leans against the railing, crossing one ankle over the other, eyes coasting the length of me as I press for her floor, then my own. "Bachelorette party."

"Everyone's getting married, huh?"

She snorts. "Not me."

Chuckling, I drag a hand through my hair. "Me neither."

The elevator dings as it stops, and Emily saunters into the hallway. One hand keeps the doors from closing as she peeks over her shoulder. "Wanna come?"

I don't miss that she leaves out the *in*, letting the innuendo hang heavy in the air.

Gripping the railing, I watch my shoe tap on the marbled floor. My gaze rises to the lump between my legs that's still kinda straining against my zipper from the ass I had my hands on less than an hour ago, and I remind myself for the hundredth time that that ass is off-limits.

Emily smiles as I straighten off the wall. *Fuck it.*

"Yup, I wanna come."

TWO
BIRTHDAY TACOS & FUCKBOYS

Jennie

YOU KNOW that icky feeling when you pull on a pair of underwear fresh out of the dryer only to find they're still damp? Or when you've got no time to heat up your leftover mac and cheese, so you have to shovel it back while it's cold and hard? Both fucking gross, exactly like the feeling I get when my dance partner watches me the way he is right now, like he can't wait to make me his next meal.

Poor guy hasn't figured out yet that I'm caviar; he can't afford me no matter how hard he tries.

Simon leans against the bench press, dropping his elbow to the bar, and flicks his head up. His brows waggle. "Like what you see?"

"Funny, I was about to ask you the same thing." I brush by him, heading to the change room. He follows, because he's a persistent little shit.

Don't get me wrong: I like Simon well enough. We've been dancing together for four years now. But in addition to his persistence, he's cocky as fuck and seems to be under the misguided impression I'm simply making him work *really hard* for it.

It's not that difficult a concept to grasp. I have absolutely zero plans of letting him inside my Disneyland. The sooner he accepts this, the better.

"This is the women's change room, Simon. You can't come in here, no matter how far back you tuck that thing."

Grinning, he slaps a hand over his crotch. "I couldn't tuck this thing back if I tried." His breath smells remarkably like beef jerky when it brushes the shell of my ear. "Can't hide a package this size."

I shove him backward, shooing him away and stepping inside the change room. "Knock that ego down, like, a hundred pegs, fuckboy."

Simon chuckles. "I'll grab a shower and meet you out front."

One of my character flaws is agreeing to plans in advance. By the time they come, I'd much rather take my bra off and not have to put it back on.

I swipe at a line of sweat making its way into my sports bra. "I've got plans tonight, and I'm pretty tired, so—"

"But it's your birthday."

"Right, and I—"

"Five minutes!" He kisses my cheek and jogs toward the men's change room. "Gimme five minutes! Gotta freshen up for my favorite birthday girl!" He winks and disappears before he can catch my eye roll.

Sure, we're friends, and yes, we spend 75 percent of our time together in intimate positions with his roaming hands on me. Still, on a pseudo–lunch date with Simon ideally isn't how I'd spend my twenty-fourth birthday. In fact, I can think of at least ten better ways to spend it, like a two-hour couch nap, jilling off in my bedroom, or taking my cat for a walk.

I don't have a cat.

But I'm partial to free food, and we wind up at Taco Cantina, which is nice—tacos are life—though I'm unimpressed with Simon's insistence to share the chips and guac as a starter. He devours all but two chips I manage to sneak.

"Oops." His fingers brush the dusty bottom of the teak chip bowl. "Kinda ate it all, didn't I?"

"You sure did."

He dismisses me with a wave. "S'okay. You don't wanna worry about the extra calories."

My brows rocket so fast up my forehead I'm worried they might fly right off. "Pardon?"

"The extra calories."

"Right, I heard you. I was giving you a chance to change your words." I sip my virgin mojito, savoring the sweet tang. "When has it ever been okay to comment on what a woman should or shouldn't eat?"

He regards me cautiously. "Calm down, Jennie. I was joking. And it's not like you're not used to it."

I am used to it, that's exactly the problem. I've spent my entire life fighting the urge to cower from the scrutinizing stares of dance coaches that nitpick any amount of softness, that scour my food logs, searching for any indication that I've been anything other than strict with my diet, something to explain why I'm moving a bit sluggish one week, or why my outfit fits a little snugger one morning. I've hugged too many toilet bowls and cried, afraid of harsh words, but more afraid to start an addiction that can too quickly turn lethal.

That I can sit here now and order three loaded tacos and a sugary drink without a care in the world or an ounce of remorse is a miracle, something I've been working toward since high school with an incredible amount of therapy. I won't let Simon's careless words steal years of progress.

And then he adds: "Plus, the winter show is next month. You don't wanna be packing on unnecessary pounds."

I keep from crushing my glass simply because this drink is banging. "You're digging your own grave. Keep it up, and I'm going to put you in it." I tack the *dipshit* on in my head.

He covers my hand with his. "You know I think you're the most beautiful girl out there, Jennie. I'm lucky to have you as a partner."

I smile up at the waiter, mouthing a silent "Thank you" as he slides a platter of tacos in front of me. To Simon, I say, "Damn right you are."

He devours half a taco in one bite. "Your brother still married?"

"It's been two weeks, so, yeah." Also, Carter's obsessed with Olivia. Good thing he's a professional hockey player. If he were in town every day, Olivia might strangle him. I'm still unsure how I made it twenty-four years without doing it myself. My brother's great, he's just a little... boisterous? Ostentatious? Self-assured? Extra as fuck? All of the above?

"Two weeks seems like more than he can handle in a committed relationship," Simon manages, showing me a mouthful of ground beef, lettuce, and cheese. How he manages to get into the skirts of every girl in the dance program at SFU is far beyond what my mind can comprehend.

"Should I remind you you're as big a manwhore as Carter was prior to Olivia?"

"I am not."

I accidentally cackle. Whoops.

Simon rolls his eyes. "How come your brother gets the chance to change his reputation, but I don't? Maybe I want to settle down too."

Do people deserve the benefit of the doubt? Normally. But I know this man. I've watched him lure in countless girls with his charm, only to sleep with one for a week or two before replacing her with another, one he likes to flaunt right in front of the former. He tosses women away without thought, all the while never missing an opportunity to hit on me.

Like right now, as he hooks his ankle around mine, pulling my legs between his under the table. He smirks that fucking smirk, and I'm reminded of exactly why I've affectionately labeled him Simon Syphilis.

"C'mon, Jennie. Let's go back to my place. Lemme give you a *real* birthday present."

"Yeah." I catch the waiter's eye, twirl one finger in the air, then point at my tacos. "Can I get a to-go box, please?" I lay my chin on my laced fingers and smile. "You know, Simon, I'd absolutely love to. Love to stay and finish this lunch too." I accept the small box from the waiter with a grateful smile and start lining up my tacos inside. "Unfortunately, I don't feel like making any fuckboy-sized mistakes today."

I stand and pop a chaste kiss on his cheek, mentally cataloging his epically surprised face into the *never wanna forget this* file in my brain. "Thanks for my birthday tacos. Can't wait to enjoy them silently and alone."

The thing about a Beckett grin is it's irresistible, even to other Becketts. My brother can't say no to me, and I've been known to take advantage of that every now and again.

So not only do I get steak and lobster at one of the fanciest restaurants in Vancouver for my birthday dinner, I devour an Oreo explosion banana split at my favorite dessert bar, too, after nothing more than a simple request and a dimple-popping grin. Carter ate two, so as I follow him down the street after dinner, I'm trying not to let the fifteen pounds I feel like I've gained tonight weigh too heavily on my mind.

Still, I'm stuffed, uncomfortable as hell, and Carter's making me walk. Plus, it's cold as balls and I'm wearing my pretty coat, not my warm coat.

I shiver, snuggling my chin into my scarf. "I'm cold. Where are we going? How come Hank got to go home after dinner, but we're subjected to walking in the snow? Don't you love us?"

Carter ignores me, but Olivia groans, both mitten-sheathed hands on her stomach. "I need to walk all that food off. I ate way too much."

I pat her adorable baby bump. "Little mama was hungry. That's okay."

"Little mama is *always* hungry."

"Big daddy's always hungry too," Carter rumbles, patting his torso.

I make a yuck face. "Please, no. Never again."

He deflates, frowning. "What? Why?"

"Because that's utterly disgusting."

"You're dramatic." He wraps an arm around his wife, pressing his mouth to her ear but not lowering his voice. "I could eat again, just not something suitable for public if you know what I—"

"Carter!" She slaps a palm across his mouth before yanking him down to eye level. "For the love of God," she whispers in that threatening teacher voice of hers. "For once in your life, stop talking."

His smirk is slow as we stop in front of a tall building downtown. "I just wanna love you out loud. Why won't you let me love you out loud?"

Olivia gives him a reassuring pat while my mom swoons and I gag. "Trust me, baby. Nobody loves as loud as you do."

Carter grins proudly and opens the glass doors. He ushers us into an elevator before I have time to admire the exquisite lobby, and as we ride up to the twenty-first floor, he finally answers the question I asked a full two minutes ago. "I do love you. Best sister ever." He pushes me into the hallway. "That's why we got you the best present ever."

"Present? Here?" My head cranks, taking in the numbered doors lining the hallway. "Carter, this is a condo building."

"Uh-huh." He slips a key into a door marked *2104*, then gestures into the space. "Welcome home, Jennie."

My jaw unhinges, feet rooted in place. "Home? For...for me?" Cautiously, I step inside the bright space, which appears to be stunning and fully furnished if the living room is any indication. I turn to my family, and my stupid eyes well with stupid tears. I hate crying, but this is an emotional time of year for me. "This is for me? You got me my own apartment?"

"Guess some might call me the best brother in the world."

He's annoying and drives me up the damn wall, but Carter always has been the best brother, and my best friend. So I fling my arms around his neck and cry out, "*I love you so much.*"

Mom's frowny face comes into view. "But you can stay with me if you want. If you want, Jennie, you don't have to move. It's not too late. Carter can back out of the lease. You can—"

Carter silences her with one giant hand over her face. "Shhh." He loops his arm through mine. "C'mon. I'll give you the tour."

Carter pulls me around the apartment, showing me the sprawling master bedroom, the attached bathroom with the sparkling glass shower. There's a second bedroom and another bathroom down the hall, much more than I need.

Not surprising, nor is him telling me he actually wanted to get me the penthouse. Carter loves to spoil his people, and he caught me looking up rentals last month. I don't have much income, and Vancouver is expensive, so my budget was giving *Criminal Minds* vibes, sans hunky Derek Morgan. The face Carter made before slamming my laptop shut, grunting out a *Fuck no*, and walking away, was both entertaining and eye-roll inducing.

When we finish the tour, I dance my way through every room three more times because I'm so in love, and I can't stop smiling.

"This is incredible and so, *so* perfect." I spin around the living room before I crush my brother in a hug and throw myself over Olivia, who's made the couch her home, and smooch her cheek. "Thank you, times infinity."

"You can move in as soon as you want," Carter tells me as we get ready to head home. "I can help you when I get back from our series next week." He hands me a rose gold key chain with an acrylic *J* on it, filled with tiny flowers. "And one of the guys lives on the top floor, which is cool. I feel better about you living alone knowing he's around. I haven't asked him yet, but I know he'll look out for you."

"Great." How like him to put me under surveillance.

He sweeps me into the hallway as the door opposite me opens. A soft giggle pierces the air, and Carter grins.

"Speak of the fucking devil. What are you doing down here? Well, I mean, I know what you were doing down here." He pumps his brows. "Your hair's all…and your shirt…" He shakes his head, still grinning, then points at me. "Jennie's moving in. Told her you'd look out for her." His expression sobers. "You have to look out for her."

"I don't need a babysitter," I grumble to nobody in particular, buttoning my coat before peeking to see which poor, unsuspecting soul has been tasked with the job. My fingers halt their work when my gaze settles on a pair of wide blue-green eyes, the mess of dirty blond waves ruffled on his head, the gray sweatpants hanging haphazardly and way too low off his hips.

Carter's right: Garrett looks exceptionally like he just had sex.

And the half-dressed blonde with her fire engine red nails wrapped around his elbow looks like she just got fucked straight into the ground. I find myself feeling oddly envious.

Garrett Andersen ranks a solid Chris Hemsworth on the fuckability scale, all glowing skin, rippling muscles, turquoise eyes the color of the ocean on the brightest day, and his sweatpants do nothing to hide that he's packing some serious heat between his legs, because why wouldn't he be? So sue a girl for wondering what a quick roll with him might feel like. It's been way too long, and I have a couple—okay, a fuckload—of cobwebs in the dungeon.

Shit, did I call it Disneyland earlier?

Bright red heat stains Garrett's cheeks as he holds my stare, and I have no idea what comes over him as he rockets away from the girl at his side, practically shoving her to the ground.

"Right, well, as I was saying." Clearing my throat, I wrap my scarf around my neck. "I don't need to be babysat, especially by Fuckboy of the Year over here." I loop my arm through Olivia's and head for the elevator, throwing one last look over my shoulder. Judging by her laugh, I'd say Olivia enjoys the way Garrett's mouth gapes as much as I do. I'm sure he wants to be my babysitter as much as I want to hear my brother call himself Big Daddy ever again.

"*Jennifer Beckett,*" Mom scolds, chasing after us. "That was mean! Sorry, Garrett! We love you!"

"I've called Carter much worse," Olivia points out. "But Garrett's a sweetheart."

My nose wrinkles. "A sweetheart who was fucking my new neighbor."

I don't mind, but it might be a little awkward to see them together in the hallway. And what if the walls are thin? Do I want to know what he sounds like when he's coming? Not particularly.

One of the reasons I avoided social media before Carter met Olivia, back when he was manwhore extraordinaire. No one needs to see evidence that someone else is getting laid.

"Maybe they're dating," I offer lamely.

"Nope." Carter's arm pushes between the elevator doors, making them spring back open. He shuffles inside. "Just fucking."

I pin my arms over my chest. "I don't need a babysitter, Carter."

He hauls Olivia into him, pulling her scarf up until it's damn near covering her whole face, despite her trying to swat him away. "Don't think of Garrett as a babysitter. Think of him more like an extra set of eyes."

"*Carter!*" I stomp twice. I've always been a bit of a drama queen. Like brother, like sister. "That's even worse! It sounds like you're spying on me!"

"I'm not spying!" he shouts back, arms waving. "I just wanna make sure you're safe!"

The doors burst open, and I strut into the immaculate lobby. "You're so annoying."

"No, *you're* annoying!"

"I know you are, but what am I?"

"Oh good God." Olivia buries her face behind her hand.

"Children," Mom warns. "Get along."

"You're lucky I love you," Carter mutters when he opens the car door for us.

"You're lucky I don't kick your ass."

His face shatters with a wide grin. "Get in the damn car."

My finger glides along the edge of the old page in front of me, the plastic that protects the pictures that have lived there for years. It's stiff and broken, sharp on the edges, and I hiss when my finger slides too quickly over a crack. A drop of blood pools on the tip of my finger, and I suck it into my mouth to stop both the pain and the bleeding as I stare down at the handsome face smiling up at me.

He's wearing a pink birthday hat and has a newly six-year-old me on his shoulders, clutching the soft, pale pink bunny stuffie he surprised me with.

My bedroom door creaks, and Mom pops her head in, smiling when she spots me still awake. She shuffles in but pauses at the edge of the bed, and I watch as years worth of unending love and heartache flashes across her eyes as she spies the photo album open in my lap. I wish I could fix it, but I know I can't.

"I miss him," I whisper, tracing the shape of my dad's face. "So much."

"Me, too, sweetie." Mom sinks down beside me, pressing a lingering kiss to my hair. "I know he's looking down on you today, crying that his baby girl isn't a baby anymore. He's so proud of you and the woman you're becoming, Jennie. I know that without a doubt."

She touches the bunny little me is clutching, smooshed into my dad's hair. Her gaze settles on the same bunny currently snuggled into my belly. "She's always been your favorite."

I pull the stuffie from my lap. Its coloring has faded, and one of the button eyes hangs by a loose thread. Years of cuddles, of towing it everywhere I went, refusing to let my mom wash it sometimes for months at a time, has made the once-soft fur coarse and dull.

"I always wanted a bunny, but you guys wouldn't let me get one. Dad got me this bunny instead." I stroke the long ears. "It was him who named her, you know. Princess Bubblegum."

"He would've given you the entire world if I only let him. He bugged me for years about getting you a real bunny. You were his little princess, and he was a persistent little shit who didn't like the word no."

"Sounds like Carter."

She chuckles. "Carter and your dad are too much alike. A dangerous duo when they got up to their shenanigans." She threads her fingers through my hair with a tender smile. "I'm sorry he's not here to celebrate your birthday with you."

"Don't be sorry." I swipe a tear from my cheek, then catch the one rolling down hers. "I'm lucky to have had sixteen years to make memories with him."

There's a quiet sadness etched in her eyes as they sweep my dimly lit room. "I'm really going to miss having you here. I'd keep you forever if I could, but you deserve to have your own life. You need space to grow."

With my face in her hands, she kisses my cheek. "Happy birthday, sweetheart. I love you, and I'm so proud of you."

THREE

MISSING: PRINCESS BUBBLEGUM
& THE WILL TO LIVE

Jennie

EVER HAVE a nagging feeling you don't belong?

It's not my attire. Nowhere to be on Fridays, I prefer minimal layers and letting the girls hang free. So the lack of pants and bra feels perfectly acceptable. I'm not even bothered by the red-rimmed eyes and extra-knotted bun I'm sporting.

It's the apartment, so pristine, so put together. It's nothing like my life, or my head.

The early morning sunshine is bright, bathing my new space in a soft glow, warming the hardwood planks beneath my bare feet. For a moment, I close my eyes and bask in the feeling, soaking in the warmth. I imagine it's how it feels to be so loved by someone, like their arms are wrapped around you, lighting you from the inside out. For a moment, the sunshine feels like love, and I live in it. For a moment, I crave it.

I'm treading water today, and the culprit is the damn photo album on my kitchen island, the one I haven't torn my gaze off since my birthday last week.

My eyes fall to the laugh lines that form creases around his wide smile and brilliant eyes. The longer I look at him, the dad I lost eight years ago today, the good-bye I never got to say, the harder it gets to breathe. My throat burns, and my teeth sink into my lower lip to still the tremor.

My hands shake as I turn away from the only face I want to see and simultaneously can't bear to look at, and I look to the boxes. There are too many, stacked in towers and lining my living room. All I want to do is bury myself in this, unpacking, making myself at home. Yet the mundane task paired with the complex waves of grief I still don't understand after all these years mix into an ugly, muddled rainbow. I don't want to go through boxes. I don't want to look at pictures and wish for more memories we'll never make. I want to crawl back into bed, pull the covers over my head, and wake up tomorrow when this is all over.

Honestly? I'd take a smile too. Something soft and genuine to remind me there's good in this world.

Coffee might be the next best thing, and the only thing I can easily access. So I pull on one of my brother's hockey hoodies, stuff my feet into my UGGs, and trudge down the hall and into the elevator.

"Hold the elevator," a voice calls, and I hammer the Close Door button fifty times before a heeled bootie shoves its way inside. "Hi, neighbor," the pretty blonde from across the hall says with a broad, sparkling grin. "Thanks for waiting."

"No problem." My gaze coasts down, taking in her lavish trench coat, the red on the bottom of her booties.

Louboutins? You've got to be shitting me.

She peels off a red leather glove and offers her hand, revealing impeccably polished, glossy nails. "Emily."

I slip my hand into hers, trying to hide the three-week-old DIY mani. "Jennie."

"You're Garrett's friend."

Nope. "And you're his fuck buddy."

She winks. "Only on days that end in *Y*." The elevator stops, and Emily gives my forearm a tender squeeze. "I'm heading down to the parking garage, so I think this is where we say good-bye. So fun to meet you, Jennie. See you around."

"Bye, Emma."

She holds my gaze, sugary smile in place. "Emily. On the off chance you find yourself feeling forgetful again, you'll likely hear Garrett calling it in the middle of the night."

I stick my tongue out as she begins to disappear behind the closing doors, and she sticks hers out right back.

I mean, ew. Haven't I already said I don't want to know what that man sounds like when he comes? I fully plan on acting like I don't know him when I see him around.

Like right now. *Fuck.*

"Jennie?"

My eyes lock with Garrett's, and my body moves faster than it ever has, darting behind a wall. Forget about not wanting to see him exiting my new neighbor's apartment, I don't want *him* to see *me* when I look like this. I've already been on the phone with Carter once this morning, feeding him some bullshit about how *fine* I am. He didn't buy it, and reluctantly agreed to pick me up later tonight for dinner instead of coming right over. I don't need my appointed babysitter running and blabbing to my big brother that his little sister is a mess.

"Jennie?" Garrett calls again, closer. "Are you hiding? You know I saw you already, right?"

I squeeze my eyes shut, plastering myself to the wall. When a throat clears, I crack one lid.

The blond giant of a man stands in front of me, wearing the exact same hoodie as me, messy hair tucked beneath a ball cap, and a tray of hot drinks in his hands from the very café I'm heading to. As his gaze rakes over me, his concerned expression amplifies.

"Oh hey, Garrett. Didn't see you there." I straighten, tugging at the hem of my hoodie, and his eyes fall to my pajama pants. I gesture at the drinks and force a chuckle. "Did you get one for me?"

His stare holds mine, brows knitting, and I can hear the question on the tip of his tongue: *Are you okay?* He rethinks his words, probably because he's terrified of me most days. "Uh, yeah, actually." He tucks one drink into his elbow and holds out the remaining two. "These are for you."

I stare at the drinks, then him. "What?"

"For you."

"I don't...I don't understand."

Garrett clears his throat into his arm. "I know last night was your first night, and I know today..." His eyes flicker as I swallow. "I know today might be a hard day, so I thought...maybe you could use some caffeine. But then I didn't know if you even like coffee, so I got you a hot chocolate, too, just in case." He places the tray in my hands and palms his nape. "There's whipped cream on it."

"That's, um..."

"It's no big deal. I was there, and I just thought…coffee."

"I like coffee. And hot chocolate." Damnit, I've got a lump in my throat. "Thank you, Garrett."

His cheeks split with an explosive grin, lighting his whole face. It's so addicting, I almost smile too. "Cool. Yeah, cool." He flicks a hand through the air. "Yeah, no problem."

Garrett ambles back to the lobby. With nowhere else to go, I trail along beside him.

"So, uh, where were you going?"

I hold up the drinks. "To get coffee."

"In your pajamas?"

"Yeah, in my pajamas. You got a problem with that, buddy?"

Eyes wide, he wags his head. He hesitates in front of the elevator. "So now that you have your coffee, are you…?"

"Going back up."

"Oh. Me too." His eyes bounce from me to the elevator, back to me, then the floor, and when they land on me, silence stretches between us for a moment too long.

"I'm gonna take the stairs," we both call out at the same time, bumping into each other as we turn toward the stair exit.

"You're gonna walk up twenty-one floors?"

I prop a fist on my hip. "It's called exercise. And you're twenty-*five* floors up. What's your excuse, big guy?"

"I'm scared of elevators," he blurts, then flushes.

I hike a brow. "Really?"

"Yeah. Terrified." He swallows, looking down the hall toward the stairs, and then does the oddest thing. "Oh, but actually…Ahhh." He grabs his knee and groans. "I hurt my knee. Banged it when I was getting coffee."

"Wow. Maybe you should take the elevator, then."

"Might be for the best." He rubs his knee and hisses in fake pain. "Think I could put my fear aside for one day."

Is this really happening? Does he know he's a shit actor?

The elevator opens when I press the button, and I shove him inside. "Thanks for the coffee. And Garrett?"

"Yeah?"

"Stick to your day job, big guy."

~

The package in my hand feels insignificant next to the extravagant bouquet and extensive breakfast spread on the small table, signs that Carter's already been here. I know Hank will appreciate the gesture anyway.

"Is that my favorite girl?"

I follow his tired voice, finding him in his rocking chair by the window.

"Just me." I pop a kiss on his smiling cheek before taking a seat next to him. He's got a great view, towering trees and green space, the peaks of the mountains not far off in the distance, decorating the North Vancouver skyline, even in the middle of this bleak fall.

"You are my favorite. And your mom. And Olivia. Love me some Cara too."

"Hate to tell you, Hank, but *favorite* requires you to put one of us above the rest."

He frowns. "You know I can't. I love you all."

"And we all love you." I set the small box on the table, lifting the lid, and sweet cinnamon sugar infiltrates the air. "I brought you a cinnamon bun."

His eyes glitter as I cut the sticky mess and lead one hand to the plate, the other to a fork. "You *are* my favorite." He gestures behind us. "Carter made you a cappuccino before he left."

I find the warm mug and wrap my hands around it, inhaling eagerly. I smile down at the cinnamon heart dusted over the foam. Carter's all about big, loud gestures, but sometimes it's these tiny, silent ones that warm me the most.

Mindless chatter fills the next few minutes, and when we take a moment to let the silence linger, Hank murmurs, "Eight years today."

I sip my cappuccino, trying to drown the tightness in my throat. "Fifteen for you."

He turns something between his fingers, and my heart lurches when I see the dainty gold band, the solitaire diamond set in the middle. "Miss my sweet Ireland every damn day."

Hank entered our lives on the worst day of ours, and the anniversary of his. His wife, Ireland, had passed seven years to the day Dad died, and we have Hank—and Ireland—to thank for saving Carter's life.

My brother was tasked with the onerous job of taking care of me and my mom that day. Impossible as it was, he did it effortlessly. My only memories revolve around the food he forced on us, the way he held us for hours on end while we thought our world was ending, carried Mom to bed when exhaustion finally took her, and laid with me until my eyes shut.

The next morning, I found him passed out on the living room couch, Hank and Dublin—who we didn't know—sitting in the corner of the room. Hank told us how he'd dreamt of his late wife, urging him out of the house, and hours later came across Carter at a bar, a drunk, incoherent mess, and stopped him from driving home, the very action that had stolen our dad in the first place.

In stopping us from losing another piece of our family, Hank became part of it.

"Too long," is the whisper that finally tumbles from my lips.

"But then every day without them is too long, isn't it?"

My chest squeezes as I imagine my mom right now. I know what she's doing: the same thing she does every year on this day. Wearing Dad's favorite sweater because the smell of his cologne still clings to it, clutching the teddy bear he won her at the fair on their first date. Crying and alone, until her heart allows her to open a space big enough to let us back in. She'll laugh and smile later today when we watch old home movies and tell stories, but she needs her space to grieve first.

"Living without your soul mate is something no one should ever have to do," Hank murmurs. He pats my hand. "I know there's something extra special waiting for you, Jennie. A love above all the rest. That's what a soul mate is. Someone with smooth edges to soften our sharp ones. Someone who fits us so perfectly, vibrates on the same frequency, makes all our best parts shine. And together? Together, everything is exactly the way it's meant to be."

I force an eye roll, laughing off his promise. "I'm in no rush. I like being independent."

"You can be independent and still share a life with someone. Your brother didn't think he wanted to share his life, and now look at him. He has a wife with a beautiful soul, a baby on the way, and the man couldn't be happier."

"I know what you're doing, old man, but I don't need a boyfriend to make me happy."

"I don't think you do either. You make yourself happy all on your own. Now, do I think finding that person who makes all the dark spots a little bit brighter when they help you hold them might open you up to a side of this world you haven't seen?" He shrugs. "Maybe." A broad grin. "Do I think you're a lot more like your brother than you let on to be, and you're scared to let someone in because love can hurt? Absolutely."

"Get outta here. I'm not scared."

I am *terrified*.

It's not that I don't crave the intimacy, the person who's always in your corner, who sees you with all your walls down and likes you even then. God, how I wouldn't love to find someone who saw everything, accepted it all. Someone all my own to share the hard things with. Maybe then all those hard things would feel manageable.

Thing is, though, when your older brother is the captain of an NHL team, when everyone wants a slice of him, it's impossible to separate the real from the fake. You wind up trudging too deep, left all on your own when you find you were merely a stepping stone, that nothing was ever real. And the ones you thought cared? When they blow your world up, they don't even glance back at the rubble and chaos left by the explosion.

It's safer to have a tight-knit circle, a few people you can trust whole-heartedly, than to recklessly let in anyone who asks, even if it is a little lonely sometimes.

Besides, who needs a boyfriend when you've got a drawer full of battery-powered ones? Men don't vibrate, but dildos do.

～

When I make it back to the condo after lunch, I'm exhausted. I've fielded messages from Carter, Olivia, Cara, and Simon all morning, constantly checking up on me. It's nice, but a lot.

I lock the door behind me. the sound of the dead bolt sliding into place echoing through my apartment before filling it with silence.

Silence makes my skin crawl. It leaves too much room for questions, for wandering thoughts, overthinking, and second-guessing.

My eyes catch that photo album, and I let it pull me forward until all I can see is his smiling face, until all that's flowing through me is the desperate urge to feel the warmth of his love instead of this sudden overwhelming lack of strength, of control.

I cover the photo and close my eyes as my chest heaves, and for some reason, Garrett's face floats through my mind. I see him standing there with coffee and hot chocolate, the smile he wore just for me, a real smile that made me feel warm. And now I feel cold again, alone, and I'm so fucking tired of being alone in my hardest moments.

Slowly, I spread my fingers, uncovering the picture a little at a time. That pink bunny stares up at me, the one clutched to my chest, and I know what I need. I know how to find some warmth again, to bring a little piece of home to me here.

With scissors, I slice through endless pieces of tape, box after box, ripping open the flaps, strewing the contents on the floor as I search for Princess Bubblegum, a piece of my dad that I can hold on to. The longer I look, the more my hands shake. The scissors break, and my chin trembles. Box after box yields the same heartbreaking result: no bunny.

I squeeze my eyes shut and shake my head, willing away the weakness that comes in the form I hate most.

I rarely lose control. Of my body, my emotions. I avoid situations that bring pain or uncertainties. I should've stayed home; home where I'm surrounded by the memories, home with my mom. Instead, I'm here, alone.

I dump out the box before me, the one labeled *bedroom*, and when nothing pink falls out, I sink to my knees and let the tears come.

FOUR

IT'S RAINING DILDOS

Garrett

"*Nnnewwwm.*"

"*Nnnewm!*"

"*Nnneeewm!*"

"For fuck's sake." Adam's solid body connects with mine, knocking me into Carter. He sandwiches the two of us between him and the boards. "Would you two shut the fuck up? Enough with the sound effects. You're not fucking race cars."

I tuck my glove under my arm and nab Adam's water bottle from where it's cradled on top of the net. Water dribbles down my neck and beneath my chest protector as I squirt it into my mouth. "You're just jealous 'cause you can't skate as fast as us."

Adam shifts his mask up and steals his water back. "When I'm wearing fifty pounds of goalie equipment? No, I can't, and I highly doubt either of you could."

Carter's chest puffs. "I could do it."

Adam snorts. "Okay, bud. Whatever you say."

"What? I could. Strap me up; let's have a race."

I snicker. "Strap me up. That's what Ollie said."

"Boom." Emmett knocks his gloved fist off mine as he laughs. "Just don't tell her I laughed at that. She's a thousand times scarier pregnant."

Carter doesn't appear to find it funny. With a battle cry that echoes across the rink, he tackles me to the ice, smothering my face with his glove.

"Get off me!" I yell, flailing my arms. "*Adam*! Help!"

"Jesus Christ," Coach mutters, spraying us with a shower of ice when he stops next to us. "Sometimes I think I'm coaching peewee, not *men's* professional hockey. My daughter is more grown-up than you two, and she's an infant." He snaps his fingers and gestures behind him. "Beckett, Andersen, off your asses and give me five laps."

Carter rolls to his feet and tugs me up. "Race ya."

I shake the snow from my jersey. "You're so unnecessarily competitive."

"Yeah, and I—"

"*Loser buys lunch!*" Frosty air nips at my cheeks as I tear down the ice, Carter hot on my heels, hollering after me. And that's exactly how, two hours later, I wind up facedown in a pile of chicken wings and pizza I don't have to pay for, with Carter still giving me the stink eye, grumbling about cheating.

"You don't know how to lose," Emmett tells him, dropping an entire slice of pizza in his mouth. "Not a good trait."

"I didn't lose! He cheated!" Carter grabs the slice from my hand. "Gimme that."

Adam slides another slice onto my plate. "Jennie all moved into her new place?"

Carter nods. "Moved in yesterday." His gaze meets mine. "You see her this morning?"

I don't lie often—this morning excluded, when I may or may not have said I was afraid of elevators, and that I hurt my knee—and I'm shit at it. But there was something vulnerable in Jennie's eyes today, something sad and uncertain hidden behind her usual boldness. Something that said she didn't want anyone to see her anything less than confident, not the way her chin trembled, the way she swallowed when I mentioned the day, or the way she hadn't bothered to dress.

So I lie. Again.

"I haven't seen her."

"I thought you might if you were sneaking outta your friend's place again."

Heat claws up my neck. "I wasn't sneaking out, and I haven't been there again."

"Finally got laid, eh, buddy?" Emmett clinks his glass against mine.

"Is sleeping with someone who lives in your building a good idea?" Amusement and concern mix in Adam's question. "Or is it serious?"

"It's not serious. And we weren't really sleeping together." At the looks I get, I relent. "Okay, but it was only a couple times. It's hard to meet girls. All you guys wanna do is look at pictures of your wives and talk about how their hair smells like banana bread or some shit. You're all pussy-whipped."

"Adam is whipped by no pussy," Carter retorts. "He's a free man, and thank fuck for that."

Adam chuckles, his cheeks pink. "Wish I could be a better wingman for you. I'm just not really ready for a relationship."

Carter shoves a deep-fried pickle into his mouth. "You could just fuck, like Garrett."

"I'm not—" I bury my face in my hands. "Ugh."

He points at me with his half-eaten pickle. "Jennie was not impressed with you, by the way."

"What? Why?" *Stupid question.* Between the wedding and the run-in at the condo, I've made less than stellar impressions. I'm hoping today fixed that, even if my original plan was to leave the drinks outside her door and never tell her they were from me.

"Something about not wanting to be subjected to you fucking her neighbor."

It's Carter's fault, but then it almost always is. Had he told me they'd be there, I absolutely wouldn't have been at Emily's. Fuck, he hadn't even told me his sister was moving in. The woman turns me on while simultaneously scaring me shitless with only the look in her eyes, which is always super fucking ferocious, and now I have to lie so we don't wind up in the elevator together.

Carter fishes his ringing phone out of his pocket. "Speak of the devil. Hey, Jennie. We were just talk—" His smile falls. "Whoa, hold on. Why are you crying? Take a deep breath." He runs a frantic hand through his hair, tugging. "I don't know how to—I don't—how can I— *I don't know how to help you from here,*" he finally settles on, half scream, and his eyes get wider the longer he listens to Jennie's frantic rambling.

My experience in dealing with upset females is extremely limited to my three younger sisters. As complicated as they are, I don't think they even tip the scale. Still, I find myself murmuring, "Remind her to breathe," to Carter.

He nods. "Okay, Jennie. Take a deep breath." He inhales deeply, over and over, winding his hand in a circle as if Jennie can see him. "Okay, good. Now tell me again." His brows tug together. "Princess Bubblegum?"

My beer slides down the wrong tube, and I cough, sputtering into my hand.

"I don't know where Princess Bubblegum is." Carter sighs. "We'll find her, 'kay? I promise. She's gotta be around somewhere."

I'm on my fourth slice of pizza when Carter hangs up the call, explaining about Jennie's missing stuffed animal, the one their dad got her, and I know the second he sets those puppy dog eyes on me that I'm fucked. Royally fucked.

I shake my head before he even opens his mouth.

"Please," he begs.

"Aw, man." I fold over the table. "C'mon."

"Just check on her on your way up. Just a minute. She wouldn't stop crying."

"She doesn't even like me! She hates me!"

"She loves you!"

"You didn't even try to make it sound convincing!" I slump in my chair. "She's not gonna wanna see me. Probably throw a pillow at my head or something."

"Nah." Carter grins. "It's the heels you gotta watch out for."

What am I doing?

Stupid condo. Stupid Carter.

No, I'm not doing it. I'm not going. I refuse. Carter can't make me. And Jennie won't know if I don't go. It's not like Carter's gonna tell her he sent me to check up on her.

It's decided. I won't go. I press for the penthouse and sink back against the elevator wall with a relieved sigh.

I watch the light above the doors bounce from one floor to the next, and as it climbs toward that *21*, I groan.

I slam the emergency stop button the moment I pass Jennie's floor, catching myself on the railing when the elevator bounces to a stop. It whirs to life when I hit it a second time, and I jab *21* just once, nice and hard, and drag my hands over my face.

A minute later, I've got my hockey bag over my shoulder, sticks in my hand, and ear pressed to Jennie's door. The silence I'm met with convinces me everything's okay. Maybe she found Princess Jellybean.

A whimper stops me in my tracks when I turn to leave. The broken sob that follows tugs on my weak heartstrings. With a sigh, I tuck my sticks under my arm and knock.

"Go away!" Jennie shouts from inside.

"Uh, I...um..." Words fail, so I knock again, quieter this time, 'cause I'm afraid to piss her off.

"*I said go a—*" The door whips open. Jennie's jaw dangles as she stares at me. Her light violet-blue eyes seem paler than usual, the rim around them dark like midnight, the contrast striking. Like the skin around her eyes, her nose is pink, lips swollen and highly kissable.

No. Nope. No, they're fucking not, Garrett.

"Uh, hi." *Am I waving? Fuck. Off to an awkward start; great.*

Jennie hiccups, dragging the back of her wrist across her eyes. "What are you doing here?"

"Uh, Carter said—"

"Oh my God! My brother sent you to check up on me? Unbelievable." She slams her hip against the door, propping it open, but it's the arms pinned over her chest that are an issue. She's wearing forest green leggings and a matching sports bra—a stark contrast from her oversized hoodie and jammies this morning. My gaze bounces between her cleavage and her toned stomach. Why isn't she wearing a shirt? She should put a shirt on.

"You should...a shirt. Please?" *Why is this happening to me?*

Dark brows rocket up her forehead. "Oh, you'd like me to put on a shirt? Would that please you? Well, I'd like you to get fucking lost!" She's screaming but still crying, swiping at the tears free-falling down her cheeks, so it's kinda more funny than scary.

Until she pins me with a glower so fierce, that smile creeping up my face drops.

"Right. Your home. No shirt." *Am I giving her finger guns? I'm fucking giving her finger guns.* I grip my stick with both hands to prevent any further embarrassing actions. "Carter didn't send me to check up on you," I lie. "We grabbed lunch after practice and he said you lost Princess Jellybean, and I thought—"

"Princess *Jellybean*? It's Princess *Bubblegum*! Ugh!" Arms in the air, she spins away.

Fuck me, those leggings. That fucking *ass*. It's not until it starts disappearing from view that I realize she's slamming the door in my face.

Flinging myself forward, I barrel through the door with my hockey bag, tumbling inside. Jennie grunts as I accidentally sandwich her between me and the wall. My arm goes around her, pulling her tight against me to keep her from going down.

"Get off me." She huffs, shoving against my chest. "Wrong apartment, fuckboy. Your hockey hooker lives across the hall."

My face flames. "She's not my—I'm not a…"

Jennie sniffles, chest heaving as she stares up at me. She shoves me once more, gently, but my feet stay rooted. That dancer's body she's worked so hard on is sculpted perfection, but I've got close to a hundred pounds of immovable body mass on her.

My hand slips to her bare waist, gripping it to keep her steady while I straighten. "I'm not looking for Emily, and she's not my…" I clear my throat. "Hockey hooker."

Jennie dusts off her boobs. Nice boobs. No dust, though. "That's not what she said." She cleans the remaining tears off her face. "What are you doing here, Andersen?"

"Carter said you were upset about Princess Jell—Bubblegum. I was passing by and wanted to see if you were okay." I take in the mess in the living room, boxes ripped open, contents strewn across the floor. "How's the search goin'?"

Jennie fiddles with her braid, scuffing at the floor with her toes. "I can't find her. I've only got a few boxes left here, and a couple in the spare bedroom."

"Hmm." I shove my fingers below my hat and scratch my head, pretending not to notice the way Jennie's eyes track the movement. I've always been fascinated by her. She's beautiful, and she knows it. Thick chestnut waves, almost always tied back in a braid, finished with a ribbon. Kinda tall, I think. Five-eight, maybe, still a whole lot shorter than me. Long-ass legs I wouldn't mind wrapping around my neck, draping down my back. A brilliant, wide grin with heart-stopping dimples, and a fierce personality, so bold and confident.

But when her eyes meet mine, it's the dashed hope in them that prompts my next words.

"I'll help you look."

"What?" Her nose wrinkles as I drop my equipment, the damp, sweaty stench wafting up to us. "You don't need to do that."

"Sure, but I don't mind." I move past her, choosing a stack of boxes before she can argue more. Picking up the steak knife resting on top, I twirl it between my fingers and glance at Jennie as she watches me cautiously, fingers curling at her stomach. "Poor Princess Bubblegum might need stitches when you're done with her if this is what you're using to open boxes."

I swear I see it, right there in the corner, the teensiest hint of a smile. Before it can bloom, Jennie's lips flatten, and she slowly steps toward me.

"I broke the scissors because I was jabbing the boxes too hard." She twirls her braid around her finger. "Uh, thanks. For helping, or whatever."

"You're welcome."

I quickly slice the tape on all the boxes so I can tuck the knife away, and we sort through each one in silence, only the quiet music Jennie has playing on her speaker drifting through the room.

"What kind of stuffie is Princess Bubblegum, anyway?" I ask, flipping through a box of photo frames. It's the last box in my stack, and the air has grown heavier with each one.

Jennie doesn't respond. I find her staring at her box, knuckles nearly white as she grips it, coaxing me slowly in her direction.

"Hey. You okay?"

"She's a pink bunny," she whispers. "My dad got her for me for my sixth birthday. She's got a ribbon on each ear and a-a—" she holds her arms out, thumbs and forefingers pinched together like she's gripping the hem of a skirt, "—*a pink tutu!*" She chokes on her words, burying her sob and face in her hands, and I race across the room, arms outstretched.

I skid to a stop in front of her, resisting the urge to touch her. "You're crying again." *Stupid.* Of course she's crying. She doesn't need me to point out the obvious.

"I'm *not* crying," she cries, jabbing a finger into my chest. "*You're* crying!"

Riiight…

"Uh, do you need a...hug?" Cautiously, I inch toward her, opening my arms in slow motion. She might, like, bite. I don't know how this shit works. My sisters are a lot younger than Jennie; their problems are easily solved with hugs.

Jennie's a Beckett. If she's anything like her older brother, there's a good chance her problems are solved with Oreos and orgasms. I didn't come prepared with cookies, and I'd ideally like to keep my balls right where they are: attached to my fucking body.

"What?" Her chin trembles. "I don't...I..." She groans, stomps, and balls her fists up as her chest heaves. "Garrett."

"C'mon, Jennie."

Taking her hands in mine, I gently guide her into me. She comes willingly, dragging her ass about it though, and I wrap my arms around her. She smells nice, intoxicating, vanilla and cinnamon and coffee. When she carefully slips her arms around my middle and lays her cheek over my heart, I find out she feels nice too. Warm and soft, like when my mom used to microwave my underwear on those extra-cold east coast winter mornings.

"Atta girl," I murmur, palm gliding down her back. It's meant to be soothing, but I forgot she's only wearing a sports bra, so my fingers dance over her bare flesh, and both of us go rigid.

Jennie pushes away at the same time I rocket backward, and I rip my hat off, burying my hand in my hair.

"I'll, uh..." I thumb down the hall. "I'll check the boxes in the spare bedroom."

"Yeah." She nods. "Yeah, cool. Good idea. You do that, and I'll...stay."

My casual stroll turns to a mad dash when I round the corner into the hall. Inside the bedroom, I press my back to the wall and breathe deeply. This is a disaster. The sooner I get out of here, the better.

There are only four boxes, and I go through the first two in no time. When I get to the third, the one labeled *toys*, I grin triumphantly, ripping at the tape.

"*Aha.*" This is it; this is the box. If this doesn't put me in Jennie's good books, nothing will. "Here I come, Princess Bubbleg—*ah! Holy fuck!*" I flip the top down and scream bloody murder. "*Help!*"

"What?" Jennie slides into the bedroom, breathless, eyes wild. "Did you find Princess Bubble—*Garrett!*" Her hands go to her face. She's screeching. I think I'm crying. *"What are you doing?"*

"Looking for Princess Bubblegum!" I shout. The box I'm crushing against my chest, the one filled with dildos and vibrators, rumbles and shakes, coming alive.

"She's not in there!"

"Spoiler alert, Jennie: *I fucking know that!*"

"This box is private!" Jennie charges at me, squishing the box between us. Something starts vibrating, trying to jump out, and I think I might be sick. "You shouldn't have touched it!"

"Why would you label a box of sex toys *toys*?" I shriek back. My back hurts and my face feels really hot. I don't like it.

"What else would you call them?" She tries to pry the box from my—for some reason unwilling—hands. A battle of tug of war promptly ensues, the box ricocheting between us. *"Give…it…back!"*

I yank the box closer—*why?*—and Jennie tumbles forward, plastering the three of us—me, her, and the box—against the wall. She huffs, puffs, and pulls. *Hard.*

The box rips apart at the seams, the most beautiful rainbow of dildos and vibrators flying through the air between us in—I swear to God— slow fucking motion. Jennie's eyes lock with mine, wide and horrified, as a particularly meaty fucker with a suction cup base slaps me across the face. It clatters to the ground, the length of it—*why the hell is it so damn long?*—pumping up and down and winding in circles, spinning around the hardwood like a bad break-dancer.

Jennie's shriek is nothing short of bloodcurdling. With both hands, she shoves me along the wall, out of the bedroom, down the hall. *"Out!"* Her tiny fists pummel my chest. *"Get out!"*

"I'm fucking going!" I trip over my hockey bag, colliding with the wall. Scrambling to my feet, I whip the door open, toss my shit into the hall, and all but throw myself out of Jennie's apartment before the door can hit me in the ass on the way out.

"Holy fucking shit," I mutter, swiping the damp hair off my forehead. I have no idea where my hat went, but I'm sure as hell not going back in to find it.

I'm almost to the elevator when a door creaks, and my heart hammers at Jennie's timid whisper.

"Garrett?"

I glance over my shoulder, finding that faint flash of violet-blue peeking through the crack in the door. "Yeah?"

She licks her lips, drops her gaze, and I barely catch her words before she slams the door. "Thanks for the hug."

I scrub my hands down my face. "Well, I'm fucking dead."

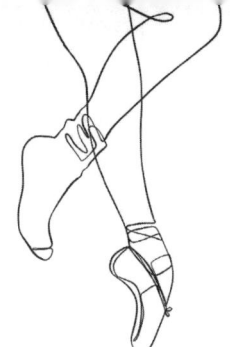

FIVE
GOLDEN DICKING

Jennie

I'M LOSING count of how many days I've sat mindlessly in a row lately, wondering what I'm doing with my life.

Here I am, in my last class of the day on a Thursday afternoon, ready for the weekend to start. I'm in my final year at SFU, about to graduate with a bachelor of fine arts, a major in dance, and the qualifications to teach it. I'm twenty-four years old, and the dream I've worked toward my entire life, poured everything into, is finally within reach.

And yet this life barely feels like mine. That future on stage? Not so sure I want it.

The only thing I'm certain about wanting is pizza. And maybe the cute corgi currently hopping around in the grass in the video on my laptop. A lot of my problems would also be solved by locating Princess Bubblegum too.

"That's it, everyone. Have a great weekend."

The YouTube compilation video of *funniest dogs* disappears as I shut my laptop and tuck it into my bag at my teacher's wrap-up call.

"Miss Beckett." Leah, my teacher, smiles and points to the door. "Can I walk with you?"

"'Course. What's up?"

"My friend from Toronto was visiting last weekend."

I wink. "Did you get a little wild?"

Leah rolls her eyes. She's only four years older than me, and I once saw her in a bar after one of my brother's hockey games. She was wasted and straddling a defenseman. Her glossy eyes were mortified when they met mine, and her entire face glowed a blushing brown. Apparently, *You go, Glen Coco,* wasn't the right thing for me to say, though I still beg to differ. Watching your teacher faceplant as she scrambles to climb off a massive hockey player is funny as hell. She was still wearing sunglasses when she came to class the following Monday, and when I opened my mouth to say something totally uncalled for, she slapped her palm over it.

She's my favorite teacher, and she'd be yours too.

"Okay, fine. I got a *little* wild." She slips a hand over her mouth, leaning closer. "One word: *quarterback.*"

"Did you show him how flexible you are?"

"That is wildly inappropriate, Miss Beckett." She stops me as I reach for the door to the dance studio, eyes wide and playful, and holds her hands out, a good foot between them. She pokes the inside of her cheek and mouths, *Fucking massive.*

I respond with a silent scream. Leah and I grip each other's arms as we bounce excitedly in place. A pair of professors slow, casting curious glances our way, and Leah promptly releases me and clears her throat before we dash ahead into the studio.

It's quiet in here, just the way I like it, and a happy hum starts in my chest.

I slip my shoes and sweater off before sinking down to a bench. "What did you wanna talk to me about, Professor Naughty?"

"So, Monica was down last week—"

"Monica? Monica from The National Ballet in Toronto, Monica? That Monica?"

"That Monica. They're looking to add another teacher to their faculty."

"Wow. That's incredible." I spent my first three years of this five-year program at the Toronto campus, following the teachers around like I was living in my own dreamland, dazed and in love with every moment of it. I never wanted to leave, but that's how the program works: three years there and two here. Plus, my family was here. They *are* here. I loved Toronto but hated the ache in my chest. "Simon will be thrilled."

"Sure, but Simon wasn't my recommendation."

I pause, meeting Leah's excited gaze. "You didn't."

"I did."

"Really? Me?" My bag spills to the floor when I rocket to my feet. "But why?"

"What do you mean why? You're the most beautiful dancer I've seen in years, Jennie."

I gesture lazily at my face. "It's the Beckett dimples and charming grin. We're irresistible."

Leah snickers and swats my shoulder. "You know what I mean. You dance flawlessly, like you were born to do it. You're also hardworking, determined, kind, and always willing to help others learn. You'd make an amazing teacher, Jennie, and the opportunities for you there as a professional dancer are endless."

A professional dancer? In Toronto? My heart patters with excitement and pride that she thought of me, but dread twists my stomach.

"I don't know…" Turning away, I scoop my things off the floor, tucking them in my bag.

"Jennie." Leah rips my bag from my hands, stealing my attention. "What do you mean you don't know?"

With a sigh, I meet her stare. For the first time in my life, I tell someone the truth. "I'm not sure it's what I want. My family is here."

"Families live apart sometimes. Your brother isn't even in the country for half the year. They won't hold it against you if you take this."

Of course they'd want me to follow my dreams. But I'm not sure my dreams involve me moving away from the only people I've been sure of my entire life, the only ones I trust to love me for me. Vancouver is part of me, this incredible place that's shaped my life. No matter how much I loved Toronto, I'm unsure it's where I belong.

"I really appreciate you thinking of me, Leah," I tell her. "When would I need to decide by?"

"You'd have to fly down in the spring to meet with the faculty. They'd need your decision by the end of term. They want someone there for the summer semester, Jennie. You'd be starting right after graduation."

"So I have time to think about it?"

"Of course." She tilts her head, smile curious. "Are you really not sure about this?"

"Just getting a little anxious, I think. About everything, you know? Graduation, getting older, moving…it feels like a new life."

"Sometimes a fresh start is exactly what we need." Leah squeezes my shoulder. "Promise me you'll give it some serious thought."

I promise I will, but it's not a safe place for my mind to get stuck right now; it can be easy for me to get lost up there. So when Leah leaves me in the studio, I throw on my headphones and turn the music loud enough to drown out incessant thoughts about a future I'm not sure of.

There's a certain freedom that comes with dancing when nobody's looking. Every worry about choices I'm not ready to make melts away as the beat carries me across the studio, my body moving effortlessly in tune with the music. A heavy weight seems to lift from my shoulders as my eyes close, and the tempo pushes me forward, letting me chase freedom at my own pace.

Large hands circle my waist, startling my breath from my lungs. My heart settles back in my chest when Simon's eyes lock with mine as he gently shifts my headphones off.

"Relax," he murmurs. "Just me."

"I thought everyone had gone home." I start to dislodge from his grasp. "I'll let you have the space."

His grip tightens as he pulls my back flush with his chest. "Dance with me."

Before I can decline, Simon queues my favorite song.

"C'mon, Jennie. Let me have you once more before the weekend."

"You're not playing fair with the song choice," I mumble, his hands guiding my hips, the rhythm of our bodies moving as James Arthur's smooth voice drenches the air around us, singing about how fast he and his lover are falling in love.

"Don't think I know how to play fair with you." He sweeps my braid over my shoulder, fingers brushing across my skin, making it pebble.

Look, I might be immune to his charms, but I won't deny that—despite the epic level of douchebaggery this man exudes like a horny teenage boy who thinks dousing himself in cologne is the equivalent of a shower—the guy is attractive. Simon is tall and lean, impeccably toned from a life of dancing and intense workouts, of disciplined eating and never taking a break. His light brown hair hangs longer on top, always perfectly styled, blue eyes forever smiling in that boyish, mischievous way that has you wondering what he's up to.

If we hadn't been partners for the last four years and I'd been emotionally available, I might have made a decision of horrendously epic proportions and let him into my pants. There were times I'd been horny enough to consider it.

Then I shook the stupid away, loaded up my favorite Lovehoney cart with some exciting new toys, and reminded myself I could fuck me better than any guy could.

And trust me, *I do.*

"I've been thinking about the Valentine's Day show," Simon starts.

"Valentine's Day? It's November, buddy."

His chuckle rolls down my neck. "I think we should use this song."

"You hate this song."

"Not true. I like it because you like it."

I slip away from him, fingers trailing down his arm to where he holds me. I can feel his eyes on me as I spin, and then he's there, pulling me right back in. With ease, he lifts me above his head, fluid like always. We're one on the dance floor, Simon and me.

I prance across the floor, Simon trailing me as I quietly sing along with James Arthur. I love the picture this song paints of a love so irresistible it's like gravity doesn't exist in their world, demanding they fall hard and fast, just like the name: "Falling Like The Stars." And yet, despite the fall, the way they can't avoid it or slow it down, they're safe.

I know that type of love exists; I've seen it with my own eyes.

I'm just not sure it exists for everyone.

Simon pulls me against him, lips at the shell of my ear as he whispers lyrics that feel too intimate, leave me feeling uneasy, and I don't know why.

Then he twirls me around, fingers curling around my hips as he forces me backward. Blood drums in my ears at the feral look in his eyes, and when I stumble over my feet, he presses me against the cold wall.

"Simon, what are you doing?"

Cupping my jaw, he tilts my face to his. "What does it look like?"

"I don't think this is a good idea," I try gently, palms on his chest to keep him at bay. "Let's say good-bye."

"You think too much, Jennie. That's your problem. Just this once, let yourself feel."

I feel just fine, that's exactly why I know this doesn't feel right, and when his lips descend, brushing across mine, I lift my knee, accidentally shoving it in his balls.

Oops.

Simon cries out, grabbing his crotch. "What the hell, Jennie?"

"I said no," I grind out, shoving against him. One hand is still gripping my waist, and I go tumbling with him, tripping over his legs on my way down. I yelp at the sharp sting radiating through my ankle, clutching it as I spew a record amount of curse words.

"What the fuck was that for?" Simon's on his back, still grabbing his junk, rolling around like a turtle who can't get up. "I thought we were having a moment!"

"Did you think that after I said it wasn't a good idea? That we should say good-bye?" I scramble to my feet, nabbing my things as furious heat rolls through me. "Not everybody wants to fuck you, Simon! We're friends. We will never *be* more than friends. Accept it, or we're done."

My ankle buckles under the weight it no longer wants to bear, and tears of fury prickle at the shooting pain as I storm across the studio. The sound of the door banging behind me echoes through the empty hallway.

If this asshole fucked up my ankle, I'm going to scream.

"Mother...fucking...*fuck*!" I slam the car door before leaning through the open window, smiling at my Uber driver. "Thank you so much, Matthew. Have a great night."

His smile is wobbly, eyes wide with fear. "Good night, ma'am."

Closing my eyes and inhaling deeply, I turn toward the minimansion in front of me. With something like seven fireplaces, it's not all that mini. Who needs that many fireplaces, you ask? My ostentatious-as-fuck brother, apparently.

The front door opens, revealing Olivia, hands on her belly as she bites her grin back. "Thought I heard my wonderful sister-in-law. Mouth of an angel, I swear." She gestures at my foot as I hobble toward her. "Dancing injury?"

"Simon Syphilis inflicted."

She pulls a face. "You need repellant."

Fucking tell me about it.

Inside, I give her a squeeze. "Hey, Pip."

Olivia frowns, crossing her arms over her chest when I release her. She's so tiny. Paired with the pregnancy, it's impossible for her to look as angry as Carter and I make her. She looks more adorable than anything.

"I'm not sure I'm a fan of this new nickname."

"But it's perfect. You're everyone's favorite pip-squeak."

There's a tall blonde sitting on the kitchen island, one long leg slung over the other. Cara hops down with a grin, swallowing me in her hold. "I called her a shrimp earlier and she tried to pull my hair. She's a feisty mama with these pregnancy hormones. Threw a hissy fit when I kept her at bay with my hand on her forehead."

"You gonna have those hormones soon or what? 'Cause I'm scared of you as it is. I need to mentally prepare myself."

Cara laughs, then frowns, nibbling the tip of her thumbnail. She huffs, and that frown turns into a full-blown pout. "Not yet. Emmett says if I sit on his dick one more time without a break longer than twelve hours, it's gonna fall off. Apparently, 'I'll kiss it better' isn't the correct response."

"It's early still," Olivia reminds her gently. "Give it some time."

Cara draws a pattern on the marble countertop. "I know. Guess it's messing with my head that Carter knocked you up by accident and it hasn't happened for us yet despite the endless sex and the fucking calendars." She runs her teeth along her lower lip, eyes hooded. "Not that I mind all the trying. I'd ride that man into oblivion. He's got a dick made of gold."

"Thanks for the mental image," I murmur, pouring myself a glass of water.

She grins. "When are you gonna get yourself your own golden dick? They're magical, promise. Just ask Ollie."

"No part of me wants to know about Ollie's experience with whatever's between my brother's legs."

"Agreed." Olivia follows me to the couch, then starts painting her lips with the ends of her hair, a faraway look in her eyes. "But if we could, like, talk about it for one little minute…" She gives me puppy eyes, and before I can protest, she goes on. "It's just that Carter's been so gen—"

"*Babe!*" The front door slams open, voices pouring into the house, and three seconds later Carter's sliding into the room, chest heaving in his three-piece suit. "Guess what I got!" He rips open a small shoe box, tosses it to the floor, and holds up the tiniest pair of hockey skates I've ever seen. "*Look how cute these are!*" His grin is so wide, and he's nearly vibrating. "Cutest skates for the cutest baby!"

"I'm not sure Baby Beckett will be able to stand, let alone skate, when those fit."

"That's what I said, Ol," Emmett says as he strolls in. He kisses Cara's cheek and slaps a hand to her ass. "Told him not to bother wasting his money. He said he was rich and bought them anyway."

Adam claps Carter's shoulder. "Leave him alone. He's a proud dad-to-be." He smiles at me. "Hey, Jennie. How's the new place? Too bad you got Garrett for a neighbor, huh?"

Before I can answer, the man in question comes inching down the hallway at the literal pace of a snail. Where I'm uneasy about seeing him after the dildo fiasco, he looks downright terrified, ears already bright red, throat bobbing, eyes wide as they pinball around the room, landing everywhere but on me.

He clears his throat, tugging on the wrist of his suit jacket. "We talkin' 'bout the baby skates?"

"Actually, we were talking about the golden dicking Jennie needs."

The teensy skates fall from Carter's hands at Cara's words, like the glass of water does from mine. I manage to catch it before it hits the ground, but not before soaking my top.

"No, we weren't!" I yell at the same time Carter shrieks, "Jennie doesn't need a dicking!"

Cara and Emmett cackle, and Adam's busy patting Garrett's back.

Because the man is keeled over, choking on his own damn spit, and I'm about to punch him right in the nuts if he doesn't reel it the fuck in.

I hate him. I hate him so much. Him and his lopsided, happy smile, and his stupid blond hair, always a beautiful, perfect disaster.

When he finally remembers how to breathe, his frightened eyes land on me.

I wish they hadn't. Why, you ask?

Ever had a box full of rubber dicks explode in front of a super-hot hockey player? Ever had one of them slap him right in the face? No? Just me?

Cool.

Well, anyway. That's why.

"Jennie needs someone to roll around with," Cara continues. "Have some fun and live it up while she's young and single."

"No fun!" Carter's still screaming. "Jennie doesn't need to have fun!"

"What about your dance partner?"

Carter gasps. "Not *Steve*."

"Simon," Olivia reminds him.

"I will break him, Jennie. Break his soul. Crush his balls." Carter squeezes the air, or rather, Simon's imaginary balls.

I check my nails while Carter finishes one of his overprotective dad-bro bullshit spiels. "Are you done?"

He leans close. "Twinkle Toes will never dance again."

"Great." Standing, I gesture at my soaked top. "Can I borrow a shirt, Ollie? I can't go to the game with a see-through shirt and a black bra."

"No, you cannot," Carter agrees aggressively, still worked up about the casual fun I'm not even having.

With an eye roll, I follow Olivia out of the room. "My eyes are on my face, Andersen," I mutter as I brush by Garrett, noting the way his gaze is glued to my chest. Inwardly, I smile as his cheeks heat like a volcano before he drops his stare to his fancy shoes. He's so damn awkward; teasing him is too easy.

Ninety percent of Olivia's shirts are bordering on crop top length due to the several inches I have on her, so the Vipers tee I settle on elicits a glare from my brother loaded with a fuckton of disapproval when I meet him downstairs.

"Wanna borrow a sweater too?" he asks. "You can wear one of mine."

"No thanks."

"You might be cold."

"It's warm in the arena."

"I can see your belly button."

"I can see that your eyes work."

"Fucking sisters," Carter grumbles, adding something about wandering eyes and dead teammates as he yanks open the door to the garage. I think he was doomed to be this overprotective, that it came with the territory of trying to fill my dad's shoes, making sure I never get hurt.

He doesn't have much to worry about anyway. I never let anyone close enough.

Carter glances back at me as the boys start to filter out, and his gaze softens as Garrett approaches. "Garrett told me he helped you look for Princess Bubblegum." He pecks my cheek. "We'll keep looking."

He steps into the garage, leaving Garrett standing there like a deer in headlights.

"Is that right?" I murmur, chin lifting. "What else did Garrett say?'

"Nothing," Garrett promises hastily, hands up between us like he needs protection. "Nothing, Jennie, I swear. I wouldn't—I would never tell him—"

"Tell him what?"

His jaw dangles, fingers plowing through his hair. "Nothing? 'Cause there's nothing to tell. So I wouldn't tell him…anything."

I smile. Garrett stares, mouth opening and closing over and over, like he can't find the words he's looking for. That's okay, because I'm trying to pretend I don't notice the way he fills out his slim-fitting burgundy suit, how the jacket stretches across his broad shoulders. His thick, mile-long legs lead down to a pair of cognac leather shoes, and my gaze lingers too long on that messy hair, the way it really ramps up the *fuck me* factor. I have an urge to bury my fingers in it, hold on tight while I take his pretty face for a ride.

I gesture at his midnight blue tie, loose and too far to the left. "Your tie is a mess."

"What?" His eyes dip. "Oh. Yeah. Okay. Thanks." He fiddles with the knot, and my brows jump at the way he somehow manages to make it so much worse. "Good?"

I shake my head, taking the silk in my hand, tugging him toward me. He comes tumbling forward, big hands swallowing up my waist to catch himself.

"Sorry!" He drops his hold, staring at his hands. "So sorry."

I unknot his tie, fix each length, crossing and looping the material.

"Thank you," he murmurs. "How did you learn how to do that?"

Memories flood of me snuggled in my parents' bed, watching my dad knot his tie, slip on his suit jacket, fix his sleeves. "Watched my dad get ready for work every morning."

Garrett's eyes flicker before his gaze falls, locking with mine. "I'm sorry we didn't find Princess Bubblegum."

"There was a locket too." The words are out of my mouth before I can stop them, and I drop my gaze to the space between us.

"What?"

The tips of my fingers flutter over my collarbone where the gold used to rest. "A locket. A heart, with a picture of my dad and I. Princess Bubblegum was wearing it." I swallow the memory, flapping a hand through the air. Garrett dodges it before it can slap him across the face, much like my dildo. "It's no big deal." *It's a huge deal.* "I'll be fine." *I'm not okay.*

"Maybe it's still at your mom's," he offers gently.

It's not; I've looked.

Correction: I've torn the house apart several times, definitely *not* while sobbing. Mom promised she'd keep an eye out, but I just know she's gone for good. Lost somewhere between the house and the condo. Recognition that I may never again see something so special to me unfurls a raw ache deep in my stomach. I quell the urge to place my hands over the pain.

A throat clears, drawing our eyes to where Cara and Olivia wait, staring. It's at this point I realize I've finished the knot long ago and am now just standing here with Garrett's tie in one hand, his face mere inches from mine.

Dropping the tie, I step back.

"Uh, I guess I'll..." Garrett thumbs toward the garage, where Carter is screaming for him to hurry up. "See you guys at the game." His tender gaze moves over me once more. "I'm sorry about your necklace." Warm fingers graze mine, a squeeze so gentle I can't be sure it's real, and then he's gone.

"That was interesting," Cara muses as he disappears.

Olivia licks an Oreo. "Super interesting."

I stroll to the fridge, hiding my face. "What was interesting?"

Cara grins. "Oh look, Liv. Jennie's playing clueless."

"Imagine all the possibilities."

"Dangerous possibilities."

"Carter would be livid.

"We should videotape his reaction."

I shut the fridge and strut down the hall.

"Where you going?" Cara calls.

"Bathroom."

I hear the smile in her voice right before I lock myself away.

"If you think the bathroom is going to save you from me right now, sweet, naïve Jennie, you're more delusional than I thought."

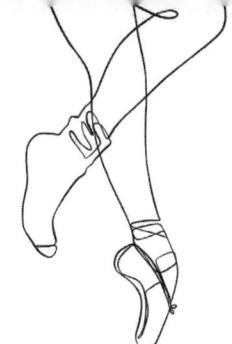

SIX
DONG RIDES & CONCUSSIONS

Jennie

"WE'RE REALLY NOT GONNA TALK about it?" Cara shoves another handful of Skittles and M&M's into her mouth. I've never been more disgusted in my entire life.

"Can you not?"

"What?" Another blasphemous handful. "Not talk about Garrett potentially taking you for a golden dong ride?"

My nose wrinkles. "Did you really just say dong?"

"I really just said dong. Bet Garrett's packing some serious heat. In fact, I guarantee it. I've got the four-one-one on *all* the dongs down there." She gestures to where the team is warming up, firing pucks off at Adam, passing back and forth with each other, or if you're Carter, grinning at Olivia while chomping on pink bubble gum. "Em's massive, obviously. So big I can't walk straight for days when I've pissed him off on purpose just so he'll hate-fuck me." She gestures at Carter. "Mediocre at best."

Olivia snorts. "*Please.*"

"Adam's our gentle giant, but he's secretly packing a weapon of mass destruction. He's definitely gonna put his future wifey in a wheelchair."

"Cara!" Olivia dunks a popcorn kernel in a container of nacho cheese sauce, tosses it back, and hums happily. Pregnancy cravings, I guess.

"And Garrett...I mean, just look at him." Cara waves her hand in his direction, and Garrett catches the motion, looking away, then back quickly. Even from here, I see his cheeks flame when he realizes he's the topic of conversation. "Such a cutie. He was the shyest thing when I first met him."

"He's still shy," I point out. It's unnerving. I grew up with a brother who never filtered his words. Now here I am, speaking most of my thoughts out loud, censorship lost. Having to guess what's going through someone's mind is tiring.

Cara shakes her head. "He's shy around you because he thinks you're hot. The safest bet is to interact with you as little as possible so Carter doesn't catch on. Bet that man's a real freak between the sheets." Another atrocious handful, paired with a brow pump. "You should find out."

"Absolutely not." When I plant my shoes on the glass in front of me, I hiss at the radiating pain in my ankle. It's definitely sprained, and now I'll have to use my other foot to kick Simon in the balls next time I see him.

"He's not my type," I continue about Garrett. Never mind that Carter would never allow me to date one of his friends or teammates. I'll have a hard enough time bringing any normal man home one day. If I ever meet one, that is.

Truth be told, I don't care all that much. I've been single virtually all my adult life, and battery-powered toys have been an outstanding substitute. Replacing them with a man almost seems like an unnecessary downgrade.

"Tell you what. If you can guarantee Garrett does, in fact, have a golden dong, I'll consider taking it for a ride."

Cara's smile widens. "Really?"

"No." *Maybe.*

Olivia huffs a long sigh and rubs her belly. "I could use a good dong ride." She lays a hand on my arm the moment my groan begins. "Don't get me wrong. It's good. Great. It always is."

"Fantastic. I was definitely wondering."

"But he's been so *gentle* lately."

Cara hammers a fist to her chest as she folds forward, choking on her snack. "Please tell me he's the type of dad who thinks he'll poke his baby in the eye if he's not careful."

"He's taken to warning the baby every time we're about to have sex." Olivia scrubs a hand over her exhausted expression. "*Okay, little buddy. Daddy's coming in. Make sure you move all the way to the back.*" Her wide brown eyes are full of disbelief. "It's the anxious chuckling that really gets me, and every time I move, he stops and asks if I'm okay. I just...I need him to fuck me, you know? *Really* fuck me." She shifts in her seat. "This baby's making me horny as hell."

Cara pokes my cheek. "Quit acting like you're gonna vomit."

"I might."

Olivia snickers before smiling softly. "Carter said Garrett helped you look for your stuffie. That was nice of him."

"Yeah, I think he really regrets that."

"Why would he regret that?"

"Because he got slapped across the face by Indiana Bones," I mumble around two pieces of licorice.

"Who's Indiana B—" Cara's question dies, words hanging in the air, before she explodes with a howl so loud the boys look up from the ice. "For the love of fucking God, tell me you slapped Garrett in the face with a dildo named Indiana Bones, please, Jennie."

"I didn't slap him in the face with it. We fought over the box it was in, the box died, and Indiana Bones soared through the air and kinda... you know." I flop my hand around before smacking the back of it against my cheek. "It's his own fault. He shouldn't have been looking."

Through the laughter, Olivia asks, "What the hell prompted him to look through that box?"

I shrug. "It might've been labeled *toys*."

"Ah." She smirks. "And he was looking for a stuffed animal, so he made a logical decision."

"Oh look! Time for the anthem." I spring from my seat. "Conversation's over."

Talk of dildos, dongs, and good, hard dickings that apparently Olivia and I are both in desperate need of are put on the back burner as the game starts. We're playing our biggest rival. Games like this require undivided attention so I can shout obscenities at the ref every time he misses something.

"Oh come on, ref!" I leap to my feet as Washington's centreman slips his stick between Garrett's legs, sending him flying forward.

"Does your wife know you're fucking us?" Cara screams as the referee continues to ignore the obvious penalty.

I slap the glass as Garrett climbs to his feet, giving his head a shake. "Hey, ref! Might wanna check your voice mail! Looks like you missed a few calls!"

The play only stops when the buzzer blares, signaling the end of the second period, and Carter gets up close and personal with the trip-happy dipshit who hasn't demonstrated any real skill so far. Whatever he says has the centreman shoving against him, and Carter glides away with a shit-eating grin.

Problem is, Cara and I have big mouths, and we're still pissed off. Countless calls and should-be penalties have been missed. We're down by one, but we shouldn't be.

"Hey, ref!" Cara hollers. "Want a pregnancy test? 'Cause you've missed two fucking periods!"

"Get off your knees!" I yell as he skates by. "You're blowing the fucking game!"

Olivia buries her face in her hands, partly to hide her laughter, partly because she's embarrassed. Every time her face winds up on TV, her high school students have a heydey with it. Her TV appearances are never her fault. The fault lies in a humiliating goal dedication from her husband, or trouble Cara and I start.

By the time we've reached the last five minutes of the game, things haven't improved. Washington is playing dirty, the ref is missing calls left, right, and center, and Cara flashed him two aggressive middle fingers and told him to shove them up his ass. On a positive note, Emmett has managed to tie the game up.

A defenseman digs the puck out of the corner and spots Garrett up the boards, open and waiting. He fires the puck up the ice and Garrett takes off like lightning as Emmett and Carter race up his sides, clearing the way for him.

Everyone's shrieking, cheering him on, and that twat centerman from earlier hops off his bench, trading spots with someone on the ice. Carter beelines for him, hollering a warning to Garrett, who winds up. His stick comes backward before sending the puck whizzing right by the goalie's head and into the net.

The sound of the buzzer is lost to the collective gasp that steals the breath of every fan in Rogers Arena as the centerman's body connects with Garrett's from behind, crushing him into the boards headfirst.

Garrett goes limp, two-hundred-plus pounds of dead weight dropping to the ice.

Silence roars, players circling our right-winger, medics on their knees tending to him.

"He's not getting up," Cara whispers. "Why isn't he getting up? Somebody help him!"

"C'mon, Garrett," I mutter, the tip of my thumbnail between my teeth. "Get up."

He doesn't, though. He doesn't move a muscle, sprawled out on the ice, and fear spreads through me in the form of adrenaline.

"Toss that asshole out!" I scream into the silence, shaking the glass as Garrett's limp body is lifted onto a stretcher. The centerman in question meets my gaze, entirely too relaxed about sending someone to the hospital. "We play real hockey in Canada, you fucking wiener!"

He smiles, wiggling his gloved fingers at me, and it's in that moment Carter throws his stick down, whips his gloves off, tosses his helmet to the ice, and pounces.

The arena erupts as the benches empty, players rushing the ice, equipment and fists everywhere. Everyone is shrieking, and there's a tiny pregnant woman trying to physically restrain me and Cara to prevent us from joining in.

At least she doesn't have to worry about her face on TV.

It's nearly midnight when the front door opens. Olivia quickly finishes slathering her Oreo with peanut butter before popping it in her mouth and leaping off the couch.

Carter, Emmett, and Adam filter into the living room one by one, all of them—*shockingly*—grinning ear to ear.

Carter has a nasty split down the center of his swollen lip, and Emmett has the beginning of a shiner. Even Adam has a puffy, red cheekbone. He looks happiest of all.

"I never get in fights! My dad's so proud of me for plowing the other goalie into the boards!" He runs a palm down his puffed chest. "Says he recorded it to show all his friends."

Olivia hands him a bag of ice. "Don't make it a habit, Mr. Lockwood. Your face is too pretty."

Garrett appears at the edge of the dark hallway with a sheepish smile, the faintest of shadows painting the skin around his eyes, exhausted but still bright.

Cara embraces him. "How are you feeling, Gare-Bear?"

He shoves his hands in his pockets, shoulders popping up and down. "Okay. Just tired and a bit of a headache. A mild concussion. Off for the next week, at least."

Cara grips his face, turning it left and right. "Why do you have black eyes?" She slaps her hands to her mouth. "Did someone punch you after you were taken off on the stretcher? Who would do that?" She slings her purse over her shoulder and starts stalking away. "Em, let's go. I'm gonna rip their puny balls off and hang them from my rearview mirror like a prize."

"Rein it in, Mrs. Brodie." Emmett takes her elbow, stopping her stomp-off. "It can happen when you hit the back of your head. Gare hit his pretty hard."

"Oh. Right. Okay then." She sinks to the couch, draping one leg over the other, arms crossed. "I still wanna castrate them."

He ruffles her hair. "I know you do, tiger."

Carter looks to me. "I told Garrett you'd drive him home."

"What? I don't have a—"

"In his car. He drove here earlier."

I open my mouth to object—I cannot be alone with this man; he saw my extensive toy collection last time, so it can only go downhill from here—but Carter silences me with a fierce look.

"He can't drive, and you live in the same building."

Right. Yeah. Garrett's slight frown at my less-than-stellar reaction tugs at my heart. "When did you wanna leave?"

He palms the back of his neck. "Uh, now? If that's okay with you, I mean."

Nodding, I stand and catch Cara's eye as she mouths, *Get that dick* to me. I flip her the sly bird while hugging Olivia, then hobble toward Garrett.

"Do you need help?" we ask each other at the same time.

My nose scrunches. "Why would I need help?"

He gestures at my foot. "You've been limping all night."

I cross my arms. "You have a concussion."

"I'm fine," he assures me.

"Well, so am I."

I see it, right there in the corner of his mouth, the tiniest hint of a smile, and I commit to being as pleasant as possible for the entirety of the twenty-minute drive.

Until I see his car.

"What the fuck is this?"

"An Audi RS Five Sportback." Smiling, he rubs his chest, like this car is his pride and joy. "Fully loaded."

"That's, like, a sixty-thousand-dollar car." I'm borderline screaming.

"Ninety-four," he murmurs.

"Garrett!" Definitely screaming. "I can't drive this!"

He opens the door for me. "You'll be fine."

"*Fine*," I mimic on a choked laugh. "*Fine,* he says. Ha."

Hand pressed to my lower back, he guides me forward. "Get in the car, Jennie."

I do, but with a groan. My seat rocks back and forth with jerking movements as I fiddle with the buttons, adjusting the position. "I don't know what I'm doing. Why isn't this working?" I throw my arms up. "See? Even your car doesn't want me driving."

Garrett chuckles, crouching down to fix the seat for me, peering at me from beneath stupidly thick eyelashes. "Good?" he asks quietly.

I grip the steering wheel, averting my gaze. "Uh-huh."

"All righty." He climbs in beside me. "Let's go."

And go I do, the car rocketing forward as I squeal, and I slam on the brakes at the end of the long driveway, Garrett catching himself on the dashboard, toque flying off his head.

"Jesus fuck." Wide eyes meet mine, and the fear is so, *so* real. "What the hell was that?"

"I haven't driven in a while! I get anxious in the snow!"

"We're not even on the road yet!"

"I know!"

He studies me for a long moment before his teeth nab his lower lip, stopping his laugh. "Just take it nice and slow. We'll be fine." Relaxing in his seat, he closes his eyes and sighs. "And don't crash my car, or you'll be working it off however I deem fit."

My jaw hangs.

He cracks one lid and a sleepy smile. "Just kidding."

The ride home is quiet and peaceful. Five minutes in, I think

Garrett's fallen asleep. His legs are spread wide, long arms between them, head thrown back on the rest, and he hasn't made a single sound. *Bad idea. Don't I need supervision?*

My favorite song comes over the stereo system, and even though I fucked my ankle during it only hours ago while Simon tried to forever ruin this song for me, I hum along quietly, singing the words under my breath. "With you I'm safe…" I glance over my shoulder before shifting lanes, approaching the parking garage. "We're fall—" Jaw clamping, I blush when I catch Garrett's eyes on me. "Sorry."

He doesn't say anything, just reaches over me, getting up in my space. My skin sizzles without permission, and my heartbeat drops between my thighs, because he's hot as balls and he smells nice and he's so close. But all he does is press the button on the visor above my head, making the garage door spring open.

"Over there," he murmurs, pointing. "Ninety-seven."

I pull into the spot and cut the engine. Garrett tows his equipment from the trunk, and it's not until he opens my door and offers me his hand that I realize I've just been sitting, watching.

I slip my hand into his. It's big and warm and swallows mine up for only a moment.

He trails behind me, and I hiss in agony as I climb the single step to the walkway, where the elevator is. His hand touches my lower back as he guides me into the elevator, and something hot unravels inside me as he stands opposite me, studying.

"What happened? To your ankle?"

"Oh, I…" I stick my foot out, moving it in a slow circle, and grit my teeth at the tenderness while I search for a lie. "Just tripped over my bag at school today."

He hums lowly, a clear indication he thinks it's bullshit, but he doesn't push.

The elevator stops on my floor, and I give Garrett a small wave.

He follows me.

"Where are you going?" I look to the door across the hall, and annoyance prickles my nape. He's got a concussion for fuck's sake. But hey: "Maybe she'll dress up and play nurse."

His brows lift at the bite in my tone. "Just walking you to your door, sunshine."

"Oh. Oops."

"Yeah. Oops." Silence stretches. "Thanks for driving me home."

"Yeah. Of course. If you need anything, help or whatever...you know where I am."

"Thanks, Jennie. Just gonna take a swim and head to bed. I'll be fine."

"A swim?" A prop a fist on my hip. "Didn't the doctor tell you to take it easy? No working out."

"It's not a workout."

"Swimming is physical activity that accelerates your heartbeat. It *is* a workout, you pylon."

His lips quirk. "Did you just call me a pylon?"

"Yeah, well, this isn't one of your brightest ideas." My hip juts with attitude; I've always had a fuckton of it. "What if something happens while you're in the water?"

He sighs, slipping a hand under his toque to scratch his head. "Look, Jennie, I feel fine. It's a precaution more than anything. I'm not gonna do any vigorous swimming. I just wanna relax a bit, loosen my muscles." At my crossed arms and pursed lips, he grins. "If you're so concerned, why don't you come with me?"

"You'd   like   that,   wouldn't   you?"   I   snap. I don't catch his response. He mutters it from behind the hand he scrubs over his mouth, but *half-naked*, *hard*, and *gonna kill me* are definitely part of it.

"Look at it this way: Carter wanted me to be your babysitter, now you can be mine. We don't have to talk. C'mon, Jennie. I won't be long."

I huff, unlocking my door, then spin back to him. "Wait a second. We have a pool?"

"Across from the gym."

"We have a gym?"

"For the top two floors," he admits sheepishly, then grins. "I can give you my code so you can use them whenever you want."

"You're damn right you're giving me that code." I prop the door open with my hip. "I have to get changed. Want to wait in here?"

The way his face lights up at the simplicity of me accepting his offer makes me wonder if he craves company the same way I do. "You're coming?"

If I'm being honest, I absolutely want to see him mostly naked and soaking wet. A mental flickpick I can file away in my Flickapedia for future usage.

Like tonight.

Yes, I'm 100 percent gonna flick it to the image of Garrett Andersen. Sue me.

"Well, duh, Garrett. I don't want you to drown."

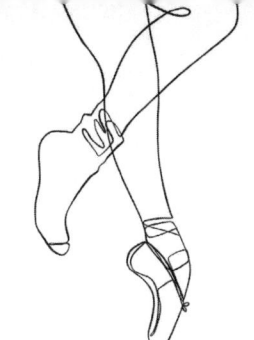

SEVEN
WE GET IT; YOU'RE HOT

Jennie

SHOULD I pay attention to the glaring neon sign in my head, the one blinking *BAD IDEA!*?

Maybe.

Ideally.

Am I going to though? *Pfft.* Don't be ridiculous.

When I step out of my bedroom, Garrett's shocked stare lands on me. "What the hell are you wearing?"

"What, this?" Fluffy, microfleece robe between my fingers, I spin. "My robe and slippers."

Not sure what reaction I expected, but it wasn't him keeled over, slapping his knee while howling with laughter.

"You look like my mom," he chokes out. He points at my outfit, my robe covered in ballerina dogs, my dog slippers with floppy ears, and opens his mouth. Instead of speaking, he shakes his head and laughs again, loud, obnoxious, and irritating. "Holy fuck."

"Yeah, well, your mom must be hot as hell then." I stomp by, chucking the hat he left here post–dildo debacle at his head. "Here's your hat, Gare-Bear."

He cackles some more, following as I strut to the elevator.

If I thought my condo was incredible, it's nothing compared to Garrett's. His penthouse is flawless, open and sprawling, a breathtaking mix of old industrial and modern, with high exposed ceilings, brick walls, and slate marble counters. With the east-facing wall made entirely of glass, he must get amazing natural light and one hell of a sunrise.

"Ready?"

I spin, stopping short when I spy him.

"Oh my God," I cackle. "What the hell are you wearing?"

His grin is electric, dipped in mirth and arrogance, a stark contrast to the sheepish half smile I normally get from him. "My robe and slippers," he parrots back. The man even punctuates his sentence with a smug hip pop.

"My robe actually covers my body. You...that..." I gesture at his sky-high silk robe, the way it shows off too much—and yet somehow not enough—of his muscular thighs. "I can't. You look ridiculous."

"I look hot as fuck." He ushers my still-laughing ass into the hall. "Carter got us these as a joke for their wedding. We had a photoshoot."

"I need the pictures." I tug his elbow. "*Please.*"

"No way, sunshine. I'm never letting anyone see them."

"But I've already seen you in this," I argue, ignoring the nickname as he leads me up one flight of stairs. I'm pretty sure he only calls me it to get under my skin. The smell of chlorine fills the air as the floor opens to a beautiful pool, the city below us lighting up the dark Vancouver skyline through the endless windows.

"And with any luck, you'll forget what I look like in this."

"Nope. Not happening. Burned into my memory, where it will remain, forever." Along with another image, which is Garrett *de*-robing while staring at me with a goofy, lopsided smile.

I swallow my groan as he reveals the most immaculate body I've ever laid eyes on.

He's pristine, all corded arms and carved muscles, leading down to a lean, tapered waist, and a bathing suit that does nothing to disguise the fact that Cara was, unfortunately, very correct: the weapon this man is carrying is big enough to destroy a small country. It's been an unholy number of years since I've been intimate with somebody, and there's a part of me—a very minuscule part—that wouldn't mind being that small country.

Sliding off my robe and slippers, I set them next to Garrett's things on the bench. When I turn back to him, I find his eyes locked on me.

His throat bobs, gaze heating as it falls, slow to come back up. In a moment of weakness, I reach for my robe, desperate to cover myself back up.

"I take back what I said earlier," he whispers, halting my actions. "You definitely do *not* look like my mom." His eyes widen, head wagging, like he didn't mean to say that out loud. He gestures at me with one hand, the other in his hair. "I mean, you have a belly button ring." He smashes his lips together. "No. No, that's not what I...I wasn't..." He covers his face with both hands, dragging them down in slow motion. "Aaah..."

Well, this is interesting. Also, I'm no longer feeling insecure. Thank you, Mr. Andersen.

To most people, I'm simply Carter Beckett's little sister. I see the struggle there, the expression Garrett wears. I'm my own person, but he's reminded that I'm untouchable by nature, *because* of my brother. There's a physical attraction, one he's battling with.

Still, when I climb into the hot tub, Garrett's head moves between me and the pool, five whole damn times, like he can't decide how close he's allowed to be to me. I rest my head and close my eyes so that he can make the decision without whatever pressure he feels he's currently under, and a minute later I hear the quiet lapping of water.

Cracking a lid, I watch Garrett swim up and down the length of the pool, and I resist the urge to snort. *Not a workout, my ass.*

Content in knowing he's not going to die, I turn the massage jets on high, enjoy the way the pain in my ankle dissipates, and relax with a happy sigh.

I don't know how long it's been when a cool, damp hand lands on my shoulder, jolting me awake with a gasp, and Garrett's turquoise eyes peer into mine.

"Sorry. Didn't mean to scare you. You fell asleep. I called your name a couple times."

My brain begs me to formulate a response. Instead, I study the shape of his lips, the way the bottom one is slightly puffier, the perfect bow that sits on top, the bit of scruff that surrounds them and makes his jawline a hundred times more rugged than it needs to be.

Towering above me, he stands there in all his flexed muscle glory, soaked to the bone, shaggy hair a rich golden color, like honey, droplets of water pooling at the tips until they drip down his face. In fact, I watch a particularly fat droplet hit his top lip, watch the way Garrett's tongue darts out to catch it. Then I find the one rolling slowly down his chest, a river etching a path through his muscles. That bad boy keeps on rolling, right until it disappears into the waistband of his bathing suit shorts.

Ladies and gentlemen, I've hit the Holy Grail in flickpick material.

Garrett's gaze drops to my chest, then ricochets back to my face. "You okay?"

"Fine," I manage, super croaky.

His eyes bounce down again, then back up. Down, once more. Up. *Jesus Christ, down again? Seriously?* I know I have boobs there, but has the guy not seen enough sets of perfect tits? What's so interesting about these ones?

Looking down at myself, I inwardly groan. My nipples are rock hard, saluting him through the bathing suit that does absolutely nothing to disguise that I'm turned on right now. Stupid fucking nipples. *Stand down, soldiers.*

I roll my eyes and flick water at him. "We get it, Garrett; you're hot. You don't have to stand there half-naked and soaking wet and rub your hotness in our face."

He beams with pride before his forehead creases. "We?"

"Yes, *we.*" I gesture at my nipples. "Don't act like you haven't noticed. Your eyes can't stay on my face for more than two seconds."

"Well, I didn't...I mean, they're...hard," he finally finishes with a sigh, followed by a barely audible *fuck.*

This guy is the most terrible combination of godawful at flirting and horrendously awkward, and part of me wants to bury my face in a pillow and scream. The other part of me finds it intoxicating, adorably charming, notching his *fuck me* factor up to a full ten.

Highly annoying. I don't like it.

Garrett claps his fist into his opposite hand, rocking back on his heels. "Um, should we...are you...let's..." He points to the door. "Bed?" His jaw hangs as he quickly attempts to backtrack, eyes full of fear as he waves his hands in front of his face. "I didn't mean together. Not, like, you and me, in bed, together. That's not what I meant."

"Right."

"I meant you in your bed and me in mine. Fuck. Gross."

My brows rise slowly. "Gross?"

"What? No. Not gross."

"You said gross."

"But I didn't mean...it wouldn't be gross. It would be great. No. That came out wrong too." He squeezes his eyes shut, head wagging frantically. "I have a concussion," he finally spits out, then holds his hand out. "Can I help you out?"

"Are you sure you want to touch me? You might get my cooties. Imagine how *gross* that would be."

Garrett cracks a grin that turns into a soft, hearty chuckle, the tension in his shoulders easing. "I deserved that. I'm ready to go, but if you want to stay longer, I don't mind hanging—"

"No." I dislodge my ass from my seat, wading through the hot water. "I'm ready for bed." I take Garrett's outstretched hand, letting him help me out.

I sink down to the bench, sliding into my slippers while Garrett fetches us some towels. Exhaustion hits me like a brick to the face, and I rest against the wall. The deck is humid and steamy, slatted bamboo walls reminiscent of a sauna, and sleep begs to pull me under.

When Garrett returns with a towel, I stand and yawn, stretching my arms overhead.

"What the—" I spin, trying to slap at my back where I feel my strap pulling, like it's caught on something. My weak ankle buckles under the pressure of the sudden movement, slipping from underneath me.

My life flashes before my eyes as I tumble face first toward the hot tub. Garrett flies forward, arms coming around me, sandwiching me between his glorious body and the wall.

"That was a close one." His chuckle dies as quickly as it starts. "Holy fuck."

His labored breathing washes over my face as he holds me tight to him. My chest heaves at the contact as my body reminds me for the umpteenth time that the man is fine as hell and battery-powered boyfriends can only satisfy so much.

He feels so nice, his skin hot on mine, the feel of his bare chest pressed against my bare—

"No," I whisper-gasp, shaking my head, fingernails biting into his shoulders.

His eyes hold pity and so, *so* much fear. "Yes."

My gaze falls, landing on my bikini top on the wet floor, halfway between us and the hot tub. My body reacts before my brain has time to catch up.

With a scream that echoes off the tiles, I shove against Garrett's broad chest, pushing him off me. Not my smartest moment. Now I'm topless and my nipples are so hard, they're sharp enough to cut ice.

But perhaps worst part of all is what Garrett wears: a massive-as-fuck hard-on, stretching his bathing suit so far that it's gaping from his waist. I'm not kidding, but I wish I were.

So I keep screaming, and pointing, one arm slapped across my boobs, the other flailing wildly in the direction of his junk, and now Garrett's screaming, too, eyes ricocheting between his tented shorts and my boobs.

"Tuck it away!" I shriek at him.

"*You* tuck *those* away!" he shrieks back.

"Stop looking!"

"*You* stop looking!"

"*Garrett!*"

"*Jennie!*"

We must cover our eyes at the same time, because one second I'm staring at his erection, and then next I'm running aimlessly. I bounce off his solid chest, and something hard pokes me in the belly button.

"I'm so sorry!" Garrett shouts. "I'm sorry, Jennie!" His hand slaps at my arm, then my shoulder, before wrapping around my neck. He turns me around and pushes me against the wall. "Just stay there, *please!*"

He releases me as I stand frozen, face smooshed against the bamboo slats that created this whole mess when they somehow managed to capture the knot in the end of my bikini string.

Slowly dropping my hands, I peek over my shoulder. Garrett reaches into his shorts and adjusts himself with two squeezed eyes and a hiss. He nabs my top off the ground, and I quickly turn back to the wall.

"Here." He shoves my top into my hand. I quickly slip it on, covering my boobs and still-erect nipples. "It's really, it's…it's not a big deal, ya know? I didn't even see anything."

"Really?" *The erection just appeared out of thin air?*

"Yeah," he lies, and not at all convincingly. "Nothing at all."

"Hey, do you see my nipple ring anywhere?" I spin toward Garrett. He's got his robe back on, though the thin silk does nothing to disguise that he's still hard, and still gigantic. "I can't find it."

"Nipple ring? I didn't notice a pierc—" His face pales. "Oh shit."

I narrow my eyes. "Yeah, oh shit, Mr. I-didn't-even-see-anything."

He rubs his nape, cheeks pink. "Well, I...I..." With a resigned smile, he lifts a shoulder. "I'm a weak man, and they're nice tits."

My stubborn nose points to the ceiling. "Yeah, I know they are."

His shy smile blooms into a megawatt grin. "I'm sorry, Jennie."

"You really look it."

"If only you could've seen something equally as embarrassing." He punctuates his sentence with an exaggerated eye roll. "Then we'd be even."

"Oh, trust me, buddy. I saw it, and I'm still seeing it."

He plants his hands on his hips, drawing my attention south. "Can't miss it, huh?"

I shove my hand in his face as I strut over to my robe. "Go back to being shy. Your arrogance is not wanted here. I have enough huge egos in my life."

Garrett chuckles softly. "Are we okay? I really am sorry."

"We're fine. This day needs to end though."

"Agreed." He points down a hallway. "Just gonna wash my hands and grab a water. Want one?"

"No thanks."

Garrett meets me at the door a minute later, slurping down his water. He screws the cap back on as he follows me out, an easy smile on his lips, much more welcome than the terrified look he normally wears.

"I'll ride down with you," he tells me, calling for the elevator.

"You don't have to."

"It's late. I should make sure you get to your door okay."

"Thank you." I study him carefully from across the elevator. The bruising around his eyes has become more prominent in the last two hours, and he looks nearly about to pass out. "How are you feeling?"

"Good," he answers too quickly, then grins at my arched brow. "My head hurts and I'm tired as hell."

"Do you need help? Like..." I wind my damp braid around my fist. "Do you need me to check on you in the middle of the night or something?"

"Nah." Palm pressed to my lower back, he guides me into the hall. "Adam's calling me every couple hours, and the guys are gonna check in in the morning."

I nod, pausing at my door. My gaze goes to Emily's apartment across the hall, and Garrett's eyes follow.

"Look, Jennie. I'm not gonna sleep with her again."

I frown. "Why?"

"Your friendship is more important to me."

"We're friends?"

His face falls. "Well, I didn't mean...I mean, I thought that we could be...friends? Or we don't have to be. If you don't want to be. Whatever."

I smile when he looks to the ground. I don't know why I find his awkwardness so endearing, especially when minutes ago he boldly asked if it was hard to miss his XL erection.

"Garrett?"

His cautious gaze rises. "Yeah?"

"You should work on saying exactly what you're thinking, all of the time, not just some of it. It's nice when people are honest, don't you think? There's no guessing."

"I guess I struggle with that sometimes when I'm getting to know someone."

"Well, I'm a Beckett. We don't censor our thoughts."

He laughs, a hearty, warm sound. "You guys really don't, do you?"

I press up on my toes and peck his cheek, smiling as it warms beneath my lips. "Thanks for the second most awkward night of my life."

"What was the most awkward?"

"The day you found my box of dildos."

Wow, I don't think I've ever seen his face so red. He buries it behind his water bottle as I open my door. I turn back to him once more.

"Garrett?"

"Yeah?"

"I'm sorry Indiana Bones slapped you in the face."

"Indiana Bones?" His brows tug together as he lifts his water back to his mouth, cheeks like a chipmunk as he guzzles.

I see the exact moment realization dawns as the wrinkle in his forehead smooths, followed promptly by the fountain of water that bursts from between his lips as he keels over, gripping his knees, choking for air.

Smiling, I slink backward into my apartment. "Sleep tight, big guy."

I leave him rooted in place in the hallway, gaping, and I strip down to my birthday suit as I head for my bedroom. Tugging open my favorite drawer, I hum to myself as my fingers flutter over my extensive collection of rubber and silicone.

I wrap my fingers around the perpetrator himself, pulling Indiana Bones from his spot in the drawer, and carry him into the shower. Slapping the suction base against the tiles, I crank the faucet with a happy sigh.

"All right, big boy. Let's raid some temples tonight."

EIGHT
WHOOPS

Garrett

THERE'S nothing like having four NHL players over two hundred pounds each in your entryway to make the twenty-two-hundred square feet of open space feel like a closet.

At least Adam brought gifts.

He shoves the massive box into my arms. I'm a little scared to open it. Will a bunch of rubber dicks jump out? I already can't look Carter in the eye. I know what his little sister does at nighttime, and I kinda wanna help her out.

Especially now that I've seen her tits.

They're nice. *Really* nice. Round and perky with super fucking rosy buds; bags of fun the perfect size to fit in the palm of my hand.

I think. I'd have to test the theory to be certain.

"You gonna open the box or keep staring at it like you wanna make love to it?" Adam laughs to himself. "It's from my mom. Express shipped it Thursday night as soon as she saw you go down on TV."

From his mom? "Oooh, fuck yeah, Bev." Adam's parents live in Colorado. They're both amazing, but Bev takes the cake as my unofficial foreign snack dealer. I can't wait to see what her post-concussion goodie box holds.

The entrance to heaven opens, bright packages staring up at me, just waiting to be unwrapped. Special edition Pop-Tarts, discontinued Dunkaroos, exciting new cereal flavors. It's the best present I've ever received, right after the one I got two nights ago, when I saw Jennie's tits and most of the rest of her body, 'cause her bikini was fucking tiny.

"When's Mama Lockwood gonna send me snacks?" Carter rips open a package of Banana Crème Pie Pop-Tarts, quickly devouring it. "Dey hab dis wimited edition Oreo in da States wight now." He struggles to swallow, crumbs littering his shirt. "It's called the—"

"You're not injured," Adam reminds him.

"But she always sends him stuff!"

"Maybe she likes Gare better than you," Emmett suggests, earning some epic sulking from Carter.

Adam and Emmett unpack my snacks and a few other care items they've brought over. Every time they put a snack away, Carter pulls it back out, investigating the package. They're annoying and overbearing sometimes, but they're my family. I'm not looking forward to staying behind, and I whine about exactly that.

"It's one road trip," Adam reminds me.

"The doctor cleared me to drive this morning. I could watch from the press box."

Carter raps his knuckles on my temple. "You don't mess with what's in here."

"I know it's frustrating, but you need to take care of yourself." Emmett gestures at the couch. "Hang out, put your feet up, watch us kick ass, and you'll be back in for our home stretch next week to help out."

"I hate watching hockey by myself."

Carter doesn't look up from the bag of Flamin' Hot Funyuns he's studying. "Go watch it with my sister. We just dropped Dublin off to her. She'll be watching, and she has no friends."

"Carter," Adam guffaws. "That's not nice."

"What? She doesn't make friends easily. She has trust issues."

That doesn't really surprise me. Jennie seems like a generally skeptical person—her side-eye is scary—and I'm not sure she believed that I wouldn't sleep with Emily again.

Carter checks his phone. "We gotta head out. Flight's in an hour, and I gotta touch base with Riley."

Jaxon Riley is our brand-new trade, straight from Nashville, and he's starting tonight. I hate that I won't be there. He's an arrogant ass, and I'm not a fan. Carter knows this, so when I grunt, he smirks.

"I'll keep him in line," he promises. It might sound empty, but where he can't keep anyone in line in his personal life, he can handle an entire team without batting an eye. He's a natural born leader on the ice and in the change room. "Don't worry, Gare. We'll miss you as much as you'll miss us."

And, really, that's it. My family is on the opposite side of the country. Having these guys and their girls around all the time makes the distance easier. Now, being forced out with an injury, and with Cara and Olivia following along for the trip, I'm feeling more alone than ever.

Maybe that's why I find myself standing in front of Jennie's door after lunch.

I raise my fist to knock but shove my fingers through my hair instead. "What am I doing? She's just a girl. She's not gonna bite."

I force myself to knock, stretching my fingers out and curling them into my palms three times while I wait. A door opens, but not the one I was hoping for.

Glancing over my shoulder, I find Emily leaning in her doorway, coy smile in place.

"Mr. Andersen. Long time, no see. Your saucy friend isn't home. She went out earlier with that cute dog."

"Saucy?" How does Emily know—

"Yeah, she keeps calling me Emma, and today she flipped me the double bird when I reminded her where she could hear my name. I might like her, and I don't think I'm the only one."

"What?" I understood roughly 5 percent of that.

Her grin is suspect. She gestures into her apartment. "Wanna come in? Gonna put on my cheerleading outfit and practice my routine."

"I-I-I-I—" I close my eyes and take a breath. I'm lonely, yes, but not enough to go back on my word to Jennie. "I can't."

"Later?"

I shake my head.

She smiles. "Thought so."

Before I can ask for clarification, she winks and disappears. I sigh, resigned to being alone tonight.

Until I get a text five minutes later.

Carter: *Jennie ended up going 2 my place for the weekend so she didn't have 2 take Dubs up n down the elevator 2 pee, cuz of her*

*fucky ankle. U can hang with her there. Don't touch my oreos or ur
dead.*

Great. But it's not the Oreos I'm worried about touching.

Is there a word for being turned on by someone's anger?

Because I'm standing on the porch, and Jennie's overcast blue eyes
are narrowed viciously at me from the doorway, her arms pinned
beneath her tits, and I'm mashing my lips together to keep from
suggesting we fuck out whatever tension this is that seems to be
constantly vibrating between us.

"What are you doing here?" Jennie asks.

I hold up the bags in my hand, and Dublin takes that as an invitation
to jump at them. "I brought food."

Her eyes sweep over me, bypassing the bags but lingering on the rest
of me, particularly my lower half. "Fucking gray sweatpants," she
mutters. "Always with the gray ones." Her gaze flips to mine. "Sorry,
what did you say?"

"Um, I brought...Thai food and snacks. Carter said you were here
alone, and I was alone, and I thought maybe we could watch the game
together and not be..."

"Alone?" Skepticism swims in her eyes. "I don't need a babysitter
just because my brother's out of town."

"No, I—can I come in, please? It's cold as balls out here."

"Maybe you should've dressed for the weather." She's all snark but
steps aside anyway. She's wearing an oversized tie-dye long sleeve that
hangs off one shoulder and a pair of spandex shorts that can't possibly
cover her ass, but I'm waiting for her to turn around before I give the
final verdict. "Do you need me to come upstairs and dress you before
you leave your apartment every morning?"

I grin, because honestly, that doesn't sound half bad. "Look, I wanted
to come. My friends are gone for the weekend, and to tell you the truth, I
was feeling lonely at home."

"You were?" Something soft and vulnerable dances across her eyes.
"And you thought of me?"

"I thought of you."

"Oh. Well, that's…" She fiddles with the messy braid that lays over her shoulder, tugging on the bright blue ribbon. I think this is the first time I've ever seen her blush. "Nice." Her nose wrinkles and she bites back her smile. "I'm sorry I bit your head off. It's a bad habit."

I'm aware, hence the nickname *sunshine* that's quickly growing on me.

Instead, I smile. Then Jennie turns, and the verdict is fucking in, ladies and gentlemen. Those shorts *do not* cover her ass. Oh fuck, are they ever cheeky.

"Garrett?"

"Huh?" *Oh shit. Scary eyes.*

"I asked if you were coming, but you were too busy staring at my ass, you wiener." She gestures at her bare legs. "Is this gonna be a problem, or do you need me to put pants on?"

I honestly don't know how to answer that. *Yes, it's going to be a problem. No, please don't put pants on.*

My expression must say it all, because Jennie rolls her eyes and rips the bags from my hands. "*Men.* If it has tits and an ass, it's good enough to fuck."

"That's not true." *Why am I talking?* "I'm pickier than that about tits and asses." *I should shut my mouth right the fuck now.*

"Oh? So do mine make the cut, or are you pickier than that?"

My brain has finally gotten the memo to shut up. Unfortunately, Jennie's waiting on a response. Wish I could formulate one.

"Garrett? I'm waiting."

"Please don't hurt me," I finally whisper.

With a smug hum, Jennie sets the dishes on the kitchen island. She hands me a beer, and when I've got a full plate, I flop on the couch, reaching for the remote.

"What were you watching?"

Jennie throws herself on my lap, nearly wearing my pad Thai, fumbling for the remote. "Nothing, Garrett, give me the remote."

I hold it over my head, intrigued. "What were you watching?"

"I wasn't—" She presses her lips together when I press Play. Simba, Nala, and Zazu fill the screen, singing about how Simba can't wait to be king. Jennie tugs the neck of her shirt up to her nose. "Shut up."

"Jesus, the Disney obsession is real with you Becketts."

"I'm a better singer than Carter," she grumbles.

"So you were singing?"

Her cheeks burn. "No."

"Sounds like you were singing, sunshine."

"Shut up, Gare-Bear." She punches me in the shoulder and steals a spring roll off my plate, settling back in her spot, feet up on the coffee table. Her left ankle has an angry, red swell to it, a bag of ice melting beside it.

Jennie sobs so hard while Simba tries to wake Mufasa up after the stampede that she starts choking, coughing, using the neck of her shirt to wipe her eyes.

"Uh, do you need a—"

"I don't need a hug!" She jabs my chest. "Stop looking at me!" She springs to her feet, slapping at her soaked cheeks. "I hate you!" she shouts, then dashes to the bathroom. It's all hobbly because of her bum ankle, and I fold my lips into my mouth so my laughter doesn't chase her.

When she returns, I've got Sportsnet on, ready for the game, and I've cleaned the dishes.

Jennie sticks her hand in the bowl of Sour Cherry Blasters I've just poured. "I'm sorry I said I hated you. It was in the heat of the moment."

"It's okay. Scar's an asshole."

"Scum of the Disney world."

I chuckle as I grab another beer from the fridge. "You want another?"

"I didn't have a first, but no, thank you. I don't drink."

"Oh."

Jennie reaches for her collarbone, like she's about to fiddle with a necklace. Instead, her fingers flutter over bare skin. I catch the sharp rise of her chest, and she quickly looks away.

Returning the beer, I grab a Gatorade instead.

Jennie frowns. "You can still drink, Garrett. It doesn't bother me. It's just my personal choice."

And it's a choice I'll support when we're together. If a drunk driver had taken someone from me, I don't know that I'd ever be able to even look at alcohol again.

Sometimes I don't know why I ever touched it myself. A childhood spent watching alcohol own my dad isn't one I'd wish on anyone. Truth be told, it wasn't much of a childhood at all. In the end, I guess I decided

I wasn't going to let him take something else from me, that I would have the control he didn't and make better choices.

I head to the couch with my Gatorade and a fresh bag of ice, and at Jennie's perplexed expression, I explain, "For your ankle."

"Oh." She hesitantly places her foot on the pillow I set on the coffee table and sighs when I cover her ankle with ice. "Thank you."

I keep my eyes on the TV as the game starts. "What happened there anyway?" I don't need to know Jennie well to know the answer she gave me in the elevator two days ago was bullshit.

"Twisted it during dance practice."

From my peripheral, I catch her nibbling her thumbnail. "Thought you tripped over your bag?"

Her head whips my way. "Why are you asking if I already gave you an answer?"

"Why are you lying?"

"You're so annoying." She shoves her hand in the popcorn bowl. "I tripped over my dance partner. There, are you happy?"

"Steve?"

She snicker-snorts. "Simon. Carter only calls him Steve to piss him off."

"Carter hates him." He's always grumbling about Jennie dropping pairs and going solo. "Says he wants in your pants."

Jennie hums dismissively, then leaps to her feet. "*Offside!* That was so offside! You're never gonna get those orange armbands missing calls like that, bud!"

With the way she keeps shouting at the officials, it takes me one minute to let go of the fact that she doesn't want to talk to me about her dance partner, and another four to realize she might be my favorite person ever to watch hockey with. I even forget about the major case of *FOMO* I had about missing the trip.

When the third period rolls around, Jennie's hoarse from yelling, and my stomach aches from laughing.

"If all you wanted to do was watch the game, you shoulda bought tickets like everyone else. You suck, ref." She tosses a piece of popcorn at the referee on TV, then a whole handful at me. "Stop laughing at me."

"I can't. Watching with you is fun. My sisters hate hockey, or they're too cool to watch. They only make it to one or two games a year, and they spend most of it buried in their tablets or making googly eyes at the guys."

Jennie snickers. "How many sisters do you have?"

"Three."

"How old?"

Skimming my jaw, I line up dates in my head. "Uh, twelve, ten, and nine."

Jennie twists my way, feet on the cushion between us. Her toes are painted pale pink, a stark contrast to her black fingernails. "Oh wow. That's a big age gap."

"My parents separated for a couple years, then got busy when they got back together. I heard more than I'd care to admit when I was thirteen and they got remarried. Nine months later Alexa came along. I learned quickly to get out of the house when they were giving each other the eyes."

Jennie snickers, stretching her legs out, toes pressing into my thigh. She either doesn't notice or doesn't care. "That's nice they worked things out. You must've been happy."

"Definitely." Mostly happy that my dad was sober for the first time I could ever remember. "What kinda dance do you do?"

"Contemporary, mostly. It's my favorite. I grew up doing ballet but fell in love when I discovered contemporary."

"Why's that?"

Her nose wrinkles. "There are too many rules in ballet."

"And you don't like following them?"

She grins. "Not really. It killed my feet too." She shrugs. "Contemporary felt more me. I don't think about anything, just listen to the music and move my body. It's freeing in a way that ballet wasn't. For me, at least. I felt too restricted, and all I wanted to do was stand out."

"That's pretty cool. It must feel nice to find your niche."

Jennie gets this super-psyched look on her face, like my youngest sister Gabby when I answer her FaceTime request. She grips my forearm. "My Christmas recital is coming up. You could come see it with Carter and Olivia. Emmett and Cara are coming too."

Her smile dissolves at my hesitation and blank expression. She releases my arm, averts her gaze, and shifts away. I watch the way her personality slips away as she shuts back down, creeping back behind whatever wall she's built to keep people at bay.

But this version of her here tonight, talking easily and laughing with me, I want to hang on to that.

"I'm heading home for a couple days over Christmas, but if the dates line up, I'll definitely come watch you kick ass on stage."

She regards me warily for a moment before her shoulders unfurl and her legs flop back down between us. "I don't wanna brag, but I'm the best one up there."

I flick her foot. "There's that trademark Beckett arrogance." She giggles, kicking my fingers away. When her feet land in my lap, my hand covers her ankles.

"Sure, but I worked my ass off to be sure of myself and my talent, so I'll own that title."

"I like that. You should be confident and proud of yourself."

Our eyes lock as we smile at each other. I take in her deep-set dimples, her heart-shaped lips, the way they curve in the righthand corner, like she's got a secret.

I've got an urge to make a big fucking oopsie, which should tell me it's time to pack up and get outta here, especially since in the time we've been chatting, the game has ended. Instead, my mouth opens, and I don't know what's going to come out until it comes.

"Wanna finish watching the movie?"

Fuck. What a fucking mistake.

Because twenty minutes later, Jennie's half-buried in some sort of blanket burrito, clutching a pillow to her chest, shaking violently as she sobs, "Can You Feel The Love Tonight" playing through the TV, and I'm just howling uncontrollably.

"Shut up!" She smashes the pillow to my face.

"It's not even a sad part!"

"It's emotional! They've found each other after all this time apart, and they were best friends, and it's-it's-it's...shut up! Stop laughing at me!"

I don't, but I do dodge the second pillow she chucks. Dublin's passed out by the fireplace, completely unfazed, even though this girl beside me has been anything but quiet all night.

"You give off this real badass vibe, but I've seen you cry three times this week, and two of them were tonight during a Disney movie."

She's not even throwing the pillow anymore, just holding it to my face, trying to smother me, her body squirming against mine. My laughter only seems to spur her on.

Jennie sends me toppling sideways, and I flop to my back as she falls between my legs.

"Shut...up...Gare...Bear!"

"I have three little sisters. You're not gonna win, sunshine."

"I grew up with Carter," she grunts, hands clasping mine as she tries to pin me to the couch. "He pissed me off daily."

"Sure." I wind one arm around her waist and flip her over, pinning her below the weight of my body, my fingers overlapping her wrists. "But I'm not your brother."

And thank fuck for that.

Jennie peers at me from beneath dark lashes, cheeks rosy, lips parted with her staggered breaths. Our chests rise and fall together, quick and heavy, like the thudding in my ears. I'm painfully aware of the warm spot between her thighs where I've settled, and my chest roars with need.

There's a voice in the back of my mind telling me to disengage, to head home before I make any mistakes I can't take back.

Because this right here? Me and her, my best friend and captain's little sister, tangled together? A mistake you don't walk away from.

But then Jennie's hazy blue eyes drop to my lips, and her hips move just slightly, an invitation, one I don't think I can turn down.

"I win," I whisper, and I drop my face at the same time she tips her chin.

My mouth covers hers without hesitation, tasting, taking. Fuck, do I ever wanna take. She's soft and sweet, eager and hesitant at the same time, and my pulse hammers the longer I explore her. I run my tongue over the seam of her lips, asking for permission. I want in, and I don't know if I'll want to leave.

She opens for me, legs winding around my waist, letting me closer than I ever thought I'd be. My tongue meets hers with a slow sweep, and when her hips lift, grinding against me, a jagged whimper leaves her mouth.

And then a gasp.

Jennie stiffens below me, and I know. I'm done. I've fucked up.

I shuffle backward the second she wriggles free of my grasp. She starts doing the crab walk, right until she tumbles over the edge of the couch with a squeal, ass in the air in her teensy, tiny shorts.

"I'm sorry." I climb to my feet and reach for her, trying to help her up, but she keeps on keepin' on with the crab walk, all the way out of the living room and down the hall, eyes wide as she gawks at me. "I'm sorry, Jennie. I didn't mean…I don't…I don't know what came over me."

She bumps into the wall and clutches the back of her head. "Ow!"

"For fuck's sake, let me help you up." I hoist her to her feet before she can slap my hands away, and she promptly darts up the stairs, hobbly ankle and all. "Jennie—"

"I'm tired! So tired! Bedtime!" She waves a flappy hand at the door. "You can just…let yourself out. Lock up when you leave! Good night, Garrett Andersen!"

She trips, falling to her hands and knees at the top of the staircase while rambling about how she just called me by my full name. Then she disappears, followed by the sound of a door slamming.

Fuck. I'm so fucking fucked. What the hell was I thinking?

I wasn't, that's the problem. Not with the head on my neck, that's for sure.

I look down at my dick. I'm thoroughly disappointed in him, and I'm about to tell him so.

"Can't fuckin' keep it in your pants for one fuckin' night, Lieutenant Johnson? C'mon, dude. Carter's goddamn little sister," I mutter, scrubbing my face as I wander back down the hall.

Dublin yawns and stretches before trotting over and licking my hand. He curls up on a cushion in the kitchen while I clean the mess we made before promptly escorting myself out the front door. I need to dip my blue balls in some snow.

"Fuck," I repeat for at least the fifteenth time in the last five minutes, softly banging my head against the door. "Fuck, fuck, fuck."

I can't leave like this. I need to apologize, and we need to talk about where to go from here. I think we should never, *ever* tell Carter, but if she wants to, I will. He'll cut off at least one integral body part, but I'll do it if she asks me to.

Quietly, I step back inside, toeing off my shoes as my neck grows clammy. I really liked hanging out with her, but I'm 99.999 percent sure I've ruined any chance of us ever being able to be in the same room again.

"Jennie?" I call tentatively, climbing the staircase. I find the only bedroom door that's closed and grip the door frame. "I wanted to apologize. Can we talk?"

Half of me hopes she's already asleep.

"Jennie, I—" I shake my head. I suck at this. "Look," I try softly, "can I come in?"

With no response, I hang my head and sigh, turning toward the stairs.

But then I hear her, softly calling my name, and I jerk my elbow into my side triumphantly.

"Yes," I mutter before opening the door and waltzing right through it. "Listen, I was—"

My words dissolve on my tongue, jaw dangling as my eyes fall on the most glorious sight they've ever witnessed.

A gentle vibration buzzes in the air, and it seems to be coming from the pink object that Jennie holds between her long, bronzed legs from her spot on the bed.

And Jennie? Pantless. And panty-less. Head thrown back too.

My hand falls to my dick when my name tumbles from her mouth once more, just like the words I can't stop tumble from mine.

"Holy shit."

Jennie's head rolls forward, eyes dazed as they float over the room before eventually landing on me, standing in the doorway, hand on my cock, which is, by the way, super fucking hard right now.

Her lips part, and I must be the densest dick on the planet to think she might say my name once more, or better yet, invite me in.

Instead, she shrieks.

Holy fucking shit, does she *shriek*. Bloodcurdling, ear piercing, and yet Lieutenant Johnson doesn't give two shits.

No, he stands on guard in all his glory, begging me to let him give her the ol' one-eyed salute, to ask her if she wants to play.

And Jesus fucking fuck, do I ever wanna play.

NINE
WE SHOULD (NEVER) DO THAT AGAIN

Jennie

I HAVE QUESTIONS.

What have I done to deserve the life I lead, particularly the one obnoxiously thrust into my face this past week? Why has this man in front of me seen me half-naked on multiple occasions? Why did my toy collection explode in his hands? Why did Indiana Bones slap him in the face? Why did I kiss my brother's best friend?

Why did Garrett just absolutely catch me jilling off with a motherfucking vibrator while maybe or maybe not—to be determined—moaning his name?

"*What are you doing in here?*" I screech, leaping from the bed. "I didn't say you could come in! You left! You were supposed to leave! I heard the door shut!"

"I-I-I—" His eyes ricochet between my lower half and my hand. "Holy fucking fuckballs."

I jerk my shirt over my hips, hiding my stupid, traitorous vagina. My occupied hand is shaking violently—the rabbit's turned all the way to ten—so I chuck that bad girl across the room.

Mistake number one. Now she's vibrating excruciatingly loudly against the hardwood, jumping around, and Garrett can't take his eyes off her.

I rush him, shoving his chest. He doesn't move, aside from his head whipping back and forth between me and my toy. "Out! Get out! And you shouldn't have kissed me!"

"I thought you wanted me to!" he screams back, face red as he comes back to life. "I misread the signs!"

"Then invest in some fucking reading glasses, hotshot!"

"I'm sorry!" Gripping my wrists, he yanks me into him. "Stop pushing me!"

"Stop yelling at me!"

"You yelled first!"

"You saw my vagina!"

"I saw your boobs two nights ago!" His eyes widen, lips mashing together. "Okay, that was the wrong thing to say. I'm sorry I saw your boobs. And your vagina. I already told you they're nice boobs." He gestures at my lower half and clears his throat. "And it's a nice, uh...vagina."

With a groan, I twirl out of his grasp, burying my scalding face in my hands. "Stop saying vagina, please."

He shrugs. "Fine, you have a nice pussy."

I whack him in the shoulder. "Garrett!"

"Ow! Christ, you're violent."

"That's not what I meant!"

He flings his arms in the air. "News flash, sunshine! I almost never know what the fuck you mean!"

"Women aren't that confusing!"

"No, but you are!" He closes his eyes, inhaling deeply. "Look, I wanted to apologize for kissing you. I was having a good time and got caught up in the moment."

Okay, maybe I did too. Garrett is kind, easy to be with despite the awkwardness, and he makes all my hot spots light up like a glow stick. The man has somehow managed to flood my basement with only one kiss.

I'm chalking it up to the lack of intimacy and physical connection in my life.

"Apology accepted," I tell him. "Now good night, Garrett."

"Okay. But don't be embarrassed. Everyone masturbates."

"Right, but not everyone gets caught by a famous, sexy hockey player who happens to be one of her brother's best friends."

His eyes brighten. "You think I'm—" He stops himself, which is for the best. He thinks I'm violent, but he hasn't truly *seen* violent yet. "I'll leave."

"Great." I tug my shirt tighter around my ass, thighs rubbing, spreading my wetness as he turns his back on me. He's tall and broad and he's got the most phenomenal hockey butt, the kind you wanna grab two handfuls of and hold on to for dear life while he fucks you up against a wall.

Or whatever.

"Wait a second," Garrett whispers, pausing. My heart thuds as he slowly spins, one finger up, seemingly lost in thought. Then his gaze zeros in on me, heated, playful, and entirely too dangerous as he takes one purposeful step in my direction, then another, and that heartbeat drops to the pit of my stomach. "You said my name."

"I did not." *Totally did.*

"Did too."

"Didn't."

His eyes roll. "*Garrett.*" He drags his name out on a moan, head thrown back. He doesn't have to grab his junk, but he does anyway, and I slink backward with each calculated step he takes in my direction. He looks like he's about to make me his snack, and I'm not sure I'll put up a fight.

I find a pillow and chuck it at his annoying, hot face for at least the twentieth time tonight. "You're supposed to be shy, jerk!"

He deflects the pillow with a veiny forearm, and when he smacks me in the face with it, I gasp. "I'm not shy, Jennie! I'm just fucking terrified of you!"

"You sure look it!" I'm running out of space as he prowls toward me, and when I trip over my bag, Garrett grips a fistful of my shirt, keeping me on my feet. I have no idea where the timid, awkward boy has gone, replaced by some sort of alpha man, oozing sex and confidence, ready to take control.

And he still hasn't let go of my shirt.

He throws a pointed look at the hot-pink rabbit still jumping around on the floor, though she's losing power, dying fast. It's the only toy I brought, and now I'm gonna have to use my fingers, and they sure as shit don't vibrate. "Don't you have someone to do that for you?"

I throw my shoulders back, judo-chopping his wrist to lose his grip. It doesn't work. "I don't need someone to do it for me. I do it myself just fine."

"No? No boyfriend?"

"If I had a boyfriend, would I have kissed you?"

A slow smirk spreads. God, arrogance looks *so* hot on him. "So you admit you were an equal participant in that kiss."

"I—" I point my nose toward the ceiling. "I admit nothing."

"That's too bad," he purrs. "Remember when you told me I should work on saying what I'm thinking?" His grip on my shirt tightens, soft cotton slipping against my skin, revealing more of my body as he walks forward, pushing me backward. "I'm thinking I wanted to kiss you, and I'm thinking you wanted me to. I'm thinking you enjoyed the hell out of it, before you told yourself you shouldn't, and then you got scared."

I gasp when my back hits the wall. Garrett's turquoise eyes fall to my lips.

"What's the matter, Jennie? Where's all that confidence gone? Nowhere to hide?"

I bite into my bottom lip to quell its quiver when Garrett slides one large hand along the edge of my jaw, angling my face toward his. His other hand lands on the edge of my thigh, fingertips blazing a forest fire along my skin as they trail up, up, toying with the hem of my shirt.

"I think you came up here to touch yourself while thinking about everything that could've happened if you hadn't run, and I think…" His ragged breath dances across my lips, gaze searing. "I think I'd like to help you. I think you *want* me to help you."

"Garrett," I whimper, trembling as his lips ghost over mine.

"Yeah," he whispers. "Just like that. That's exactly how you sounded when you moaned my name."

I lift my chin and lick my lips, eyelids fluttering closed as I wait.

And wait.

The heat of his body is replaced by the cool chill of rejection as he releases me, his smirk nothing short of smug pride when my eyes flip open, and he steps backward.

"I'd sure hate to misread the signs though. So if I'm right, if you want my help…" He skims a thumb across his rugged jawline, scraping the stubble that wasn't there two days ago. "You'll have to be explicitly clear."

A growl rumbles in my throat, and before I have time to comprehend my actions, I've thrown myself at his chest and buried my fingers in his hair. He clasps my ass, lifting me to him, my legs winding around his waist as my back collides with the wall.

The way his mouth takes mine is nothing short of possessive, ownership in its purest, most simple form. He can have my mouth, and just about any other part of me right now, and I don't even know why I'm willing to give it to him.

Heels digging into his ass, I spur him on, pulling a groan from his throat as I arch against him. I'm hot and wet and I've never wanted anything the way I want Garrett right now.

Pinning me to the wall with his hips, he tears my shirt over my head. Never have I seen something as ferocious as his scorching gaze as it drags over me, lighting every nerve ending on fire in its wake. With a fistful of my hair, he buries his face in my neck, his warm mouth teasing, nipping, leaving a wet trail as it glides.

"Are you gonna let me take care of you tonight, sunshine? 'Cause it's all I can fucking think about."

God, *yes*. I drag his mouth back to mine, right where I want it. His tongue sweeps inside, exploring, tasting, taking. I want more, and it's been *so damn long* since I've wanted anything, since I've felt like somebody wanted me—just *me*—this much.

Dropping me to my feet, he grips the back of my neck, spins me around, and presses me to the wall. Fingers dance over my hip, my belly, until his delicate touch kisses the spot I ache most, and I claw at the wall as tears of desperation prickle.

I don't want the teasing; I just want him to fingerbang me into next year. Is that too much to ask?

So I beg a raspy, "Please," when he traces the inside of my quivering thighs.

"Tell me what you want, Jennie."

"Touch me," I whisper, hanging my head. His grip on my neck tightens, forcing my eyes to his over my shoulder. "Please, Garrett."

He skims my clit, pulling a shaky burst of air from my lips. "Here?"

"Fuck, *yes*," I gasp as he strokes me slowly.

"Jesus, you're wet." His tongue slides up the length of my neck. "So fucking wet." He sinks two fingers inside me and smiles against my shoulder when I cry out. "You gonna let me fuck this pussy one day?"

"*Holy shit*," I cry. The dirty talk is doing me in, paired with the touch of another person, intimacy I've craved for so long, even if I've been denying it. "Who are you?"

His low chuckle sends shivers down my spine. Releasing my neck, he presses two fingers to my clit. "I can't wait to feel you come on my fingers."

"Fuck." I grip his hand, lacing our fingers, pulling him closer and pushing him away all at once. He shoves a knee between my thighs, spreading them wider, and thrusts his fingers deeper, harder, taking me further than I've ever been able to take myself. "*Garrett.*"

His fingers move quickly, pushing me closer to that edge, the one I want him to throw me right over.

And does he ever throw me over it. Brings me up that peak, drags me right to the edge, and when he looks me in the eye and demands *come*, he tosses me over and watches me free-fall into oblivion, buckling at the knees.

Without missing a beat, Garrett winds an arm around my waist and tosses me to the bed. His knees hit the mattress as he tears his shirt over his head, and he crawls toward me, hitting me with a wink that has the heartbeat between my legs pounding.

"Do you want me to taste you, Jennie?" He taps my knees and they fall open for him. "'Cause I wanna fuckin' taste you."

I can't answer, but he's not waiting. He shoves his arms below my legs, grabs my hips, and yanks me down the mattress. Our eyes lock and his mouth descends right as I forget my own name.

"Oh *shit*," I weep behind my palm. He wrenches my hand away in time for his name to come ripping up my throat as his fingers pierce through me, tongue flicking, mouth sucking.

Peering up at me with a smile so broad, so handsome, *so fucking wicked*, he licks his lips. "My name sounds so much better coming from that mouth when you're screaming it for an entirely different reason."

His thumb replaces his mouth on that swollen nub as he drags his lips up my torso, then licks an achingly slow path around one taut nipple. "These tits are fuckin' perfect. Perfect tits, perfect pussy." He pulls one nipple between his teeth, tongue swirling before he pops off, presses a searing kiss to my mouth, and disappears between my legs again.

Garrett's mouth is exactly how I imagine heaven, warm and incredible, like sunshine between my thighs, utter perfection that forces my fingers into his hair, urging him closer. Each lash of his tongue is fluid, the thrusts of his fingers deep and powerful, and his eyes meet mine as he sucks my clit into his mouth.

My head falls to the mattress as his name leaves my lips again, my body shaking, quivering with the type of orgasm you only read about in books, the kind I didn't think were real. And Garrett just buries himself between my thighs, drinking up every ounce like he'll die without it.

He withdraws his fingers and gives me three languid, reverent passes with his tongue, licking me clean as I collapse, arms over my head. The light scruff on his jaw tickles my inner thigh when he wipes his face off there, and I shudder, trying to breathe again.

Garrett falls beside me, the mattress bouncing beneath his weight. "Fuck, you taste amazing," he croaks out, all gravel. Our eyes meet, and when his drift down my body, I heat with sudden nerves under the intensity of his stare.

I scramble off the bed, reaching for my shirt, clutching it to my chest. I toss Garrett's to him. He takes it for the sign it is, though I see the confusion coasting through his eyes, marring his forehead.

It's less confusion, more curiosity, if I'm being honest. He doesn't know what this means, and neither do I. That felt good. *Amazing.* But it can't happen again.

Can it?

I slip my shirt on, sink to the bed, and pull my knees to my chest as Garrett stands and covers his ridiculous abs.

"You should go," I say. There's no force behind the words. I'd like him to stay, and I'd like to ride his face until I pass out from too many orgasms. Is that a thing? It should be. Anyway, if he gave me any push-back about leaving, I'd fold in a heartbeat, despite the confusion.

Unfortunately for me, he nods. Five times.

"I should go." He adjusts the giant lump in his pants, and though he's not asking, I wish I could return the favor. But it's been a while, and I'm kind of…unsure. He's probably had the Holy Grail of blow jobs. I'm competitive as hell and hate being bad at anything. Finding out I'm bad at blow jobs is not something I'm prepared to handle tonight. "But was that…?"

"Great," I answer breathlessly, swiping my damp hair from my forehead. "Yeah, super great."

"Oh good. Great. I'm glad. And you feel…?"

With trembling hands, I gesture at my sweaty face, then at my legs, still shaking with the aftershock of my orgasms. "Amazing."

His head bobs as he claps his fist into his opposite hand. "Amazing.

Good." He backs toward the door, pointing at me with two finger guns. "We should do that again sometime."

"Uh, absolutely."

His face lights up. "Cool."

I squeeze my eyes shut, shaking my head. "No, we shouldn't."

He frowns. "No, we shouldn't."

"Carter."

He nods, solemn. "Carter."

"So…good night?"

He waves. "Night."

Instead of leaving, Garrett continues to stand there, the two of us staring at each other. I'm still naked from the waist down, and I'm sitting in an explosion of my own fluids. It's uncomfortable, but more than that, staring at him right now, his hair a mess, cheeks flushed, it's making my lady bits all tingly again.

"So, uh…good night." His eyes widen like he's forgotten something, and he darts back over.

My heart hums as he looms over me, warm hand sliding along my jaw, fingers tangling in my hair as he cups my face and tips it up. His lips cover mine in a slow, heated kiss that lights a fire deep in my belly, and I fist the collar of his shirt, wanting to keep him close.

"Good night," Garrett says again when he pulls away, then drops his lips to mine once more. "Night." He jogs back to the door, waving at me over his shoulder. "Bye." He pulls the door open and looks back at me, eyes sweeping over me, bright like the smile he hits me with when our gazes finally lock.

"Have a good sleep, Jennie," he whispers, and then, for real this time, he leaves, footsteps thudding down the stairs, the front door closing behind him, the beep that tells me he's locked up for the night.

I fall back against the mountain of pillows behind me, clapping a hand to my sweaty forehead.

Fuck me. Indiana Bones is going to have to step it up.

TEN
USAIN BOLT

Garrett

JENNIE'S BEEN IGNORING me all week.

Four days ago, I called after her in the lobby. When she saw me, she bolted. Literally ran, across the lobby, out the door, throwing herself in the backseat of the taxi waiting out front, fucky ankle and all.

Two days ago, I knocked on her door. Without opening it, she shouted back in—I think—a horrendous mix of Spanish and English, claiming to be someone named Gloria, because Jennie didn't live there anymore. I said I knew it was her because I'd seen her get into the elevator. She was silent for an entire thirty seconds before replying, "Me no hablo English."

I'm frustrated as fuck. Despite the mind-blowing orgasms, I'd thought there'd been a shift in our dynamic, like we were finally becoming friends. She'd stopped being so utterly terrifying to the point that I could speak full sentences to her. If that's not friendship, I don't know what is.

Plus, we left on good terms—I kissed her good night—so why is she avoiding me? She's normally good at talking and yelling and all that; I'm the one who can't string words together.

Should we repeat the orgasms? Probably not. Would I like to? Abso-fucking-lutely yes. But if she can't look me in the eye, how will we ever be in the same room together? We need to talk this thing out before it blows up in our faces.

The door next to me opens. I straighten off the wall as Jennie strolls out of her apartment, singing what I'm pretty sure is the soundtrack to *Frozen*.

She's wearing skintight plum leggings, highlighting her out-of-this-world ass, a pair of those comfy, warm boots my sisters love, and a baggy hoodie. A toque dangles from the tips of her fingers, headphones slung around her wrist. Casual has never looked better than it does on her.

"Morning, sunshine. Your ankle looks better."

I wonder if she'll ever not shriek at me, but know today isn't the day.

She leaps into the air, dropping her shit to the ground, screaming out a string of curses. "Mother...fucker." She scoops up her stuff before whacking me in the shoulder. "Was that necessary?"

"Based on the way you've been ignoring me for the last week? Absolutely."

"I've been..." She looks around for the rest of her sentence. "Busy."

Shit, she's as bad at lying as I am.

"Thought you moved out. What happened to Gloria?"

She folds her guilty smile into her mouth. "Oh, she...just a...friend...sleepover...girl's night." She waves a flappy hand through the air. "Pillow fights in our panties and all that."

"Uh-huh. Listen." I take a step forward and she plasters herself against the door, terrified. I'm pretty sure I'm the least terrifying person ever, based on the amount of blushing and stuttering like a jackass that occurs when she's around. But I stop anyway, because we aren't in the bedroom, which happens to be the only place I like being a little terrifying. "We should talk about what happened last weekend."

"What happened?" Her voice rockets up an entire octave. "Nothing happened. Did you happen?" She squeezes her eyes shut. "Fuck."

I like this messy side to her. It makes me feel like I get under her skin as much as she does mine. Makes it less of a lonely place to be.

Maybe that's why I take another step toward her, then another, until she's staring up at me with those wide eyes that give way to the innocence I think hides under all her bold.

"C'mon, sunshine. You can't possibly think I've forgotten. The way my name sounded leaving your lips on repeat is burned into my mind, just like the way your mouth opened when you came around my fingers, and again on my tongue." I trail a finger over her hip before slipping my hand below her hoodie, wrapping my palm around her bare waist. "Would you like a reminder?"

I don't have a clue what I'm doing right now. And Jennie is, without a doubt, *the last* person I should be doing it with. I guess I've decided—in this moment, anyway—I have no fucks left to give. Not based on the way I drop my lips, letting them hover above her mouth as the tip of my nose skims hers.

Jennie clings to me, chin lifting, plush pink lips reaching for mine. They part on a jagged inhale, cheeks flush under the intensity of my stare, the words I shouldn't have said.

And then she comes back down to earth, shaking her head and essentially bodychecking me across the hall. She twists back to her door and jams her key in the lock.

Okay, she doesn't, but she sure tries. She misses, like, twenty times, repeatedly stabbing the door, marking up the white paint.

"I'd love to chat, but I gotta go! Gotta take a shower." She forces out a laugh that's teetering on the edge of unhinged. "I stink."

My eyes go to her hair, piled on top of her head and— "Your hair is wet."

Never mind that she was *leaving* her apartment, not coming home. Also, she smells super fresh, with hints of vanilla, cinnamon, and something sweet, like she spent the morning baking Christmas cookies.

I'd like to eat *her* cookie.

No. No, Garrett. That's what got us into this whole mess in the first place.

Jennie's dimples disappear when she realizes she's been caught in another lie, and she finally gets that damn key in the lock. The door springs open, and she tumbles through it.

"Greasy. Super greasy. My hair. Yeah, I haven't showered in…days." Her nose scrunches with disgust at her lie. "So it looks wet, but it's just…" She circles a hand around her damp bun and sighs, resigned. "Greasy."

"Jen—"

"*Okay-bye-Garrett!*" The words fly past her lips with the same speed she slams the door, and the sound of chuckling draws my attention over my shoulder.

Emily leans in her doorway, arms crossed as she grins at me. "Knew it."

I scrub a hand over my eyes. I'm so fucking tired, and I don't know what to do with my life anymore. "Knew what?"

"That you two were gonna fuck. You can smell the sexual tension from here."

"We didn't—ugh." I rub the back of my neck. "She seems tense?"

"*So* tense. Girl wants your dick and hates that she does."

I chuckle and Emily smiles. This should be weird, but it isn't. In the years I've known Emily, she's had plenty of boyfriends and girlfriends in between our casual hookups. I'm not worried that Emily caught… whatever the fuck that was. Maybe nothing. Probably nothing.

Or maybe something. Jennie's impossible to read.

Except last weekend when I ate her pussy like the Last Supper. Pretty hard to misread the signals when she's yanking on my hair, grinding her pussy against my mouth, and moaning my name as she comes. Twice.

"Things with Jennie are a little…"

"Challenging, best friend's little sister, and all? Those are some serious balls, Andersen!" Emily knocks my shoulder. "Proud of you."

I slip my fingers up the back of my toque and scratch my scalp to distract from the fact that I'm feeling a stupid amount of guilt. I let my blue balls do the talking, and now I'm gonna spend the rest of my life trying to hide it from one of my best friends.

"It was only the once. Won't happen again."

The truth is more disappointing than it reasonably should be.

Because as it turns out, offering to take care of Jennie's needs might've been, like, the teensiest bit of a mistake, and a highly addicting one too.

On the plus side, her sprained ankle seems to be healing well. Girl can bolt faster than Usain.

~

Adam has a breakfast date tomorrow, and now I'm fucked.

"You're not fucked," he says for the third time. I might've accidentally said the words out loud when he told us the news two minutes ago. "It's one date. It might not work out."

How does something not work out with a guy like Adam? He's the very best person I know, which is exactly why I'm fucked. He'll settle down, and then I'll really be lonely.

"I'm gonna be the only single friend," I mumble absently.

"Jaxon's single," Carter tosses out. "You guys can pick up chicks together."

"I don't wanna—I hate—ugh." Cheek on my fist, I glance at my lunch menu, then Adam. "Where'd you meet her?"

"At the grocery store. Cereal aisle. She said she likes dogs. That's good, right?"

"Considering you have a dog, that's probably for the best."

Adam swirls the straw in his chocolate milk. "I haven't been on a date in forever."

Emmett looks up from his phone. "Cara wants to know if we can run a background check on her and also if she can dress you for your date."

I tune out the conversation as I consider my future, what I want it to look like. My friends are trading nights at the bar for phone calls in the hotel room with their wives, and hangovers for early morning trips to Ikea, spending all their free time together, nothing but brightness looming in their futures.

I'm not bitter; I'm envious. There's only so much *COD* a guy can play alone on his couch while his friends are doing coupley shit together, like how Cara extended the sympathy invite to Adam and me to cut down Christmas trees with her, Emmett, Carter, and Olivia. They're moving forward, and I think I'm...stuck.

Emmett pulls my attention, poking me. "Hey, what about that girl? She's staring at you. Ask her out."

The pretty brunette approaches, and I roll my eyes. Gaze locked on the back of Carter's head, she tucks her hair behind her ears and takes a deep breath before tapping him on the shoulder.

"Excuse me. I'm Arianna."

Carter doesn't look up from his menu. "I'm married."

I lift my own menu to hide my snort.

Arianna opens her mouth, and Carter cuts her off before she can use it.

"Happily." He looks up with a grin and shows her Olivia's smiling face on his phone screen. "Isn't she beautiful?" He flips through his photos. "Here she is on our wedding day. Fucking gorgeous, right? And here's the baby she's growing right now. That's my baby. What do you think? Girl or boy? We're not finding out. We want to be surprised. I'm trying to convince myself I see a penis, though, 'cause girls are scary."

Huh. Arianna might be faster than Jennie. She's back on the other side of the diner before I can blink.

"That's exactly why it's hard to meet someone, though," I point out, and Adam nods. "I have no idea when someone is genuinely interested in me, or the rich hockey player."

"What about your neighbor?" Carter asks. "You guys still fucking?"

"Nah, nothing's going on. She lives across the hall from your sister." Wishing I'd left off that last bit, I bury my warming face in my menu. I'm shit at lying, even worse at hiding things. If Carter prods even a bit, there's a good chance I'll accidentally shout that I tongue-fucked his sister. "You said Jennie was uncomfortable with the neighbor stuff, so I figured since we're, like, friends by association, I wouldn't do it anymore."

Cautiously, I lift my gaze. Then I deflate. Carter's not even looking at me. He's blowing bubbles in his fucking chocolate milk.

"Jennie can be a bit scary sometimes, but she said she had a good time watching the game with you."

My mouth falls open and my brows skyrocket before I demand my brain lower them back down to their home. I chug my drink to hide that I'm barely hanging on right now. "She did?"

"Yeah, said you ate good. Something about the dessert you brought being, and I quote, orgasmic." He rolls his eyes. "She's so dramatic."

"Wonder where she gets that from," Emmett mutters.

At least I think that's what he says.

I'm too busy choking on the chocolate milk that's gone sliding down the wrong tube.

Carter rambles on about a good meal being the only thing Becketts need to keep them happy, and while I'm gasping for air, my entire life flashes before my eyes, especially at the hard, suspicious gaze Adam watches me with.

If it's my time to go, at least the dessert was orgasmic.

Lunchtime games on Saturdays are my favorite. I get my workout in extra early, hockey's done before dinner, and we get a rare Saturday night off.

Emmett keeps labeling Cara's twenty-sixth birthday party tonight as *lowkey*, but I'm not sure that word belongs in any sentence with Cara. I doubt there will be girls dancing on her kitchen counters like last year at the bar, so I guess that's lowkey.

"How was your date this morning, bud?" I ask Adam as I drop to my knees beside him, spreading my thighs and stretching my groin. My morning skate went well, and getting back on the ice feels exceptionally good. Coach has me on limited ice time tonight to ease back in, but at least I'm playing. I've been wound tight from nine days without hockey, among other things. The arena is buzzing, the chill from the ice feels refreshing on my cheeks, and I'm not gonna look at Jennie the entire game. Nothing can go wrong.

Adam sighs. "She definitely doesn't like dogs."

"But she told you she did."

"Well, I kinda wanted out at the end of breakfast." He chuckles at my expression. "So I told her I had to head home to walk Bear before the game. She insisted on coming."

"Dude. You're too nice."

"I didn't have the heart to tell her no! She was pouting up at me, with these big fucking eyes..." He sighs as we climb back to our feet. "Bear jumped up to say hello before I could stop him. Licked her face. She, uh...lost her shit, to put it nicely. About the slobber, the hair..."

"Aw, c'mon." Bear's next level on the cute scale, a giant, furry suck. "She's out, right?"

"If she hadn't already been, she definitely would've been when she asked if he'd be around much longer."

"Speaking of dates." A spray of snow slashes my face and covers my visor as Jaxon Riley, our new defenseman, stops in front of me. He spares me an absent glance. "Andersen."

"Riley."

He's already on my shitlist. To be honest, he's been there for years. He's an arrogant prick who shoots his mouth off nonstop. It gets him into a lot of trouble, hence why he's been traded here from Nashville after his second suspension of the season. Coach thinks he can straighten him out and get the most out of him. We'll see.

"Speaking of dates," he repeats. "Who's the rocket?"

I follow his gaze into the stands and reply on autopilot. "Cara and Olivia."

"I know who they are. I'm talking about the one with the dimples and the killer rack."

Yeah, I was hoping that wasn't the case.

My eyes sweep over Jennie, sandwiched between Cara and Olivia. Between the three of them, they appear to have bought the entire snack bar.

Jennie looks alarmingly pretty today. Hair down instead of in one of her signature braids, her thick chestnut tresses roll in waves around her shoulders, highlighting her broad smile and deep dimples when she laughs. She's also wearing a skintight tee that, as Jaxon mentioned, showcases her stellar rack. I bite my tongue to keep from bragging that I've tasted them.

Looking away, I nab a puck, spin around the net and stuff it behind Adam. "She's off-limits."

"Yours?"

"No."

"Then I guess she's not off-limits." His grin is self-assured, and I can't wait to wipe it off.

I smile back at him, extra megawatt. "Hey, Carter?" I call as he zooms by us, using his stick as a guitar. "What's Jennie's relationship status? Asking for a friend."

"Nobody touches my baby sister." It's half scream, half song, and Jaxon's face falls. "Oh hey." Carter follows me to the bench and leans on his stick, popping a pink bubble in his mouth. "Speaking of Jennie. Can you ride home with her tonight? I don't like the idea of her taking an Uber late at night by herself."

My first thought is the backseat of a car late at night is the last place I should ever be with Jennie. My second is she's a grown woman who'd likely lose her shit if she knew Carter was organizing supervised rides home for her. My third thought is—*oh fuck.*

"Your sister's coming to the party tonight?"

Carter nods, and my pulse thunders.

"Why is Jennie coming?" I accidentally ask out loud as Emmett joins us.

He gestures to where the girls are cackling on about something. My eyes lock with Jennie's before I immediately tear them away. "'Cause she's one of Cara's best friends?"

"Since when?" I stupidly demand rather than just saying, *Sure, I'll ride home with her.*

"Uh, since Olivia and Carter started dating, and now the three of them spend all their time together?"

"Oh. Right." *Fuck.* I look to Carter and start waving one floppy, gloved hand through the air. I might as well be holding a neon sign that reads *I ate your sister's pussy and liked it.* "Um, I think I'm gonna…drive." I wasn't going to, but if Jennie's gonna be there, I absolutely need to stay sober. I can't have alcohol impeding any of my decision-making capabilities—which are already flawed and weak—because I'll try to talk myself into a place I want to be but shouldn't, like between her thighs while I locate her G-spot with the tip of my tongue, or my cock. Plus, Jennie doesn't drink, and being supportive of that feels like the right move in our fucked-up friendship.

"Perfect. You can take her home." Carter cups his gloved hands around his mouth. "Hey, Jennie! Garrett's gonna give you a ride tonight!"

Give her a ride? That's exactly what I want to do and what I'm actively trying to avoid. Instead, I attempt to swallow down my entire Adam's apple as I meet Jennie's gaze.

At least she looks as terrified as I am about what type of ride I might take her for.

I wonder which one of us has better self-control.

ELEVEN
PLAY WITH ME

Garrett

HOW THE FUCK did she get those on?

Judging by the way I'm trying to decide on a plan of attack for getting her out of them, Jennie's high-waisted jeans appear to be painted over her round ass and wide hips. I'm not allowed to undress her though.

But these fucking jeans. The tight, washed-out denim flares below her knees, and I swear those legs go straight to heaven. I'm already mentally cataloging all the different ways I can wrap them around me (hint: position number one is over my shoulders). She's also wearing this stupid crop top that shows off her stupid belly button, and all I'm thinking about is shifting that shitty excuse for a shirt up and swirling my tongue around the tiny plum-purple gem that dangles there.

I need to get her the fuck out of my system.

"You don't drink?"

"Huh?" I drag my gaze away from Jennie, unimpressed that it's Jaxon Riley who's made me do so.

He gestures at the can of sparkling cherry-flavored water in my hand. "You're drinking water."

"I'm driving tonight."

"Why?"

So I don't make any *captain's little sister*–sized mistakes that have the potential to prematurely end my career via shattered bones?

"Uh, 'cause?" is the intellectual response I give him.

Jaxon's gaze follows mine as it bounces back to the girl in question, and he smirks. Leaning next to me, he murmurs, "The thing about her being Carter's little sister is that he's only my captain, whereas he's one of your best friends. Where she's off-limits for you, she's free game for me."

I snort. "Good luck walking outta here with that type of logic."

"Tell ya what. I'll make you a bet."

"No." I'm not entertaining this jackass. "What's the bet?" I'm entertaining him a little.

"I get her to come home with me tonight."

My grip on my can tightens. "I think the fuck not."

"Because you want her?"

"Because you'll fuck her once and ghost her, and we'll be short a defenseman when Carter knocks you the fuck out." I drain my can and crush it between my hands. "Jennie deserves better."

Jaxon grins, pulling two beers from the ice in the kitchen sink. He tosses his words over his shoulder as he wanders toward Jennie. "I'll treat her real nice, Andersen. Promise."

I'm highly unimpressed with the state of Olivia's bladder. She's left me here alone, and I'm about to have to be friendly with a fuckboy.

The new trade saunters toward me, a smug grin on his smug face. "Pretty girl like you shouldn't be alone." He holds out his hand. "I'm Jaxon."

I lift my sparkling water to my mouth. "I know who you are."

Speaking loosely, of course, about having to be friendly.

Jaxon Riley, NHL bad boy, fuckboy extraordinaire, and Vancouver's newest defenseman, chuckles, taking his hand back. "All right. That's cool. I know who you are too." He offers me one of the beers laced between his fingers. "Brought you a beer."

"I don't drink."

I catch a snort of laughter, and my gaze flits over Jaxon's shoulder, finding Garrett's amused eyes on us. I'm not proud to say I suddenly become a lot more interested in the man in front of me.

Jaxon's nice to look at, so it's not an onerous task. All messy brown hair, hazel eyes, broad shoulders, and a full sleeve of tattoos decorating his left arm, I'm entirely into it. Top-shelf Flickapedia material, without a doubt. A welcome reprieve from the mental image I've been flicking it to every single night since Garrett destroyed me after catching his name leaving my lips.

I lean into the new defenseman, squeezing his forearm, and drop my voice to a purr. "But thank you so much for thinking of me. That's incredibly sweet of you."

His smirk is too proud. "That's why they call me Sugar."

I inwardly roll my eyes, trailing my fingertip over the flowers decorating the cuff of Jaxon's wrist as Garrett crushes his can in his fist and reaches for a new one. "Really? I heard that was for an entirely different reason."

Jaxon takes the bait, stepping into me. "Dessert might be my favorite meal of the day."

"Mmm..." I bat my lashes while Garrett aggressively chugs his water. "Mine too."

I spy the platter of double fudge cupcakes sitting on the counter, right next to Garrett's elbow. I walk toward him, his face heating the closer I get.

"Excuse me." I brush against him, reaching for a cupcake. "Dessert," I murmur with a wink before heading back to Jaxon. "I've been craving something sweet all night long." I swipe my finger through the fudge frosting, then slowly suck it into my mouth, all the while noticing how Garrett demolishes another can of sparkling water.

Jaxon's hooded gaze tracks my finger, my lips, the way my tongue darts out to make sure I don't miss a single bit of decadence. He brushes a lock of hair off my face before his fingertips skim my waist. "Come home with me."

Behind him, Garrett's fist ends the life of what I'm pretty sure is his third can of cherry sparkling water in the last five minutes.

Garrett

Well, that won't work. Absolutely not. If I can't have her, nobody else on this team gets her.

"Eh, Carter," I call across the kitchen.

Jennie's icy stare widens. She takes a frantic step away from Jaxon, confirming my suspicion that she's doing this to get under my skin.

Carter ambles over. "What's up?"

I incline my head in Jennie's direction. "Nice to see Jennie and Jaxon getting along."

Carter's head whips around, and his fist destroys his beer can. "The fuck he is," he grinds out, tossing his can in the sink and stalking toward the happy couple.

Well, Jaxon's happy; Jennie's not.

Jaxon's about to be broken, not happy.

I'm happy.

Jennie

I hope Garrett's had a good life, because I'm about to end it.

I shove Jaxon's hand away and pin my brother with a grin, extra dimply. "Hey, you! Enjoying the party?"

Carter's in full grump mode, angling himself toward Jaxon, strategically blocking me from his line of vision and any further physical contact. "Riley. I see you've met my sister. Baby sister. Only sister. *My* sister."

Oh Christ. Here we go. Garrett's not even bothering to hide his triumphant grin behind his fourth water. I hope all the bathrooms are occupied when he soon needs one.

Fuck you, I mouth, flipping him the bird behind Carter's back.

You'd like that, is I'm pretty sure what he mouths back.

"I was just introducing myself," Jaxon says. "She's been very welcoming. She's beautiful."

"I know she is," Carter snaps back. "She's also twenty-four."

Jaxon leans around Carter, grinning. "I'm twenty-six."

Carter sidesteps, the human barrier I didn't ask for. "Two years too old for her."

I frown. "You're almost three years older than Olivia."

Carter's head swivels in slow motion. I mash my lips together at his expression, mostly to keep from laughing in his face. He may look threatening, but I'm fully aware he's a giant teddy bear who spends his time singing Disney songs, carrying his dog, and plastering his ear against his wife's stomach in case today's the day he can hear the baby.

"Hey, Carter, I was thinking, with your permission—"

"Riley." Carter drops his head, shoulders shaking with his chuckle. He lays a heavy hand on Jaxon's shoulder. "Look, I like you. You're a good hockey player, nice enough guy." He steps into him, and Jaxon's easy smile melts off his face. "But if you finish that sentence—"

"Carter—" His palm covers my mouth, halting my words.

"Now, I know what you're probably thinking. *But Carter, she's a grown woman.*"

"Yes," I mumble behind his palm. "I am.

"*But Carter, she can make her own decisions.*"

"I can."

"*I'll treat her right, blah blah blah.*" He shakes his head. "The answer is no. You can touch my sister over my dead body."

I smile weakly at Jaxon. This is futile, and I don't care enough to argue it with Carter. "Nice talking to you."

When Jaxon darts off, Carter turns back to me with a sigh and a dopey grin.

"Sorry Riley was bugging you. Thank fuck Garrett tipped me off."

My eyes zero in on the man in question, the one who's watching, wiggling two fingers in a wave.

"Yes," I murmur. "Thank fuck."

Garrett

I changed my mind. I want her, and I'm gonna have her.

Carter walks away, leaving his sister glaring at me, and when she flips me the double bird, I know that only God can help me now.

Fuck me, I'm going for it anyway.

Jennie

What is he doing? Why is he looking at me like that? Is he walking this way? He's walking this way.

Get back, demon boy.

But also, come a bit closer.

No, stop right there.

Fuckballs. I can't make up my mind.

I drag my clammy palms down my thighs, glancing away. He's probably not coming this way.

He's definitely coming this way.

My jaw drops, he grins, and I do what I do best.

I run.

"I'm gonna make a mistake," I mutter, slipping through the crowd. I climb the stairs two at a time and beeline down the hall. "If he talks to me, I'm gonna make a mistake. A *huge* mistake. I won't be able to stop myself. I will *not* be able to stop myself. Huge mistake, Jennie. *Huge.* No. Nope."

I heave open the linen closet and throw myself through it.

Safe.

The door swings open a moment later, and the moonlight filtering through the window in the hallway illuminates a pair of piercing eyes as the intruder sweeps into the tiny space and shuts us in.

"Great thinking on the closet, Jennie." Garrett's gravelly voice sends a shiver down my spine. He smacks the wall, lighting the space with a warm glow via the tiny chandelier hanging above us, and the man has never looked so sinister. "Think we lost them."

My heart leaps to my throat as he steps into me, towering. This man right here is all devil as he slowly crowds me, gaze locked on mine as he pins my hips to the wall.

"Now tell me about that huge mistake you wanna make."

Garrett

"Lemme guess…" Jennie's hands sweep up my biceps, roaming over my shoulders. She tangles her fingers in my hair, twining it slowly. The way she turns her confidence on and all the way up to ten without batting an eye cranks my gears in a way I can't explain. "You heard the word huge and figured I must've been talking about you."

"Hey, if the shoe fits."

"Ego," she whispers, dragging my neck down until my lips hover over hers. "The word you're looking for is ego." Her mouth bypasses mine, lips skimming my jaw, and my cock starts gearing up for a quick fuck in the closet.

Except I don't want there to be anything quick about the way I fuck Jennie.

"Remarkable how well your ankle healed over the past week," I murmur as she leans back. "Couldn't even tell you sprained it tripping over your bag, hurting it during practice, and tripping over your dance partner, by the way you sprinted up those stairs."

Jennie checks her nails. "Yes, well, they had me stay home and rest it for the week so I didn't aggravate it. It feels fine now." Her gaze flips to mine. "I'm sorry your head isn't any better."

"I scored a goal and got an assist today."

"Oh, I'm not basing it on your ability to play hockey. Simply on the way you seem to keep making…" Her tongue pokes the corner of her mouth. "*Ill-advised* decisions."

I drop my gaze, watching my finger trace the waist of her jeans, the way her exposed skin jumps at my touch. "I don't recall making any *ill-advised* decisions. In fact, I've been told the dessert was…" Dipping my fingers below the waist of her jeans, I tug her forward. She catches herself on my chest with a strangled gasp. "Orgasmic."

A tiny vibration, right there in her throat, as she tries to hide her snicker. "The popcorn was delicious." Her fingers brush my collarbone as she fixes the button on my shirt. "Are you having fun playing this little game of yours?"

"Funny you should ask. That's exactly what I wanna do." I capture her hands in mine, pinning them on either side of her head. "I want to play."

A beat of silence echoes between us as the words settle. Jennie laughs lowly.

"You think I'm gonna let you into my Disneyland just for fun? Oh, Garrett, you're adorable. What makes you think I'd agree to something like that?"

I press my lips to the thundering pulse point on her neck. "Besides the fact that your body's giving away how much the idea intrigues you? Our chemistry is off the charts, don't you think? I go all tongue-tied, you scream at me 'til you're hot and bothered, and all the while I'm thinking about throwing your legs over my shoulders and gorging on my favorite dessert." I kiss the hollow spot below her ear, reveling in her shiver. "That's you, sunshine. You're my favorite dessert."

With my hand on her throat, I haul her into me until her lips wait just below mine, fingernails biting into my shoulders. Breathless, she clings to me as I whisper my next words.

"C'mon, Jennie. Play with me."

Jennie

This motherfucker thinks I'm gonna give it up.

"That's sweet, but you're not really my type, big guy." I'm hoping the lie isn't as blatant as it feels, but the chances aren't great. My gaze heats as it crawls down his body, slow to come back up, and my tongue absently glides across my lower lip as I remember the way his mouth tastes. When dark amusement flashes in Garrett's eyes, I know. I'm as wrapped up as he is, as he wants me to be, and he knows it.

His thumb nabs my lower lip, gently tugging. "This is fun to you, isn't it? The forced indifference, the teasing. It's part of what makes things so electric between us."

Said electricity buzzes through me like a live wire dipped in water, but I keep playing. "It must be incredibly difficult for you to wrap your head around. Rich, successful, sexy hockey player, and yet I couldn't possibly be less interested."

"Rich, successful, and sexy," he murmurs. "Sure sounds like I'm renting a space in your brain, sunshine."

"You're not letting a few simple adjectives go to your extremely large head now, are you, Mr. Andersen?"

His grin turns wicked, and I gasp when he fists the hair at my nape, pulling my head taut. His gaze drops, hooded and heated, and he watches with a heady, starved look as my bottom lip slides between my teeth.

"Anything else?"

"You're too timid and gentle," I whisper, needling him on as I toy with his collar. "You don't know how to take what you want."

My heartbeat settles at the cleft of my thighs when he flips me around without warning, pushing me against the wall, his chest flush with my back. I give my ass a little wiggle to see how far I can push him, and bite back my moan at the weight of his desire pressing deeper against me.

His lips linger at my ear. "This sudden confidence of mine? That's courtesy of you, Jennie. Knowing you want me as much as I want you makes me feel like I'm on top of the world."

"I don't want you," I breathe out, even as I let my head fall onto his shoulder, our fingers tangling as he shifts the neck of my shirt over.

His teeth skim across my shoulder. "No?"

"N-no."

Garrett's fingers dance down my belly, and every muscle clenches as he pops the button on my jeans. My sharp inhale spirals into an unashamed moan, and I arch off his chest, pushing myself into his hand, begging for attention where I want it most.

And then he releases me. "'Kay."

I whip around in time to see him adjusting the lump in his jeans. "'Kay? 'Kay what? What are you doing?" I watch in horror as he reaches for the door. "Where are you going? You can't...You can't do this. *Garrett!*"

He sweeps a soft, slow kiss across my cheek. "Enjoy your night, sunshine."

I hate him.

I hate him and his stupid, hot face and his stupid, hot body so motherfucking much.

Garrett

Fuck, she wants me so bad. It's written all over her face, the flush of her high cheekbones, the murderous way she glares at me every time she finds me staring, 'cause she's mad at me for not finishing what I started.

Cara slaps Jennie's ass as she moves past her, remarking how incredible her jeans make her ass look, and I'm ready to rip them right the fuck off her.

Should I tell her? I should tell her.

Jennie

"You look angry."

"I am angry," I grumble to Cara. I pin my arms over my chest, then promptly drop them at the look of approval on Garrett's face when I push my own tits up. *Fuck you,* I mouth to him.

"Angry sex is the best sex," Cara tells me sincerely.

"I wouldn't know."

"You could find out." Cara winks, a finger on her lips. "I'm great at keeping secrets."

Sometimes avoidance is the best policy, so I reach for the closest thing, which happens to be the fridge door. I pull it open, staring at nothing.

Cara's chin lands on my shoulder. "Forced proximity does wonders for two horny, single hotties."

"I'm not—*ugh*."

Another wink before the birthday girl sashays away, and I swivel back to the fridge, content with letting the cool air nip at my warm cheeks.

I know the second he's behind me. My body reacts before my mind does, which is irritating. I'd like to tell him to get fucking lost, but my mouth isn't forming the words, and my body's trembling with desire. Desire to touch, feel, let myself get lost in this man until nothing else matters.

Garrett leans over me on the pretense of reaching into the fridge, fingers fluttering over the bottles of beer, though he never does grab one. His hips press against my ass as he whispers, "Do you have a preference in how I take these off you later? I can try to be gentle and peel them off real slow, but I'm leaning toward option two."

I swallow. "What's option two?"

"I destroy them. One way or another, they'll be on my bedroom floor tonight, and you'll be beneath me, saying my name." His mouth dips low as he skims my bare waist with his frosty fingertips. "Over and over again."

"Can you take us through the McDonald's drive-thru?"

I glance at Carter in my backseat. "Put your seat belt on."

He somehow manages to squeeze his sasquatch frame between the front seats, right between me and his sister. "I'll put it on if you take us to McDick's."

"You've gotta be kidding. There was so much food at the party."

"I want an Oreo McFlurry." He taps Olivia's shoulder five hundred times. She's halfway to passed out beside him. "Want one, pumpkin? Extra Oreo? Gare-Bear's takin' us."

She cracks a sleepy lid, smiling at me in the mirror. Sighing, I switch lanes. You don't say no to a pregnant woman who wants ice cream.

"Pushover," Jennie mumbles under her breath.

Carter swings his arms over both seats. "I'm so happy you're friends now. It makes me so happy." His forehead flops to my shoulder. "I'm so happy."

I'm happy when he disappears inside his house, Olivia shouting both an apology and a thank you over her shoulder while she munches her ice cream.

Jennie looks the opposite of happy, glowering beside me, but then again, she almost always looks this way.

"Don't look so glum, sunshine. We'll have a pleasant, quiet ride home, just the two of us."

"I'm no one's sunshine," she barks back. She's been especially snippy since I left her in the closet.

I swallow my snort. "Clearly."

"So stop calling me it."

"But it suits you so well, what with the way you sprinkle it every-where you go."

I swear those arms of hers have a permanent spot folded over her chest. "I hate you."

I reach across the console, skimming the edge of her thigh. Her hands fall to her lap and her lips part as she tracks the movement. "Sure you do, sunshine."

A growl rumbles and she slaps my hand away, angling herself toward the window. The air between us sizzles like an electric current every time I catch her peeking over her shoulder at me.

At the condo, we ride the elevator in silence, and she fumbles with her key when I hang over her shoulder in front of her door.

"You're not...you can't..." She points at me, then her door, and wags her head. I smile, 'cause I think we might've switched roles.

I lean forward and she plasters herself against the door, each breath heavier than the last. Our eyes lock as I step into her. She tips her chin up, wets her lips, and I turn the key in the lock.

Jennie tumbles backward before I catch her via a fistful of her coat.

The look she hits me with has me thinking my jockstrap might be useful for more than blocking pucks.

"Night, sunshine."

Jennie

"Stupid…motherfucking…cocky…son of a goddamn bitch." I yank open the drawer in my bedside table, rooting through the rainbow of rubber and silicone. "He thinks he can play me like that?"

A bitter chuckle escapes as I select one of my best friends: the womanizer, or, as I've affectionately labeled her, Ol' Faithful.

"I don't need him. I didn't need him before, and I don't need him now. It wasn't even that good."

I tug my jeans aggressively down my legs and climb on the bed, feet flat and legs wide as I fix Ol' Faithful over my clit. I press the power button six times, cranking her right up to max, and my lids flutter closed as I sink into the pillows.

"Oh yeah," I murmur, that little bud tightening. Everything feels ultrasensitive, tingly like Pop Rocks, and I settle in, ready to take myself for a ride. My toes curl as I climb higher, pushing that little hunk of magic closer, and my lips part on a moan as—

"Damnit. What the hell? C'mon, girl. You earned your name for a reason; don't fail me now." I hammer the button, desperate for more. More power, more friction, *more, more, more.*

But she doesn't give me more, and what she does give me, quite frankly, isn't enough. It's always been enough.

Frustrated and desperate, I reach down with my free hand and swipe my fingers through my slit. I'm wet, so that's good. Drenched, really. So I skip one finger and go right to two.

"Oh yes," I moan. "Dual stimulation. This is what I need. So good. So perfect." My hips lift as I arch into my palm. "Abs, abs, abs," I chant. "He's got great abs. And fingers. Oooh, and that tongue. He does wonderful things with that tongue. Yes, yes, yes."

The feeling wanes as quickly as it builds, and I pump harder, faster, begging my body to work with me, to give me a release I've never so desperately chased before.

But for every step forward, I take two backward. Pretty soon I'm just miserably flicking it while I glare at the wall, an annoyingly attractive and newly arrogant man's face smiling back at me, reminding me for the umpteenth time that the little object between my thighs can only do so much. It's not those fingers that stroked me so meticulously, that tongue that ate me so savagely.

And above all else, it lacks the heat, the determination, the ferocity with which Garrett promised to wreck me.

All waves of pleasure die down to a gentle ripple, and I chuck Ol' Faithful—*new name required*—across the room before I sprawl out on the mattress, defeated, miserable, and horny as fuck.

Garrett

I fix my track pants low on my hips, choosing to forgo a T-shirt. It won't stay on anyway.

Making my way to the kitchen, I pour myself a glass of water and wait, eyes on the stove clock.

I smile to myself when the banging starts. Loud and aggressive, like her, and when I leave her hanging a minute longer, it turns to slapping.

Eight minutes. Huh. I gave her fifteen. She's always surprising me.

I unlock the door and pull it open.

I appreciate that she put her shirt back on to come up here, even if it is inside out. Her jeans made it back on, too, unbuttoned and hanging off her hips, and the long cardigan she's added does a mediocre job at best of hiding this mess of an outfit. Those heeled booties she wore earlier didn't make it back on her feet, but her puppy slippers complete the look.

Jennie's scowl is particularly ferocious, cheeks rosy as she breathes heavily. She whips off her cardigan and steps toward me.

"I wanna play."

TWELVE
RULES? DO WE HAVE TO?

Garrett

My back hits the wall with a thud when Jennie pins me there, her warm fingers and fiery gaze roaming my torso, leaving a trail of want in their wake, so deep, so hot, my skin singes.

She drags her tongue slowly across her lips before murmuring, "So fucking hot." Her eyes flip to mine, the challenge there. "Keep grinning like a jackass and I'll walk my ass right the fuck back out of here."

I flip us around, hips pressing her into the wall, fingers circling her wrists as I hold her hands on either side of her head. Her mouth lifts to mine, seeking, hungry, *so fucking eager*. "You won't go anywhere, sunshine."

"Rules." Jennie gasps as I bury my face in her neck, legs wrapping around me as I hoist her up to me. "We should set some rules."

My tongue trails the columns of her throat. "Do we have to?"

"Carter would never approve."

"And I don't want to die at the ripe age of twenty-six. It'll be our little secret." I flick my tongue over the spot below her ear. "Spoiler alert: it's not little in the slightest."

"No sleepovers."

"Excellent. You seem like a bed hog."

I yank her top over her head and die a little at the lacy mocha bra, the pink rosebuds peeking out from behind the scant material. I want them between my teeth while she sinks her nails into my shoulders and cries out for *more*.

Jennie's eyes are hooded and dazed as she watches me, starved, a desperation I've never seen before but vow to cherish for as long as I get to be on the receiving end of it.

I bury my fingers in her hair and my tongue in her mouth, swallowing her moans as I grind her against the weight of my craving for her. I'm gonna need to fuck her hard and quick so that I can start over and take my time with her. We've got all night.

But then she chokes out her next rule, the two words a garbled mess lost somewhere in my mouth.

"No sex."

I chuckle. "Cute."

"I'm serious, Garrett. I won't have sex with you."

My mouth pauses on her jaw and my hands still their kneading. I drop her slowly to her feet. "Are you a virgin?'

"What? No!"

"Then why won't you have sex with me?"

"Because I...well, I'm...I'm just..." Her eyes scale the wall behind me as she aggressively twines her hair around her fingers until it knots and gets stuck. When I free it, she shoves the tip of her thumbnail between her teeth, nibbling.

Taking her hand gently in mine, I pull it away from her mouth. "Jennie."

"It's been a while," she admits quietly. "A few years...or so."

Or so. "Oh."

"Yeah. I'm just...not really ready to go there again."

"Oh."

Heat floods her cheeks the longer she waits for me to say something more substantial than *oh*, and I'm trying, I swear to fucking God. Nothing's coming.

The light in her eyes dims, and she steps away, picking up her shirt. I've never seen her so vulnerable before, and something inside me hurts at the sight of her.

"Forget it," she whispers. "This was stupid. I knew you wouldn't go for it. Why would anyone?"

I grab her wrist. "Hang on." *What am I doing?* "It's fine." *Fine?!* Lieutenant Johnson screams at me from where he's way too restricted in my briefs. "No sex. I can handle that." *I think the fuck not,* he argues. Thing is, though, I've already seen Jennie naked. I've seen her *I'm fucking coming* face. Not only would I like to see it again, but I'd like to be the reason behind it.

But more? There's something going on here, something that ruined this for her. Not all sex is special, but some is supposed to be, and when it should've been, I can tell it wasn't. I don't know if it's related to her lack of friends, or the trust she doesn't give easily, but if I can give her those things—friendship, trust, respect—I'll do it happily. I want whatever pieces of herself she's willing to give me.

Jennie watches me warily. "You can?"

"Taking control of your sexuality and setting your boundaries is fucking cool, and I respect that." I gesture at the shirt she's clutching to her chest. "Now ditch the fuckin' shirt, sunshine. I'm gonna worship all of you tonight."

It's not until I start stalking toward her, a sinister grin on my face, that she fully comprehends what's happening and frantically tosses the shirt. She lets out a yelp when I scoop her up and toss her over my shoulder. Dropping her to her feet in my bedroom, I bend her over the bed with my palm between her shoulder blades.

These jeans are a fucking sin, hugging her wicked hips, that little gap at the back of her waist just big enough for me to slip two fingers down and take a peek at the heart-shaped ass hiding beneath. They're the kind with all those strategically placed rips, like through one thigh and over her knee. But my favorite one...

I slip a thumb below the frayed, narrow rip slicing its way across the back of Jennie's left thigh, a mere inch or two below her ass cheek. Whoever designed these jeans...I would fall to their feet.

My thumb glides over Jennie's heated skin. "These new?"

"I bought them last week."

"Part of the current collection? Great."

Jennie frowns. When I dip four fingers below the slit and smile, her lips part in horror.

"Garrett," she warns.

But it's too late for warnings. I'm already pulling, and they're already ripping, shredding into a beautiful mess.

Jennie gasps, trying to turn around. I press myself against the backs of her thighs, fisting her hair to keep her in place as I admire her.

"Jesus Christ." My brain is short-circuiting. I trace the edge of her panties and her skin pebbles. "This ass is out of this fuckin' world." I clap a hand to her ass cheek, grinning at her murderous gaze. "Send me the link. I'll buy you a new pair."

"I hate you," she growls.

"Furthest thing from it, gorgeous." I drop my pants to the ground, flip her onto her back, kneel before her, and start working her jeans off. "Any other rules before I get started? I'm fuckin' starving."

I part her legs, pressing my lips to the inside of her knee, nibbling a languid path up her thigh. She fists the sheets, head rolling as she whimpers my name. But I want to hear her scream it.

"Rules, Jennie."

"I don't want to be one of many," she says on a gasp as I brush her clit through her damp lace. "I know it's casual, but I want to at least feel…" Her eyes lock with mine as I gently rub her.

"Special?" When she nods, I chuckle. "You're already special, sunshine." I wrap my palm around her neck and bring her lips down to mine. "Committed friends with benefits?"

She sucks her bottom lip into her mouth, wide eyes moving between mine, and nods.

"Deal. No one but you."

"Just like that? Even without the sex?"

"Just like that. I don't need to use my dick to fuck you. My fingers and tongue work just fine."

Jennie comes to life with an electric, flirty grin, slinging her arms around my neck. "Yes, they do." She tilts my head back, her mouth claiming mine. "In case you were wondering, blow jobs are still on the table."

My body stills as my cock roars with need. "They are? I'm clean, I promise. Are you sure? It's okay if—"

"Just because we aren't having sex doesn't mean I'm not gonna pull my weight. I'm still gonna suck your cock."

If my dick had arms, he'd be jerking one back into his side triumphantly. Since he can't, I do. "Fuck yeah you are!" I tug her to her feet and seat myself on the edge of the bed. "On your knees, sunshine."

Her mouth gapes. "But I—"

"Knees," I repeat on a whisper, squeezing the back of her neck. Jennie falls to her knees, and I thread my fingers through her hair. "So fuckin' sexy when you're on your knees and, for once in your life, speechless." I run a thumb over her parted, swollen lips. "You okay with a little bit rough?"

Her eyes pinball between mine, and her innocence throws me for a loop and spurs me on all at once. "Rough?"

"Mmm." My grasp on her hair tightens and her breath hitches, heat climbing her chest as she grips my thighs. "There's something about your bossy-as-fuck attitude that screams 'boss me the fuck around in bed.'"

I hook her fingers in the waistband of my boxer briefs, and Jennie hesitantly works them down. Her eyes widen and she leans back as if she's scared. Lieutenant Johnson bobs around, happy and proud as he greets her, letting her know she has nothing to be scared of. He'll be real gentle with her.

"I-I-I—" Jennie stutters, which is super fucking new, and super fucking hot.

"What's the matter? What happened to all that attitude?" I haul her forward, lips at her ear. "Am I in charge?"

Fingernails bite into my thighs as I dip my hand and stroke two fingers over the seam of her soaked panties. "*Garrett.*"

"Say it," I demand.

"You're in charge."

"Fuckin' right I am. Open your mouth, Jennie."

She does, without hesitation, slender fingers wrapping around me. A drop of cum beads at the tip, and Jennie's gaze flutters to mine. She looks nervous, unsure maybe. I'm about to tell her she doesn't have to do anything she's not comfortable with, but the words die on my tongue as hers flicks out, tasting me.

"Holy fuck." The words rumble in my chest as her mouth engulfs the head of my cock.

I take her face in my hands, eyes locking as her pink lips slide down my length, as much as she can take until I hit the back of her throat. When I groan, those pale eyes light with excitement. The corners of her mouth lift as she smiles around me, and it's in that moment I realize what she needs.

Encouragement. Reassurance. Praise. She needs to know she makes me feel as good as I make her feel. Her signature Beckett arrogance doesn't own this part of her life, but if I have any say, it will.

It won't be hard; she sure as hell sucks my cock like she was made to do it. I'm about to cheer her on until she believes it.

"Fuck yes," I hiss. "Just like that, Jennie." With her hair around my fist, I force her gaze to mine. "Eyes on me, sunshine. Always on me."

Jennie whimpers, shifting, rubbing her thighs together. She's desperate for affection, attention, friction, and I'm gonna give it to her, just as soon as I come.

I guide her head, watching her swallow as much of me as she can, cheeks hollowing as she slides backward. She pauses on the tip, tongue swirling, hand working the base, before she swallows me back up again.

"Shit. Don't stop. Fuck, Jennie, don't you fucking stop."

She grows louder, moves faster, slurping like it's her damn job. I lose my words, and Jennie's smile blooms. Her eyes dance with pride as my balls tighten, and when I tell her I'm gonna come, choking on the words, she keeps going, gaze fixed on mine as I empty myself down her throat.

"Holy fuck."

She licks the corner of her mouth. "How was that?"

I chuckle, grabbing her by the waist and tossing her onto the pillows. "You wanna know how that was?" My knees hit the bed, and I crawl toward her. "How 'bout I show you how that was?"

My mouth takes hers, stealing her response. There's something about the taste of me on her lips that makes me a little wild, and when Jennie arches off the bed, rubbing her soaked pussy on my cock, I'm worried I'm gonna try to convince her to let me take something that doesn't belong to me.

"Jennie," I warn on a snarl.

"Please." Her nails bite into my shoulders as she slides herself against my length, up and down, coating me in her. Her smell, her wetness, her heat. "It feels so good."

And *fuck*, I can't say no to her.

My fingers sink into her plush ass as I squeeze her to me with one hand, the other running along the edge of her jaw, angling her hungry mouth to mine. It's every bit swallowed moan, sweeping tongues, nipping teeth as Jennie's hips lift and I slide through her folds over and over.

Her nails rake down my biceps as she tears her mouth from mine, gasping for air, and I pull one pink nipple into my mouth. My tongue rolls over the taut peak before I tug it between my teeth, and a shiver of pleasure rockets up my spine when Jennie's nails score down my back, my name leaving her lips on a moan. I'm going to come, and Jennie's going to spiral with me.

"You gonna come, sunshine?"

Jennie's eyes roll down from heaven, and she smirks that Beckett smirk. "You gonna make me, Gare-Bear?"

I steal her grin with my own, and heat spreads like wildfire throughout my body. On the next rock of my hips, I reach down and spear her with two fingers, replacing my cock with my thumb as I rub her clit without mercy. Jennie explodes around me, mouth opening on a cry, cheeks and tits flushed and rosy, and when I catch sight of that swollen, glistening pussy, my cock pulses.

"Jesus fuck." I roll off the bed as my cock empties all over my hand, seeping through my fingers and to the floor, which is definitely not what I planned and *what a fucking mess.* "I've never done that before."

Breathless, Jennie sprawls over the mattress, swiping her chestnut hair from her damp forehead. "Came in your hand? Or dry-humped?"

"There was nothing dry about that. Fuckin' Niagara Falls down there."

Standing before me, she trails a fingertip along her collarbone, peeking up at me from beneath dark lashes. "I was thinking about Chris Hemsworth."

"The fuck you were." I clap a hand to her ass. "Bathroom. Shower. Now."

"You know, you're turning out to be a little bit bossy."

"And you're a fuckload bossy." Gripping her nape, I steer her into the bathroom and crank the shower. "Now get in there so I can make sure you're thoroughly cleaned."

She does, and I do. Several times over, 'cause being thorough is super important, and I'm nothing if not detail oriented.

It's nearly four in the morning when we ride the elevator down to Jennie's floor, hair damp and both of us squeaky clean.

Jennie turns to me with this coy little half smile as she unlocks her door and starts backing in. "Thanks for the ride, Andersen. A solid six outta ten."

"Six outta ten, my ass. I rocked your world, sunshine."

She fingers a wet lock of hair that hangs down my forehead. "I'll only have to use Indiana Bones once tonight."

My chest rumbles as she grins, and she grips a fistful of my shirt, hauling me into her. Her tongue slides into my mouth as my hands crawl up her top, circling her warm waist.

I start walking her backward, 'cause now I'm thinking round four sounds real nice, but Jennie disengages, slapping my hands away.

"G'night, Gare-Bear," she sings, then promptly slams the door in my face.

Hands on my hips, I look down at Lieutenant Johnson, snug and content in my track pants. "We did it, big buddy. We did it."

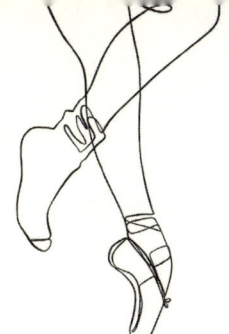

THIRTEEN
NAILING IT

Jennie

IN ONE EAR, out the other. That's what's happening right now. To be fair, Mom's been on about Olivia's baby shower plans for forty minutes now. She's surpassed overthinking territory, so I've resorted to staring out the coffee shop window.

Fat snowflakes fall slowly, turning downtown Vancouver into a winter wonderland. It's pretty to watch, mesmerizing, even if I'm counting down the days to spring. Sleet and snow bring dangerous driving conditions, along with a lot of unnecessary anxiety, and the fleeting daylight hours are depressing.

"Jennie? Are you listening? I don't want to disappoint Olivia."

I leave the bleak, gray day on the other side of the window and look at my mom. Her wide-eyed expression is half-annoyed, half-worried.

"Please, Mom. Olivia's already reached maximum disappointment levels; she married your son."

"*Jennifer.* I swear, the teasing between you and your brother is ridiculous."

Beside me, Hank sips his coffee. "Teasing is the love language of siblings, Holly."

Truth, but Carter's love can, on occasion, be a touch suffocating. Like right now as I check my phone.

World's Best Bro: *dance practice done @ 5? i'll pick u up.*

World's Best Bro: *u can have dinner with me n ollie*

One guess at who named his phone contact.

Me: *Taking the bus home.*
World's Best Bro: *don't think so. it'll be starting to get dark.*
World's Best Bro: *or u could take one of my cars. have 5.*
Me: *Thanks, but no.*
World's Best Bro: *thx, but ya. pizza? or indian?*

With a sigh, I flip my phone upside down and give my mom a look. "Your son doesn't take no for an answer."

"He didn't get that from me."

My phone dings again, and I'm ready to tell my brother where he can shove all five of his cars. Instead, my cheeks heat at the bear emoji lighting my phone.

Bear: *Play tonight? We fly out in the morning for a few days.*

Telling him I can't makes me sadder than seems reasonable. For years I've been happy with my personal satisfaction and growing toy collection. In a few measly days, Garrett's managed to throw that all out the window.

I tack on something about Carter being a demanding shit with his insistence to kidnap me for dinner. Otherwise, the answer would be a resounding *yes*, and one of us would be on our knees within thirty seconds of being behind closed doors.

Bear: *I'll pick u up. Tell him u got a ride with a friend.*

Garrett must sense the incoming argument when he sees those three dots jumping around—mostly because Carter knows my only friends are his friends and Simon, and he'd have a shitfit and burst a carotid if Simon were driving me home—because another text comes in before I can finish mine.

Bear: *Give me attitude and I'll give it right back, ur choice.*
Me: *Don't threaten me with a good time.*

Bear: *I'll be out front at 5, sunshine.*

I don't know much about Garrett, but I do know a switch has been flipped, one I don't want him to turn off.

"Gosh, you know, I really hope this baby doesn't take after Carter in the size department," Mom's busy saying, jotting down notes in her planning journal as I sip my drink and rejoin the conversation. "Poor Ollie will be split right in half."

My cappuccino slides down the wrong tube, scorching my windpipe. I slap a hand over my mouth to catch the sputtering liquid.

"I think that's exactly what Carter's hoping will happen," Hank supplies. "Nothing would make him prouder than making a monster-sized baby to match his monster-sized—" Hank cuts himself off, skin around his eyes wrinkling as he tries not to laugh. "Sorry, sorry. That boy's really rubbed off on me after all these years. My Ireland would be washin' my mouth out with soap for that kind of language."

I snicker, breaking off a piece of my apple pie muffin.

"Wow, Jennie, are you having lunch with your grandparents?"

My skin prickles at the voice I've come to know well over the last four years. Krissy stares down at me with the same self-absorbed grin she always wears, along with her two blonde lackeys, the Ashley's. Yeah, they're both named Ashley. Well, technically, one is Ash*lee*, two *E*'s.

"That's *so* cute," she continues. "My grandparents used to be my best friends, too, when I was a kid, but I'm older now."

I sling one leg over the other. "And now that they've gotten to know you, they realize they don't like you all that much?"

Krissy gives me a smile nearly as tight as the ridiculous buns on either side of her head. "You're so funny, Jennie. We should hang out sometime."

I hate the way my face lights with intrigue. If I can feel it, she can see it, and I don't understand my reaction. No part of me desires being part of this clique. Every compliment is backhanded, every conversation a whisper while they're tucked in the corner of the dance studio, a secret I'm not in on. And yet all these years I've struggled with envy for the relationship they share.

Because they have each other, and I have no one.

I don't need the negativity people like them would undoubtedly bring, but I wouldn't mind having *some* people in my life that haven't come via my brother, ones that'll take me for me.

Mom's gaze follows as Krissy and A² sashay away. She blinks at me in silence, several times over, before her expression morphs into outrage. "Did she just call me a grandma?"

"You're about to be a grandma," I point out.

"To a *baby*, Jennie, not a twenty-four-year-old woman!" She swivels in her seat, and I hide my face in my cappuccino. She's about to demonstrate that she can be as embarrassing as Carter, though she claims he didn't get it from her. "*Hey!* Yeah, you there, with the Princess Leia buns! I'm young, okay? I still get my period!" She stands, sweeping both hands down her body. "You *wish* you could look this good when you're my age!" She plops back down, slicing an aggressive hand through the air. "Pfft. *Grandma*."

"They thought Holly and I were married?" Hank's grin is so wide as he dusts off his shoulder. "I always knew I was hot stuff."

And, you see, I'd rather have a thousand Moms and Hanks than one Krissy and two Ashleys.

～

"Missed you last week, Jennie. Glad you're back."

My fingers trail down Simon's arm to his hand, where he takes mine as I spin away before he pulls me back in.

"C'mon." He grips my waist, lifting me into the air. The landing feels all wrong, but I push through it. I'm desperate for this to end so I can go home and make Garrett flick my bean. I'm also hoping for snacks. "You really not gonna talk to me?"

I'm *really* not gonna talk to him.

"No, no, no, no. Stop. Stop the music." Mikhail, our dance coach, buries his face behind the wad of papers in his hand as silence fills the studio. Eyes closed, he holds one hand up, waiting, and I stand with my hands on my hips, trying to catch my breath. With a heavy sigh, he flings his arms wide, tossing the papers in the process. "What is happening? What is going on? I call you two my diamond dazzlers for a reason. You were born to dance together, and when you do it right, you—" clap, "both—" clap, "dazzle—" clap. "I don't know what that was, but it was *not* dazzling."

Mikhail expects perfection; it's what he always gave. Born in Russia some fifty-odd years ago, the man's been dancing since he could walk, and on stage at a professional level for forty-two of those years. He's magical and terrifying all at once, like a mythical creature, and when he walks through the hall, every voice falls silent. Most people stay in his good graces by simply keeping their mouths shut and doing what they're told. I'm one of the few that gets to work my charm on him every now and then, but whether it works is a crapshoot I never know the answer to until I've given it my best shot.

"Jennie, your ankle looks great, but you're stiff out there. You're like a…" He lifts his arms, waving them awkwardly. "Like a damn puppet. It's horrifying, utterly horrifying. It's like you're not comfortable with Simon."

Correct.

He drums his fingers against his pursed lips, then shrugs. "Should we increase hours this week? Maybe the two of you can book the studio and do some after-hours bonding."

"I think that's a great idea, Mik," Simon eagerly supplies.

"Uh, no." *Oops, meant to think that one, not say it.* "I'm just not feeling my best today." Hand on my stomach, I pull a sick face. "Went to this sketchy sushi place last night and—"

Mikhail holds his hand up. "Was it Sushi Paradise? On Mainland? I swear, that place is *the worst*." He claps twice. "Say no more. Let's call it an early night. Jennie, go home, hydrate, and get an early sleep. Take it easy, you hear? Let someone else do all the work tonight."

"Can I get that in writing?" I joke, then wave off my own laughter at his expression. Today's not the day. Garrett would've laughed though. I can probably still convince him to do all the work anyway. He likes a full to-do list. I scoop up my things before Simon can say anything that might get him kneed in the nuts, and wave over my shoulder. "Night!"

We're done a half hour early, so I text Garrett, letting him know I'll grab the bus. I get a photo of the front of the building from behind a wet windshield, and the words *already here*, so I make a beeline there, ignoring my name as Simon hollers it.

The snow is heavy and wet, the kind that melts and turns to slush as soon as it hits the ground. My feet slip through it as I make my way to Garrett's car, and I roll my eyes as Simon bursts out the doors behind me.

"*Jennie*! C'mon! You can't ignore me!"

"You know, when people tell me I can't do something, it only makes me wanna do it harder." I turn, jabbing him in the chest with my finger. "I'm gonna ignore the fuck outta you, you twat-waffle."

"Oh come on! Your ankle's all better. No permanent damage."

"Yes, thank goodness I didn't permanently damage my ankle when I was running away from you. Not only did I manage to avoid any lasting damage that might've jeopardized everything I've worked so hard for my entire life, I also managed to avoid a venereal disease!"

Simon rolls his eyes. "Don't be so dramatic. I'm clean, and you didn't need to run."

"Really? *No* didn't seem to be working. Or is that word just not in your vocabulary?" I turn my back on him, continuing my trek through the snow. The ground is slick and wet, my UGGs have zero traction, and I can barely see.

"Look, Jennie, I'm sorry. I thought you were into it. You're always flirting with me. Maybe stop sending me mixed signals."

Every muscle in my body tenses, locking me in spot.

"Pardon me?" I ask lowly, taking one step toward him, then another. Another, as he backs up, and on my fourth supposed-to-be-threatening step in his direction, my boot goes sliding through gray slush, legs splitting. I start falling backward after a shitty attempt at regaining my balance by grabbing onto air, which, by the way, doesn't work. I'm less pissed about the slush I'm about to wear and more pissed I've lost the fear dancing in Simon's eyes.

A thick arm wraps around my waist, quickly righting me on my feet, and Garrett's blue-green eyes peer down at me. The confusion and anger marring his forehead is an expression I haven't seen before, one that stops my breath. With a hand on my lower back, he guides me forcefully to his car, all but stuffing me into the passenger seat.

"The fuck's he talking about?" Garrett demands, gaze raking over me. "He hurt you?"

"I'm fine," I grumble.

"Did. He. Hurt. You?" His gravelly, harsh tone has my mouth gaping and butterflies erupting. Bossy looks so, *so* good on this man.

I gesture haphazardly toward my previously injured ankle. Garrett's gaze hardens before he stalks off.

Garrett's not a fighter. He's a carefree, laid-back guy, that east coast twang making his words languid and happy. It takes a lot to rattle his cage. Judging by the way he looms over Simon, forcing him backward, I'd wager this is one of those times.

I watch as Simon nods repeatedly at whatever Garrett's saying, hands coming up between them like a shield before he finally scrambles back inside the building.

When the normally shy, awkward man slides into the driver's seat without a word, I'm equally turned on and annoyed.

"What did you do, Garrett?"

"Nothing."

"Bullshit. Why did you get involved? I can handle Simon."

Garrett glances over his shoulder before pulling into traffic. "Carter would kill me if he found out you hurt your ankle after that douchebag tried to kiss you, and I didn't do anything about it."

"Right. Carter." Because it always goes back to him, every fucking time.

Silence and anger drench the air between us like a heavy fog. My skin crawls.

"I don't need a boyfriend," I snap, shoving a finger into his shoulder. "And I certainly don't need a chaperone who thinks I can't take care of myself and only looks out for me because of some ridiculously misplaced sense of duty to my brother."

Garrett nabs my finger, wrapping his hand tightly around mine in an effort to control my violence. For the most part, I strive to be controlled by no man. But I kinda like the way he controls me, you know, physically, and while naked. Slightly messed up.

"I didn't ask to be your boyfriend. I asked to—respectfully, I might add—wreck your body in a way that both of us enjoy *immensely*, based on the way I can't keep my tongue out of there and you keep trying to detach my hair from my scalp. But that doesn't mean I'm gonna sit by and let someone disrespect you or your boundaries just because we aren't dating. I'm still gonna have your back."

Okay, not exactly the response I was expecting. Still, I yank my hand back and cross my arms over my chest, grumbling quietly, "I don't need protecting."

"I'll keep that in mind for the future. But if, in the future, I happen to accidentally punch Simon Syphilis in his smart-ass mouth, don't think of it as protection. Think of it as karma."

The corner of my mouth twitches. "*I* call him Simon Syphilis."

Garrett graces me with a lopsided smile. "For the record, I didn't do that just because of your brother. I'm sorry it came out that way. This thing between you and me has nothing to do with him. And I know you can take care of yourself, Jennie, trust me. I've been on the receiving end of your wrath many times. But from what I gather—since you won't come out right and tell me—you told him no. And nobody fucking touches you. Except me," he adds with a wink. "With your permission, of course, because I don't have a death wish."

I giggle quietly as my anger dials down to a simmer.

Garrett clears his throat, gesturing at the Starbucks cup in the middle console. "I, uh, got you a drink. Figured 'cause it was cold and snowy, plus you're probably tired."

"Oh. Thanks." I bring the warm drink to my nose, inhaling the scent. It smells delicious, like Christmas, robust and heavenly, with hints of cinnamon and nutmeg.

"I didn't, uh..." He shoves his fingers beneath his toque and scratches his head. "I didn't know what you like, but you always smell like cinnamon and coffee, so...yeah."

I smile against the lid. "It's perfect, Garrett. Thank you."

The car rolls to a stop at a red light, and Garrett's eyes flit between me and the road, fingers drumming the steering wheel. On the fourth look, I face him, prepared to tell him to spit whatever the fuck it is out already.

But he leans over the console, pressing a quick kiss to my lips.

"Uh, hi," he says, as if we haven't been together for the last several minutes.

"Hi," I laugh. "You don't have to kiss me when we say hello or good-bye. We aren't dating."

"I guess, but I like kissing you, so it's not a big deal as long as you're cool with it. Unless you're not cool with it. If you're uncomfortable, then I will...stop." He stares straight ahead, eyes wide like he has no clue what he's doing.

I don't know, either, to be honest. I haven't been in a relationship since my senior year in high school, and it wasn't particularly healthy. So friends with benefits? Not only do I have no idea where the lines are drawn, I have no clue how normal people in consenting relationships act *ever*. I guess I can think of this thing between us as my test run.

"I don't mind," I finally say as Garrett pulls into his parking spot. "I just don't want you to feel like you have to do boyfriend crap because we're getting naked together."

"I don't mind doing boyfriend crap, like picking you up and getting you coffee. If it makes you feel better, we can call it committed friends crap." Garrett takes my bag and my hand, helping me out of the car. "Besides, if you were my girlfriend, I'd tell you to carry your own shit."

"As if. You're a sap."

"Nope." He directs the elevator to the penthouse as his eyes glide over me, heating on the way. "Then you'd yell at me for making you carry it, and I'd tell you to get over it and stop acting like a princess." He steps into me, lips sweeping my jaw, pausing at my ear as he slips a hand below my top. "Just to push your buttons a little further, get you all riled up." He grabs my hand and tows me out of the elevator, down the hall, and inside his condo. "Couch or bedroom?"

"Couch," I answer breathlessly as he pulls his shirt over his head.

He yanks my leggings down and I fumble out of them, gripping his forearms while he walks me backward, wearing that self-righteous smirk I love/hate.

Garrett spins me around and shoves me over the arm of the couch, his chest against my bare back when he tugs my shirt off. "And when you were good and angry, I'd bend you over the couch, just like this." Pushing my panties aside, he swipes two fingers along my slit. I'm embarrassingly drenched from a few simple words, and God, I fucking want him. "And I'd fuck you right...here."

I shoot forward with a gasp, clawing at the leather as his fingers pierce my entrance, and Garrett spends the next hour showing me exactly what I'm missing with my no-sex rule, and how lucky his future girlfriend is going to be when she's on the receiving end of his body, his attention.

Garrett steps out of the bathroom, shaking his shaggy hair out in a towel while I pull my panties on. "You hungry?"

"I should go, no?" I'm starving, but I'll order in when I get home. I don't want to overstay my welcome now that the naked fun is done.

"Nah. Why? There's a game on, and we're playing the home team this week." He tosses a hoodie and a pair of sweatpants at me. "Let's order pizza and watch." He strolls from the bedroom, where we wound up somewhere between the third Big O and the shower, right out to the living room, not sticking around to let me overthink the simple invite.

So I'll overthink something else, like his clothes in my hands. I should put on my own. But he offered, didn't he? So it's not weird, right?

His sweats swallow me whole, engulfing me in warmth. They smell like him, this homey, comforting scent, like fresh laundry and cedarwood. It's nice, and I make my way down the hall, pulling the strings at my waist tight.

Garrett's still shirtless, sweatpants hanging low on his hips, showing off those dips right above his perfect hockey butt as he roots through his pantry. "Pizza will be here in forty," he mumbles around a mouthful of food as he turns toward me. "But I couldn't wait." He holds up a blue box and swallows. "Want one?"

"What the hell are those?"

His expression is a perfect mix of confusion and disgust. "Pop-Tarts?"

"No, I know they're Pop-Tarts, but..." I take the box from him. "Cinnamon Sugar Pretzel? I've never seen these ones before." I yank another package from his other hand. "And Dunkaroos? I haven't had these since I was a kid! I didn't think they even made these in Canada anymore."

"They don't. Bev gets them for me."

"Bev?"

"Yeah, Beverly; Adam's mom. She lives in Denver. She's my snack dealer."

"You get your friend's mom to send you snacks from the States?"

"Fuck yeah, I do! They got the best shit." He gestures at his pantry. "Check out my stash."

I root through the bags and boxes of foreign cereals, special edition cookies, candy I've never heard of, stopping when I get to a yellow bag. "Flamin' Hot Funyuns..." I wrinkle my nose. "These sound horrendous."

Garrett tosses his head back, moaning. "They're fucking amazing." When I gag, he grins. "Don't knock 'em 'til you try 'em.

I nab a package each of Pop-Tarts and Dunkaroos, and Garrett follows me to the couch. "New rule: no Funyuns before we make out."

"Fine, but they're free game after I've rocked your world, sunshine."

He stretches out on the couch, pulling me down between his legs as he turns on the hockey game. I peel back the wrapper on my Dunkaroos, and Garrett shoves his fingers inside, stealing a cookie and dunking it in my frosting.

"Oh hey. Can you tickle my back?" I ask.

"Tickle your back?"

"Please." I shove the snacks into his hands, place a pillow on his chest, and flop onto my belly. Shifting his hoodie up my back, I guide his free hand there. "It feels nice and helps me relax before bed. My mom used to do it when I was younger."

Garrett places a Pop-Tart between his teeth, pushes a frosting-covered mini-cookie between my lips, and winds his legs around mine before trailing the tips of his fingers up and down my spine, around my shoulder blades. "Yeah?"

"Yeah." I sigh, nestling my cheek into the pillow as I wrap my arms around him.

"Look at us," he boasts. "Killing the whole friends-with-benefits thing. Knew we would."

I hold my fist up, and he bumps his against mine.

"Nailed it!"

FOURTEEN
HI, MOM. I RUINED THE CARPET.

Garrett

I'M A GODDAMN GENIUS.

Friends with benefits with the hottest girl I know, no strings attached? *Come on.* I'm reaping all the benefits of an exciting, new relationship without all the boring crap that comes with a long-term one when the novelty wears off and things start to get mundane.

Besides, the mundane stuff is kinda fun with Jennie. Like watching TV, eating pizza, and tickling her back. I didn't even mind when she fell asleep in my lap. And when she woke up an hour later, sucked my cock like a queen, then told me it was time for her to go, I didn't mind then either. I walked her to her door, gave her a kiss, and got to sprawl out in my own bed all alone.

You know what you can't do when you're in a relationship? Sleep diagonally.

Sure, the no-sex rule was a little disconcerting at first, but exploring all the adventurous ways we can get each other there is fun as fuck.

And best of all? I don't feel so lonely anymore when my buds immediately pull their phones out to text their wives postgame. Even Adam has a text from Olivia, who's currently pup-sitting Bear for him while we're away. He proudly flashes us the attached photo of Bear and Dublin sprawled out together in front of the fireplace.

Hiding my smile, I open my own waiting message.

Sunshine: *Tough loss, big guy. No congratulatory BJ for you.*
Me: *Consolation BJ? Lieutenant Johnson is sad and only u can cheer him up *sad emoji**
Sunshine: *Not sure it's in the cards for you.*
Me: *I checked, and it is. Gonna fuck ur mouth when I get home later this week, then I'm gonna eat dessert.*

Those three little dots pop up before disappearing, reappearing, then disappearing again. I love watching this side of Jennie bloom. She's bold as hell but a little hesitant in the bedroom. The more time we spend together, the more confidence comes roaring out. She's up for anything, eager and willing to learn. Also? Watching her walls slowly drop is really cool.

She's still working on the sexting though. There's something about seeing the words that leaves her a bit speechless.

My phone vibrates as I'm tucking it away, and I die a little at Jennie's picture: just a red popsicle, her pink lips circling it.

I don't have time to appreciate it. Carter curses loudly, and I jump, slamming my phone to my chest. *This is it. It's my time to go.*

Carter frowns at his phone. "Ollie's been feeling the baby move so much, but I can't feel anything. He's been moving all night, apparently."

My heart restarts and I force myself to focus on my skate laces, formulating an answer, and breathing. "What is she now? Five months? I couldn't feel my sisters consistently 'til my mom hit the third trimester. Soon you'll be able to see the baby move, too, which is cool but also creepy."

"And you keep saying *him*," Adam points out. "Baby Beckett might be a girl."

Carter grunts, rolling his hockey socks into a ball. "Nope. I saw a penis."

Emmett sighs. "I've told you a thousand times: that was an arm. Your baby does not have a gigantic penis."

"His daddy does," is Carter's smug response.

I hesitantly peel my vibrating phone from my chest, sighing when I see it's just an email from Levi's. Apparently, I have three pairs of ladies' jeans arriving in five-to-seven business days.

I type out a quick text to the perpetrator.

Me: *Funny, when I gave u my credit card info, I thought u were only gonna replace the jeans I ruined.*
Sunshine: *Funny, I thought you'd respect my outfit choices rather than ripping them off my body.*
Me: *I'm gonna disrespect the fuck outta your body just for that.*
Sunshine: *J–1, G–0*

God. Damn. Genius.

I wonder how long this will last. Jennie's smart, strong, sassy, and sexy—all the very best *S*'s. It's only a matter of time before somebody else realizes, and I'll be forced to let her go. I'm also not sure how far we can push our luck with the oblivious man in front of me, propping his phone up on one of the cubby shelves.

"Garrett, come do this dance with me."

I yank off my skates. "I'm not doing another one of your fuckin' TokToks, Carter."

"*Tik*Toks. C'mon. I got so many likes on the last one you were in. All the girls think you're cute when you dance. *Riley*!" He catches Jaxon on his way to the showers. "I'll teach you the dance real quick."

Jaxon flings an arm out, free hand covering his junk. "I'm naked!"

"Great for ratings," Carter mumbles. He props his fists on his hips and starts barking out orders. With the entire team lined up, he turns his stare on me, brows lifting. "Garrett."

"No. Fuck that. I'm not doing your damn dance."

Famous last words. An hour later, I'm sitting at our hotel bar, watching our team do some ridiculous trend that has an entire team of NHL players dropping it low before they spin around and shake their asses for the camera. Most of us are half-dressed in equipment. Jaxon is less fortunate, covering his dick with a hand towel. The video already has over a hundred thousand views. Carter's only ever looked prouder when Olivia said *I do*.

There's a fuckton of girls here tonight, swarming the team. Jaxon's already made out with one, Adam keeps trying to swat away the fingers trying to twine around his curls, and when a leggy brunette slides her hand along my shoulders, I start panicking, shrugging away from her touch.

"Uh, no thanks. No, thank you. Thanks."

Emmett arches a brow as she walks away. "No, thank you? A month ago you were bitching about us stopping you from getting laid. No one's stopping you now."

I bury my deflection behind a handful of nachos.

Emmett waits for me to swallow. "What?"

"Uh…" I scratch my jaw as my gaze coasts the table, landing on Adam as he politely lets another girl down, explaining they don't want the same things. "Netflix and chill," I blurt, then backtrack. "I think I'm growing out of this scene. I'd rather hang out at home with someone who makes me laugh." *Not a lie.* "Netflix and chill," I repeat. "Or whatever."

Adam grins. "So you want to date."

"Garrett wants a girrrlfriend," Carter sings, sucking a chicken wing clean. "I'm sure you'll find someone."

"It can't be all that hard. You did it."

His bone clatters to his plate, hardened gaze slowly rising. "I'm a catch, jerk."

I snicker. "Yeah, Ollie's lucky she didn't *catch* a disease."

"Fucker." Carter reaches across the table, and a game of slapsies quickly ensues as our hands fly, before Dad gets in the middle of it.

Dad is Adam. Emmett is the bad uncle who sits in the corner, egging us on. Jaxon's the drunk aunt making out with a random.

"We should let natural selection take care of you," Emmett says when we disengage. "Only the toughest survives."

Carter flexes a bicep before kissing it. "That's me."

"As if." I stretch my arms out, veins popping when I make two fists. "I'm tough as fuck."

"Whatever. My sister could bring you to your knees."

She absolutely can, already has, and I'll gladly get down on them a thousand more times to taste the sweet spot between her thighs while she yanks my hair and chants my name, begging for more.

I try to recenter my thoughts and focus on the new conversation at hand, which is the additional time Adam's been spending at the children's home.

"I found my family in a home just like this one, but I know not everyone is that lucky. To think some of those kids have been sitting there for years, waiting for someone to take a chance on them…" He shakes his head, frowning. "It's heartbreaking."

"I think it's great you're using your own experience with the foster system to help other kids," I tell him.

"You're adopted?" Jaxon asks now that his mouth is free.

Adam nods, and Carter adds, "His dad is Deacon Lockwood."

Jaxon's brows jump. "Deacon Lockwood, retired quarterback for the Denver Broncos and five-time Superbowl champ, Deacon Lockwood?"

Adam chuckles. "He was so bummed when I chose hockey over football. Really, though, I couldn't have asked for a better family. Sometimes you're not born to them; you find them."

Jaxon claps a hand to his shoulder, and I fight the urge to roll my eyes. I haven't warmed to him yet. "Glad you found your crew, bud."

"I've been thinking about fostering, but it's impossible with my schedule. They've been through enough, and they need consistency, someone who can show up every day for them." He shrugs. "Maybe in the future, if I ever get married."

Emmett laughs softly. "You're gonna meet someone incredible and have an amazing family together, in whatever way you decide to make it."

"What happened with Courtney was shit," I chime in, "and I wish you hadn't gotten hurt. But you deserve so much better than what she was giving you. I'm not sure you would've walked away if she hadn't given you a reason."

Adam's relationship with his ex was on shaky grounds for a while, and he reached a point where he was desperate to make her happy. In doing so, he neglected his own happiness. If he hadn't found her with another man, I'm not sure he would've done what was best for himself.

Adam focuses on the drink in his hand before he looks up, smiling. "Yeah. Fuck yeah. Fuck her."

"Ay-yo!" Emmett punches a fist through the air. "That's the spirit, Woody! Round of shots for the table!"

I wish I could enjoy mine with the team.

Instead, it stays in my hand, halfway to my mouth as my jaw dangles, stare fixed on the picture peeking up at me from my phone.

One small, purple, and glittery, the other gigantic, black, and veiny as fuck, two dildos stare up at me. A simple question accompanies the photo.

Sunshine: *Hey big guy, if I were considering sleeping with you in the future and wanted to give myself time to adjust to your size, which one would I fuck?*

Jennie's doing great with the sexting. Fast learner. Superfast.

I, on the other hand, am not doing so well. My brain might be melting, and my dick has turned to steel.

A second picture comes in, Jennie's fingers wrapped around the small, purple dildo.

Sunshine: *Mr. Itty Bitty it is.*

"Why're you making that face? Who're you texting?" I slam my phone against my chest at Carter's questions, thankful X-ray vision isn't real—*that I know of.* When I leap to my feet, my chair topples to the ground. "It's my mom." *Shit, that was so high-pitched.* "I-I-I—" *Fuck.* "I gotta go!" I lift my phone way up, and shake it, for whatever fucking reason. "She needs me. Mom needs me. I gotta...*bye!*"

I dash across the bar and into the lobby, fingers flying over the screen.

Me: *Mr. Itty Bitty? I think the fuck not.*
Sunshine: *Gonna head to bed to take care of myself. Talk to you tomorrow.*
Me: *Don't u fucking dare.*

I jab the elevator call button nine hundred thousand times and fall inside when it opens.

Me: *Jennie???*
Me: *I swear to god if u go to bed right now I will fly home early and wake you up with my cock down your damn throat.*
Sunshine: **kiss emoji* Night Gare-Bear*

"No. No, no, no, no." Agitation barrels through my veins as the elevator climbs. My foot won't stop bouncing. Pretty sure my eye is twitching.

I claw at the doors when the elevator stops, and it takes me seven tries to successfully swipe my card through my door slot. My shirt gets stuck over my face as I go tumbling into my room, and Jennie answers my video request on the third attempt, because she's a little shit who likes to get me going.

"Mr. Andersen," she purrs. "To what do I owe the pleasure of a late-night phone call?"

I trip over my feet stepping out of my pants, stumbling forward and bouncing off the side of the bed.

Jennie's cackle electrifies the air. "What are you doing?"

"Gettin' naked." Jennie gets an eyeful of my dick as he springs free from my boxer briefs, bobbing around.

"Oh my. Lieutenant Johnson sure looks happy to see me."

"He sure as shit is, and you're gonna need to ditch Mr. Itty Bitty. My fingers can fuck you better than he can." I grip the base of my cock and flick my head. "Now lose the clothes, sunshine."

Dragging the blanket away, she reveals those stellar curves inch by aching inch. "What clothes?"

My eyes roll to the ceiling as I groan. "God, I wanna fuck you."

I'm baffled when her smile turns shy. Does she not know how mind-blowingly sexy she is? I'd sell my left nut for a VIP all-you-can-ride ticket to her Disneyland. All-you-can-eat works just fucking fine for now, though.

I roll onto the bed, prop the phone up on the side table, and wait for Jennie to do the same.

She tucks her hair behind her ears, a purely innocent move that makes my cock throb. It's down and long and messy, and I wanna drag my fingers through it before I wrap it around my fist and make her look me in the eyes while she comes.

"So, uh, how does this...work?"

"I'm gonna fuck my hand while I watch you fuck your pussy, and I'm gonna try not to make a mess when I come. You, sunshine, can be as messy as your heart desires."

A shiver rocks through her body, and she shakes her head. "Two weeks ago you couldn't even string an entire sentence together."

"Yeah, 'cause you're hot as balls and you intimidated the fuck out of me."

"And not anymore?"

"Nah, not so much. Not now that I know I can boss you around just as well, but in a different way." I watch her body flush, glowing skin kissed pink by nerves, lashes fluttering as her gaze bounces away, then back again. "It turns you on. You like the way I talk to you."

"Well, duh."

"What do you like about it?"

She lifts a shoulder. "I donno."

Bullshit she doesn't know. She's playing shy, afraid to say it out loud, so I'm gonna help her. She doesn't get to hide with me, not anymore.

"I like that I can make you shy. Take the boldest, bravest girl I know and make you speechless, even for a second. And then you get this big smile on your face and come to life, like my words spur you on. You're the best mix of shy and confident when you're naked, and I love watching you get there."

Teeth press into that plush lower lip. She trails her finger over her thigh. "I like...I like when you tell me what you want to do to me. It makes me feel..." Her cheeks blaze as she looks away.

"Makes you feel what?"

"Wanted," she admits on a murmur. "I haven't felt that way in a long time."

The truth is, I'm not sure I've ever wanted anyone the way I want her, so I tell her just that, ignoring the way she rolls her eyes like I'm feeding her a line.

"Besides your banging body, pretty eyes, and perfect smile, Jennie, you're a smart-ass who can hold her own. You dish it out without missing a beat, and you push yourself. You're also funny as hell, and you yell at the refs when they make shitty calls. I always wanted to know you better than I did. I'm glad I get to now."

Jennie's cute nose wrinkles, and low and behold, a fucking *giggle* slips past her lips. "Yeah, whatever, fuckboy."

"Call me whatever you want, I'm the one you think about when you're home alone, fucking your rubber cocks."

"And my pussy is the one you're thinking about when you lock yourself in your hotel bathroom, fuck your hand, and come in your sock." Feet flat on the bed, she spreads her legs, showing me that immaculate, pink pussy. She swipes one finger along her slick slit. "Too bad you can't have it. It's a fuckload softer and warmer than your hand."

My gaze follows the slow fingers that circle her clit, mesmerized as my words tumble out. "I fucking own it…"

"I'm the only one that owns this pussy." Agonizingly slow, she sinks two fingers inside, back arching off the pillows, lips parting with a low gasp. "I just let you use it sometimes."

"Fuck. Christ. Shit." I run my palm over my mouth before taking my cock in my hand, stroking. "Show me how wet you are."

"Ask nicely."

"Please, Jennie. I wanna see how wet you are."

Jennie pulls her fingers out, glistening and dripping. "Soaked."

I groan, squeezing my cock. "Taste yourself, Jennie."

Desire sparkles in her eyes, but so does uncertainty.

"Don't go shy on me now, sunshine. We both know that's not you. You're my favorite flavor, so go on and taste."

She paints a finger over her lower lip, making it shine, and I stop breathing when she drags her tongue across it. With her eyes locked on mine, she takes her fingers into her mouth, a throaty moan filling the air as she cleans herself off.

"Use your fingers," I order gruffly.

"You're not the boss of me."

"The fuck I'm not. Ride your fingers, gorgeous, and pretend it's my cock."

A devilish smirk before she drags her fingers through her soaking slit, making herself quiver and flush. Jennie moans quietly as she pushes two fingers inside, heated stare fixed on my hand as I work my cock. I'm not going to last, and it's her fault. Watching her love on her own body, appreciate all her curves and edges, is the biggest turn-on.

"One more," I demand. "Can you do one more?"

Jennie doesn't hesitate, plunging another finger, arching into her palm as she straddles that line. She squeezes a nipple, palming her perfect, round tit, her breath coming in spurts, and then her hand falls down her body, finding her clit.

"Fuck, Jennie. You're so sexy."

"Garrett," she whimpers, eyes dazed. "I'm gonna come."

So the fuck am I. My balls tighten, spine tingling, and the second Jennie cries out, slamming her thighs together, head falling back, I'm a goner.

"Fuck." I roll off the bed, leap to my feet, and accidentally empty my entire load onto the carpet. "Oh shit."

Jennie's giggle quickly spirals out of control. "Did you just jizz on the floor?"

"It was an accident! I wasn't prepared!" I grab a pillow.

"Not the pillow! Gross! Someone's gonna put their face on that!"

"I'm overwhelmed!" I yell, running to the bathroom. I grab a wad of toilet paper, which, as it turns out, is a terrible idea. It starts disintegrating, leaving white clumps all over the carpet as I wipe at my mess. "This is gonna cost me."

"Best money you've ever spent," Jennie retorts smugly.

Groaning, I collapse on the bed in time to catch Jennie rolling herself in her blankets. "So…"

"So…good night?"

"Good night? That's it?" I chuckle. "Do you wanna, like…talk?"

She picks at her blanket. "Do you?"

"Well, Adam's not back yet."

"So you wanna talk?"

"If you wanna talk, we can talk."

"It sounds like you wanna talk, Garrett."

I clear my throat, rubbing my nape. "Guess we could talk."

Jennie grins. "Let me wash up and grab a snack."

I follow suit, and when Jennie rejoins me, it's with a bowl of cereal, wearing the hoodie I dressed her in when I last saw her.

"What's that?" she asks.

I hold up the jar I just dunked my cookie in. "Cookie butter." I shove the whole thing in my mouth. "Fwom da States. You gotta twy it. I sabe you some."

Jennie giggles. "Okay, tell me about your night prior to ruining the carpet."

"We were hanging at the bar with the team. Adam was getting hit on."

"Just Adam?"

"And Jaxon."

She waits.

"Okay, me too." I swipe another cookie through my dip. "So I told the guys I wanted to date, not fuck."

"Adam's the only one pure enough to buy that."

I agree, so I tell Jennie about his dream to one day foster, and she smiles softly through the whole thing before telling me about her day.

"Ollie and I took the pups for a walk, and then she made me make her a tray of brownies before the game. Cara and I yelled at the refs through most of it, and Ollie passed out in my lap during the third period."

I smile, watching as she lazily wipes away the milk that dribbles down her chin and licks the corner of her mouth. She meets my gaze, smiling back, and I search for something else to say. I guess I'm not ready to say good night. Talking about nothing with her...it's nice.

"I, uh...told Carter you were my mom."

Her nose wrinkles. "What?"

"When you sent me that picture," I clarify. "I couldn't even talk, and he didn't see it or anything, but he asked me who I was texting and I..."

Her eyes glitter with her grin. It's big and cocky, exclusively Beckett. "Said I was your mom."

"My brain shut off. It almost always does when you're involved."

My head snaps as the door beeps, opens partway, and then promptly slams against the swing lock.

"What the fuck?" Adam jiggles the handle, shoving against the lock. "Did you lock me out, you fucker?"

"It was an accident!" I scramble off the bed, pulling my pants up with one hand. I trip for the second time tonight, nearly faceplanting in the mess I made. "Hang on a sec!"

Jennie shakes with laughter, hand clamped over her mouth, and I shoot her a look.

"Night, sunshine," I whisper.

She winks. "Night, Gare-Bear."

I shove my phone into my pocket, smooth my hand down my chest for no reason at all, then open the door. Adam stands there, brows high on his forehead, and I'm already coming up with excuses in my head.

Then he steps forward, tumbles into me, and I realize he's drunk as fuck.

He peels his clothes off on the way. "Can I have some cookies?" He nabs the package and jar off my bedside table, not waiting for a response.

He stops abruptly, gaze falling to the ruined carpet. The tips of my ears burn.

I scratch my neck as Adam stares at me. "Uh, that's...I was...well, see, I was—"

"I don't even wanna know." He wobbles by, shaking my cookie butter in my face. "This is mine now, 'cause I'm not gonna tell anyone about that. Deal?"

Fucking deal.

FIFTEEN
IT'S A NO FROM ME

Jennie

"I THINK IT'S A FANTASTIC IDEA."

"I don't." In my head, my response sounds more like, *You're delusional like always, turd muncher.*

Mikhail pulls a frowny face. "And why not? Simon just said he's on board."

Simon's always on board; that's part of the issue.

And being on board about the two of us posing as a couple in love to *really sell the performance*? I'd rather submerge myself in a shark tank during shark week—mine, not the Discovery Channel's.

"I'm not comfortable with it," I tell my dance coach honestly. "I don't like lying."

"It's called acting, Jennifer."

He slings one arm around my shoulders, the other around Simon's, and starts walking us forward. I have no idea where we're going, and if I had to guess, neither does Mikhail. He's all about dramatic conversations, which usually means a lot of aimless wandering, staring at nothing but pretending you're seeing his vision, and clapping out syllables.

"It's too late for the Christmas show. Jennie, you need some work on your acting. I need to *feel* how much you love Simon. We can get there in time for the Valentine's recital, though, and that's the one that matters most."

He stops and twirls, painting his hand through the air in an arc. "Just imagine: the two of you dazzling the stage on Valentine's Day, the day meant for love. You put on the most magnificent performance this school has ever seen, and you finish it with a kiss." He clasps his hands under his chin. "But not just any kiss. The kind where you, Simon, sweep you, Jennie, off your feet, tip you back, and go for it, full movie effect. And the crowd goes wild." Another spin. "You turn the biggest cynics into believers. Everyone falls in love with my Diamond Dazzlers, and everyone wants to fall in love out there in the real world. And the best part? Ticket sales skyrocket for our year-end recital in April because everyone wants to see the happy couple shine on stage together."

Simon grins. "Honestly, Mik, I love it. Your best idea yet."

It's the worst idea I've ever heard in my entire life. This guy has a teaching degree? Someone take it away. "I don't think—"

"Jennie and I have great chemistry too. We'll nail it." Simon slings his arm around me, grinning, all teeth. I'm not a dentist, but I'd love to yank one or two of those things out. They might be useful in identifying his body one day, should it ever come to that.

Mikhail trots away, rambling on about magic and love and chemistry. He waltzes right through the door, chuckling, and I realize he's as delusional as Simon.

I slap Simon's hand from my shoulder. "I didn't agree to anything, and I'm sure as hell not kissing you."

"It's a ways away," Simon says, following behind me. "You have some time to think about it."

"I've thought about it. It's a no from me."

Simon sighs, plopping down on the bench as I pull a pair of sweatpants over my shorts. "Jennie, you can't stay mad at me. Please. I can't take it. You're my friend."

"Didn't really seem like it when you were trying to shove your tongue down my throat."

"I made a mistake. I've always wanted to explore things with you, and I had to shoot my shot while I had it. We were alone, dancing, and I donno…" He lifts a shoulder, giving me those eyes. "Felt kinda romantic. But I got it: no feelings on your end. Loud and clear. Won't happen again." Simon folds his hands beneath his chin, pouting. "Please forgive me. I don't want to lose your friendship, and I can't bear the thought of replacing you as my dance partner."

I roll my eyes and head for the door. "Obviously. I'm magnificent out there."

Simon jogs after me. "So...a second chance? Please?"

With a sigh, I stop, pinning my arms to my chest as I watch him. He's not the most genuine guy, but the sad truth is he's been the only friend I've had here, the only person other than my teachers who's consistently sat and drank coffee with me, talked about more than whether I think my brother's going to take his team to the Stanley Cup again this year.

God, I hope I don't regret this. "I don't give third chances, Simon."

"*Yes!*" He punches a fist through the air before wrapping me in a hug. "I won't let you down, I promise!" He steers me down the hall. "Wanna grab a coffee?"

"Mine will have to be to-go. Carter's picking me up on his way home from the airport."

"I can't believe he's cool with you dating one of his teammates."

I fumble a step. "What?"

"Garrett Andersen?"

"I'm not—" My head wags rapidly. "No, I'm not dating Garrett."

"Really? 'Cause he told me he was gonna put my balls in a blender if I hurt you again."

I fold my lips into my mouth, swallowing my snort. Okay, so I might've given Garrett a hard time about approaching Simon—strong, independent woman and all that—but I gotta hand it to him, that's a good one. BJ worthy, even. Not that I need an excuse to suck his cock. But it's fun to pretend like he needs to earn it.

"We live in the same building," I explain. "He was picking me up on his way home. We're just friends, and he's only protective 'cause of Carter."

Simon's expression is suspect, but instead of trying to convince him, I change the subject, and he takes off with another hug when he sees the long line at the coffee kiosk.

I shoot off a text to Garrett while I wait for my cappuccino.

Me: *Balls in a blender? Really?*
Bear: *U'd be surprised, but a Vitamix can turn anything into soup.*
Me: *You're ridiculous.*
Bear: *Just prepared to make some fucknut soup if I need to.*

Bear: *I'm almost home. Wanna bang?*
Bear: ***hang*

I huff a laugh, grinning at my phone. *Men.*

Me: *Going to Carter's for dinner, sorry.*
Bear: **sad emoji* but I wanna kiss u*

Okay, well that's kind of sweet.

Bear: *Oops, autocorrect. **Kiss ur pussy*

There it is.

"Jennie?" the barista calls, holding my drink up. His gray eyes move over me, and my cheeks heat when I take the cup from him, our fingers brushing. He's tall and lean with a messy head of ebony waves, tattoos decorating his arms.

"Hey." He his head toward the bakery display. "It's a cold one out there. How about a warm ginger molasses cookie for the road?" He winks. "On me."

I bat my lashes. "You trying to buy me with cookies?"

His elbows hit the countertop as he leans closer. "You don't seem like the kind of girl who can be bought." He tucks the cookie in a paper bag and holds it out to me. When I reach for it, he pulls it closer. "Tell you what, though. How about in exchange for the cookie, you let me buy you dinner?"

Butterflies take flight in my stomach. I've never been on a real date. The idea is as thrilling as it is scary. I like how things are going with Garrett, but what if I could have it all? What if I could have the pleasure, the fun, the friendship, and the love, all wrapped up in one person?

"So you want to buy me cookies *and* dinner?" I tug the treat from his hand. "I might be able to squeeze you in."

His eyes hood, grin deepening, pulling in a dimple in his chin. "I love squeezing in. Tomorrow?"

My stomach somersaults. I tuck a loose wave behind my ear. "That works."

"Great. Should I pick you up at your brother's?"

My heart stops, sinking. "What?"

"You're Carter Beckett's sister, right? Do you live with him? I'd love to meet him. I can pick you up at his place and you can introduce us. We don't even have to do dinner. My friends are having a party tomorrow night." He nabs the end of my braid, winding it around his finger. "They're big fans of your work."

My throat runs dry as my pulse races. "My dancing?"

The barista—his name tag says Nate—smirks. "Sure. Let's call it that."

Fiery hot blood rushes to my face, drumming in my ears. I crush the cookie in my hand as my fists clench, bile rising in my throat. The chatter in the cafeteria grows muddled and muted, like I'm underwater. Without another thought, I toss the cookie at Nate's chest, my drink in the garbage, and hoof it out of there.

It would be just my luck that Krissy and A² have caught it all.

"Yikes." Krissy grimaces. "That was tough to watch. Must be hard being the second-string Beckett sibling." She rubs my shoulder like she cares about me. "You okay?"

"Fine," I lie.

"Rejection must be hard."

Pressing my fingers to my forehead, I close my eyes to the impending headache. I'm not in the mood to entertain Krissy's shit. I'm hovering on the goddamn edge, not sure if I want to cry, scream, or be sick. Truthfully, the only appealing idea is letting Garrett make me forget all about this, remind me why this—no strings, no feelings, just pleasure —is better.

"We missed you last weekend," Krissy continues. "Shopping, dinner, drinks, dancing...It was weird having all the dance girls there except you."

"You didn't invite me."

"Didn't I? Shit, I must've forgotten."

I turn toward the door, ignoring the pang of hurt that sweeps through me. It may not make sense, but that doesn't make it any easier to ignore that it's always been there.

The older I get, the more prominent my status as a loner becomes. But the thing is, I don't want to be alone. Maybe that's why it's getting increasingly difficult to balance the *I hate them and wouldn't be caught dead wasting my life with people like that* with the *I wish they'd invited me.*

"Maybe next time," Krissy says.

My smile is weak, and I hate it. I hate this part of me, my inability to make authentic and meaningful friendships, the urge to fit in, even when I don't really want to. I want to be unapologetically me, and what I wouldn't give for people to love those parts. More than that, I want to believe they do.

I'm tired of the doubt, of tucking pieces of myself away in hopes that someone might take me in. No matter how much I starve it, the fear grows like weeds. I'm a tangled web of uncertainties and insecurities, and I don't recognize myself.

Yet when Carter pulls up out front, the tension in my shoulders immediately melts away.

Krissy might as well be purring as she follows behind me, like she's planning to climb in with me. "Is that your brother?"

"No," I answer bluntly, loading myself into the front seat, narrowly missing Carter's face when I aggressively toss my bag into the backseat. "It's my grandma." I slam the door and sink into my seat. "Yes, Krissy, you fucking doorknob. It's my brother."

Carter grins. "Ah, my sweet, charming sister. How I've missed you."

"*Carter!* Why are my cookies above the fridge?"

I prop my elbows on the countertop, watching my tiny, pregnant sister-in-law as she turns into Spider-Woman and tries to crawl up the stainless-steel fridge.

"Son of a...goddamn...bitch," she grunts, slapping at the top of the fridge, which is as high as she can reach.

Carter waltzes into the kitchen. "You asked me to put them somewhere you couldn't reach. You said you were eating too many."

"I'm pregnant," Olivia growls. "And *you* made me this way! *And another thing!*" She stabs an angry finger into his chest. "I'm allowed to eat too many cookies!"

Carter leans into me, hand over his mouth. "She's been especially aggressive and emotional lately."

I roll my eyes. "I'll grab—"

He bars his arm across my chest, stopping me. "I like to let her go for a couple minutes. It tires her out, kinda like an overstimulated kitten."

God, I hope I'm here the day Olivia finally decides to let him have it.

This right here is where I need to be, watching my mom yell at Carter for hiding his wife's cookies, then him and Olivia fighting over said cookies, and Hank sneaking a whole handful of them. Any residual anger from the day fades away, replaced with a soft, warm feeling in my chest that only comes with family.

The warmth still lingers a half hour later, when Carter, Hank, and Olivia, all smiling happily with their stacks of Oreos next to their plates of lasagna, are seated around the dinner table.

Hank twists a cookie apart. "How's school, Jennie?"

"Good. Great." I sigh when everyone pauses eating. "I'm ready for it to be over," I admit.

Carter points his fork at me. "Steve's dragging you down. You should ditch him."

Reason one why I'm not going to tell him Mikhail wants Simon and me to pretend to be a couple. I do, however, finally open my mouth and tell my family the secret I've been hanging on to.

"There's a job opening at The National Ballet in Toronto after graduation. And, uh…" I fold my napkin, unfold it, then fold it again. "Leah recommended me for the job."

"Jennie," Olivia murmurs. "That's incredible."

Hank finds my hand and clasps it, pressing a loud smooch to it. "Way to go, kiddo."

Carter springs from his seat, engulfing me in a hug that's teetering on the edge of suffocating. He only pulls away when somebody starts wailing, choking on their sobs.

It's my mom.

"Aw, Mom." I go to her, hugging her from behind. "What's the matter?"

"I'm fine," she cries. "Totally fine!" Another sob. "It's just that I'm equal parts so happy for you and so sad for myself." She buries her face in my neck. "I don't want to lose my best friend, but I want you to have everything you want and deserve, and I don't know how to express that all, so it's coming out as tears!"

A heavy ache rips through me as she clings to me. "You'll never lose me, Mom. I don't think I'm going to go."

"You have to go," Carter interjects, arms in the air. "It's your dream!"

Is it though? How can I go after something without being 100 percent certain it's the future I want?

Another choking sob pierces the air, and tears start streaming down Olivia's cheeks.

"Nooo." I scrub my face. "Not you too!"

"I'm just really happy for you but I also really want you to stay because you're going to be the best auntie ever and you're one of my best friends, and your mom is sad and that's making me sad, and my mom's on the other side of the country and I miss her so much so I don't want to miss you, too, but you should pursue your dreams, and also I'm just—" she gasps for air, flapping at her face, "—*feeling really, really emotional right now!*"

Carter meets my gaze as Mom and Olivia collapse into each other, weeping.

Help me, he mouths.

"Uh, right. I love you both," I tell Mom and Olivia, kissing their heads as Carter leaps to his feet. "I promise you'll never lose me. Carter's driving me home now."

"You're gonna leave me here with these two?" Hank calls after us in disbelief.

"You were made for this," Carter yells over his shoulder as he ushers me down the hallway. "Good thinking," he mutters as he hands me my coat. "I think Mom might be entering *the phase*."

"*Carter!*" I whack him in the shoulder.

"What?" he asks, sweeping me into the garage. "Oh, are you on your period?"

I shake my head in disbelief. "How in the fuck has Olivia not killed you yet?"

His grin is oddly proud as he runs his palm over his torso. "She tries on a weekly basis."

I roll my eyes as I turn toward the cars. Olivia's beat-up old Corolla sits on the end, unused in months. I've seen her out here petting it, like she can't bear to part ways with it. "Which car are we taking?"

"Any one you want." Carter taps on the hood of his BMW. "You could take the Beemer." He scoops up a set of keys and swings them around his pointer finger. "Or you could have the Benz."

I pinch the bridge of my nose. I'm too tired for games, my heavy emotions are creeping back up, and there's a sexy hockey player at home who's eager to put his face between my thighs. "What are you talking about?"

He pets the hood of his graphite Mercedes Benz. "I think you want this pretty lady."

I fold my arms over my chest. "Carter."

"We don't need all these cars, Jennie."

"Then why did you buy them?"

"Because I'm ostentatious," he murmurs, leading me to the driver's seat.

"Carter! This is ridiculous!" I grip the door frame when he tries to shove me inside. "You can't give me a car! You already gave me an apartment!"

"You don't have your own car."

"I'm gonna get one!" In the summer maybe, when I hopefully have a job.

"C'mon, Jennie. For the winter, at least."

"I don't like driving in the winter! The roads are slick and-and-and accidents happen!" My chest hurts, and I don't even know why.

Carter's eyes soften. "It has four-wheel drive and snow tires. Let me make life a little easier for you. You're a safe driver."

"Oh great. Now you've jinxed me."

Carter wraps an arm around my waist, lifts me off my feet, and stuffs me into the seat. He clicks the seat belt in place and drops the keys in my hand, folding my fingers around it. "Just give it a week, okay? If you hate driving that much, I'll take it back."

My hands reluctantly glide over the leather steering wheel. This car is pretty, no doubt about it. "I'd look pretty dope rolling up to the grocery store in this, eh?"

"*So* dope."

I sigh. "Okay. I'll try it."

Carter shows me all the features, and he doesn't open the garage until I promise to text him to let him know I made it home safely.

"Oh wait." I roll down the window. "I forgot to mention this a couple weeks ago, but your wife wants you to fuck her like you mean it."

Carter stares. "What?"

"You cannot poke your baby in the eye, Carter."

He glances at his crotch. "Are you sure? I'm pretty well-endow—"

"Stop." I hold up a hand. "Please stop. My God, what is this life I'm leading?" I sigh. "Okay. Thanks for the car. I'll take care of her, hopefully. You take care of your wife. Bye. I'm going now. Good-bye."

~

Okay, this car is *pretty* cool. It has a banging stereo system, and I can text using my voice, and somehow the car sends it. That's how I wind up yelling at Garrett over "Dear John."

"Can you meet me in the parking garage? It's important!"

"Bear said, 'Did you slash my tires? I get to spank you if you did.' Do you want to reply?"

"Yes," I tell Veronica, which is the name I've given my new car. *"Note to self: find something to slash tires with."*

That's basically how Garrett finds me sprawled across the hood of Veronica when the elevator doors open, revealing him in all his messy hair, sweatpants, and dry-fit T-shirt glory.

"What the fuck is this?" he asks with a chuckle. His eyes coast over me, then the parking garage, before he slips his hand beneath my coat and wraps his palm around the curve of my waist. "Hi." His soft lips sweep across mine. "Your brother did not willingly allow you to take his Benz."

I pull my dimples all the way in. "He did."

"Damn, he loves you way more than I thought. This wasn't a good idea. We need to break up. No more special friends."

"Please. You couldn't kick me out of your bed if you tried." I pop off the hood with a wink and reach for the waistband of his sweats. "I suck your cock too damn good."

His bright eyes sparkle as he pins me to the car with his body. The only thing gentle about it is the way his lips ghost over the edge of my jaw until they find my ear. "Keep talking, sunshine. I'll shove you in this backseat and make you suck me dry."

"Perfect." I slip my hand down his pants, palming his thick length. "I'll be done in two minutes."

Thirty seconds later, we're pinballing around the elevator, hands and mouths everywhere.

"Ow." Garrett pins my wrists on either side of my head. "You ripped out my hair."

"You bit me."

"You like it," he growls, mouth opening on my neck.

My fingers sink into his hair. "So do you."

"This is so incredibly entertaining," a voice murmurs, and my blood freezes. "You're so wrapped up in each other you haven't even realized the elevator is stopped and I'm standing right here."

SIXTEEN

LADIES & GENTLEMEN, THIS IS ORGASM #5

Jennie

WIDE AND FULL OF FEAR, Garrett's eyes stare into mine. I fist his shirt, too terrified to move. Maybe if we stand still, we'll blend into the walls.

Finally, I peek over his shoulder.

Emily stands in the doorway of the elevator, arms crossed, looking mighty pleased with herself.

"*Fuck*," I gasp, the word garbled. I swat Emily's arm. "You scared the shit out of us!"

"You're really playing with fire, aren't you?" She trails the tip of one nail across her lower lip, arches a brow, and shrugs. "I don't know much about your brother, Jennie, but he seems like the kinda guy who wouldn't be overly thrilled with his friend's dick saying hi to his little sister's belly button while riding the elevator." She gestures at Garrett, and I slap a hand over my eyes, groaning when I see what she sees.

Garrett grins sheepishly, cute cheeks like lava. He claps his hands over his super-erect monster cock. "Sue me for being a little excited."

"Oh, buddy." Emily laughs. "There's nothing little about how excited you are right now."

I may or may not snort a laugh—*to be determined*.

"Oh, don't let me stop you." She steps aside, gesturing for us to move by her. "Get in there and get your fuck on. Don't forget to wrap it before you tap it."

"God, I think I might like her. How the hell did that happen?" I fiddle with my keys, swatting at Garrett's face, which he's buried in my neck while I'm trying to unlock my door. *"Garrett."*

"Hurry up."

"I'm trying, but there's something hard poking me in the ass."

"Just letting you know how much we missed you. We've forgotten what you look, feel, and taste like, so we need to spend the next several hours getting reacquainted."

We go tumbling inside my apartment when I finally get the door opened, and I snicker as Garrett starts stripping, hopping on one foot as he peels his pants off. He falls forward, sandwiching me between him and the wall, keeping me there while he discards the rest of his clothes. Then he hoists me off my feet, tosses me over his shoulder, and carts me down the hall.

"How was your day?" Garrett drops me to the bed and yanks my leggings down. "How was school?"

"Good," I say on autoreply, then shake my head. I reach toward the ceiling as he works my shirt off. "It was okay."

His movements slow as he peers at me. "Doesn't sound like it."

I shrug, then swallow when he pulls his boxers off. Are dicks meant to be attractive? Because, God, Garrett's got the Chris Evans/Captain America of dicks, in that he might be the absolute perfect specimen who vibrates at peak efficiency.

Garrett pushes me to the pillows and drags my panties down. "Wanna talk about it?"

"Uh, right now?"

"Sure."

My ears grow hot. "It's not a big deal."

"Sounds like it is, so we're gonna talk about it."

His broad body settles between my thighs, corded muscles in his back rolling like waves as he moves lithely. I reach for him, raking my finger through his hair, wanting one more taste. His smile is that perfect amount of lopsided, a gorgeous mix of sweet and arrogant, the kind that has the power to make even the smartest of girls reckless.

He lifts me to him, cupping my cheek and tilting my chin.

"Hi," he whispers, then covers my mouth with his, sweet tongue slipping inside. "I'm sorry you didn't have a good day, but mine got a hundred times better when I saw you sprawled out on the hood of that car. So tell me all about your day and why it sucked. But first..." Soft, plush lips coast over my breasts, down my torso, one hand gliding up my leg, thumb skimming my inner thigh, making me quiver. "Spread your legs. By the time we're both done, you won't remember why it was so bad."

"Garrett," I whimper, and he grins.

"Yeah. If I do my job right, that's the only word you'll be saying by the end of it."

"I—*oooh*." My head lands in the pillows as he licks one languid stroke up the center of my heat.

"Your day, sunshine. Tell me about your day."

"I-I—" My fingers plunge into his silky hair, tugging. "Fuck. It was… Mik…my coach…he wants…*oh, Garrett*."

Eyes locked on mine, he inserts a single finger painstakingly slowly. "Focus, Jennie."

"He wants us to pretend to date," I finally—*barely*—manage.

Garrett's brows tug down. "You and Steve?"

"Simon." I gasp as he pumps faster.

"Mmm, nope." He sucks my clit into his mouth, rolling the swollen nub gently between his teeth. "Don't like that. I licked it. It's mine."

A giggle bubbles in my chest. "It's just for show."

"Don't care. Not interested in sharing, even for show." He rolls off me, and a mortified gasp leaves my lips as he stands. He smiles down at me. "Don't worry. I'll be right back."

"Where are you…" My words die as he slowly tugs the bedside drawer open, gaze holding mine, and my heart thumps as he dips a hand inside.

"Are you uncomfortable?"

Am I? I've been destined to live a life in the limelight because of my brother. You can find out everything about me with a simple Google search, except for a few rare things Carter's PR team works hard to keep off the internet. This part of me right here, how I take my sexual experience and needs into my own hands because I haven't been able to trust someone else with them for so long, it's the most intimate part of me. It was fun and exciting to tease him when he was hundreds of miles away, but now he's here. I'm anxious, yes, but does sharing this with Garrett make me uncomfortable?

I bring my knees to my chest. "I've never shared this with anyone else. It's always been just me."

"I'd be honored if you shared it with me, but I understand if you don't want to." Garrett takes my hand in his, tracing each finger. "I won't ever push you to do something you're not comfortable with. I promise, Jennie."

I think I've known that since this whole thing started, but it's nice to hear anyway. Maybe that's why I nod. "Okay."

Garrett smiles, and I'm super confused when he shuts the drawer and proceeds to crawl onto the bed with empty hands.

"What are you doing, Andersen?"

He wraps his arms around me, nuzzling into my neck, trailing kisses along my shoulder. "Cuddlin'. I can still rock your world later, though, if you're up for it."

"That's great. Kinda thought you were gonna rock it now, and, you know...with something made of rubber."

"What?"

"I said okay."

He sits up abruptly, nearly punching me in the face as he scrambles. "But I thought you meant...I thought you were just, like...acknowledging my promise." He balks at my expression, then gets low on the mattress, like an animal about to pounce. "You really want me to?"

"I really want you to."

He makes a sound in his throat. It starts high-pitched and enthusiastic but finishes a deep, vibrating growl—still equally as enthusiastic—as he grips my wrists, straddles my hips, and hovers above me. "Say it. Tell me you want me to fuck you."

Lifting my hips, I grind against him, watching with pleasure as his face contorts, forced to resist the urge to plow inside me. Am I pushing my luck? Absolutely. Is it fun? *Phenomenally.*

"With a fake cock."

"I don't give a fuck, Jennie. Just fuckin' say it."

Winding my legs around him, I pull his body tight to mine. I've never felt as warm as I do when I'm with Garrett. I know this relationship is physical, but the way he treats me tells me I'm his friend first, and he'd take that over the rest if he had to. He knows when to be rough, commanding, possessive, while also knowing when to give me his patient, gentle, and goofy side. But above all, he's always genuine with me, and it's refreshing to no longer have to guess what's going through his mind when he looks at me.

With my wrists still in his grasp, I lift my chin. Garrett drops his mouth to mine, and I turn at the last moment, lips grazing his ears as I roll my hips.

"I want you to fuck me."

A carnal sound rumbles in his chest as he crushes his mouth to mine, releasing my wrists to dig his fingers into my waist as we move together. Everything is hot and wet, and a need so deep, so feral, burns through my blood.

Garrett pushes a hand between us, forcing me backward before he rolls off the bed. His hand disappears in the drawer, but he gets distracted, suddenly changing direction. He produces a tiny, pink glass plug with a gem on the end, and his forehead creases as he studies it. His mouth pops open, the light in his eyes dancing as his gaze pinballs between me, the pink plug in his palm, and down to his XL cock.

"Don't even fucking think about it, Andersen." I'll try almost anything once, but I'm not remotely close to being ready to try *that*.

"Yeah," he agrees, head bobbing, as if it'd actually been up for discussion. "Yeah, too big."

He tucks the plug away and pulls out a purple silicone wand. The slim body gains girth toward the head and curves in the most delicious way to ensure it never misses your G-spot.

Garrett places my feet flat on the mattress, spreading my legs wide as he crawls between me. "Your day," he murmurs. "What were you saying?"

"You can't seriously expect me to finish telling you about my day when you—*oooh*." My toes curl and my head falls backward, fingers gripping the sheets as Garrett places the vibrating head against my clit, making my legs quiver and my spine shake.

"Your coach wants you and Simon Syphilis to pretend to date."

"And you said no." The words are a garbled cry as he teases me, slipping the toy through my slit, prodding without actually penetrating, circling my clit until I'm on the verge of tears. "*Garrett*."

"It physically pains me that he gets to put his hands on you. No need to give him more than he deserves."

My breath leaves me on a choked exhale as he pushes in just a touch, and when he pulls it out while smirking, I might combust.

"I swear to God, Garrett, if you don't f-f-f-*fuuuck*. Oh my...*oooh*." My back arches as the wand slides inside, stretching me just right, finding that spot that makes me shiver.

"Look at you, sunshine. Taking all of this cock like a good girl." He presses warm, wet kisses to the inside of my thigh as he pulls the toy out and sinks it back in, slow, twisting as he goes. "What else? Tell me more."

One broad thumb finds my clit, rubbing gently with agonizingly slow circles. All I can think about as I pant under his control is how badly I wish it were him inside me.

"*Jennie*. Tell me, or I stop."

"Krissy was being rude for no reason other than that she likes to exert her superiority over me just so she can hurt my feelings," I blurt, tossing my head back with a moan as that magical wand hits my favorite spot, harder this time.

"Who's Krissy?"

I tear at the sheet as Garrett plunges faster. "Another dancer. All the girls got together last weekend and she said…she forgot to… *invite-me-oh-my-fucking-God*, yes, please." His thumb matches the tempo of the dildo thrusting inside me, making me whimper. "I don't know why they don't like me."

"Fuck 'em. You don't need them. You've got me. *I* like you."

Garrett's mouth trails up my thighs, trading between gentle nips and the wicked lash of his tongue, all while never giving up on the pumping, the delirious way he fucks me that makes me want to scream for more. Part of me wants to give it all up, and I'm talking about more than my body.

I can't, though, so I'll tuck it away like I always do. I'm so used to giving up only pieces of myself, I don't even know how to be whole with someone anymore.

"Anything else?" Garrett asks, tongue swirling around my belly button. He takes the purple gem between his teeth, giving it a little tug, and the simple action tows me closer to that cliff. I'm about to throw myself off it, watching as he lowers his face. "Go on, sunshine." He flicks his tongue over that tight bud of nerves, teasing me. "Answer the question."

"I-I-I—" I shake my head, clapping my hands over my face. What's happened to me? What has he done to me in only a matter of weeks? I'm losing my mind, and instead of caring, I fist his hair, holding him in place as he laps and laves, and I spill my guts about the job offer, the potential new life that waits in Toronto after graduation.

Garrett's tongue stops its lashing, and he slowly removes the toy. He lays his cheek on the inside of my thigh, pouting up at me.

"Why are you looking at me like that? And more importantly—" I gesture at my crotch, "—why are you not finishing dessert? I'm not above sitting on your face and making you."

Garrett chuckles. "You can sit on my face any day, sunshine." Slowly, he sinks the wand, smiling at my throaty groan. "I'm looking at you like this because you just put a time limit on the best fun I've ever had."

I rock into his hand, silently asking for more, but he doesn't relent. "The best fun? You aren't even getting laid."

"Don't really give a fuck."

"I don't know if I want to go," I admit.

His brows tug down. "Why not?"

"I'm not sure it's, *oooh*, the future I want for my-my-myself." I throw my head back as a mangled sound leaves my throat, part irritation, part pleasure. "Garrett, *please*."

"We'll talk about this later." His gaze holds mine, playful, teasing, as he licks a leisurely path up my slit. "Now I'm gonna finish fucking you." He promptly impales me with the dildo, his grin self-righteous and pleased when I cry out his name.

Garrett's mouth suctions over my clit as he thrusts in and out, faster, harder, hitting that spot every time until I'm nothing but a whimpering, quaking mess, begging to come. He grips my throat, gliding up my body, the touch of his gaze possessive and feral. A pleasure so fierce unfurls in my belly as he brings me higher than I've ever been before.

"I fucking love watching you come, and I fucking love being the one to get you there." His mouth takes mine in a searing, plunging kiss that leaves me breathless. He rests his forehead against mine, watching me unravel. "Come for me, sunshine," he demands, and I do, nails shredding his shoulders as I cling to him, and he swallows his name as it leaves my mouth, over and over.

The pads of his fingers press deeper into my throat as he forces me to meet his gaze.

"You see how you could still talk through that? That won't happen when it's my cock inside you."

~

"You gonna tell me why you don't wanna take your dream job in Toronto?" Garrett's hand closes around mine, bringing my spoon to his mouth, and I frown as he swallows my Corn Pops. He's already had two bowls.

"Why does everyone keep saying it's my dream job?"

"Isn't it?"

"Yes. No. I don't know." At the look on his face, I laugh. When he reaches for my spoon again, I shove it in my mouth. "I wanted to dance, and I wanted to teach it. It's just…" I lift a shoulder. "My mind changes all the time. I spent my childhood dreaming of being a ballerina, dancing in The Nutcracker in New York. But then I grew up, and all my ballet dreams flew out the window."

"So you don't want to teach anymore?"

"I don't know. I loved ballet, and it served its purpose in my life. It fueled my love of dance. But it's not me. How do I teach something I'm not passionate about anymore? My passion lies elsewhere."

"Contemporary?" Garrett asks, draining the milk from my bowl once I scoop out the last of my cereal.

I lean my elbows on the counter, drop my chin to one hand and twirl my hair with the other. "Can I tell you something I've never told anyone before?"

"'Course."

"I…I want to open my own studio. For kids. I want to teach kids to express themselves, to have fun. I want them to love dance as much as I did, as I still do. I don't want to be that strict dance teacher, the one that makes you second-guess every piece of food you put in your mouth, that tells you your life doesn't exist outside of dance. There has to be a healthy balance between loving something passionately and letting it be a part of your life, but not the whole thing. And honestly? I already miss my dad; I don't want to put myself in a position where I'm forced to miss the rest of my family."

Garrett stares at me for a long moment that makes my skin crawl with apprehension, luring me back into that cave I should've never crept out of. It's when he grins, taking my face in his hands and pressing a loud, sloppy kiss to my mouth, that my shoulders sag.

And I creep a little further from the shadows I've been so content to hide in.

"I think it's great you're able to be honest with yourself. That you acknowledge what you want and what no longer serves you, or when you aren't exactly sure what your next step is. I also think it's awesome you can look back on your dance career and recognize what didn't work and what you don't want to repeat one day when you're the teacher. I'm really proud to be your friend, Jennie."

My nose wrinkles as I drop my gaze to my feet, swinging from my stool. "Thanks, Garrett."

He takes my hand, pulling me down. "Let's go watch TV in bed. I'll tickle your back."

"Are you sure? You've got morning skate in seven hours."

He twirls me into him, his mouth drowning my words. "Don't care." He smacks my ass. "Get in there."

Tonight has been exactly what I needed to forget about my shit day. I have Garrett, and he makes me smile. I feel light again, and the disastrous bed makes me happy. One of us—Garrett says it was me—tore the sheet off the bed during orgasm number…four? Five? Five.

Okay, it was me. Sue me.

I find my dildo in the rumpled blankets and tote it to the bathroom for a good cleaning. She kicked ass tonight.

"Thanks for tonight, girl. You felt amazing." I hug her to my chest and tuck her away. I turn to the now-made bed where Garrett's lying, hands behind his head, ankles crossed, brow arched high on his forehead. "What?"

"Should I point out the obvious?"

I climb on top of him, straddling his hips. "What's that?"

Fingers tangling in my hair at the nape of my neck, Garrett brushes a kiss across my lips. "That I would feel even better inside you."

"Mmm. I think *you're* forgetting the obvious." I rock into him, grinding down. His cock twitches and he moans, and I smile because I know. The only thing that made it back on my body earlier was his T-shirt. I'm soaked, again, and now his boxer briefs are too. "I haven't had a cock inside me that wasn't made of rubber for years. It's like I'm brand-new down there." My mouth slides along his collarbone, up his neck, hovering at the shell of his ear. "Tight. Warm. You've never felt anything like me, and it's the only place you want to be. I don't even know what it's like to be with a real man, and you're dying to show me." Reaching down, I collect the moisture between my legs, showing Garrett my glistening fingertips before I slowly suck myself clean. "So if anyone's thinking about how good it would feel to have you inside me...it's you, big guy."

Garrett flips me onto my back, wrists in his tight grasp on either side of my head. "Trust me, sunshine. I haven't forgotten." He nips my jaw. "I can't wait for you to let me in one day."

"You think I'm just gonna let you into my Disneyland?"

"You're not just gonna let me in; you're gonna invite me in." He drags his thumb along my lower lip. "Might even lock the gate and keep me from leaving." Bending his neck, he trails the tip of his nose along my jaw. "I'd treat you so much better than your ex did too."

My blood runs cold at his harmless words, except they aren't harmless to me. Garrett's heated gaze turns to one of confusion and then concern as he watches me shut down. He shakes his head, but it's too late; I'm already shoving him off me.

"Jennie. I didn't know...I don't...Fuck, I'm so shit at talking sometimes." He runs an aggravated hand through his hair. "I'm sorry. Forget I said anything, okay?"

But I don't know if I can. Today has been one reminder after another that there are people who never wanted to be in my life for the right reasons, and the first person to own one of those special titles was the very ex Garrett is referring to. Kevin greedily took whatever I was willing to give and left me with nothing. Why I prefer self-suffiency begins with him and continues with people like Krissy and Nate.

And the reminder is suffocating.

But as I scurry into the bathroom, closing myself in, I tell myself Garrett isn't Kevin. He's not Krissy, or Nate. He has no reason to want me for anything other than me. Garrett is kind and genuine, *and he's not them.*

Leaning against the door, I lay my palm over my pounding heart. As I focus on breathing, it slows to a gentle trot, leaving me with the silence that stretches beyond the door. Have I scared him away? Did he leave before things could get more awkward?

I don't know why my heart starts galloping again when I find him tucked beneath the blankets, scrolling through Netflix.

He pats the spot beside him. When I slide in, he pulls me into his side, winds an arm around me, and trails his fingertips over my back. It's when he brushes a kiss to my hair and tells me he likes lying with me that I open my mouth and blurt out the only bad part of my day that I left out earlier.

"Somebody at school asked me out today."

"Goddammit." He groans. "I thought I had more time."

I giggle softly. "I'm not going."

"What? Why not? Not cute?"

"He was very cute. He just..." I watch my finger trace a random pattern into the bed sheets. "He didn't want me. He wanted Carter."

And something else, maybe. My mind flashes back to those words, the ones he spoke after mentioning Carter. *My friends are big fans of your work.* I close my eyes to the feeling, swallow down the fear, and tell myself the parts I want to keep safe are safe. I just hope it's not a lie.

"His mistake. He's missing out on the chance to know an incredible woman." Garrett forces my gaze to his. "Don't make this your problem, Jennie. It's a reflection of him, not you."

But what if I never get the chance to show someone who I am beyond my last name? What if nobody bothers to look? That's...that's what hurts the most.

Instead, I lay my cheek on Garrett's warm chest and nod.

We choose *Brooklyn 99*, laughing quietly together as he tickles my back, any lingering tension melting away.

"Hey, uh, listen." His fingertip dips around my shoulder blade, then loops down my spine, and I'm pretty sure he's writing his name. He clears his throat. "I can't come to your recital next week."

"Oh." Without thinking, I start rolling toward the edge of the bed, putting distance between us. Garrett pulls me right back.

"Hey, stop it. You're not going anywhere." He drops his lips to the spot below my ear. "I'm flying home on the twenty-third for Christmas, but I checked out the program online, and there's gonna be a livestream."

"You're gonna watch still?"

"Fuck yeah. I don't wanna miss you kick ass up there."

My face warms, nose wrinkling. I grin at him. "I'm gonna be the best."

"I know you are." His fingers land on my ribs, tickling, and I all but shove a knee into his crotch as I roll around like a feral animal trying to escape. He shoves me to my back and climbs aboard. "Your grand finale should be you nailing Simon Syphilis in the balls. Your standing ovation would never end. You'd hear me all the way from Nova Scotia. Woohoo," he whisper-cheers. "Fuck yeah, Jennie!"

I giggle, struggling against him.

He trails the tip of his nose across mine and touches a kiss to my lips. "Gonna kinda suck not seeing you for a few days."

There's that damn gallop again, no rhyme or reason. "I'm irresistible. One can't help but miss me when I'm not around."

Garrett turns me back over so he can go back to trailing his fingertips over my back, and my eyelids flutter closed.

"It's true," he says as the motion of his hand on my back lulls me to sleep. "You are very missable."

When I wake in the morning, it's to a package of Banana Crème Pie Pop-Tarts on my pillow and three text messages from Garrett.

Bear: *U snore like a trucker. Had to get the fuck outta there before I smothered you with a pillow.*
Bear: *Just kidding. U looked cute as fuck. Didn't wanna wake u.*
Bear: **kiss emoji* Have a good day at school, sunshine.*

I can't remember the last time my smile felt this genuine.

SEVENTEEN

ARE GIRLS REALLY THAT GRUMPY ON THEIR PERIODS?

Garrett

JENNIE'S ANNOYING ME.

It's been three days since I've seen her, and she's thwarting all my attempts. She ignored every FaceTime request, didn't come to our home game yesterday with the girls, but sent me multiple lewd messages while she was in her classes. I'm super confused. I hate being confused.

Plus, I leave tomorrow for three nights on the road, then fly home to the east coast for the holidays. I wouldn't mind seeing her first.

I shoot off a quick text and knock on Adam's door.

Me: *U done being a brat?*
Sunshine: *Literally never.*
Me: *Let's bang tonight.*
Me: *Oops, autocorrect got me again. **hang*
Sunshine: *No thanks.*

The door opens, and Bear leaps up on my chest, tongue in my mouth the second I open it.

"Sorry 'bout him." Oddly enough, Adam doesn't sound the least bit apologetic. "You know he likes his kisses."

"I prefer a woman's tongue, Bear, but yours will do." I carry him into the house, setting him down when my face is good and wet. Adam looks tired, so I bet I already know the answer to the question I'm about to ask. "How was your date last night? What was she, number six?"

"Eight." He sighs, tugging at his hair, which leads me to believe it was as underwhelming as the previous seven.

"What was it this time?" I follow him into the kitchen, where he hands me a plate stacked with sandwiches made of toasted rye bread, salami, prosciutto, the works, and this is exactly why the dating stuff isn't working out for him. He's too good for most of this world. Nobody deserves Adam's sandwiches. Except me, obviously.

"Vacation property. She wanted to know if I had any."

I don't know whether to laugh or cry, and Adam looks the same. There are plenty of girls out there that money and fame mean nothing to —we've already got three of them—so why is it so difficult for a guy like Adam to find one?

"I need to meet someone who's never watched hockey," he grumbles. "Knows nothing about the sport and doesn't have a single clue who I am. Maybe then I'll know if they actually like me for me."

This version of Adam, ready to call it a day, is sad. It's not the Adam I know. I want him to find the good he's looking for; I know she's out there.

"I'm sorry, buddy. Give it some more time. I bet she comes around when you're least expecting."

"Hope so." He checks his Apple Watch. "Jaxon should be here any minute, then we can take off."

"Jaxon? What? No. He's coming? C'mon. That guy?"

Adam's doorbell rings, and he chuckles. "He's a good guy."

"He's annoying," I counter, following him down the hall as I stuff the rest of my sandwich into my mouth. I'm not sharing.

"Carter's annoying, and you're friends with him." He levels me with a look that tells me to play nice. "I think you'll like Jaxon if you give him a chance. C'mon. He's uprooted his whole life and moved to a new country. He doesn't have anyone here."

"Fine, but he's sitting in the back."

Adam opens the door, and Jaxon grins at us from the porch.

"I call shotgun!" he yells, then promptly dashes to Adam's truck, and I fucking hate him.

"Did you have to get the biggest one?" Adam grunts as we shove my Christmas tree into the back of his pickup.

"*I* got the biggest," Jaxon argues.

I shove him through the pine needles. "Like fuck you did."

"Biggest tree to match the biggest cock."

"You're the biggest dick, that's for fucking sure."

Adam sighs. "I should've gone with the couples. Then I wouldn't be feeling like a single dad right now, and I would've had my Christmas tree two weeks ago."

"Yeah, and you'd be missing all the fun," I say, then clap Jaxon's hand in a high five.

Okay, so he hasn't been the worst today, but he hasn't been the best either. Tolerable. A couple funny jokes here and there. He's okay. Plus, I know what it's like to come out here on your own and hope someone will take you into their crew.

Still, by the time we're wrapping up at lunch, Jaxon doesn't seem that lonely. He's managed to get both the hostess and the waitress's phone numbers without them knowing about each other. He's taking one for dinner tonight, Adam's heading to Second Chance to volunteer, and I'm arguing with Jennie via text.

"I could probably get both girls out tonight and you can join us, Andersen," Jaxon says when we climb into Adam's truck. "If you need help getting a date."

"I don't need help getting a date, you douchewaffle," I grumble as I shoot off a text.

Me: *Can u at least come be a brat at my place?*
Sunshine: *OMG! It's like you're obsessed with me or something.*
Me: *Accurate. Please? I leave tomorrow n won't be back til after xmas.*
Sunshine: *I can't, ok?? I'm on my period.*
Me: *Ok, and??*

"Did you just call me a douchewaffle? What the fuck even is that?"

I honestly don't know. I've been spending a lot of time with Jennie. Her insults are colorful, to say the least, and she's rubbing off on me. A few days away from her over Christmas will probably do me well.

But it's not Christmas just yet, so I shoot off another text with ten question marks.

Sunshine: *I'M. ON. MY. PERIOD.*

I lean between the front seats. "Hey, why would a girl not wanna hang out when she's on her period? Are they really that grumpy?"

"What's the nature of the relationship?" Jaxon asks.

My nose scrunches. "Huh?"

"Physical or emotional?"

"Uh, physical." *Right? Maybe emotional too? Ugh, I don't know.* I like eating her pussy, tickling her back while we watch TV, and it's cool when she tells me things no one else knows. "I don't know," I admit on a groan, sinking back in my seat.

Adam's suspicious, scary gaze meets mine in the rearview mirror.

"Physical," I quickly clarify. "Just a girl I'm…fucking around with." I frown. That doesn't sound right. Jennie means more to me than that.

"There's your reason," Jaxon replies. "If she's on her period, not a whole lot of fucking around you can do."

"Oh." I drum my fingers on my knees, then lean between them again, hands on their shoulders. "Does that mean she doesn't wanna hang out with me if there's no sex involved?"

Jaxon smiles slowly. "It means she's giving you an out, dude. She's telling you now so you don't come over hoping to get some. Be grateful."

I guess, but the longer I mull over the words, the more they don't sit well with me.

That's probably why hours later, when the tree is up and dinner is on the way, I make my way down to the twenty-first floor.

"Go away!" Jennie yells through the door when I knock.

I knock again, louder.

"I already told you, Emily! I don't have any fucking wine! Sorry I'm sober! Unless you've got a pint of Ben & Jerry's for me, leave me here to *die*!"

Huh. I've never been more grateful to have six provinces between me and my little sisters.

I try the handle, pleased when the door swings open. The second I step inside, though, I'm considering turning right the fuck back around.

Jennie's sobs are fierce, hair piled in a mess on top of her head, where it hangs off the edge of the couch. Tissues litter the ground, and an open tube of cookie dough sits on her coffee table.

She throws a popcorn kernel at the TV. "I hate you, you evil...*snail*! You should've never taken him in if you couldn't take care of him." She flings her arm out, gesturing at the cartoon fox on the TV. "Look at his sweet face! How could you do this to him? He's your family!"

"Jesus fuck. You're riding the hot mess express, eh?"

Jennie shrieks, rolling off the couch and crashing into the coffee table. She sits up, hair spilling out of her bun. She blows a thick wave off her face, illuminating her tear-streaked cheeks and red eyes. "*Garrett*! Get out! Why are you in here? Who let you in? What are you doing?"

"Watching you cry, apparently. Again."

She gestures violently at the TV. "The old lady's leaving him in the forest all by himself! It's dark and raining, and he doesn't understand! She's supposed to love him! You don't leave someone you love!" She swats at the tears streaming down her face, and I pull her to her feet, wrapping her up, rubbing her back as we sway.

"Shhh. It's okay. I know."

"She's so mean," Jennie cries softly, wiping her face on my shoulder. She hiccups and pulls back, scrubbing her eyes with her fists. "Tod doesn't deserve it."

"No, he doesn't, you're right." I kiss her forehead and pat her ass. "Go put pants on. You can't ride the elevator in your underwear, and you're not spending all night in here crying over Disney movies."

Jennie's nose is pink, lips swollen, but when the words finally settle, she still manages to look like she could rip my balls off. "I'm on my period."

"Yeah, you said that. So what?"

"So you don't wanna hang out with me on my period! I'm hungry and growly like a bear, emotional like a toddler who missed nap time, and you're not getting any!"

"I hate to break it to you, sunshine, but you're always hungry, growly, and emotional. But, hey." I take her damp face in my hands. "You're *my* hungry, growly, emotional bear." I kiss her lips. "Come on. I need help with something. And I promise to feed you."

She disappears slowly and backward, eyes skeptical as she watches me, and I survey her mess. Beyond the tissues and cookie dough, a framed picture lays facedown on the coffee table. I turn it over, smiling at the blue-eyed brunette grinning from ear to ear from her dad's shoulders, clutching a pink bunny—*Princess Bubblegum*. A silver locket hangs from her neck, barely visible in the photo, and my heart aches for my friend.

When Jennie reappears, she's draped in my hoodie and sweatpants, and I'm content in knowing I'm never getting them back.

I follow her out the door and into the elevator, and she sighs.

"I really hope you have ice cream, Garrett."

"First thing I put in my cart for you." I lead her into my apartment. "I'll make you a sundae, but first you have to help me—" I point at the tree, the boxes of decorations on the floor, "—with that."

Jennie squeals, clasping her hands. "We're decorating?" She dashes to the tree, fingers fluttering over the pine needles, eyes glittering with wonder. "We haven't decorated since my dad died. It makes my mom too sad. I thought it made me sad, too, but now…now I think it's just one more thing we're missing." She graces me with a grateful, breathtaking smile before hugging me tightly. "Thank you for including me." Her eyes light up. "Do you have hot chocolate? We need hot chocolate if we're gonna decorate. And Christmas music. Can I put the star up top? My dad always put me on his shoulders. It was my favorite part." She squeezes me once more, then rips open a box of decorations.

"Do you want marshmallows in your hot chocolate?" I ask as she tears around my living room. At this rate, she'll be done before I've even heated the milk.

"Yes, please! Just bring the whole bag!"

It's an odd request, but I do as I'm told, all while Jennie hooks her phone up to my speakers and starts pumping old Christmas tunes.

She's maybe the cutest thing ever as she sings to herself, hips swaying back and forth as she works. She asks for the story behind every handmade childhood ornament and takes a hot chocolate break every two minutes. It's essentially her spooning the marshmallows from her mug into her mouth, then dumping another handful on top.

"Garrett," she coos. "Oh my God. Is this your tiny hand?" I wrap my arm around her waist and drop my chin to her shoulder, examining the glass ornament she holds delicately in her hands. There's a small, white handprint on it, and each finger is decorated like a snowman. I spin it, showing her my sloppy handwriting, the backward letter *G*, and the 5 that tells us how old I was.

Her beam is so bright. "Do you have any paint?"

"Paint?" I follow her gaze to the box of six glass globes. "You wanna make handprint snowmen?"

She grins, head bobbing.

What did I say? Cutest thing ever? Feeling like a pretty accurate statement right now.

Forty-five minutes later, our hands are covered in grayish-blue latex paint that won't come all the way off, there's paint on the tip of Jennie's nose and above my left eyebrow, and our miscolored snowmen hand-prints hang side by side on my tree. Jennie's the happiest I've ever seen her.

She's snuggling in on the couch while I put the finishing touches on our ice cream sundaes when my phone starts vibrating across the room.

"Uh, you have a FaceTime request," Jennie tells me, her tone uncharacteristically reserved. "Someone named Gabby."

"Oh perfect." I set the ice cream bowls on the coffee table and flop down next to Jennie. Taking my phone, I wait for my littlest sister's face to appear. "Hey, Gabs."

Out of my periphery, I catch the way Jennie's shoulders drop, and she scoots a little closer.

"*Garrett!*"

"What's up, kiddo?"

Gabby heaves an exaggerated sigh. "I miss you so much. Alexa is annoyin' me. Maybe she'll be nicer when you get home."

"Shut. Up. *Gabby!*" Alexa yells from the abyss. She's three years older than Gabby, and a fuckload sassier. She and Jennie would get along well.

"See what I mean?" Gabby rolls her eyes, and when she notices the bit of Jennie she can see, her face lights. "Who's that?"

"This is my friend, Jennie." I flash the phone her way, and Gabby gives Jennie a big wave. "We're about to eat our ice cream sundaes."

"Friend? Like, girlfriend?"

"No," Jennie and I say at the same time, laughter echoing off the walls.

Gabby's eyes sparkle with mischief, and she grins, showing off the gap between her front teeth. "Sure. That's what they all say." She twists. "*Mom!* Garrett has a girlfriend!"

"Is she coming for Christmas?" Mom shouts back, and Jennie buries her face beneath my arm.

"No, she can't make it," I tell them, smiling down at Jennie. "She's about to die from embarrassment because the idea of us in a relationship sickens her."

"*Ha!*" Mom snorts from afar. "I like her already!"

Gabby giggles. "Well, I guess if you're eatin' ice cream, I should let you eat it before it melts. I can't wait to see you, Garrett."

"Me too, Gabs. Love ya."

"She's your twin," Jennie murmurs when I set my phone down. "She almost looks like she could be your daughter."

I chuckle, handing Jennie her sundae before I dive into mine. "Yeah, me and Gabs look just like our mom. Alexa and Stephie look like our dad."

"You must be so excited to see them. I always wished I had a sister." She steals a chunk of banana from my sundae. "Will you see anyone else when you're home?"

"My old high school crew gets together every time I'm back. There were only sixty of us in our graduating class, so most of us were pretty close. Almost everyone still lives there."

It's hard to tell what lingers behind Jennie's smile. It looks part wistful, and maybe a little sad.

"What about you?" I shove her spoon aside, digging into her bowl after emptying mine. "Are you still close with your high school friends?"

Jennie pauses on sucking her spoon clean. "No." The simple answer is soft but firm, final, and the way she starts putting space between us, no matter how little, tells me not to push it.

"Whadda ya wanna watch?"

"I don't care."

I highly doubt that. We've watched several movies and TV shows together, and I've only ever been allowed to choose when it's a pre-approved movie or show on her list.

I flip mindlessly through Netflix, focusing instead on Jennie from the corner of my eye. She's pulling at the frayed hem of the blanket draped over her lap, tugging at the cuff of her sleeves, twining her hair around her fingers, all while looking anywhere but at me.

I don't like the apprehension she's wearing, the rosy flush of her cheeks because she's trying to withhold her emotions, the way her gaze wobbles just slightly.

I pick up her phone. It's still connected to my speakers, so I exit her Christmas playlist and click on the one titled *J's Favs* while she watches me curiously.

"I can't dance like you, but I can do a mean slow spin around the living room. You shoulda seen all the girls I got at the Spring Fling in eighth grade. Started so many fights between friends." I hold out my hand, and when she hesitantly slips hers into mine, I pull her to her feet. "C'mon, Jennie. Dance with me."

Her grin is a slow explosion, lighting her whole face as all that apprehension fades away. "You'll dance for me?"

"I'll do anything for you." Spinning her into me, I wind an arm around her back. When our fingers lace, she lays her head on my chest. "Although it's secretly killing me that I'm slow dancing to Justin Bieber right now."

We sway together, a comfortable silence that wraps around us, the twinkly lights from the Christmas tree making her glow in my arms, but I think she always glows.

A new song starts, and Jennie makes a soft, happy noise, her body molding into mine. I listen as she hums along to the music, and as the words dance around my living room, the familiarity of the tune sinks in.

"This is your favorite song," I murmur.

"How'd you know?"

"When you drove me home after my concussion, it came on the radio. You turned it up and sang along." I looked it up later that night, learning its name: "Falling Like The Stars." I remember the quiet way she sang the words, the way the air in the car changed, heavier some-how. I knew then I wanted to know her better, so I came up with my genius swim plan. She'd never let me go alone.

"I thought you were sleeping."

"Nah. Just couldn't look at you."

"*Garrett*," she guffaws, delivering a swift smack to my shoulder.

I chuckle, catching her hand and tangling our fingers again. "Not like that. We were alone in my car, and you looked so hot sitting in the driver's seat. I was afraid I was gonna derail us and toss you in the backseat."

She giggles quietly, and I revel in the feel of her in my arms, like she was made to be a part of my life in some way.

"Jennie?"

"Yeah?"

"Can I ask why?"

"Why what?" Her body doesn't even tense, her hand soft and warm in mine, head on my shoulder while she hums along. I'd like to tell myself it's because she trusts me, that she feels safe here with me. But she's relaxed because she has no idea I'm about to go down this road. She thinks she's surrounded by skyscrapers, but they're only walls. Walls that lower day after day, letting me peek into her life, her past, even if she has no idea I'm looking.

So, why what? How do I put it into words without scaring her off? Why has it been years since she's had sex? What happened, and who did it? Is she okay? How can I help her?

"What did he do?" is the question that finally comes. I'm not sure it's the best option, especially when she stiffens in my arms.

"I think I'm gonna head out," she replies quietly, her hands slipping through mine.

"What? No. No, I—" I watch as she makes her way to the door, looking for her slippers, and when she finds them, I grab them. "Don't leave."

"It's not a big deal," she lies. "I'm just tired."

"No." I tug her into me, burying her in my body while she puts up a half-assed fight. "Please, Jennie," I whine. "Don't leave me."

She sighs, giving up the fight, letting me smother her in my hug. "I don't want to talk about him."

And so we don't. We settle together on the couch, under piles of blankets, Jennie between my legs, her small hand fisting my shirt, as the Whos down in Whoville prepare for Christmas.

I shift my hoodie up her back, trailing my fingertips over her smooth skin. "Jennie?"

"Yeah?"

"I'm sorry I upset you."

A tired sigh, and she snuggles deeper, nuzzling into my chest. "Garrett?"

"Yeah?"

"Thanks for making me feel better today. I'm lucky to have you."

But I think it's me who's the lucky one, and when she falls asleep ten minutes into the movie, I don't wake her. I don't wake her 'til after midnight, and even then, I'm considering saying *fuck it.*

Instead, I pick her up, wind her arms around my neck, legs around my waist, and take her back to her apartment, leaving with a kiss on her lips when she stirs, gazing up at me with a dazzling, sleep-drunk smile.

EIGHTEEN
THE F-WORD

Garrett

EAST COAST WINTERS SUCK.

I don't often find myself missing them, unless Vancouver has a particularly mild winter and pond hockey is off the table. I've been here two days and have spent hours whipping around the frozen pond with friends or taking my sisters out for a skate.

But right now I'm on my ass in the snow on the front lawn of my childhood home, getting pummeled by snowballs.

A particularly hard and icy one smacks me dead in the nuts, and I fall to my back, groaning.

"Oops," Alexa says, which is how I know she did it on purpose.

"Garrett! Are you okay?" Gabby scrunches her nose, grits her teeth, and with a battle cry that echoes in the frigid air, charges at Alexa. The two of them collide, tumbling to the ground, shrieking as the snow swirls around them.

Stephie's face appears overtop of me, blocking the sun. "Me and you are the only normal ones," she says plainly, then tries to pull me up. She's ten, all scrawny, gangly limbs, and probably seventy pounds soaking wet. I'm two hundred plus. The effort is there, but it's not working.

I lie there lifeless, and eventually she gives up, dropping on top of me, knocking the wind from my lungs.

She rolls off, lying beside me in the snow, and smiles. "I really miss you when you're not here. I wish you could come home more."

"I think we should convince Mom and Dad to move to Vancouver. Then we'd never have to miss each other."

"Fat chance. Dad says you guys don't have good lobster there."

You can get good anything anywhere if you make as much money as I do, but there really is nothing like east coast lobster. It's why I wound up wearing one of those plastic bibs last night at the Harbour Lobster Pound. Conversation was limited, the moaning at top peak. I ate so much I crashed early and missed Jennie's call.

In fact, with our clashing schedules, we haven't talked much since I last saw her. At least I get to see her during her recital tonight, even if it's only on TV.

When the sun starts to dip, the chill in the air too damp to be fun anymore, we retreat to the warmth, and I text Jennie.

Me: *Can't wait to watch u kick ass. Hope u can hear my cheers from here, sunshine.*

"*Garrett's texting his girlfriend!*" Gabby shrieks as she leaps over the back of the couch and onto my back, trying to tackle me to the ground. "*He called her sunshine!*"

"She's not my girlfriend, you little monster." I wrap my arm around her head and tickle her ribs, laughing as she tries to fight me off. "Jennie's just my friend."

She spins out of my grasp and jumps to her feet. Breathless, she swipes her dark blonde hair from where it's plastered to her cheeks. "Yeah, a friend you watch Christmas movies with and make ice cream sundaes for." She sticks her tongue out, dashing away with a squeal when I lunge for her.

"Jennie," Mom murmurs from where she's working over the stove. She casts me a glance over her shoulder. "Not Jennie Beckett?"

When I don't respond, her mouth gapes.

"Garrett Andersen, please tell me you're not dating your captain's little sister."

"Okay. I'm not dating my captain's little sister."

She pops a fist on her hip, expression unamused.

"What? We're not dating. We're just friends." *Technically not a lie.*

"Does Carter know you're friends?"

"Uh, yeah. We live in the same building. He knows." *Still not a lie.*

"Okay, let me rephrase my question. Does Carter know you're watching movies at night with his little sister and making her ice cream sundaes?"

I cross my arms and look away, grumbling, "Shut up." Gabby meets my gaze from where she's partially hidden behind the wall. I point a finger at her. "You're in trouble."

A maniacal giggle leaves her mouth. "Alexa has a boyfriend too! Jacob Daniels!"

"*Gabby!*" Alexa shrieks.

"I saw them holding hands at recess!" Gabby screams, running down the hallway, bedroom door slamming shut moments before Alexa collides with it.

Stephie meets my gaze. "What'd I tell ya? The only normal ones."

"What about you?" I poke her side. "Any boyfriends?"

Her cheeks blaze and she looks at her hands in her lap.

"I'll take that as a yes."

Her eyes lift, searching mine. "What if I want a girlfriend instead of a boyfriend?"

I tug her into my side, kissing her hair. "Then you want a girlfriend; that's all there is to it."

Stephie sinks against me, and the phone on the wall rings before my mom grabs it. My parents are the only people I know who still have a house phone.

Mom turns away, voice low. "Well, what time can we expect you? Your son is only home for a couple of days…I didn't say that. I know you're being safe. It'd just be nice if you could spend some more—okay, okay. We'll see you when you get home." She hangs up, giving me a tight smile.

"Everything okay?"

"Your dad's going for dinner with the guys from work."

I'm not surprised. He's mostly made himself scarce since I got in yesterday morning. He picked me up from the airport, and it was an awkward drive home, forcing conversation that didn't want to come.

I love my dad, and I know he loves me, but I also know he feels an overwhelming sense of guilt for his absence in my childhood and the pain he caused. He went through a lot of therapy, made the effort to repair our relationship when he returned to our lives, but I think it's been easier for him with me gone all these years. Sometimes I feel like nothing more than a reminder of his struggles.

I'm glad my sisters got a different version of him, but it doesn't stop me from wishing our relationship were different now, especially when he eventually walks in the door and my sisters rush him, hugging him.

"Hey, Gare." He squeezes my shoulder. "Sorry I missed dinner. What are you guys up to?" His eyes are tired and red rimmed, and his gaze doesn't linger long on mine. My brain tells me to search the air for any hint of vanilla spice, the smoky aroma of his old drink of choice. My heart reminds my brain that we trust him.

"We're gonna watch Garrett's girlfriend's dance recital," Gabby tells him as I set up the livestream.

"She's *not* his girlfriend," Alexa mumbles.

I shake her knee. "Thanks, Lex."

I sink into the couch as a group of ballerinas take the stage, and Gabby snuggles into my side, Stephie between my legs on the floor. Alexa looks at me and Gabby and slowly, so damn slowly, starts inching closer.

Grinning, I grab her, jerking her into my side. "Come here, you."

She giggles, relaxing against me, and my dad smiles down at us.

He claps his fist into his hand as my mom finds a space. "Uh, do you mind if I...join you guys?"

"Of course you can," I tell him. The way he grins, going instantly from awkward to ecstatic, reminds me so much of myself during those first few encounters with Jennie.

He brews mugs of hot chocolate for everyone, extra marshmallows, and turns the lights out. "Which one is your girlfriend?"

"She's not my—" I sigh, scrubbing a hand down my face, but when the spotlight illuminates the next dancers, when the music starts and Jennie's body comes to life, I lean forward. "There she is."

I'm not sure I've ever seen anything so stunning. Draped in a deep emerald dress, long hair braided back with a champagne ribbon, she outshines everyone as she floats across the stage. Every leap, every spin, everything she does looks effortless and natural, exactly like she was born to do it.

Jennie and Simon are an extension of each other, always connected in some way. He seems to know where she is even when he can't see her, and a strange feeling surges through me, like I want to take her hand and tug her into me, hide her away for only me.

I push the thought from my head, focusing on my favorite person as she dances several times throughout the ninety-minute recital, all while my family comments on how beautifully she moves. When it comes to an end, Jennie the last on stage, my chest swells with pride, and I stay up late so I can tell her just that when she calls.

When Jennie's bright beam fills my screen, it hits me why *sunshine* is the perfect nickname for her—because she's radiating, and when she wears that wide smile, deep dimples pulled in, stormy blue eyes shining with excitement, she fucking glows.

"What did you think?" She might be vibrating.

"You were incredible, Jennie."

Her eyes spark with excitement. "You really think so?"

"I'm so proud of you. You were breathtaking."

She fiddles with the bow at the end of her braid. "I was thinking about you up there. I...I wasn't sure you were still going to watch. You didn't answer my call last night, so I thought maybe..." She lifts a shoulder and lets it fall. "I donno. Forget it. It's stupid."

"Tell me."

"I don't know. I guess I thought you went home and maybe forgot about me." Her face flames and she waves a hand through the air. "Stupid."

I haven't quite figured it out, but Jennie brings an ache to my chest that wasn't there before her. She's an enigma, this bold, confident woman who refuses to settle yet always seems to be waiting for the other shoe to drop. It's like she's expecting me to walk away at any moment, like this relationship isn't as valuable to me as it is to her.

"Haven't we already covered that you're very missable?"

Jennie flips her braid over her shoulder. "So true. You'd never survive without me."

I chuckle, stretching out on the small bed, folding an arm behind my head. "I'm sorry I missed your call last night. I ate so much lobster I passed out at nine and slept for fourteen hours straight. Did you think I was ignoring your call?"

She pulls her knees to her chest, smile guilty. Her teeth descend on her bottom lip, gnawing until she finally works up the courage to say what she wants to. "Will you do me a favor? When you want to stop this, like if you meet someone and you wanna hook up or date or whatever, will you end this before anything happens with them? I don't want to feel stupid or anything."

Her question catches me off guard, but every time she shows me pieces of her vulnerability, I'm surprised. She used to say she wished she could see inside my head, but lately I'm finding I wish I could see inside hers.

"Committed, remember? There won't be anyone else."

Jennie rolls her eyes. "Garrett, you're a rich, professional hockey player. And you're hot as balls. You're meeting girls all the time."

"Sure, and when that's all they see, they're not it for me."

Shame slashes her delicate features. "I didn't mean…I know there's more to you than that, Garrett."

"I don't want you being insecure about this. Yes, I meet lots of girls, and admittedly, I could do this with any number of them. But there's a reason I'm doing it with you. I like you, Jennie. You're fun and you make me laugh. I like to boss you around in the bedroom and you like to boss me around the rest of the time. We're compatible, and the chemistry is explosive, which is why I think this works so well. On top of that, you're quickly climbing your way to the top of my best friend list."

Her nose does that cute wrinkle thing. "You're just saying that."

I'm not though. I don't know when she became my favorite person to hang out with, but she is. I find myself thinking about her when I'm out with the guys after a game, or warming up on the ice. I text her for no reason at all, simply because I like talking to her.

I'm having fun here, seeing my old friends, spending Christmas with my family, but I can't wait to get home, spend a night reminding Jennie how much I enjoy her company. Because for some fucked-up reason, I think she might see herself as disposable.

"Plus, our snowmen handprints look bomb next to each other on my tree."

Jennie laughs, and any lingering tension dissipates, her shoulders falling as she chats animatedly about the recital, the dinner Carter took everyone to afterward.

It's two in the morning here and ten at night there when I ask Jennie, "If you could wake up tomorrow and have the thing you wanted most for Christmas, what would it be?" I regret the words as soon as they leave my mouth, and even more so when Jennie's gaze flickers, the light in her eyes dimming.

I know the answer. It's the same for any person who's lost someone special.

More time. One more hug. The good-bye they never got.

Jennie reaches for that invisible locket, the one that's supposed to be hanging from her neck. "Princess Bubblegum. It's stupid, I know. It's just a stuffed animal, just a necklace. I can't get my dad back, but...at least I got to carry him with me."

She surprises me then with a smile, wide and brilliant. Even with so much lingering sadness, it's easily the most breathtaking smile I've ever seen.

"Have you ever seen *The Parent Trap*? It was my favorite movie when I was younger. Annie and her butler had this secret handshake. It was this huge thing, super extravagant. My dad and I, we spent hours learning it. We'd do it every day. Every single day. Before he left for work, before he tucked me into bed." She smiles wistfully at the memory. "I think if I could have anything, something that were actually possible...it would be cool to do that handshake again." She waves a hand through the air. "What would you ask for?"

My thoughts drift to earlier tonight, the way my family was whole as we sat on the couch together and laughed, just...existed together, happy and carefree. So I tell Jennie exactly that.

When I'm done, she asks, "You and your dad don't have the best relationship?"

"It's just strained. He carries a lot of guilt, and the time away from each other allows the distance in our relationship to grow."

"What does he feel guilty about? You don't have to tell me if you don't want to."

"It's okay. I don't mind." With a tired sigh, I drag a hand through my hair. "My parents were high school sweethearts, and my mom had me when she was seventeen. When I was six, they got married. My dad...I guess he felt like he missed out on a lot of things, becoming a father so young. He started drinking a lot, and it spiraled out of control pretty quickly. My mom decided enough was enough when he forgot to pick me up from hockey practice when I was nine because he was drunk at a bar."

Jennie's expression is careful while I tell her about my parents' short-lived marriage, my dad's struggle with alcohol, even after my mom left him, but her eyes shine with hurt for me, hold the betrayal I felt all those years ago when the person I was supposed to be able to rely on most was never able to be there for me because he wasn't coherent enough to do so.

"When I was eleven, my dad took me for dinner. We went to this shady dive bar. It was dark and reeked like stale beer. I ate my pizza in silence while he drank. One hour turned into two, and eventually it was after ten on a school night." My hand slides along my jaw at the memory that makes my throat tight. "I drove home because he couldn't."

"Garrett." Jennie gasps softly. "You were only eleven."

"Our neighbor saw me trying to drag him up the pathway and into the house. My dad lost his license and all visitation rights."

"I'm sorry, Garrett. That sounds so difficult. I wish I could hug you."

"It is what it is. In the end, it was for the best. It was the push he needed to get help, and he did. He put the work in, and he hasn't touched a drop of alcohol since. I'm proud of him."

"You're a good son."

"When you told me you didn't drink, I had to kind of sit on that for a while. Maybe I'd made the wrong decision by drinking after everything my dad went through, after what he put me and my mom through. Should I have avoided it?" I shrug. "Maybe. Probably. But I guess I didn't want to let his past mistakes control my life."

I see the wheels turning as Jennie contemplates my words. "Do you think I let the way my dad died control my life by choosing not to drink?"

"I don't think that at all, Jennie. I think you saw the devastating effects alcohol could have on a family and you decided you wanted nothing to do with it. We handle it differently, and neither of us is wrong."

"I'm glad you don't let your dad's past affect you."

"Sometimes I think it does. Not much, but a little. When he was drinking, he said a lot of things he didn't mean, or maybe he did. A lot of hurtful things, regardless, so eventually I learned it was safer to keep my mouth shut. If I was quiet, I was less likely to be on the receiving end of his words. Sometimes I still have trouble speaking my mind, like I'm worried someone might not like what I have to say."

Guilt tugs at Jennie's mouth. "I'm sorry I made you feel like you couldn't speak freely with me before."

I shake my head, chuckling quietly. "I appreciate the apology, but it's not necessary. Sure, I was intimidated by you and that made it hard for me to talk around you. But that's because you were sexy as hell, spoke your mind, and I wanted you but knew I could never have you. There was a good chance anything I said was gonna get me de-dicked, by either you or your brother."

She flashes a grin, dimple-popping and extra charming. "I would never de-dick you. I love your dick."

"You'd love him more if you let him inside your Disneyland."

Jennie laughs, but there's a strain behind it, a sign she's retreating just a little. She drops her gaze, and silence beats between us. I don't know when the fuck I'll learn to keep my mouth shut, to think a little harder before I speak. Ironic, considering the conversation we just had. But now that I've gotten to know Jennie, I feel at ease with my thoughts. I don't feel like I need to withhold them from her so much, because I know she appreciates my honesty.

So while the intent behind my words may have been innocent to me, I can recognize they might sound different to Jennie.

"Hey, I'm sorry. I'm not trying to push you to have sex with me, and I realize it must sound like that. I respect your decision, and I won't bring it up again."

Jennie nods, tracing some sort of pattern on her bedspread.

"You can talk to me though; you have to know that."

Her head lifts, blue eyes careful. "Talk to you about what?"

"About what happened."

Her gaze goes hazy and dark. "Did Carter tell you?"

"No, Jennie. Carter didn't tell me anything."

I wish I were there to have this talk with her in person. Her first instinct is always to run, and mine is to hug. All I want to do is wrap her in my arms and promise her there's another side to whatever happened, an ending where she's able to move past it and stop letting it impact her life the way it does.

"You shut down every time we go down any direction that leads toward high school, exes, and sex. That's how I know. And I want you to know that if you ever want to share it, I'll keep it safe." *I'll keep* you *safe.*

She picks at her blanket, licks her lips. "Do you think we'd be friends even without Carter? If you sat down next to me in a coffee shop?"

"I think we share a connection that goes beyond your brother. With or without him, I wouldn't hesitate to place you in my life and keep you there."

There's something so heartbreaking about the spark of life those simple words bring to her eyes, the way she bites back this trembling smile that wants to spring free, like she's never felt so wanted and she doesn't know what to do with the feeling. It makes me want to dedicate the rest of my life to making sure she never goes without it again.

"I'd like to tell you one day, but I'm not ready." Jennie's eyes search mine, begging for patience. "Is that okay?"

"When you're ready, Jennie, I'm here."

The gratitude shining in her smile throws me for a loop. It's like all she's needed all this time was for somebody to give her the chance to navigate a new friendship, a meaningful relationship, time for her to feel at ease to open up and be herself. I'm happy and honored to be that person, but I'm sad she's spent years without one. I want her to feel safe to be herself with me.

But I have one more question, one that's been hanging like a heavy cloud above me. "Jennie? I just have to know one thing." When she nods, I ask, "Did he hurt you?"

Her hand goes to her braid as her gaze falls. "Not physically, no."

"Please don't brush off whatever happened because he didn't leave bruises on your body. Bruises you can't see can hurt just as much as the ones you can."

Her eyes lift cautiously to mine, showing me unshed tears. "They hurt a little less when I'm with you," she whispers. "Thank you for being my friend, Garrett. I think I really needed you."

The heaviness wanes as Jennie asks me about my sisters, what we've been getting up to. She laughs and smiles, and I revel in each one she graces me with as I sit here thinking about that fucking f-word, the label I was so eager to shove on us.

Friends.

What the fuck was I thinking?

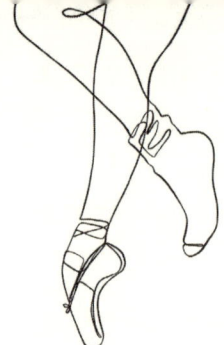

NINETEEN
SO THIS IS CHRISTMAS...

Jennie

I KEEP WAITING for Christmases without him to get easier, but I'm learning that's not how grief works.

I don't know that grief even has set rules, only that it pretty much always does the opposite of what you think it will. You think you know what to expect because you went through it last year, and the year before, and the one before that. You'll be prepared this time. Right?

Grief's not that simple. It's a fucking mindfuck.

My heart feels jagged and fractured, a deep, dull pain that won't wane, even as I snuggle beneath the covers, hugging the frame with the photo of me and Dad a little bit tighter, wishing for just one more Christmas with a heart that's whole.

My phone buzzes, and I shove it under the pillow, not ready to wear a smile that feels extra empty today.

But it keeps buzzing, over and over until I yank it out, accept the call before I realize it's a FaceTime, and growl out a rather aggressive, "*What?*"

Garrett's bright eyes blink back at me. He grins. "Merry Christmas to you, too, sunshine. Jesus Christ, who shit in your Corn Pops this morning?"

I don't know how the man manages to do it, but I crack a smile. A little one, like, super tiny. But the wider his gets, the bigger mine grows, until I'm rolling my eyes and laughing.

"Sorry. I didn't look to see who it was before I answered."

"You fell asleep on me last night, so I wanted to—"

"Are you on the phone with your *girrrlfriend*?" a voice teases.

"*Get outta here, Gabby!*" Garrett tosses a pillow, and even through the sound of a slamming door, I can hear Gabby's shrill giggles. He sighs, dragging his fingers through his mussed hair. "She's been calling you my girlfriend for the last three days."

"Better set her straight then. Tell her I had no choice in having a brother as a hockey player; I'm not going to voluntarily date one. She'll understand one day."

He turns away, rubbing the back of his neck. "Yeah, well, Gabby can't be tamed. She says and does whatever she wants, kinda like you."

"Ah, so you're surrounded by strong, powerful women."

"Something like that," he says on a long exhale. "Just toss the word *wild* in there."

My eyes narrow. "You're gonna get pinched for that when I see you next."

"Nah, I'll just tie your hands behind your back so your pinchy fingers can't get anywhere near me. Plus—" he lifts one arm, flexing his bicep, and growls playfully, "—this body was built by the gods. I don't have an ounce of body fat on me for pinching purposes."

"You hockey players are all the same: cocky little shits." I won't touch on the fact that my lady parts are tingling at the thought of him tying my hands behind my back. But, like…maybe I'll touch on it in the future.

"You can't lump me in with the rest of them. I'm in a league all my own."

I can't say I really disagree. Garrett's nothing like the players you see in the news. He's like a soft, gooey cinnamon roll. A lot of women would jump at a shot with a man like him.

I tuck the thoughts away, because I'd prefer to remain oblivious to the eventual good-bye I'll have to say to the only meaningful relationship I've ever had, the deepest, most genuine connection I've found with a person. Good-byes suck, and no part of me is ready for the one with Garrett that looms somewhere in the future.

"What are you doing still in bed, anyway?" Garrett asks.

"You're still in bed," I point out.

"I'm *back* in bed. We already had coffee, ate breakfast, and opened presents."

"But you're not wearing a shirt."

"Wanted to give you something to look at."

I laugh, a full belly one that feels good. "Okay, hotshot."

"You could take yours off, too, if you want."

"We're not having Christmas morning phone sex when your family is down the hall."

He runs a palm down his chest and sighs. "Can't blame a guy for trying. But seriously, can you do something for me? I need you to run up to my place for a minute."

"But I'm in bed!" I peel back the blankets and aim the phone at my fleece pajamas with dogs dressed as Santa. "I'm wearing my jammies!"

His gaze rakes over me, an amused brow quirking. "Really leaving a lot to the imagination there, aren't you?"

"Shut up, you donkey." I slip out of bed and stretch, yawning. "Fine, I'll go. But I'm going like this, and I'm not putting a bra on."

"Braless Jennie is my favorite Jennie."

I ride the elevator up to Garrett's penthouse and key in the code as he recites it to me. It's bright and toasty in here, the morning sun drowning the space in golden warmth. Multicolored lights make the Christmas tree twinkle, drawing me to it. It's been so long since I decorated for Christmas that I hadn't even thought to put up a tree of my own.

"There's a box under the tree," I observe, spotting the gift wrapped in brown paper with shiny red reindeers stamped all over it, topped with an extravagant gold bow. I turn our snowmen ornaments in my hand, smiling at our initials on the bottom, right next to our ages. "You didn't forget one of your sister's presents, did you?"

"No. I just wanted to be with you while you opened your gift."

My gaze falls to my phone, finding Garrett's soft smile. "What?"

"The gift is for you, Jennie."

I sink to my knees in front of the gift. Sure enough, *Sunshine* is scrawled across the tag. A lump forms in my throat, tight and heavy, one I can't swallow down. "You got me a gift? But I...I didn't get anything for you. I didn't know...I—"

"Stop. I'm sure this crosses some sort of imaginary friends-with-benefits line, but I wanted to get you something. So go on and open it."

I cross my legs and prop the phone up so Garrett can see me. There's a slight tremor in my hands, both excited and nervous to see inside. I run my finger along the edge of the ribbon before tugging, watch the bow fall apart, then promptly rip into the wrapping paper.

When I open the box, a giggle bubbles in my throat, and I pull the first item out.

"So we can have dance battles," Garrett says, watching me turn the *Just Dance* video game in my hand.

"I'll destroy you. Is your ego built to handle that?"

"Maybe I've been practicing."

"Practice all you want, Garrett, I'm still gonna bury you alive." I set the game aside and pull out a sweatshirt, laughing again as I read the silver words that loop across it. "*Sparkling Personality*? Really?"

He's doing a shit job at hiding how funny he thinks this is, snicker-snorting as he vibrates. "Get it? 'Cause you're so pleasant and sweet."

"Uh-huh." The next item is clothing too. A pale blue and purple romper made of ultra-soft fleece, zipping in the front. When I spy the word on the butt, Garrett's laughter quickly spirals into hysterical territory.

"They say *angel* on the ass," he wheezes. "*Angel*."

"Unbelievable. You're really on a roll right now, aren't you?"

"I'm sorry." He swipes at a tear. "I couldn't help myself. Plus, they're super cheeky, so your ass is gonna hang out of them." He wipes both eyes again and pushes a heavy breath out, trying to get control of himself. Both actions annoy me, yet for the life of me I cannot stop smiling. "There's one more."

I pull the skinny silver wand out of the box, the claws attached to the head that make it look like some sort of extra long fork.

"It's a back scratcher," Garrett explains, "but I thought, if you use it gently, you could tickle your own back when I'm away."

I extend the wand and slip it down the back of my pajama top. My eyes flutter closed as I moan. "Oooh, Garrett. You might've just inadvertently replaced yourself, big guy."

"Fuck that. Nothing replaces these fingers."

"They are my favorite fingers." I look down at the pile of gifts. "Thank you so much, Garrett. I love everything."

"It's no Princess Bubblegum, but I hope it brought you a little happiness anyway."

"It did. Thank you for thinking of me."

My gaze drops to my slippers as my own words register. Because at the busiest time of the year, between juggling his busy hockey schedule, the holidays, and traveling home to see his family, this man thought of *me*, and I honestly can't think of the last time somebody did.

"I can't remember the last time I got any gifts from someone who wasn't family."

Silence hangs between us like an anchor, keeping my eyes downcast. I'm worried I've taken us into unchartered territory, somewhere Garrett had no intention of going with a simple gift.

"But I think you are my family," he finally replies softly, urging my gaze to his, patient and kind, full of compassion. "The guys, Cara, Ollie…they're the family I found here, the one I chose, and I think you're part of it, too, now. I want you to be, at least. You feel like you belong in it."

I turn away in time to catch a sneaky tear that finds its way out of my eye and tries to roll down my cheek. Stupid holidays and big, cocky hockey players who are secret teddy bears.

"I'm not crying," I tell him, sniffling. "I have this, like, leaky tear duct thing. It's a condition."

His laugh is my favorite sound, his smile my favorite sight.

"Merry Christmas, Jennie."

"Merry Christmas, Garrett."

~

"What in the sweet fuck are you wearing?"

"What? This?" Carter looks down at his shirt, tugging so the single word is visible, as if it weren't already large and in charge. DILF. "Ollie got it for me."

"It was meant to be a joke," Olivia murmurs, "but it's his favorite gift. He won't take it off."

"Wanna see the best part?" Carter pulls Olivia into his side, beaming proudly. "Show 'em yours, pumpkin."

Her face flushes. "No, I don't think I will."

"C'mon." He shakes her arm. "Be loud, be proud, Ollie girl."

She does it, but she sure drags her ass about it, slowly pulling her sweater over her head, and I don't know whether to laugh at her or cry for her.

Because the shirt she wears underneath sports one simple sentence: *I HEART DILFs.*

"Pip," I whisper to Olivia, my shoulders shaking, laughter rumbling in my chest. I try to hold it in, I swear. "What did you do?"

Her shoulders slump, eyes downcast. "I fucked up."

"What's a DILF?" Mom asks, which only makes me laugh harder, and when Carter joins in, Olivia storms down the hallway. *"It was just a question!"*

Beside me, Hank smiles. "I feel bad for all the people who will never get to experience a Beckett Family Christmas."

I feel bad for Olivia, because now she's doomed to a lifetime of them.

I'm glad to have her, though, because I haven't seen Carter this happy at Christmas since our dad died. His smile never wanes as he hugs her into his side, linking their fingers, kissing her shoulder or temple every time he passes by.

I think Olivia brought him back to life. Now he's always the same brother I grew up with—goofy, outrageous, with a massive heart—not just when the cameras aren't around.

So when he tells us he has an exciting Christmas activity for us to do as a family, I'm not surprised.

Still not surprised when he rips the sheet off the kitchen table, revealing several boxes of gingerbread houses, the kind you build and decorate yourself.

A little surprised they're made of Oreos, though.

"I'm just saying." Carter slathers a cookie with icing, sticking it to his cookie roof. "Whoever thought of this is a genius. A whole village made of Oreos?" He makes a sound, like he's having a revelation, and turns, wide-eyed, to Olivia. "What if we name the baby—"

"No."

"But—"

"Not happening."

Carter frowns, grumbling something about the Grinch being a five-foot-one pregnant woman, and Olivia steals a mini-cookie out of his hand, tossing it in her mouth. It turns into a fight over cookies and edible decorations, and eventually Carter's holding everything above his head and laughing while Olivia tries to climb his body to retrieve said items, all the while Hank's eating whatever he can get his hands on beside me.

"Hank." I snicker. "You're supposed to be putting them on your house, not in your mouth."

"Oops." He pops another cookie between his lips. "Am I not putting them on my house? Couldn't quite tell. I am blind, after all."

"You're not using that as an excuse to eat your cookies, are you?"

"I can do whatever I want," he says simply, and it's a wonder he and Carter aren't actually related, because when the cookie village is done, that seems to also be Carter's motto.

"There!" he exclaims, putting the finishing touch on the last of his three houses. "All done!" His eyes glitter with pride as he takes in the village that sprawls across his kitchen table. Then he reaches down, grabs hold of a chimney, pries it off, and throws it in his mouth.

"*Carter!*"

He stops, eyes round with fear, like he's been caught red-handed by his wife doing something he's not supposed to. Like eating the cookie village. "What?"

"You're not supposed to eat it yet! You're supposed to leave it on display for a few days! One, at the very least!"

"What? You want me to stare at cookie houses all day and *not* eat them?"

She jabs at one of the boxes, pointing to the village that's on display in the picture behind the happy family, the one that looks nothing like ours right now. "Those are the rules!"

He flings his arms overhead. "You know I don't follow rules, especially when Oreos are involved!" He breaks a wall off one house and looks Olivia dead in the eye as he stuffs the entire thing in his mouth. "Wha' now, pwincess?" he mumbles, then dashes away with a squeal when she lunges for him.

Hank whistles along to the tune floating from the speakers. "So this is Christmas…"

~

Christmas snuggles are the best snuggles, especially when it's your mom's arms wrapped around you and you're wearing matching jammies.

She hugs me tight, sighing into my hair. "I missed our sleepovers."

"I missed *you*." My gaze wanders through the open door, down the hallway, where I can see the twinkle of lights. "I can't believe you decorated this year."

"With the baby on the way, I figured maybe it was time to start again. They deserve to have a magical Christmas experience, no matter where they go."

I turn, looking at my beautiful mom. "What about you?"

"What about me?"

"Don't you deserve it as well?" I link our fingers, pulling our clasped hands to my chest. "Don't you want someone to spend the holidays with? Share your life with?"

"I have my family. I don't need anyone else."

"I just want you to be happy, Mom." The words are more a plea than anything. I don't know if finding someone to share her time with will bring happiness, but if she thinks it might, I wish she'd try.

This house used to be filled with so much laughter, and while it still is, it's also home to a gut-wrenching, silent loneliness. It's my mom snuggling up alone on a Friday night to watch her favorite movies, the cheesy rom-coms my dad gladly sat through with her head on his shoulder. It's the far-off look in her eyes while she works in the kitchen, the memories of my dad hanging over her shoulder and begging for a taste of whatever she was making, pulling her away so he could spin her around the kitchen while he sang to her, loud and obnoxious until her laughter drowned out his voice, and he sealed it with a kiss.

Sometimes the silence is louder than the laughter, an ear-piercing roar that has you begging for it to end.

"I don't need a man to make me happy, Jennie." There's no uncertainty in her eyes. She's sure of her decision, but I suppose that's what brings her peace. "I'm happy with the life your dad and I created here while we had the chance. I'm thankful for the memories we made, and I'll always wish for more, but he's with us in every new memory we create too. I can feel him, and I just…I don't want to fill his space with someone else."

A tear rolls across the bridge of my nose, dripping onto the pillow-case. "What if one day you find space for someone else?"

"If one day I find space, then I'll let someone in." She pushes my hair back, tucking it behind my ear. "But what about you? When will you let someone in?"

"I don't need a man to make me happy," I parrot back, making her laugh.

"No, you don't. What you need is a partner, a best friend. Someone who's patient with you, who waits for you to open up when you're ready and wants to walk through all your battles with you. Someone who makes you laugh, who complements your incredible qualities. You have such a big heart, Jennie, and I wish you'd open up a space in it for someone. I know you're afraid. But life is too short to be afraid."

Her words wiggle their way into my brain, setting up shop in the corner, gathering cobwebs, until I'm thinking back on them over and over, even two days later while I'm lying awake in bed as the sun rises, and a deranged murderer decides to knock on my door.

Not literally, but seriously, what the fuck? My bare feet slap against the floors as I storm down the hall, not bothering with the rat's nest on my head that most people call hair.

"In what world is it socially acceptable to knock on someone's door at—*Garrett.*"

He smiles down at me from where he waits in my doorway, golden hair curling out from beneath the forest green toque he wears, dusted in snowflakes, just like the shoulders of his coat and the duffle that hangs at his side.

"I have one more Christmas gift for you." He steps beneath the threshold, his presence overwhelming, making my senses run wild. When he extends his hand to me, my heart leaps to my throat.

"What are you doing?" I whisper.

"C'mon, Jennie. Take my hand."

I do, tentatively slipping mine into his. It's cool from the elements, but his touch still manages to make my skin tingle with heat, desire.

And as we stand there staring at each other, slowly shaking hands, I've never been so confused.

Until he pulls his hand free and lays it palm down in the space between us.

My memory floods with hundreds of happy mornings, my dad's sly grin as a regular handshake spiraled and turned into one of our favorite pastimes, something special for just the two of us.

"C'mon," Garrett whispers again, and my chest heaves as he smiles, waiting patiently for me to lay my hand on top of his.

When I finally clap my hand on top of his, his face shatters with a grin, and tears prickle my eyes as a burst of laughter bubbles from my throat, the two of us in my doorway, slapping hands, bumping hips, switching spots, and finishing right back where we started: with a simple handshake.

He opens his arms and I barrel forward, burying my face in his chest, inhaling his scent. He's the same, rich mahogany, clean and citrusy, but the dampness from the snow he's just escaped from makes him different too. Earthy and fresh, like rain and pine needles.

I soak it all in, because the truth is, I feel a little bit more me when I'm with this man. He sees past all the bravado, sees both the bold and the quiet, the gentle that simmers below the fierce, and instead of turning away, he takes my hand and walks with me.

When we press the same whispered words to each other's bodies, something warm lights inside me.

"I missed you."

TWENTY
I THINK WE BROKE ADAM

Garrett

"I WIN AGAIN." Jennie gathers her chestnut waves, piling them on her head and securing them with a velvet scrunchie the color of champagne. "How you feeling? Tired? Angry? Emasculated?" She wiggles her brows, cheeky grin in place. "Want me to hold you and tickle your back while you cry, big guy?"

"Shut up." I shove her to the couch and turn off the stupid dancing video game. "You cheated."

"Whatever helps you sleep at night."

You know what's *not* gonna help me sleep? The image of Jennie dancing around my living room in nothing but a pair of lacy red panties and my T-shirt. No, that image is definitely going to keep me up tonight. We're riding together to the New Year's Eve party—Carter's idea; can't wait for him to regret that one—and Jennie came by early to hang. She showed up at my door in this shimmery midnight blue dress painted over her ass, then promptly discarded it so we could have dance battles. Dance battles were delayed by other types of battles, and I accidentally held her to the wall by her throat while I made her come on my fingers. The throat thing was because she already had her makeup on, and she didn't wanna ruin it.

I wanna ruin all of her.

"What are you doing?" Jennie asks as I tear open a bag of snacks.

"Eating my feelings," I mumble, tossing a handful of Flamin' Hot

Funyuns in my mouth. They're crunchy and spicy, bursting with flavor, kinda like Jennie. Everything I want in a snack.

"Ew. Have fun making out with yourself tonight."

"Nah." Another handful. "Gonna dwag you off ta da closet, shub ma tongue in yo mouf."

"You're absolutely not coming anywhere near me tonight."

I swallow, wiggling my red fingers at her. "That's what you think."

Jennie's face twists with disgust, and she gags when I lick my fingers. "That's utterly disgusting. I can smell your breath from here."

I tuck the bag away and wash my hands. "You wanna smell it up close and personal?"

She pins her arms over her chest and crosses her ankles on my coffee table, ignoring me as I creep toward her. "Keep your breath away from me, Andersen, or else."

"Or else what?"

"Or else I'll kick your ass."

"Creative." My fingers circle her ankles, spinning her on the couch and opening her legs so I can crawl between them.

"I'll karate kick your ass so hard you'll be playing tonsil hockey with your balls."

I bite back my laugh, straddling her hips and pinning her wrists on either side of her head. "I've never met a more violent person in my life. Lucky for me, I've learned my size means I can hold you down, and you very much enjoy me doing so."

She wiggles her hips, lifting them off the couch, smashing her pelvis against mine as she tries to kick me off. My grip on her wrists tightens as I cover her body with mine.

"*Garrett,*" she warns lowly. She's got the wild eyes going on. I love the wild eyes.

"C'mon, Jennie." I purse my lips, making smooching sounds. "Lemme kiss you."

"*Garrett!*" Shrieks of giggles fill the air as she rolls around beneath me, trying to shake me off. When my fingertips descend on her rib cage, tickling, she starts wheezing, crying as she laughs and gasps for breath at the same time, begging me to stop.

When I think she's on the verge of passing out or nailing me in the nuts, I ease up on the tickling. Circling her wrists, I pin them beside her head and chuckle, skimming the length of her nose with the tip of mine.

When she's able to breathe again, I roll off her, heading for my bedroom.

"Where are you going?" Jennie swipes at her hair. She's gonna need to fix that before we show up to her brother's house.

"To brush my teeth. I wanna spend my night kissin' you." I hit her with a wink. "Secret kissin', of course." I grip my junk. "I like getting blow jobs. Can't do that if I lose my dick tonight."

Jennie chucks a pillow at my face. "Go brush your teeth, you brussel sprout."

An hour and a half later, we're rolling up to Carter and Olivia's house, and I've spent the entire twenty-minute drive trying to slip my hand under Jennie's dress.

"Are you sure you don't want to drink tonight?" She slaps my hand and stuffs it in the middle console. "We can take an Uber home."

"Nah, I'm good."

"Well, if you change your—"

"I won't. I'm gonna fuck your mouth later, and something about me being drunk and you being sober while I do it doesn't sit right with me."

Jennie doesn't even miss a beat as she stares out the window. "Whether you're drunk or sober isn't gonna stop me from sitting on your face and coming all over your tongue." She looks my way with a dazzling grin as I leave the car idling on the street, slack jawed, and she squeezes my thigh, right next to my cock. "Ready, big guy?"

I wasn't ready.

I had to hang back and tuck my dick into the waistband of my boxers while Jennie went on ahead; I'd accidentally pitched a tent in my jeans.

Now it's two hours later and she's been flirting with Jaxon all night long, batting her stupid lashes at him, licking her stupid lips, smirking at me over his stupid shoulder. She mentioned something about me decorating her ass with my handprint later tonight. I guess this is her way of ensuring it'll be fucking permanent.

"Watching you fall is adorably hilarious."

I trip over nothing, catching myself on the wall. My cherry soda water sloshes and fizzes, coating my hand. "Fuck, Care. Why are you always sneaking up on me?"

Cara grins. "I'm very, very sneaky."

"And annoying," I grumble, then cover my shoulder when she punches it. "*Ow*! What was that for?"

Her eyes slice sideways, landing on Jennie and Jaxon. *J&J. JJ. J².* Those all sound stupid. Stupid *J*'s. *G&J* sounds way better, if I were to put any two totally random letters of the alphabet together.

"Poor baby. Did the green-eyed monster get you?"

I frown. "What are you talking about? Stop speaking in codes."

"Okay, Garrett. I'll stop speaking in codes." She backs me against the wall, fiery eyes making my neck clammy. She's tall and fierce and scary. "You've been staring at Jennie all night, and every time Jaxon touches her, you look like you're on the verge of popping this vein right—" she pokes my neck, "—here."

"Carter doesn't like him talking to her." *Oooh, good one. Quick thinking, Gare.*

"Carter's not the only one."

Jaxon chooses this moment to saunter over, tipping his beer to his lips. "What're we talking about?"

"Oh hey, Jax." Cara gives his shoulder a squeeze. "Gare-Bear was telling me how he doesn't like you talking to Jennie because he has a crush on her."

"*Cara*." I fling my arms wide. My drink fizzes again, soaking my left sock. I look back at Jaxon. "I didn't say any of that. She's being a...a...a Cara." *Smooth.* "She's drunk."

Adam appears out of nowhere, swinging one arm around my shoulders. "*I'm* drunk." His tone is as proud as his broad grin. "There's a cute girl here. Her name is Stacey. Samantha?" His brows crumple. "Maybe it's Sarah. She likes hockey, and I showed her a picture of Bear, and she said he was cute. Should I ask her out?"

"Oh, sweetie." Cara pats his chest. "No. No, you shouldn't."

He frowns. "Yeah, I thought so. New year, same single me."

"Man, even *I'm* rooting for that guy to find someone," Jaxon mumbles as we slip away, heading into the dining room where a game of beer pong has just ended.

"Garrett!" Carter bounces a ping pong ball off the walnut table. "I need a partner."

"I'm not drinking."

"They're not drinking either." He gestures across the table where

202 | BECKA MACK

Jennie and Olivia are fixing their cups. "Gonna plow them into the ground, alcohol or no alcohol."

Jennie's eyes meet mine, brows lifting, a challenge. "Andersen doesn't have it in him."

"Uh, Liv and I took the entire tournament last year," I reply, high-fiving Olivia in the process.

"You guys cheated," Carter grumbles.

Olivia smiles sweetly. "You know what they say. You have to learn to lose before you can truly appreciate winning."

His eyes darken. "*Garrett*! Get over here!"

The thing about those two is they both hate losing. Carter might seem like the type of guy to let his wife win to shield her feelings, but he never willingly loses. So it's always highly entertaining to watch his tiny wife beat him at nearly everything.

Including the first beer pong game, in which Olivia and Jennie sink all six fucking cups in a fucking row, and Carter demands a rematch.

"How is it even possible?" I murmur.

"I don't fucking know," Carter mutters. "Fucking horseshoes up their asses."

"Nothing to do with luck, bud," Emmett chimes in, but maybe luck is on our side this time around. Because Olivia misses one shot, Jennie two. Carter's more focused, refusing to look at Olivia when it's his shot, relentlessly taunting her when it's hers, and I'm as good as I've always been.

With two cups left on each side, tensions are high. The girls are up first, and Cara runs in, smacking both their asses.

"I want to see them *cry*, ladies."

Jennie bounces her ball three times then bends, poised at the edge of the table.

"Hey, Jen—*ah*!" Carter bends, clutching at the toes I've accidentally stepped on.

"Whoops," I say. "Sorry 'bout that, bud."

With her brother distracted, Jennie lets the ball fly, sinking it with ease, and poor Carter's gonna be so drunk by the end of this.

He's apparently decided to try his hand at another distraction tactic for this last round. When Olivia steps up to the table, he drags his shirt up his torso in slow motion, one finger on his lip as he gives her the eyes.

"Like what you see, princess? Want me to take you upstairs and—*ah, for fuck's sake!*"

That, my friends, is the sound of Olivia sinking her last shot, all while looking her husband dead in the eye.

"Hey, c'mon now." I clap Carter's back as he whines. "We've still got a chance. We've got as many cups as they had. We can do it."

He grips the edge of the table, swallowing. "You go first."

You're going down, Jennie mouths to me.

One way or another, I definitely am. Down on her, or down in this game. Either way, when I effortlessly sink my shot, I know I'm not at fault for whatever happens next.

With a shaky exhale, Carter steps up. He rolls his shoulders, bending his neck left, then right.

"Any cup, Carter," I tell him, rubbing his shoulders. "Any cup."

It's in this moment, as he's poised and ready to throw, that Olivia makes eye contact with Emmett, and he tips his chin just slightly, an instruction.

"Don't look at her," I growl at Carter. "Don't you fucking look at her."

But does he listen? No, of course not. Carter never listens.

Olivia twists away, slow as hell, bending, and Carter snorts a laugh.

"Don't even try it, Ollie girl. I'm not falling for…"

I see it all happen in slow motion. The water sloshing between her legs, covering the floor as she gasps, the color draining from Carter's face as Olivia cries out that her water just broke. His eyes widen with fear as the ball slips from between his fingers, bouncing once, twice, three times on the wooden table before clattering to the ground. Through it all, I don't miss Jennie snickering in the corner.

"Ollie—"

"*Ha!*" Olivia twirls back to us, face shining with arrogance, and she crushes the empty water bottle between her hands. "Gotcha, sucker! You missed!" She claps Jennie's hand before Emmett embraces her.

"I told you he'd fall for it!" he shouts, and Carter curls over with a snarl.

I chuck a ping pong ball off the table. "I knew I shoulda been Ollie's partner again this year. Carter sucks."

"I thought my wife was in labor! This isn't fair! It's cheating! I call a rematch!"

"That was the rematch," Jennie reminds him. "You keep losing."

"I'm not losing! I didn't lose! I-I-I—"

"You lost," Cara cuts him off. "Twice. And you lost three times last year. Your wife continuously beats you at this game, and yet you continue to have hope that the next game might be yours. It's inspiring, Carter, but it's also sad." She pats his chest. "Midnight is in five. We don't have time for you to find your balls."

Chaos ensues as everyone piles into the living room and the kitchen, and the temperature in the house instantly spikes. Too many people, too many bodies crammed onto the main level as everyone starts pairing off with their respective partners. Adam and Jaxon are gathered at the island, lining up shots for all the single guys and girls. There are so many people in this space that it's hard to see anyone other than the person standing next to you.

For me, it's hard to see anyone other than Jennie, the way she stands at the edge of the living room like she's damn well trying to disappear, eyes moving anxiously around the space. Her glowing personality has been shoved aside, replaced with this shell of who she is, preferring to hide away than be part of the excitement.

I slip through the kitchen and into the dining room before I loop back around to the dark, empty hallway, right behind Jennie.

My fingertips dance their way around her waist until I splay my palm out on her belly, and she gasps, jolting.

My lips touch her ear as the countdown drops to the final minute. "Come with me."

"What are you doing?" she whispers as I usher her up the stairs. "What if Carter sees?"

"The only thing that exists in your brother's world in this moment is his wife." I peek into a bedroom, the same one I first tasted Jennie in. "He won't notice we're gone."

"I'm playing amnesia if you're wrong."

I pull her into the dark room, pressing her against the wall. "And I'll jump out the window and you'll never see me again."

Downstairs, people start counting backward from twenty.

My hand curves around Jennie's neck, and my thumb settles over the pulse point hidden below her warm skin. It thuds violently, and I love being the reason she's coming back to life right now.

Fifteen.

"You gonna let me be your midnight kiss?"

Ten.

Her wild eyes jump between mine. "Maybe."

Five.

"Not the answer I'm looking for."

Four.

Three.

Two.

One.

"Then maybe you should just take what you want."

Our mouths clash in a frenzy, fingers plowing through hair, hips grinding, tongues sweeping, all while the house erupts with cheers and hollers below.

My hand slips up the back of Jennie's dress and I give her ass a light smack. "Bite me one more time and I'm gonna make you scream."

Her fingers curl around my hair as she kisses me deeply, teeth sliding along my lower lip before she tugs. "I'd like to see you try."

I swing the bedroom door shut and shove her into the bathroom, flicking on the light as I lock us in. Her cheeks are flushed, rosy lips swollen, chest heaving as I stalk toward her.

"Take off your panties."

"Gar—"

"Now."

I'm playing with fire, but I can't find it in me to care. I've had to stare at her from a distance all night, and all I wanna do is taste her.

Jennie's not moving fast enough, so I spin her around, push her against the wall, and with one swift yank, her panties are balled up in my fist.

One hand wraps around the base of her throat, the other dipping between her legs. "Guess what happens when you scream?"

"People hear," she whimpers.

"People hear. Do you want people to hear?"

She gasps as I slide my fingers through her soaked warmth. "No."

"Then you're gonna have to be a good girl and stay quiet."

I swing her up into my arms before depositing her ass on the countertop, bunching her dress up around her hips as I spread her legs wide. In the mirror, her pussy glistens with need, and my mouth waters.

"You're gonna watch yourself come for me, and you're gonna try not to be loud when you do it."

Her wide eyes stare up at me with wonder as my palms sweep over her thighs. When I open my mouth on her neck, her lips part with a raspy inhale that quickly spirals into a moan the second I stroke her clit.

I tsk, give my head a small shake. "Not off to a good start, sunshine."

Her hips buck, eyes pleading with me as my touch ghosts over her, almost giving her what she wants, taking it away at the last second.

My mouth trails the columns of her throat, along her jaw, stopping at her ear. "You want me to fuck you with my fingers?"

Jennie's a sight to be seen, bare and open to me, vulnerable as she peers up at me, head thrown back over my shoulder. When she nods, I realize I've rendered her speechless for the first time since I've known her.

Maybe that's why I put her out of her misery, keeping our gazes locked as I sink one finger inside her. When her mouth opens on a moan, I clamp my free hand over it, drowning out my name as it leaves her lips.

I plunge a second finger. "What did I say?"

Her hands reach back, frantic, looking for something to grab hold of. One grips a fistful of my shirt, the other the counter, and when I pump harder, faster, her eyes roll to the ceiling as she whimpers into my hand. My thumb finds her clit, pressing, edging, driving her wild.

"I want you on your knees when we get home," I whisper in her ear. Her walls start squeezing around my fingers as she thrashes in my arms, toes curling against the mirror. "And I want to see how far back you can take my cock."

Jennie moans loudly behind my hand, making me squeeze harder, and she starts ripping at my hand between her legs, trying to pull it away as her orgasm barrels down.

Her body trembles and quakes as she gives up the fight, head lolling backward as she screams my name into my hand, and when she finally stills, coming down from her high, her blue eyes are glossy and dazed.

I cover her mouth with mine, coaxing it open with my tongue, and she sighs as she sinks into my hold.

Two minutes later, I'm trying to figure out how to tell Carter he needs to sanitize the bathroom in his spare bedroom while Jennie gets dressed.

"Go make sure the coast is clear," she whispers, producing a container of wipes from the cabinet. "I'll clean up."

I creep into the dark bedroom and crack the door. Light and noise from downstairs filter in, but the hallway is empty.

I tiptoe back to the bathroom, where Jennie wraps her arms around my neck, pulling me in for a kiss.

"First orgasm of the new year. Solid six outta ten, Andersen."

"Get outta here, sunshine. I rock your world night after night." Linking my pinky with hers, I tow her into the bedroom. "I checked. The coast is—"

"Not clear," Cara finishes for me, from where she's standing in the doorway of the bedroom. "Those were the words you were looking for, right, Garrett?"

Behind me, Jennie cowers, pressing herself into my back, her face peeking out beneath my arm. Beside Cara, Adam's jaw dangles.

"We-we-we..." *Oh fuck.* "We, uh..." *Think, Garrett. Think!* "We sanitized."

Adam claps both hands over his eyes. "No, no, no, *no*. I can't know about this!" He spins, dashing off down the hallway. He doesn't make it far, based on the crash we hear, then the way his broken voice calls out, *"Caraaa."*

"Yes, my sweet angel," she shouts back, eyes on us. "I'm coming!"

Her smile doesn't waver as her eyes pierce ours, one red fingernail tapping on the door frame. My entire life flashes before my eyes as I contemplate all the ways Carter is going to hurt me, torture me slowly without ever actually killing me, just so he can do it all again.

"We are *so* going to talk about this," she finally says, simply, like this isn't the last time I'll have all my limbs, and with that, she turns on her heel and leaves us.

"So it's over."

"Over."

Jennie takes my hand, towing me into the elevator. "Because Cara said she wouldn't tell."

I nod, pressing for the twenty-first floor. "She did."

"Because she thinks it was a one-time thing."

"She does."

Jennie's foot bounces. "So we shouldn't push our luck."

I follow Jennie to her door. "Definitely not."

Her hand trembles as she jams her key in the lock, and when she finally gets the door open, she stares up at me. "So we're in agreement? We're done?"

"Done," I whisper, leaning toward her.

"Totally done," she murmurs, lifting her chin.

I bend my neck. "Done like dinner."

Her breath ghosts over my lips, warm and sweet. "Stick a fork in me, I'm done."

Jennie's back hits the wall with a thud as we crash into it, the door slamming behind me. I kick my shoes off, ditch my coat, and don't wait for Jennie to take her heels off before I tear her dress over her head and hoist her up to me, winding her legs around my waist.

"Not done," I growl against her neck as we pinball down the hallway. "Not fucking done."

~

"I think we broke Adam."

"We *definitely* broke Adam."

Jennie hands me a plate of cold pizza. "Will he be okay?"

I devour an entire slice before I answer, mostly because I need time to think. "I'm honestly not sure." I tried talking to him outside, but he kept putting his hands over his ears and singing, *I'm not listening, I'm not listening.* He was pretty drunk. I might be able to pretend this was a figment of his imagination.

When I'm finished, I set my plate on the bedside table and yawn.

"Are you leaving?" Jennie takes my hand in hers, tracing the length of my fingers. "Could you stay a while longer? We could cuddle."

A slow grin spreads up my face. "Cuddle?"

She lifts a shoulder. "If you want."

"If *I* want, or if *you* want?"

"You." She giggles, slapping my hand away when I reach for her waist.

I crawl toward her. "You know, you're turning out to be a huge snuggle bear. Who woulda thought?"

"Am not."

"Admit it, Jennie." I knock her down to her back, straddling her hips as I loom above her. "You're a cuddler. You like cuddling with me."

"Nope."

"C'mon, Jennie." I nudge her jaw with my nose. "Admit it."

"*Never.*"

For the second time today, my fingers descend on her rib cage, and I watch with pleasure as Jennie writhes below me, shrieking and giggling until she's breathless.

Laughing, I hug her to me. "I can't believe I was ever so scared of you."

"Yes, clearly I need to get my fear factor back." Jennie snuggles into my side as the tips of my fingers circle her shoulder blades, dancing down her spine, over the back of her waist. "Can I tell you something, Garrett?"

"Of course."

"I don't make friends all that easily. I have a hard time trusting people. I've learned to be okay with keeping my circle small, but you... you've made everything better." She sleepy blue eyes stare up at me, showing me the vulnerability that lurks beneath them. "I think you're my best friend." She drops her gaze to my chest, cheeks radiating with heat. "It would really hurt me to lose you."

Hooking a finger under her chin, I force her gaze to mine. I don't know what happened to make friendships so challenging and unattainable for her, to make her trust a prized possession, but the fear is so real for her, the fear that I'll just leave, that she'll lose this all.

Is that why she's refusing to see what's right in front of her, what we might be able to have? Because she'd rather have me as a friend than nothing at all?

I can't promise her forever, not when I don't know what tomorrow holds for us, not when she's not ready to go down the road that takes us from friends with benefits to something more. But I can promise her one thing.

"Best friends don't lose each other, Jennie. I'll be right here, always. I promise you that."

TWENTY-ONE
MY NAME IS GARRETT ANDERSEN, AND I HAVE A HOCKEY BUTT.

Garrett

"DAMN, I LOOK GOOD." Carter pivots, watching himself in the mirror. He tugs on the lapels of his tailored suit jacket. "I'd fuck me."

He hands his phone to Emmett before he presses his palm to the floor-length mirror, sticks his butt out, and looks back at us over his shoulder. "Take a picture. Gonna send it to Ollie. Let her know what she's in store for tonight."

Emmett shoves a stool toward Carter. "Hike your leg up." His head bobs as he snaps pictures. "Yeah, that's good. Ollie'll like that."

Adam crosses his arms, watching the mini-photoshoot. "Damn, these pants are really good." He gestures at Carter's ass in his burgundy suit. "Doesn't even look like you're gonna split 'em open, Carter. I'm impressed."

Carter holds his arms out and drops down to a squat, bouncing. "It's all the stretch. They're fantastic. Give it a try."

We do, all of us. To be clear, it's our entire team. All twenty-five of us are standing here, fully decked out in designer suits specifically tailored to athletes with muscular lower halves, dropping it low. We get called in for a ton of different marketing and commercial shoots, but I think this might be my new favorite. I look bomb as fuck.

"Fuck." I place one hand on my thigh, the other on my left ass cheek as I lunge forward. "These are incredible. So comfy." I sink into the stretch, feeling the burn in my groin, groaning. As a dancer, Jennie's incredibly flexible. I'm not. She gets these ideas and I go along with them, but if I can be honest, keeping up with her is hard sometimes.

The photographer giggles, snapping my photo. "This is great." Her raven hair is tied back in a tight pony that hangs halfway down her back. "Forget the posed photos; we should have just let you guys go for it. You're all naturals."

When I smile, she grins. Her name is Susie and I'm 99 percent sure she's been flirting with me for the last hour, mostly 'cause mine is the only suit she seems to think needs to constantly be adjusted. She's cute, but I haven't said more than five words to her; there's a saucy brunette occupying most of the space in my brain.

"You pull your groin?" Carter asks as I straighten and rub at the throbbing spot. "How'd you do that?"

The tips of my ears burn, the back of my neck growing damp, especially when Adam's eyes meet mine. He hasn't said a single word to me about New Year's Eve. Is it possible he forgot, or am I just dense enough to hope so?

Cara promised not to tell anyone, but only on the caveat it was a one-time thing. She was all for it being ongoing but said she wouldn't be able to keep her mouth shut if it was. I'm surprised she kept her promise. Emmett's been floating around me for the last week without a clue in the world I've had any of my body parts inside Jennie.

"I slipped on ice," I finally explain, or lie, depending on how you look at it. "Yeah, I slipped, and my legs, they went, like—" I make finger-legs with my pointer and middle fingers, then split them, because apparently, I'm under the impression *I slipped* requires a visual, "—this. So...yeah. Hurts."

"Jennie's got this awesome massage thingie," Carter says. "I call it the thumper. It beats the shit out of your sore muscles. You should borrow it."

"I'll definitely do that, yeah. I'll borrow her thumper." Wish I could stop my head from bobbing.

"Get her to show you how to use it. You're gonna be moaning nonstop."

Uh-huh. Definitely.

I'm still searching for a response when Adam asks, "What's the line again?" He fixes his cuffs, eyes moving over himself in the mirror. He's dressed in all black and looks sharp as fuck.

"My name is Jaxon Riley, and I have a hockey butt," Jaxon answers.

Adam clears his throat. "My name is Adam Lockwood, and I have a hockey butt."

I snort. "Add a little flair, at least."

"Yeah, it's like this." Carter rests his palm on the mirror again, looking over his shoulder. "My name is Carter Beckett, and I have a hockey butt."

"It's more like this." I clear my throat and wiggle my shoulders, getting into position, one hand on the knot of my tie, the other on my hip. "My name is Garrett Andersen—" I peek over my shoulder, "—and *I* have a hockey butt."

Carter shoves me out of the way with his hip. "My name is Carter Beckett," he murmurs, husky and low. He swings his head over his shoulder, eyes hooded as his hip juts, sliding one hand over his right butt cheek. "And *I* have a hockey butt."

I flip up the tail of my suit jacket and squat low, casting a heavy, heated glare over my shoulder. It's the kind I reserve for luring Jennie to the bedroom. "My name is Garrett Andersen…" I bounce into my squat, hand moving in a circle over my butt cheek, and pump my brows. "And *I* have a hockey butt."

"Damn," Carter murmurs, head bobbing slowly. "Yeah. Yeah, that's it."

"This is great," Susie says, snapping photo after photo of a team of hockey players dropping into squats, popping their hips, patting their own asses. "You guys are so fun and candid. We should get a couple of group shots, and then the videographer will pull you aside one by one."

She steps up to me, reaching for my tie.

"Is my tie loose again?" I shove my hands in my pant pockets as she starts fiddling with the knot.

She giggles. "I don't know how it keeps happening."

Me neither, because the only person who keeps touching it is her.

"This suit looks really good on you."

"Thanks. I like it. It's super comfy." It's the performance stretch-tech. Tapered waists and legs, but enough space and stretch to accommodate our thick thighs and—you guessed it—hockey butts.

"You're really tall. How tall are you?"

"Six three," I answer, ignoring Carter and Jaxon's snickers.

"Wow," Susie murmurs wondrously.

I point at Adam, trying to deflect her attention. She's sweet, but I'm not trying to give her any wrong ideas. "He's six-five."

She barely spares him a glance. "Yeah, he's so big. So, is your girl-friend tall too?"

"Um, I..." I scratch my nose. "I don't have a girlfriend." It's not a lie, but it feels like one.

Her face brightens. "Oh."

"Do you have a boyfriend?" Carter asks, sauntering over, annoying grin on his annoying face.

Susie shakes her head, grinning expectantly at me, and Carter swings an arm around my shoulders, jerking me into his side.

"Well, isn't this fun. You're both single, and Garrett's looking to get into the dating game. Right, buddy?"

Well, fuck me sideways. This isn't good.

Pregnant women are scary.

Jennie's got, like, half a foot on Olivia, and she's still trying to disappear into the couch, flinching away from Olivia's glare.

"Would you stop looking at me like that?" Jennie finally shouts at her. "I get it, you don't like the Christmas gift I got Carter! I'm not trying to die today!"

Olivia gestures aggressively to where Carter is standing in the center of their living room with a microphone, singing the words that scrawl across their TV. "Two weeks, Jennie! He's been singing every day for two weeks!"

"Well, they were on a road trip for five—" Jennie clamps her mouth shut at the murderous expression on Olivia's face. "Yeah, got it. Two weeks. Karaoke machine was a terrible idea."

Jennie and Cara share a wide-eyed look, trying not to laugh, but when Carter turns around and captures Olivia's hand, tugging her to her feet and spinning her around while he sings "Kiss the Girl" from *The Little Mermaid*, they burst with laughter.

"Okay, Jennie," he heaves when the song is done, swiping at the sweat on his brow. "You and me. *Frozen*?"

"Fuck yes!" She leaps from the couch, grabbing a second micro-phone, and I don't know what the fuck has happened to my life that I'm a twenty-six-year-old man spending a rare free Friday night watching my friends sing Disney karaoke.

And yet I wouldn't change a thing. There's just something about the way Jennie looks so utterly free and at ease, like she feels in her element here with these people, free to be herself.

"Sometimes," Olivia sighs, "it's like there are two of them."

I pat her hand. "And you're about to add one more. So brave of you, Liv."

"I need help. So much help."

I chuckle. "Can I grab you something, little mama?" She's snuggled into the couch, managing to look both uncomfortable and comfy as hell. Her baby belly is cute, but for such a little person, it sure takes up a lot of her, and I'm certain she's hurting.

"I would love a tea and my Oreos. Carter put the cookies on top of the fridge where I can't reach, and the tea bags are in the pantry."

Adam ambles over to me in the kitchen while I'm getting the kettle ready, looking awkward as hell, and a little scared too.

"Look, buddy," he starts cautiously. "I love you."

"Love you, too, man."

"I want you to be happy," he tries again.

"Thanks, buddy. Appreciate that." I pour the steaming water over the tea bag, watching as it changes colors. "I want you to be happy too."

"Uh, right. But in order to be happy, you have to, uh…" He runs an anxious hand through his hair, eyes darting around the room before he leans close and whispers, "Stay alive."

I resist the urge to laugh, only because his concern is genuine, and also because not dying is preferable. Truthfully, I'm surprised it took him this long to bring up. I bet he's been stewing all week.

I steal a quick glance around the room. Everyone's busy, and most importantly, Carter's still singing. "Look, it was only the once. It won't happen again." Lying to Adam feels weird. I don't like it.

"It shouldn't have happened at all," he whisper-yells. "You made a mistake!"

I throw my arms out. "I make mistakes all the time, man!" I place a hand on my chest to calm my erratic breathing before this gets any more heated. Plus, Cara's eyeing us from the living room. I don't need her sticking her nose back in here. It's a miracle we got it out in the first place. "Look, all we did was make out."

"You said you sanitized!"

"Oh c'mon, man! Were you even drunk? How do you remember?"

"Why would you need to sanitize if all you did was kiss?"

"Uh, because J—*she*—she's a...a sloppy kisser. Yeah, super sloppy. She's got this disorder, I guess, where she makes extra saliva." I shudder. "Super weird." She's gonna have my balls if this gets back to her. "Still good, though."

Adam rolls his eyes. "Great, because I was definitely wondering how she rates on the tonsil hockey scale." He leans closer, accusing eyes fierce. "What were you even doing in the upstairs bathroom alone with her to begin with?"

"All the bathrooms were full."

"All the bathrooms were full at exactly midnight while everyone was celebrating the ball drop?"

I fold my lips into my mouth. "Mhmm."

Adam shakes his head.

"Well, what were you and Cara doing going to the upstairs bathroom together?" I'm deflecting, not accusing, but he still slams his fist against my shoulder at the implication.

"Because all the bathrooms were full *after* midnight when we both needed to go, and Cara said she didn't wait for anything or anyone, you dipshit."

I snort a laugh, 'cause I kinda like seeing Adam riled up, name-calling and all that jazz.

He sighs, running his fingers through his dark hair, blue eyes exhausted. "You promise it was only the once? That you're done?"

I scratch the corner of my mouth, mumbling, "Promise," into my hand, hoping Adam will forgive me one day

"So you'll call that girl then?"

"Girl? What girl?"

"The girl from today! The photographer!"

"Ohhh, right, right. Her. Yeah, I'm gonna call her." *Already deleted her number.*

Susie was fine. She was cute and sweet and very friendly. If I were available, maybe I'd take her out. But I'm not available. I don't think I'm available. Right?

Well, anyway, she's not Jennie, and that's the only thing that matters. She's the only woman I can't take my eyes off.

When Adam's finally satisfied enough, she wanders into the kitchen.

She takes a mug down, and I fill it with hot water. She dips a tea bag. "What was that about?"

"Just wanted to make sure nothing was going on."

Jennie leans against the counter, hiding her smile behind her mug. "Poor Adam. I feel bad lying to such a sweet man."

"Me, too, especially when his main concern is I stay alive."

Jennie hums, nodding. "Valid."

I lean next to her, and when our hands brush, I link my pinky around hers. "Was the karaoke machine a gift for you or for Carter?"

Jennie snickers. "So what if I like to sing too."

"I think you were born to be on stage."

"Born to shine, baby." The current song wanes, and Jennie lifts both brows at me as she pulls her hand back and starts walking toward the living room with her tea. "Garrett's up next! He wants to sing *Moana*!"

I'd rather not, but Cara jumps up, declaring she'll sing with me, and before I know it, I've sung half the soundtrack and Jennie hasn't stopped laughing the entire time. I love being the reason behind her laugh.

When I finally sit down, breathless and hungry, Carter bursts my happy bubble.

"Garrett has a date."

My jaw dangles, gaze darting to Jennie. "What? No I don't."

"Well, not yet. He got the photographer's phone number from the shoot today."

"She-she-she...she gave it to me!"

"They were flirting the entire time," Carter continues. "They were so into each other."

"No, I-I-I...she was, but I was...I was..." *Fuck.* The second my eyes meet Jennie's, she averts her gaze, cheeks a furious shade of red. Cara's own gaze pinballs between the two of us, a sly grin creeping up her face. Adam just looks fucking exhausted, or disappointed, maybe both.

"I wasn't flirting," I mumble, but the words are lost as Carter and Emmett burst into song, duetting to *Frozen*'s "Do You Want to Build a Snowman," and for the next hour, all I do is steal glances at Jennie.

By the time we're headed back to the condo, I'm royally confused. She won't look at me, and she barely said a word the rest of the evening. Every time somebody addressed her, she asked them to repeat themselves. I tried to tuck my pinky around hers under the kitchen island when we were all lined up to fill our plates, but she twisted away and acted like I wasn't there. The most I've gotten out of her was when she handed me the keys to Carter's car and asked me to drive home, because the snow was making her anxious.

"It's nice how close you and Carter are. You can tell just by watching you two."

She keeps her gaze trained out the window. "Yeah, we always have been. He's my best friend."

"And me, too, right?" I poke her thigh and chuckle eagerly. I don't know why I'm poking her. Everything is awkward and all I wanna do is touch her, put my hand on her knee, twine my fingers through hers. "Jennie?" I prod, poking once more.

She peeks at me, giving me a weak smile. I don't think that's an answer. If it is, I don't like it.

"Well, you're my best friend." Because I can't stop talking. "So, tough cookies." *Tough cookies? Holy fuck, please stop.*

I drive for another three minutes in horrible silence, and when we stop at a red light, I can no longer resist the urge to keep my hands off her. I lay my palm face up, fingers spread, and wait.

Jennie watches me but doesn't take the bait, so I shake my hand.

"C'mon, Jennie. Hold my fucking hand, please. I wasn't allowed to touch you all day, which is, coincidentally, the only thing I was thinking about."

The corner of her mouth quirks, and it's not enough, but I'll take it. She slides her palm along mine, and when our fingers tangle and she clasps my hand, my nerve endings sizzle. I wonder if I make her feel warm the same way she does me, like a mug of hot chocolate after coming in from the cold, or stepping outside in the spring and feeling the sunshine on your face after a long winter.

Back at the condo, we ride the elevator in more silence, but she keeps her hand tucked softly in mine. When we get to her door, she slips inside, and the way she starts closing it before I can follow makes my heart thump too quickly. She's upset, and I don't want her to be.

She gives me a smile, but I hate it. It's small and sad and kind of shy, half-hidden by the door she's gripping, barely pulling in her dimples. "Hey, I'm gonna head in alone. I'm pretty tired."

"Oh. Okay. Are you sure? We could just watch a movie or something? I can tickle your back in bed."

"Yeah, no, it's okay. Just gonna go to sleep."

"Okay." I rub the back of my neck. "Um…good night, I guess." I lean forward, and she turns her face so minutely I wouldn't even notice, except that I get the corner of her mouth rather than her lips when I kiss her.

And that fucking sucks.

Silence floats between us as we stare at each other, making my skin itch. I don't know what's happening between us. I know I don't feel the same as when this started, when all I wanted was an innocent taste. Maybe it's my fault, for bending rules, giving her more than she ever asked for, the movies, the cuddling, the fucking sweatpants.

But I can't read her, and right now, when my own feelings are new and confusing and I'm not sure of their depth, I don't know how to proceed, other than knowing I need to tread lightly. Patience has always gotten me so far with Jennie. Is it farfetched to hope a little more will take me where I want it to? All I know is she scares easy, and scaring her off is the last thing I want to do.

Jennie fiddles with the tip of her braid. "Oh hey, um, if you're gonna call that girl—"

Knew it. She's jealous. Does this mean she likes me? I think this means she likes me.

"I'm not gonna call that girl."

"Well, if you change your mind—"

"I already deleted her number."

Jennie blinks once, twice. "Oh."

"Yeah."

"Um, well." She winds her braid around her hand, tangling her fingers, and her cheeks turn pink as she tries to free herself. I reach forward and pull her hand from her hair. She promptly starts picking at imaginary lint on her hoodie. "Just remember that we should end this before you start seeing someone else, because I don't want to feel stupid, or be embarrassed, or whatever."

"I'm not seeing someone else, Jennie, and we're not ending this. Is that all?"

"Is what all?"

"You don't want to feel stupid?"

Her nose wrinkles as she pulls her bottom lip into her mouth and drops her gaze again. I'm not sure I'll ever get used to the shy bits of her that peek out here and there, but I'm learning that I like them just as much as her loud, confident bits. Whether she roars or whispers, she's still beautiful, strong, and uniquely perfect to me.

"What else would it be?"

My eyes roll to the ceiling with my sigh. She likes to do this every now and then, answer my question with one of her own. It's how she avoids any serious conversation that might force us to address where things are heading, or at least where I want them to head.

So with a dopey grin, I clasp a fistful of her hoodie and tug. She comes tumbling into me, grasping my biceps to catch herself, and I angle her face up to mine.

"You're fuckin' infuriating sometimes, sunshine. You know that, don't you?"

There it is, right there in the corner, the hint of a smile. Her dimples start pulling in, and when her beam blooms across her face, I wanna kiss them right off her cheeks.

"I'm no one's sunshine."

"Fuck, I love when you're wrong." My mouth covers hers, coaxing it open, and her tongue meets mine for a slow, sweeping kiss. "You're *my* sunshine."

TWENTY-TWO

FUCK.

Jennie

"The reservations are for seven."

"And everyone's coming?"

"*Everyone*. It's gonna be amazing. I've got us on the list at Sapphire for afterward."

"*Sapphire*? How did you make that happen?"

The tip of my pen taps incessantly against the desktop, and my eye twitches as I dream about shoving my turquoise-blue BIC right through Krissy's eye socket.

Is it extreme? Maybe. Is it necessary? Also maybe.

Simon takes the weapon from my hand, replacing it with a Starburst. I can't put a Starburst through Krissy's eye. Plus, it's a pink one. I'm not wasting that.

"Have some candy. You look like you're plotting a murder." He opens his laptop and fucks around on YouTube until he finds one of those funny dog videos he knows I like. He checks it's muted and flips the screen to me before focusing his attention back on Leah at the front of the lecture hall.

I'm wound tight right now. Krissy's sitting directly in front of me, talking loudly about their Friday plans, putting emphasis on the *everyone* who's coming.

I'm not part of the *everyone*, and I definitely don't care. It's not like they're going to the best, most exclusive dance club in Vancouver, and it's not like I love to dance. It's not like the entire graduating dance class is attending, and it's not like I care that I've been sitting on the sidelines all these years.

I've been an outlier from the beginning, the rich girl who didn't have to try to get accepted to one of the most elite dance schools in the nation, the scholarship that was handed to me.

Except I'm not rich, and I never have been. And that scholarship I rode in on? I earned every cent of it by busting my metaphorical balls for seventeen years, when all I ate, slept, and dreamt about was dance.

My fate was set the moment Carter Beckett's little sister strolled in on the first day of orientation, and like I'd learned to do, I accepted it, choosing instead to sink back into the shadows, to be my own friend.

I'm tired, but now the fear of rejection is all too real for me to even try.

My friendship with Garrett has shown me the types of connections I've been missing all these years, and has sparked a deep craving for more. Coming to this place where I'm forced to hide inside myself is draining. I want the freedom I feel with Garrett, the one that lets me be unapologetically myself, and I want to experience it always, everywhere I go.

Is the connection we share the kind you find regularly? Is it the type of connection you create with all your friends? Or is this connection unique to him? To us? Is it fleeting and rare, the powerful kind that allows a deep and meaningful relationship to bloom? The kind you grab hold of and tell yourself, no matter what, don't you dare let go?

My mind sees Garrett, and it clasps onto his face.

Things have been quieter with him, gentler. Like we're both treading lightly, tiptoeing that line but careful not to cross it, afraid even.

It's confusing, daunting, and maybe a bit frustrating. Does the line even exist anymore? I don't know where it's drawn, but I know what sits on the other side of it, and that makes things all the more frightening. Because where there's something beautiful to be found, there's something beautiful to be lost too.

When I thought Garrett had a date, a tsunami of feelings I'd been refusing to acknowledge rushed through me. Feelings that had been simmering on the back burner for weeks, growing stronger with every *good morning* text, every kiss hello, every night in on the couch, watching movies with mugs of hot chocolate, every quiet, mundane conversation in bed where his fingers drift up and down my spine before we eventually say good night.

The logical part of my brain examines each of Garrett's actions, his words, every smile he graces me with, the way his gaze floats down my face before he presses his lips to mine. That part convinces me there's something vibrating between us, something strong and tangible. So tangible I can feel it even when he's not right next to me.

But then there's that weak part of my brain, or rather, my heart. The pieces that have been shattered and bruised, those still-jagged edges, they remind me that sometimes not everything is as it seems. That some people are so good at convincing you they care, or worse, that they love you.

My judgment may be flawed, but every part of me knows Garrett's not that person.

But that doesn't mean he feels what I feel. I've been wrong before, and I don't want to be wrong about Garrett. That feels a lot like losing him, and he's not a loss I'm willing to risk.

"That's it for today. Have a great weekend, everyone."

Leah brings a welcome end to my spiraling thoughts, and chairs skid across the linoleum floors as everybody rushes out of the lecture hall.

Simon packs up his laptop while I wait for Krissy and A² to leave. Ashlee—Ashley number two—smiles at me, waving. She's always been nice, quiet, and I don't understand why she hangs around with this group. Maybe she's as desperate as I am to fit in somewhere, anywhere.

Simon takes my hand, helping me to my feet. "Wanna be my date to Sapphire tomorrow night?"

"Thanks, but I'm not going."

"What? Why?"

"You know exactly why."

Simon sighs. "C'mon, Jennie. Come with me. We'll have fun."

"I don't think that's a good idea. I wasn't invited." I'm never invited. "Sapphire sucks anyway." It's amazing, impossible to get into unless you have a rich connection, like, for example, a professional hockey player for a brother.

Going to a dance club with your overprotective older brother is not fun, by the way. Carter conned his friends into forming a barricade around us girls that made the Great Wall of China look like a white picket fence. I stomped off the dance floor two minutes later, and Carter made it up to me with a chocolate banana milk shake topped with crumbled Oreos on the way home.

"*Krissy!*" Simon calls, cupping his hands around his mouth. "Jennie can come tomorrow, can't she?"

Her mouth quirks as she looks me over. "I didn't know you liked to dance, Jennie."

I bite my tongue to keep from calling her a giant twat, because I'm a fucking dance major, the same as she is. "You know, for fun," she adds. "Of course you can come."

Simon's as oblivious to her attitude as he always is, or maybe he just doesn't give two shits. He barely spares her the time of day anymore, and sometimes I think that's what bothers Krissy most about me. I get the attention she wishes she had.

He pops a loud smooch on my cheek. "See? Told ya you could come." He starts jogging away. "I'll text you tomorrow before I pick you up."

Krissy's tight smile lingers on me. "I was just saying to the girls, I don't know why you never come out for drinks with us."

I'm about to remind her they've never once invited me, but Ashley number one beats me to a response.

"Jennie doesn't drink."

"What? You don't?"

I shake my head.

Krissy's nose wrinkles. "Ew. Why?"

My chin juts, because her tone is pissing me off. "I don't need alcohol to have or be fun." While true, it's not my reason. But I don't need to explain myself to anyone.

She shrugs. "Guess we'll see you on Monday then," she tosses over her shoulder as the three of them walk away, leaving me standing here, wondering why being sober means I've suddenly been uninvited.

Krissy pauses, and I hate how my body buzzes, eager, hopeful for inclusion, when she calls my name.

"Yeah?" My grip tightens around the strap of my bag, waiting.

"We heard you've been recommended for the job in Toronto. I won't be at all surprised if you get it."

My face beams with pride, tension in my chest easing, shoulders dropping. "Thank you. I'm really excited about the opportunity."

"Apparently talent isn't their priority this round, which is why I'm not going to bother applying. I heard they're looking for someone willing to follow blindly like a sheep. It makes sense Leah thought of her favorite student. They know you won't stir any dirt up there. You're so…" Her gaze drifts down, then back up. "Vanilla."

I open my mouth to tell her to go fucking fuck herself, but instead, my chin trembles. My teeth quickly descend, biting into my lip, trying to still the quiver before she can derive any pleasure from seeing it, from knowing she's succeeded in hurting me.

I don't know what I've done to make her dislike me so strongly over the years, not when I've worked so hard to stay in my own lane.

But staying in my own lane doesn't make me vanilla. Following the rules because I see no need to break them doesn't make me boring.

Does it?

"I'm a good dancer, and I've worked my ass off," finally leaves my mouth. "I *always* work my ass off."

"Oh, of course."

"I deserve to be considered."

Krissy gives me a condescending pat on the shoulder. "I didn't mean anything bad by it. There's nothing wrong with being predictable."

"It's called being reliable."

"And it certainly doesn't hurt that your brother is Carter Beckett. I'm sure that plays into this. Think of the extra publicity, the donations… They have so much to gain by having his little sister teach there."

My fists clench, nails biting into my palms. "My brother has nothing to do with this."

Krissy gestures for her friends to follow her. "Anyway, Jennie. We'll see you on Monday."

Ashlee lingers, giving me a small wave paired with a sympathetic smile. "Have a good weekend, Jennie."

I watch their retreating forms, demanding my brain to drop it, to not let it get to me. But then the sound of heels clicking in the hallway echoes in my ears, matching the pounding of my pulse, and my throat feels thick and tight when I try to swallow.

"Jennie! There you are. How's my favorite student? I wanted to ask you how you're feeling about the job, with graduation getting closer."

My eyes shift, barely meeting Leah's. The lines in her face soften, her brown eyes full of compassion as she steps into me, clasping my elbow.

"Hey, are you okay? Wanna go grab a bite?"

Is this what Krissy was talking about? Aside from Simon, my teacher is my only friend at school, the only other person who invites me to sit with her in the cafeteria, who just fucking…*talks to me.*

No, I tell myself, squeezing my eyes shut and shaking my head. *Don't let her make you doubt yourself. Don't fucking let her, Jennie.*

"Jennie," Leah urges softly. "What's going on? Let's grab a coffee and sit down."

"I…" I feel like an idiot. I feel alone. I feel so…*vanilla.* I don't fit in with the rest of them, and while I've always known that, today it feels heavier and darker than it ever has. *Is there anything special about me?*

"I have to go," I finally mumble, peeling Leah's hand off.

She calls after me, but I'm already out the door, stepping into the blustery afternoon. The damp wind slaps at my cheeks, making my skin sting. It was mild this morning, rainy, but the temperatures have taken a sharp dive and the rain has turned to snow. It's that thick, heavy kind, sleet that makes every step an icy hazard as it coats the ground.

I slip twice on my way to the car, barely catching myself before I face-plant. I whip the door open and shove my coat and bag in the backseat before climbing in. The snow falls heavier the longer I sit here, gripping the steering wheel, telling myself these people aren't worth my tears, but that doesn't stop them from prickling my eyes. By the time I'm creeping out of the parking lot, the blowing snow and my flooded vision make it nearly impossible to see.

My heart slams against my rib cage and my pulse thunders in my ears as I approach a four-way stop sign, and when I tap on the brake, the car skids forward.

And forward.

The car going through the intersection blares its horn.

Every muscle in my body tenses and my knuckles turn white as I grind down on the brake as hard as I can and swing the wheel. My tears finally spill at the crunching of metal.

TWENTY-THREE
INDIANA BONES TO THE RESCUE

Garrett

"YOU CALL THAT GIRL YET?"

My thumbs pause on my game controller and my heart skips a beat. "Huh?"

Emmett looks at me. "The photographer? The one Carter hooked you up with."

"You're welcome," Carter mumbles around a carrot stick. Apparently Olivia's on a health kick because she's getting down on the way her body's changing the later she gets in her pregnancy. She's banned cookies from their house, and Carter's trying to be supportive by not eating them. We're at Emmett's, and Olivia's not here, so I'm impressed he's sticking with it.

"Uh, no," I finally answer, hoping we leave it at that.

"Why not?" Carter asks. "She seemed nice."

"Yeah, Garrett," Cara chimes from the kitchen. "Why not?"

"Uh, I donno." I rub the back of my neck. I'm tired of doing this, dodging questions about my relationship status, or why I keep going back to my hotel room early and alone. "I don't think we'd be a good match."

"How do you know?" Emmett asks. "Maybe you'd really get along if you gave it a chance."

"I just wasn't feeling her." I keep my eyes on the TV screen as my player nabs the puck then barrels down the ice.

"You're never feeling anyone lately," Emmett points out. "I don't think I've seen you entertain anyone for the last two months."

"Yeah, what gives?" Carter asks.

"How come nobody asks Adam these questions?" I grumble.

"Adam's not here right now," Emmett reminds me. "And he's still sorting through his shit. And don't even think about bringing up Jaxon. That guy's got three girls in his lap on any given night."

"Well, maybe I'm sorting through some shit too."

"What shit?"

Sighing, I toss my controller to the coffee table. The words are out of my mouth before I can stop them. "Look, I'm seeing someone." Cara's infuriating, shit-eating grin comes into view, and I drop my gaze like it's on fire. "Kinda, or whatever. It's complicated."

Carter dunks a carrot stick in a bowl of blue cheese dip. "Complicated how?"

"I don't think she's ready for a relationship. A bit of trust issues." Not a lie.

He chomps away, mumbling, "Need welation-sip a-bice?"

"Relationship advice? From you? Absolutely not."

"Why not? I'm great at relationships."

I snort a laugh. "You've been in one."

"Yeah, and I'm married to her, 'cause I fucking nailed it the first time around."

Rolling my eyes, I fish my vibrating phone out of my pocket. A single sunshine lights my screen, and I hit Decline as I stand and stretch. "I'm gonna get going."

"If you change your mind, you know where to reach me."

I'm typing out a text to Jennie while carrying my glass to the kitchen when she calls again.

"Sunshine," Cara murmurs over my shoulder, making me jump. "Who's sunshine and why is she calling you?"

"Jesus Christ, Care. A little privacy?"

"I've never been good at that," she muses, watching me load my glass into her dishwasher. "Seeing someone, huh?"

"It's not what you think."

Her smile is slow and scary, but she's almost always scary. "And what do I think, Garrett?"

"Uh…" *Is this a trap?* "Nothing?"

She takes a step closer, then another, until I'm pressed against the counter, the word *help!* on the tip of my tongue.

"I think you and *sunshine* lied to me when you said it was a one-time thing. I think you've been fooling around for a while, maybe since she moved into your building. Quite ballsy of you, Andersen. I didn't think you had it in you, Carter's baby sister and all."

"*Shut up,*" I seethe, gaze bouncing to the living room where Carter's still preoccupied with his video game.

"You know what else I think?" She winds the strings of my hoodie around her fists, yanking me closer. "I think you have feelings for her now, and I bet that's something you didn't plan for."

My phone buzzes against my chest, and when I pull it away, there's that damn sunshine again.

"You better get outta here. Sunshine's calling."

I've never busted my ass so fast to get outside in the cold and all the snow, to get away from Cara. I start backing out of the driveway and connect my phone to my speakers to call Jennie.

"Garrett," her strangled voice cries as soon as the call connects. "I need you."

~

"Fuck."

"He's gonna kill me."

"I mean…" I slip my fingers up my toque, scratching at my head. "It's not that bad. The most important thing is you're okay."

I drag my gaze over Jennie for at least the tenth time in the last three minutes. My hands have roamed every inch of her, checking for damage. They came up empty, other than the kink in her neck and the finger gouges on the insides of her palm. But it's the broken look in her eyes that says there's damage I can't see, damage that can't be fixed with bandages.

"*Garrett,*" Jennie cries, gesturing at the front bumper of Carter's Benz. "It's awful! Look at that dent!"

"Tell me again what happened."

"It was snowy and icy and I-I-I was having trouble seeing." She swipes the cuffs of her sweater across her eyes, the skin around them red and raw. "I came up to a stop sign and I tried to brake but the tires just kept spinning, and someone was going through the intersection and I thought I was going to hit them, and then somehow, at the last second, the wheels turned, and I went up on the curb and hit the stop sign."

I shake my head, sighing. "I wish you'd called me to come get you. You could've been hurt, Jennie, or worse. It's not worth driving when you're upset and anxious and the weather's bad."

Her lower lip trembles, hands wringing at her stomach.

Palming the back of her head, I haul her forward and kiss her forehead. "I'm sorry. I was just worried. I'm glad you're safe."

Worried doesn't begin to describe how I was feeling twenty minutes ago. I flew home, blowing through two stop signs at empty intersections, and when I found her crying on the curb in the parking garage, I nearly suffocated her in my choking hold. Her feet left the ground and I didn't put her down until she started pummeling her fists against my shoulders.

She averts her eyes. "I don't want to drive anymore, not in the snow."

"And you don't have to. I'll pick you up whenever I'm in town."

Her gaze floats back up, wide eyes grateful but cautious. "You'd do that?"

"Of course. Now the real question is…" I crouch down, inspecting the dent in the bumper. "What are we gonna do about this?" I rub the pad of my thumb across my lower lip, and when an idea pops into my head, I don't know if I'm a genius or deranged. "Go get Indiana Bones."

"What?"

"Indiana Bones," I repeat, pressing on the dent. It flexes and bounces, and I'm hopeful enough to think this just might work. "Go get him."

"Garrett. You cannot be serious right now."

"Oh, but I am."

"*Garrett!*"

"*Jennie.* Go. Get. Him."

With a face-scrunching glare and her fists balled at her sides, she stomps off toward the elevator.

She returns a few minutes later, hugging her backpack to her chest, eyes bouncing wildly around the garage. "Got him," she whispers. "Are we…um…" She thumbs at my car. "In there?"

My grin spreads slowly, and when it's at megawatt levels, I fail at containing my laughter. Jennie frowns, and I tear her backpack away, dipping my hand inside, finding the girthy fucker.

Man, this thing is fucking massive. Thick. Veiny. Firm, but with just the right amount of flop. This thing could do some damage. I give it a jiggle right here in the parking garage, and Jennie gasps, darting forward, smashing it between us when she wraps her arms around me and slams her chest against mine.

She growls at my snickering. "Stop laughing."

"I just realized how lucky I am to still have both eyes."

"Oh my God. I hate you." Indiana Bones starts buzzing, vibrating between us, and Jennie's lids flutter closed as she breathes deeply through her nose.

"Were you about to let me fuck you with this in the backseat of my car?"

"What?" She shoves away from me, nabs her monster dildo, turns off the power, and slaps him against my shoulder. "Of course not."

"Uh-huh."

She winds her braid around her fist. "So what are you…" Her mouth pops open when I sink to the ground, and when I slap the suction cup base to the dented steel, she gasps. "Garrett!"

I chuckle at the way the rubber cock hangs there, bobbing, and I flick the head. The suction on this thing is mighty as fuck, which makes sense given the size and weight of it. I wrap my fingers around it and place my foot against the bumper, gaze locking with Jennie. With a smile, I give Indiana Bones a swift tug.

I topple backward, and the dick comes with me, smacking me in the chin. Jennie's squeals echo off the walls, and a moment later she's on top of me.

"You did it," she wails, peppering my face in kisses. "Thank you, thank you, *thank you*! I love you, Garrett!" She rolls off me, fingers fluttering over the bumper before she flings herself at the car, hugging the hood.

I'm kinda stuck on those three words she just said, paired with my name, but instead of circling back around to them, I stand and tuck her dildo in her backpack. "There are some chips in the paint, but I have a guy who can fix that for you. I'll call him tomorrow."

Jennie sits in silence, staring at her brother's car. Finally, her eyes lift to mine, and the sight of them makes my heart heavy. They're foggy blue swimming pools, brimming with tears, and when she blinks, they slide down her rosy cheeks. "Thank you for helping me, Garrett."

Taking her hands in mine, I pull her to her feet, then into my arms. She buries her face in my chest and my fingers sink into her hair, tangling in her braid.

"What happened, Jennie?"

"I told you. The car—"

"Not the car." I inch back, hooking a finger beneath her chin. "What happened at school today? What made you so upset?"

Her eyes cloud over, riddled with confusion, anger, heartbreak. All I want her to do is tell me how I can fix it.

"Do you think I'm good enough to teach at The National Ballet? Or do you think I got offered the job because of Carter? Because my brother's famous? Do you think…am I boring? Am I too vanilla? I—"

"Hey." I cup her face, keeping her gaze steady on mine. "Stop spiraling. Carter has nothing to do with your job offer. I know fuck all about dance, but I know you rocked that stage on Christmas Eve. My dad gave you a standing ovation in our living room, and now all three of my sisters want to be dancers. And fucking vanilla, Jennie? Jesus Christ, you're red fucking velvet."

Her bottom lip wobbles, and her next whisper breaks my heart. "Then how come nobody wants to be my friend? Nobody is interested in getting to know me. I've never even been on a proper date. I can't remember the last time I went to the movies with anyone other than my mom."

I haven't even processed my idea before my fingers are moving, and when I put my phone to my ear, Jennie's brows pull together.

"Well, well, well," Carter hums when he answers my call. "Look who came crawling back for relationship advice."

"The last thing I need is your version of relationship advice, Carter." Jennie's eyes widen, and I keep her at bay with my palm on her chest when she tries to rip my phone away. "Hey, listen. I ran into your sister in the parking garage. She's had a bit of a shit day, and I think she could use a distraction. Mind if I take her out?"

I'm met with silence, and a moment later, the call disconnects. I think I just fucked myself, but then Jennie's pulling her ringing phone out of her pocket as her face drains of color.

"Hi, Carter." She presses her hand to her forehead and twists away, voice low. "I'm fine. Just the usual mean girl bullshit." She kicks at the curb. "No, I don't need you to come get me...Carter, I don't need you to babysit me every time something—no, I know." She sighs. "I love you too."

She tucks her phone away, and seconds later mine buzzes.

Carter: *thx 4 looking out 4 her.*

"What the hell was that?" Jennie asks, arms wide.

"C'mon, sunshine. I'm taking you on a date."

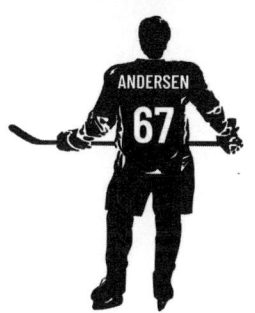

TWENTY-FOUR
WE MIGHT NEED SUPER GLUE
FOR THIS ONE

Garrett

I NEVER EXPECTED NAILING a date with Jennie Beckett with her brother's permission would be so easy.

Okay, that might be a stretch. I don't think Carter really understood what he was agreeing to. Still, I'm out in public with Jennie, alone, and I'm allowed to be.

I'm alive, and Carter has no plans to kill me.

I wish I'd had more time to plan, to really rock our first date and convince her we should do it again. Judging by the glow of wonder on Jennie's face while she takes in the atmosphere at Udupi Palace, my favorite Indian restaurant, I'd guess she's enjoying herself regardless.

I can't take my eyes off her, watching her shoulders drop with each passing moment, her small smile turning to happy, nose-scrunching giggles, her eyes rolling as she hums with each bite of food. She's a kid in a candy shop, and by the time I'm tugging her out the door, it's like her entire day never happened.

"Bye, Rudra!" she calls to our server, waving. She places one hand on her belly. "It was *so* good!"

"See you soon, Miss Jennie!"

"You hear that? See you soon?" She pokes me as we head to my car. "You have to take me back. Rudra said so."

I open the door for her. "Is that what he said?"

"Uh-huh." She grins, pressing up on her toes, and I bend my neck.

"Oops," she whispers, pausing halfway. "Forgot. No kissing in public." She tucks herself into the front seat, and her glittering eyes tells me she's finding immense pleasure in how difficult this is for me. "C'mon, Gare-Bear. Places to be."

Rules fucking suck. Not kissing her is hard, but the hardest part is not holding her hand.

It only gets harder as we ride through Stanley Park on the open-air train, cruising through the trail lit with twinkling lights. All I wanna do is pull her into my side, feel the warmth of her body spreading to mine.

"Good call on wearing my warm coat, Gare-Bear."

"Told you your pretty coat wouldn't do."

"So you're saying this one's not pretty?"

"I—what?" I nudge her side. "I'm not walking into your trap, Beckett."

Jennie chuckles softly, shifting closer, resting her arm against mine. "I wish I had a mug of your hot chocolate. You make the best kind."

"Half a bag of mini-marshmallows and a couple mouthfuls of the hot stuff?"

"Yeah." Her sigh is wistful as she stares out at the trees, the lights, the stars that dance above us. "Thank you, Garrett. This is the best date I've ever been on."

I huff a laugh. "It's the only one you've ever been on."

"Yeah, the competition is nonexistent." She slips her mitt off and carefully hooks her pinky around mine before turning her gaze back out on the way this Vancouver night glows. Then she murmurs, "I think it'd still be the best."

∽

"Can we get popcorn, Garrett?"

"We can get popcorn, Jennie."

"Can we get extra butter on the popcorn?"

"We can get extra butter on the popcorn."

Jennie spins around, eyes sparkling. "What about Skittles? I like the tropical kind. Do you want to share a drink? Maybe root beer? I haven't had it in *years*."

I chuckle, making a mental note to plan more movie dates in the future. Her happiness is contagious, and all I want to do is feed it.

My phone buzzes, and I pull it out of my pocket.

"Is that my brother again?"

"Yup." It's the fourth time he's texted tonight, and the question is the same every time.

Carter: *what r u doing now?*

If I don't respond within the first minute, he sends me exactly seven question marks, so I've learned to be quick. It helps, because if I'm replying to his texts, it means my hands aren't anywhere they're not supposed to be.

Loaded up with snacks, we hike up the stairs of the theater, finding two private seats off to the side, right next to the aisle.

We're halfway through the popcorn before the trailers are even finished, and Jennie conveniently misses the bag on her next grab, grazing my dick.

"Oops." She snickers. "Didn't see you there, big guy."

"Keep it up and we won't even make it out of the parking lot before Indiana Bones is raiding your temple, sunshine," I mumble, stuffing a handful of popcorn in my mouth. "I'll have you sprawled out over the leather while you scream for me."

Beside me, Jennie stiffens, and I'm about to apologize if I've taken it too far, but her eyes are glued to a group of guys heading up the stairs. Her hand leaves my thigh, gripping the armrest between us, and her chest lifts and falls rapidly.

I nudge her shoulder with mine. "You okay?"

She swallows as the men climb closer. "I want to go home."

"What?"

One of the guys looks our way, a slow smile spreading as he spins his backward hat to the front.

Jennie turns quickly, knocking the popcorn off my lap. "Shit. Shit."

"Hey, what's going—"

"Garrett, please." Her eyes meet mine, frantic, pleading. "I want to go home."

"Jennie fucking Beckett." The douchefuck wearing the Toronto Maple Leaf hat stops beside us, grinning down at Jennie. "Shit, it's been, what? Six years, give or take?"

She doesn't answer, just stares up at him, hands balled into fists.

"You look good. We should hang sometime. I've missed you." He laughs lowly, looking back at the screen where the previews are still playing. "You know, I always thought it'd be you up there on the big screen."

Jennie's fingernails dig into the armrest.

I don't know who this guy is, but when his gaze settles on mine, arrogant and amused, I'm about this close to punching a person I've never met before in the face. In fact, I already hate him more than Simon.

"What's up, man?" He extends a hand. "I'm Kevin."

"I don't really give a fuck who you are."

His smile falters. "What?"

"You heard me." I gesture at Jennie. "You're clearly making her uncomfortable, so you need to go."

He barks an incredulous laugh. "That's ridiculous. I'm not making you uncomfortable, Jen, am I?" When he reaches down and brushes his thumb across her chin, all I see is red. "Fuck, I always loved this mouth."

I'm out of my seat before my brain even sends the message for my feet to move, and I step in front of Jennie, shoving Kevin backward.

"Don't fucking touch her," I growl as Jennie's hand slips up the back of my hoodie, gripping a fistful of my shirt, tugging me closer. "Don't fucking talk to her. Don't even fucking *look* at her."

"Easy." Kevin's hands come up in surrender. "We go way back."

"Then there's a good fucking reason you aren't in her life anymore." I scoop up our coats, grab Jennie's hand, and pull her out of her seat. "Come near her again and you'll need your face reconstructed."

Her hand trembles in mine as I march into the parking lot, and I'm busy chanting to myself in my head about how I need to calm the fuck down. I don't want Jennie feeding off my energy right now, not when she needs to feel safe.

I all but stuff her in the passenger seat, then take a moment in the bitter, damp night air to tamp down on the urge to go back in there and knock Kevin's teeth out for whatever he did to make this wild girl question all her best parts, to stomp on her trust to the point that she's wary to ever give it out again.

Inside the car, Jennie quivers, small hands shaking on her thighs. I cover one in mine, and just like that, her body stills as she looks down at our clasped hands.

"Do you want to talk about it?" I ask. She shakes her head and I bring her knuckles to my lips. "Let's go home."

I don't know what she needs from me, but I know I want to give it to her. Snuggles on the couch? Sure. Back tickle in bed? You got it. Fuck, I'll even give her space if she asks me twice.

What I don't expect is for her to bypass my hand as it reaches for her floor in the elevator, to press for mine instead, keying in the penthouse code.

I don't expect her to kick off her shoes inside my door and look me in the eye as she unbuttons her jeans. I don't expect her to slide them over her hips and drop them to the ground before she takes my face in her cold, trembling hands and fuses our mouths together.

My hands slip under her shirt and glide over her back, pulling her against me. She sighs, tilting her head back when my mouth moves down her chin, over the columns of her throat. I hoist her up to me, winding her legs around my waist, carrying her to my bedroom.

She pulls her shirt over her head when I set her on the bed, lips parting as she watches me undress. When my knees hit the mattress and I pull her below me, a cherry red flush creeps up her chest, staining her creamy skin. My lips follow its path, feeling the heat that warms her, stoking the fire between us.

"Garrett," she whispers as I unhook her bra, sliding the straps down her shoulders. She's got the teensiest freckles dotting her skin here, barely noticeable, but I notice everything about her. I press my lips there, then nibble along her collarbone, finding the hollow spot at the base of her throat as she quivers below my touch. "I want to...I want to have sex with you."

My body stills, lips hovering on her neck, and my cock betrays me by throbbing where it rests, right against the spot she says she wants me.

But she doesn't really.

"Jennie..."

Her fingers fall from my hair, and she shifts, like she's trying to hide, like she doesn't know how badly I want her.

My hand slides along her jaw, forcing her to look at me. "Stop. If it isn't clear enough, there's nowhere else I'd rather be than inside you." My eyes move between hers, noting the uncertainty, the insecurities, the fear. "Tonight is not the night. You've had an overwhelming day, and you're feeling vulnerable, and that's okay. But I want you to want me because you actually do, because you're certain about it. I won't take something from you unless you're without a doubt ready to give it to me. And you're not, Jennie."

She pulls her bottom lip between her teeth. "But what if you get bored of me?"

"Jennie." Burying my face in her neck, I chuckle softly, then tug her lip free. "Today I used one of your dildos to fix a dent you put in your brother's car, then watched you moan over every single bite of your dinner and lick your fingers clean. Being with you is like watching my favorite TV show. I'm always on the edge of my seat, waiting to see what comes next."

She beams. "I'm your favorite?"

"My fucking favorite."

She tangles her fingers with mine. "Can you show me?"

I do, five times over, showing her all my favorite spots on her body, whispering against her skin about everything she does that makes my life better. Later, when her body curls into mine and my fingers dance down her spine, she opens her mouth and tells me what really happened earlier today.

"That's bullshit and you know it, Jennie," I say when she finishes. "You got that job offer because your teacher thinks you deserve it, not because of who your brother is, and not because you follow the rules."

She traces her name on my torso with the tip of her finger. "It's hard not to think about it when someone puts the thought in your head. I hate doubting myself."

"And in doing so, you gave Krissy exactly what she wanted. She wants you to second-guess your talent. She wants you to be as insecure as she is. Because in the end, that's what it comes down to. She's insecure and jealous."

"Do you think that's why she doesn't like me?"

I lift a shoulder. "I bet Krissy doesn't even know why she doesn't like you. Because it's got nothing to do with you and everything to do with her. She's got her own shit that needs working through."

"It makes sense. It's just...sometimes it feels like I don't fit in with anyone."

"You weren't made to fit in, Jennie. You stand out way too much to hide in the shadows."

She lays her warm cheek on my shoulder. "Thank you, Garrett."

I tickle her neck with the tip of her braid. "For what?"

"For talking to me. Listening to me. Helping me. But most of all, for trapping me in a closet and forcing me to play with you."

"I'm not sure that's quite how that went."

"The orgasms have been wonderful."

"Wonderful enough to ditch the toys?"

"Oh, Garrett." She gives me a pitying, humoring laugh, patting my chest. "Let's not get carried away. Men don't vibrate."

"Maybe not." My tongue flicks over that spot below her ear. "But real men make you vibrate."

Giggling, she snuggles into me, and soon she's sound asleep in my arms. I turn on Netflix, telling myself I'll wake her up after and walk her home. But the longer I lie here, the more unwilling I am to let her go.

She's stunning, a breathtaking masterpiece with chestnut waves tumbling out of her braid, splayed over her neck, dark lashes resting against her rosy cheekbones. I don't know what she's dreaming about, but the more her nose scrunches in her sleep, the more she sighs happily and smiles, the more I hope to God it's me.

I can't stop myself from picking my phone up and hitting that red Record button. I want to see this face exactly as it is right now, whenever I want to, and when an hour's passed, I decide to say a big ol' fuck you to the rules. I turn off the TV and settle into the darkness, pulling Jennie tighter to me.

Her hand coasts up my arm, fingers sinking into my hair. "Garrett?" she murmurs. "Do you want me to go?"

"I want you to stay."

I wait for her to argue the way she likes to, to say it's not a good idea. But instead, after a moment that seems to last forever, she shoves her leg between mine.

"Thought you said I snore."

"Nah, you're being extra cute in your sleep tonight. I took a video so I can remind myself next time you're acting like a brat."

She laughs, then stills. "A what?"

"A video. Don't worry; I hid it."

She shoots up, nearly hammering me in the face when she flings herself over me, slapping at the lamp until it floods the room with light, making me all squinty. "Delete it."

I rub my eyes with my fists. "What?"

"Delete it. Now."

"You can't see anything. It's just your face. You're doing this cute thing with your nose, all scrunchy, kinda like a bunny, and you keep smiling, and—Jesus, Jennie, watch it." Her knee narrowly misses my balls as she crawls over me. She rips my phone from the charger, swiping frantically through my photos, searching for the video.

"Where is it?" She shoves it against my chest. "Delete it. Right now."

"Okay, Jennie. I'll delete it. Calm down."

"Don't tell me to calm down." She storms around the room, snagging her underwear and fumbling her way back into them. "You don't take a video of someone without their permission, Garrett! What the fuck were you thinking?"

What was I thinking? I was thinking I wanted to feel like she was beside me the next time I'm hundreds of miles away from her. "I guess I wasn't," is the lame excuse I offer, rolling off the bed. I show her my phone as I delete the video. "There. It's gone." She pulls her shirt over her head, and I follow her into the hallway, cupping my balls, wishing I wasn't naked right now. "What are you doing?"

"Leaving."

I rub my temple, right where a headache is forming. "I thought we were gonna…you were gonna…stay?"

"We don't do sleepovers, Garrett. We have rules."

My pulse thunders in my ears as she buttons her jeans and steps into her shoes. "We don't have to have rules. We don't—we can—" *Fuck.* I tug at my hair. Here I go again. It's not that hard to have difficult conversations. I just want her to stay. I just want *her.* "Jennie—"

"This was a mistake." She mumbles the words to herself, but I hear them, and they hurt.

"Because of the video? I don't understand."

Jennie scoops up her things and flings the door open. I reach out, wrapping my fingers around her elbow.

"Wait, Jennie—"

"Don't touch me!" Her face flames, eyes piercing as she reels on me, chest heaving with each ragged inhale. Her gaze flickers as a thousand emotions pass through them, and I don't recognize a single one, except the heartbreak, the deep-seated betrayal. I may see them, but I don't understand them, not why she wears them with me. "I shouldn't have let you in. I'm better off alone."

Fury builds in my chest and bursts through my veins, fists clenching at my sides as the words sink in. She regrets this. Regrets me. Her past hurt rules her life, and I'm tired of sitting by and letting it. "That's bull-shit and you know it, Jennie. Nobody is better off alone."

I watch it all in slow motion, the way her eyes dim, the fire in them dying, replaced with an emptiness I haven't seen before, a distance that makes her feel an entire world away as she shuts down on me far worse than she ever has.

"I am," is her simple reply, right before she lets the door slam shut behind her.

"Fuck." I snap my pants up off the ground. "Fuck." I head to the kitchen and fill a glass with water, drain it quickly, then fill it again. I've gone from blissful to mindfucked in a matter of two minutes.

Done my fucking ass. She likes to be in control, to act like she calls the shots, but I refuse to let her decide this one on her own. She keeps telling herself I'm someone else, convincing herself she can't trust me, the same way she shouldn't have trusted the people who broke her.

But I'm not them.

I don't want to break her; I want to show her she's already whole. I want to be her best friend, the person she comes to when she needs help, like she did tonight. I want to be the one she opens herself up to without holding back. I want her to show me it all while I promise to keep those parts safe.

I know she's wired this way after all these years, conditioned to believe no one could ever want her for everything she brings to the table. She thinks she's safer in her bubble, keeping out the people who have the power to hurt her, but in the end, she only hurts herself more.

She's determined to keep parts of herself hidden, hell-bent on keeping me on the outside.

It's ironic, really, because on the outside is where she hates to be. Right now, she's the one putting herself there.

So maybe that's why I'm stunned when there's a knock on my door at the crack of dawn as I'm standing in my living room, watching the sun rise with a cup of coffee in my hand, my desperate attempt at curing the headache caused by the muddled mess in my brain, the utter absence of sleep as I sat on my couch and typed out fifty text messages, never sending a single one of them.

Because when I open the door, Jennie stands there in a pair of plaid sleep pants and my hoodie, thick hair weaved in her signature messy braid, draped over her shoulder, the smooth skin on her face framed by all the loose tresses that spill from it.

Her cool blue eyes are red rimmed and exhausted, shattered, and her chin quivers as she peers up at me. "I'm sorry, Garrett."

The words are fractured and hoarse, and when my arms open, she falls into them, burying her face in my shoulder as she trembles in my hold, and I know: My heart hasn't ever beat so hard for another person.

TWENTY-FIVE
SAFE LANDING

Jennie

THE DOOR HADN'T EVEN FINISHED SLAMMING behind me and I already knew I'd be back.

There hadn't been a shred of doubt in my mind as I bypassed the elevator and sprinted down the staircase, as I'd let go of the irrational anger and let the grief take over, tears spilling down my cheeks, blurring my vision for the umpteenth time.

Irrational anger because Garrett's not the person I'm angry with, nor does he deserve to be on the receiving end of it.

Grief because I'm just giving up the fucking fight here. I've lost so much, *too much*. Missed out on meaningful relationships, avoided intimate connections, tucked so many pieces of myself away for so long I've begun to forget where I've hidden them.

I'm tired of being a victim of my circumstances. I need to move forward, but I don't know how. I make strides every day with Garrett, but there are these small steps, the last few at the top of the mountain, the ones I just don't know how to climb. Each time I try, my steps are too wobbly. I tell myself to close my eyes and do it, but nothing done blindly is ever easy.

All I know is this right here—my face buried in his chest, his arms wound around me, his soothing voice in my ear telling me everything will be okay—feels like exactly where I'm meant to be.

Garrett's my solid and my steady. He's the constant in my life, the smile always waiting for me, the friendship that never wanes, the connection that grows stronger each day. He's the warm arms that hug me, the fingers that drift down my back, the quiet voice that eases my worries at the end of the day and promises to be my safe place to land.

And that's why I knew I'd be back. That's why I spent my night weaving through periods of broken sleep, pacing my living room, curled up on my couch, waiting for sunrise so I could come back, ask him to listen.

The bags under his heavy, bleary eyes say he got as much sleep as I did, that I could've come back at any time and he would've been here, waiting, ready.

He's always ready; I'm the one that takes too many steps backward instead of forward.

Garrett's large hands bracket my face, pushing my hair off my cheeks. His blue-green eyes are full of compassion, patience, more than I ever thought I'd find. When the pad of his thumb brushes my bottom lip, I sink into his touch.

"Thank you for coming back."

"I'm sorry I yelled at you."

"You're allowed to have feelings, Jennie, and it's okay if that feeling is anger."

"But it's not you who I'm mad at."

He sweeps my braid over my shoulder and kisses my forehead. "Will you come in and tell me who you're mad at?"

There's a tightness between my shoulder blades that's been there since yesterday. It started with Krissy and eased with Garrett, but the moment I spotted Kevin climbing the steps in the theater, it came roaring back. Krissy and Kevin are one and the same, the type of people who thrive on making others feel small and insignificant. I like to live my life loud and proud, but when they're around, all I find myself doing is curling into myself, hoping to disappear.

Garrett takes my hand, giving it a gentle squeeze, a reminder of the answer he's waiting for. When I nod, he leads me to the couch and drapes a blanket over me, before promising he'll be right back. When he returns, it's with the swankiest mug of hot chocolate I've ever seen, topped with whipped cream, crushed candy cane, and blue marshmallows shaped like snowflakes.

I wrap my hands around the steaming mug. "You're really stepping up your hot chocolate game."

"You have the effect on me," he murmurs. "Making me want to be better."

"You don't need to be better. You're already the best person I know."

"And I feel the same way about you, but I get the feeling that's not how you feel about yourself. Not about some things, at least." He stretches his arm across the back of the couch, angling himself toward me. "You don't need to change anything about yourself to get someone like Krissy to like you, Jennie. You're so much better than people like that."

It's something about me that doesn't make sense. Not to people like Garrett who know me, and not to myself. I'm not a follower. I'm perfectly fine to carve my own path, and I don't want to give up my personality to fit in with anybody. So why do I crave acceptance so much?

"I think I just want to feel like I have a space in this world, people that love me for me."

"But you do," Garrett argues.

"Not really. Everyone who's important in my life came through Carter."

"So? I mean, I get it. But finding them because they found Carter first doesn't mean they don't love you for everything you are. I know for a fact Olivia and Cara feel so lucky to have you. Do you doubt that?"

I think back on the way Olivia cried over my job offer, the thought of me moving across the country. How, just like my mom, she wants me to follow my dreams but wishes I could do so right here, next to her, our family. I think about Cara, so easily swayed to keep our secret from not only Carter but her own husband. The way she gave my hand a squeeze and whispered *as long as you're happy* in my ear before she danced back to the party.

"They got two Becketts for the price of one, Jennie, and so did I. We all love you for the person you are, not for who your brother is. I'm sorry anybody ever made you feel like all you brought to the table was being Carter's sister. That's simply not true."

I take a sip of my hot chocolate to let his words settle, to feel the love he says is there, to let myself believe it. When I move the mug away, Garrett chuckles.

"What?" I swipe at the corner of my mouth. "Whipped cream?"

His palm curves around my neck, hauling me closer, and his lips touch the tip of my nose. When he pulls back, his tongue flicks out, licking the whipped cream from his lips. He sits back, patient, waiting, smiling.

I take a deep breath and jump.

"Kevin was my boyfriend in high school." My *only* boyfriend. "I don't even know why I liked him. Maybe I was being shallow. He was cute, popular, and the captain of our football team. Everybody loved him. I thought I was so special when he started pursuing me. It was shortly after my dad died, and I think…maybe I was missing some of the love I'd lost. Everything was hard. My mom was barely functioning, and Carter was hardly in the country. I knew I wasn't alone, but I felt that way a lot of the time. Kevin made me feel seen, and he cared about me." I swallow the lump in my throat. "Or he acted like he did."

Garrett's jaw flexes, fists clenching. He's thinking the same thing Carter did—that Kevin was taking advantage of me, the way my grief rocked me to my core. I can see it now clear as day, but I couldn't then. Carter and I got in too many fights about it to even recall.

"Kevin wanted to have sex, but I wanted to wait. I didn't feel ready, and I was intimidated. He was experienced, and he'd even been with some of the girls in older grades. He said he was okay with waiting, but it didn't stop him from asking me every single time we were alone. By the time senior year rolled around, all I felt was pressure. Pressure to skip classes, to drink with my friends, to have sex like everyone else, to just…fit in."

A sharp pit of pain roots deep in my chest, each breath shallower than the last. Garrett's fingertips skim the back of my neck, easing the tension enough for me to breathe.

"Kevin started dropping hints that he was getting bored, that he could go somewhere else to get what he wanted. The me now would've told him to go fuck himself and get lost, but the me back then was too afraid to be alone. He had a big party one night while his parents were away, and everyone was pressuring me to drink."

Fire flashes in Garrett's eyes, angrier than I've ever seen, and I don't blame him. I was and still am within my right to decline alcohol. Nobody needs an excuse to avoid it, but that alcohol stole my dad from me was more than enough of a reason. That my friends didn't respect this should've been enough of a red flag.

But the worst part of all?

"It was a couple days after the anniversary of my dad's death. Carter was on a ten-day road trip, and I was just...*struggling*. I was tired. I wanted to forget." Garrett slips an arm around my waist, tugging me into his side, and I lay my head on his shoulder. "I don't know what I drank. It smelled like gasoline and burned like fire. I went upstairs with Kevin, and we were fooling around on his bed, and I told him I wanted to have sex."

"You didn't want to," Garrett speaks for the first time. He looks at me, a soft understanding that coasts my face. "You didn't want to have sex. You just wanted to feel something else. And he took advantage of you feeling that way."

Many years separate Garrett now and Kevin then, but this man beside me is exactly that—a man. A *real* man. What I felt last night is what I felt all those years ago. I wanted to feel anything other than the anger, the hurt, the betrayal, so I offered up the last bit of my body to Garrett in hopes he'd take those feelings away, help me feel something else.

And he said no.

He saw my struggle and instead of taking something he wanted, he gave me what I needed. Patience, compassion, connection. With one simple action, he reinforced what I already knew: that I could trust him.

"It felt like it went on forever. He said he wanted me to feel good. At the time, I thought it was sweet, that he just wanted to make sure my first time was pleasurable."

My throat constricts, and my eyes sting with tears begging to fall. I don't want to let them. I've given Kevin far too many.

"It started to feel good. I was..." Heat floods my face, clawing its way to the tips of my ears. "Getting vocal. Making noises." My vision blurs and Garrett presses his lips to the crown of my head. "He flipped me over suddenly and right before he pushed back inside me, he told me...he told me to scream for them."

"Them?"

Tears tip over the edge of my lids and free-fall down my cheeks as I'm flooded with memories, as I tell Garrett about the way the door to Kevin's bedroom sprung open just as I called his name, how half of the

248 | BECKA MACK

football team stood on the other side, phones pointed at us while they laughed and cheered Kevin on while he finished. The way Kevin smacked my ass when he was done, told me it was no big deal, how he left me there to clean myself up, and then watched me leave while he stood in his kitchen, drinking beer and laughing with his friends.

I slap at my cheeks, trying to swipe my tears away, but it's no use. They keep falling as I tell him how Kevin wouldn't return my calls the next day, how I walked through the halls at school on Monday and listened to my own moans being played back to me from everyone's phones, how I found my boyfriend standing at his locker with his arm around my best friend, all the people I had considered friends surrounding them, laughing at me.

"I lost my virginity, my boyfriend, my friends, and everything else that mattered in one night. He took everything from me, Garrett, worst of all, my pride." The words are strangled as I rub my eyes, and Garrett pulls me tight to him. "By Monday night, there were videos all over the internet. You couldn't see my body, but you could hear...*everything*. Carter Beckett's little sister's sex tape," I murmur, remembering the headlines of the gossip articles, the ones Carter's PR team still works to take down every now and again when they pop up.

"I told you it'd been years since I'd had sex. What I didn't tell you was it only happened once. I wanted to." God, how I wanted to. So badly, I craved an intimate connection. "But I was too scared. Too scared to trust someone again. I let him steal that from me."

Garrett curses under his breath, fingertips biting into my skin. "I should've put him through the fucking floor."

"Carter took care of him. He flew home the next morning, stormed through the parking lot at school, found Kevin standing around his car, and didn't stop until I begged him to."

Carter is a lot of things, but he's the best brother anyone could ask for. As soon as his eyes met mine, when he found me sobbing, needing him, his entire face softened. He stood up, broke the phone of the person nearby who was videotaping, gave Kevin one final warning, then wrapped me in his arms and took me home.

"I finished the semester, took my exams, and never went back. Carter sent me and my mom on a long trip, and the next fall I finished my diploma online. That's why I'm a year behind. I should've finished my degree last year, but I needed time. Time I probably should've taken after my dad passed, rather than throwing myself into a relationship that left me feeling empty, like a shell of the person I had once been so proud to be."

"Are you proud of who you are now?"

"I want to be, but sometimes I'm not even sure who that is anymore."

Garrett smiles gently. "I know who you are, Jennie. You're a dedicated friend, sister, and dancer. You're hardworking, competitive, and you always strive to be better than you were the day before. You're committed and loyal to the people you care about, even though not everyone has been loyal to you. You're sassy and sarcastic, and you don't hesitate to clap back most of the time, shut everyone up and put us all in our place."

He picks up a wayward lock of hair, letting it slip between his fingers before he tucks it behind my ear, letting his knuckles graze my cheekbone.

"But you have a quiet side too. A side that craves downtime, that likes to snuggle in bed and whisper about the best and worst parts of your days. You overanalyze everything because you think about every possible ending. You hate that you do, but you care too much about what people who don't matter think about you. You have a big heart, and you cry at every single Disney movie, even the parts that aren't sad, because all that love hits you hard. You're a secret softie, but you like everyone to think you're a little bit scary, that you're unshakable.

"But here's the thing, Jennie. You don't have to be strong and confident all the time. You're allowed to have insecurities, to be afraid, to feel lonely. Those things don't make you weak; they make you human."

His thumb traps a tear that drips down my cheek. "I hope you're proud of yourself, but if you're not, know that I am. I've watched you take step after step, learning to trust me and open up to me even though everything inside you probably begs you not to." His eyes rake over me, like they're cataloging every passing emotion. "I'm sorry somebody was so careless with your heart. Thank you for trusting me with this."

I fiddle with a loose string on the hem of his shirt. "Sometimes my brain tells me not to trust you, but I'm learning not to listen to it."

He captures my chin, forcing my gaze back to his. "I'm not like them. I care about you, and when you're hurting, I'm hurting. So whatever I need to do to show you that you can trust me, I'll do it. I want you to feel safe with me, Jennie."

I look at the way our fingers lace together, and I know without a doubt I've never felt safer than I do with him. "I do feel safe with you. That's why I came back. I wanted to share this with you. But that doesn't mean putting my trust in someone new is easy. It's scary, not knowing how this ends, the thought that I might get hurt again."

He squeezes my hand, smiling tenderly. "Blind leap of faith? Promise I'll catch you."

"Honestly? It doesn't feel so blind right now."

The pad of his thumb skates across my bottom lip. "I know your walls are there for a reason. All I ask is that every once in a while you let me in and show me around. I'll hold your hand while you do it, and I promise I won't let go."

In lieu of words I can't find, I climb onto his lap and wrap my arms around his neck, snuggling into him as his hand runs up and down my back.

This entire time I've been thinking I can't have him. That this is temporary. Garrett's empathy, his unending patience with me, it's something I'm not used to finding. I may be scared to let people in, but he's the only person who's stayed long enough, tried hard enough to wiggle in.

I don't know how or why, but something inside me settles when I'm with him. I remember who I am, not who I tell myself I need to be. So would it be foolish of me to want to try? To see if this, us…if we could work? Would he want that? Would he be willing to try?

The question is on the tip of my tongue, but the insecurities and fears that don't disappear overnight, the exhaustion stealing every ounce of my energy, they keep me from asking. The last thing I remember before my eyes close is Garrett's lips at my ear as he promises I'm safe with him.

I'm not sure how long I've been asleep when I wake to his fingers fluttering over my cheek, coaxing my heavy lids open. I find his gentle smile waiting for me as he crouches in front of me.

"I'm sorry to wake you." He frowns, like he's not sure of his next words. "Your brother's on the way over."

My eyes shut again with a groan. My head is in agony, desperate for rest. I can't handle Carter's worries today.

Garrett's thumb sweeps the sensitive skin below my eyes. "It's okay. There were a couple pictures of what happened at the theater yesterday. Carter called because you weren't answering."

"I didn't bring my phone. What did you say?"

"I was honest." He shrugs. "As honest as I could be without risking my balls, at least. I told him what happened, that we left and you went home upset. I said you came back this morning because you needed someone to talk to, and you fell asleep afterward. All he cares about is you, Jennie. He wanted to make sure you were safe. I told him you were still here, and he said he was on his way."

"If he knows I was sleeping, then I can go back to sleep, right?"

"You sure can, sunshine." His eyes drop to his hand as he plays with the strings of his hoodie, the one I'm still wearing. "You can keep it on if you want."

I want to, but I can't, so I let Garrett peel it off, leaving me in my T-shirt before he tucks the blanket back around my shoulders.

I grip his shirt, tugging him back to me. "Kiss me, please."

He does, long and deep, warm hands on my face before he whispers a "Sweet dreams" against my lips and pulls away.

It's not long before knocking on the door wakes me.

Knocking is the wrong word. It starts that way but quickly spirals to slapping and knob-jiggling, Carter's irritating voice chanting, "Gare. Gare. Gare."

I direct my brain to sleep through this, ignore the onslaught of questions. But even without seeing him, his presence is overpowering.

"Where is she? Is she okay?"

"She's okay," Garrett whispers. "She's sleeping still."

"What did he say?" Carter demands. "Did he fucking touch her?"

I tune out the conversation, but my eyes flutter open when a pair of soft hands land on my face, and Olivia's smiling face comes into view.

"Hi. I brought you a cinnamon bun cappuccino."

I manage to sit up, rubbing at my eyes with my fists. "You came with Carter? Why?"

A flash of hurt dances in her dark eyes. "Because you're my sister, one of my best friends, and I love you. If you're hurting, I don't want you to do it alone." Her arms come around me, a suffocating, wonderful hug. "We're stronger together, Jennie."

My heart thumps at the promise, the love, and I jump when her stomach kicks against mine. I pull back, looking at her round belly. "Holy shit. What the fuck was that?"

Olivia smiles. "Your niece or nephew saying hi to their aunt."

"Are you fucking kidding me?" Carter whines, marching across the living room. "Jennie felt him move?"

"Or her," Olivia mutters. "Baby Beckett loves Auntie Jennie."

I squeeze her hands. "Thank you for coming."

Carter sweeps me off the couch and crushes me against his chest, my feet dangling above the floor. "I'm sorry I wasn't there for you."

"I'm okay," I remind him, the words muffled by his shoulder. "Garrett was there."

"It should've been me."

Carter was born a protector. It's part of what makes him a good leader, an amazing captain. His team is his family, and he won't let anybody touch them. It also makes him an incredible brother, even if a little—or a lot—overbearing at times.

But when our dad passed, when Carter put taking care of me and my mom above taking care of himself, and when my boyfriend and friends broke my heart? It pushed him to a whole new level. He struggles with guilt, believing he failed at protecting me, and now he's hell-bent on keeping me safe from heartache.

I get it, I really do. But he couldn't protect me then, and he can't protect me now. Hearts break and people get hurt. It's inevitable, and it's unrealistic for him to think he might be able to keep me safe forever.

But now, as I meet Garrett's stare over Carter's shoulder, I'm painfully aware that there's one heartbreak I never want to experience, one person I never want to lose, and right now, he's wearing a gentle, patient smile all for me.

So do I keep allowing fear to tighten its grip on me, to control my life?

Or do I take Garrett's hand and ask him to jump with me?

TWENTY-SIX
THE GREEN-EYED MONSTER

Jennie

"I'M GONNA VOMIT."

"You are not. Quit being dramatic."

"I am. I'm gonna do it." I'm not lying.

"If she doesn't, I will." Olivia places one hand on her stomach, the other over her mouth. Her face pales right on time, and Cara rolls her eyes, yanking her candy dish into her stomach.

To be fair, Olivia might actually vomit. She's been on this pregnancy health kick lately, but we went for lunch earlier and she kinda said *fuck it* and threw it all out the window. She had a platter of tacos and a basket of chili cheese fries. She's been moaning and groaning for hours now.

"There's nothing wrong with my snack." Cara sticks her hand inside, grabs a whole-ass handful of Skittles and M&M's, and dumps them—together—into her mouth. "It's de-wish-us."

Olivia gags, lurching forward, and I gather her hair at the nape of her neck and rub her back. She's become such a good actor since becoming a Beckett. I'm so proud of my Pip-squeak.

With another exaggerated eye roll, Cara hauls her candy to the kitchen. "You guys fucking suck. If you'd just try it, you'd like—"

"Absolutely not." I release Olivia's hair and sink back, picking up my plate of Pop-Tarts. Garrett left me a box of my favorite kind before he left: Frosted Hot Fudge Sundae.

Cara lifts a brow at me from where she shovels her snack into her mouth at the island. "We don't have that flavor here, Jennie. That's exclusive to the States."

I hum around my bite.

"You know who always has fun flavors of Pop-Tarts?" This handful isn't big enough to hide her shit-eating smirk. "Garrett. Yeah, gets them sent special from Adam's mom."

"Really? Wow. I've never met Adam's mom. Is she as sweet as he is? Sounds like it." *Deflection: A+.* Cara opens her mouth, but I shove a snack between my teeth and point at the TV. "Boys are on."

Cara sinks beside me with an acceptable snack, and Olivia snuggles into my side as the boys start zipping around the ice, warming up for their game.

It takes Olivia approximately ten seconds to go from snuggly to growly, shoveling popcorn into her mouth while she mutters beneath her breath, scowling at the TV.

"What are you on about, Pip?" I ask, stealing a queso-covered nacho chip from Cara.

Olivia gestures wildly at the TV. "Look at them! Damn vultures. Swoop right in."

"Who swoops in?" I answer my own question when the camera pans over the half-dressed women shaking their signs behind the glass.

Beckett, show me a hat trick and I'll show you a sex trick!

You can put it in my 5-hole, #87!

My nose scrunches with disgust. "Ew. Don't worry; he's not paying them any attention." In fact, he skates over to one of the cameras at board level, and when he stops there to talk to it, the camera on the TV switches to that feed.

"Hi, princess!" he shouts from behind the glass. "Miss you!" He skates away with a wink, and Olivia's entire face lights, body humming happily.

"See? Nothing to worry about. We didn't even have to fly to Montreal so you could bump 'em with your belly and show 'em who's boss."

"Oh look." Cara grips my forearm. "Garrett's got his own fan section tonight too."

I hate the way my head whips and the frantic "What?" that leaves my lips. But worst of all? I dropped my nacho chip.

My eyes trail the rink on TV, and I find Garrett without hesitation. He's tall and broad as he floats around the ice, right before he crashes into Carter from behind, shoving him into the boards. It's followed quickly by Emmett crushing both of them to the boards and Adam dog-piling on top when they sink to the ice, and I'm too annoyed with the group of women two rows up to find it cute.

Marry me, Andersen!

Can I handle your stick, G Baby?

"Stupid. Those are stupid signs. They're not even creative." I nab the pack of Swedish Berries off the coffee table, tear it open, and dump half the contents into my mouth. "Handle his stick? Whatever. What does that even mean? Handle his stick." I snort. "Whatever."

"You've said that twice," Cara murmurs.

"No I haven't."

"You did, actually," Olivia observes, eye cocked as she examines me.

I shake my head, looking back to the TV. Terrible timing; one of the women has made her way down to the boards, and my brother seems to be facilitating conversation between her and Garrett.

"Pee." I rocket to my feet. "I have to pee. In the toilet. Excuse me." I'm turning into the man who fingerbangs me straight to heaven. Highly embarrassing.

I stay in there for five minutes, until I'm sure I'm safe to return. When I do, I glue on my best carefree smile, pick up my plate of Pop-Tarts, and squeeze myself back between my friends, both of whom steal a Pop-Tart from my tray.

"Tell Garrett thanks for the Pop-Tarts."

It's not Cara who says it. It's Olivia.

"I'm hot."

"We love a self-aware queen," Cara murmurs into my hair. "Yes, Jennie, you're gorgeous."

"No, I mean, physically I feel like I'm on fire."

I'm currently sandwiched between two women—one tiny and pregnant, the other tall and lanky—who have decided to make me their bedtime bitch for the night. Those were Cara's words. Olivia told me she simply missed snuggling with her husband. She'd already told me she hadn't been sleeping well without Carter, and the dark circles under her eyes were proof.

So when she held up a pair of pajamas, gave me that pouty face, and asked me to stay the night, I couldn't say no. Cara said if Olivia got to sleep with someone, so did she. Now here we are, the three of us snuggled together in one outrageously large bed, after a FaceTime call with Carter, Garrett, Emmett, Adam, and Jaxon that lasted way too long and had Carter asking Olivia to sneak off alone to the bathroom once, and Cara and Emmett *actually* sneaking off.

"It's me," Olivia says on a sigh. "I'm hot all the time. I'm like a furnace. I can't turn it off." She pops up on her elbow, eyes dancing in the moonlight. "Hey, remember when Carter bought me a furnace when we started dating because mine was broken and he didn't want me to be cold?"

"He's so ostentatious."

"He does love his big gestures. But he's so thoughtful." Another sigh, this one happy, and Olivia flops back down on the mattress and shoves one leg between mine, snuggling closer and upping my body temperature another ten degrees. "You Becketts are the very best at snuggling."

The full, content feeling that hums in my chest makes me smile. "Cara, I wouldn't have expected you to be so snuggly."

"Oh, I'm a sprawler. Yeah, I like to get right on top of Emmett and just give up for the night. Can't tell you how many times that guy's woken up with his head tangled between my legs, and not for the right reasons."

I snicker, and my mind coasts to Garrett. I've fallen asleep wrapped around him countless times, woken up in the middle of the night to his head between my legs for the *right* reasons. But without fail, I wake up alone each morning, trying to remember the way his warm body felt locked around mine, the feel of his fingertips drifting over my back, his lips sliding along my shoulder.

My forever has been a lonely one so far. I hadn't realized the weight of the emptiness until Garrett filled it so effortlessly, lifting everything heavy off my shoulders, my chest, letting me stand taller and breathe deeper.

The night is quiet and still around us, the soft sound of steady breathing in my ear, the gentle rise and fall of chests on either side of me, and I sit in the silence, the love, basking in it.

A pair of arms squeeze around me, and when I open my eyes, I find Olivia's dark ones gazing sleepily at me.

"What's up, Pip?"

"I don't want you to leave," she whispers, and there's something heavy and vulnerable in her voice, something on the verge of broken. "I don't want you to go to Toronto when you graduate, and I feel so selfish for that." The moonlight streaking through the balcony doors slices across the single tear that peels away across the bridge of her nose. "I want you to be successful, and most of all, I want you to be happy. But, God, I don't want you to have to leave to do it."

I think Cara's asleep, but she tangles her fingers with mine. "We'll always be together, no matter where we are. But it's always a bonus when we don't have to be far."

And maybe forever doesn't need to be lonely. It sure doesn't feel that way with these people surrounding me.

Cara had this fun idea.

I use the word *fun* loosely, of course.

She woke us up this morning by ripping us apart, grinning down at us like some sort of deranged convict who'd just found her next victims.

Let's make the boys work for us, she'd said with a maniacal giggle.

Apparently, that meant getting dressed up, leaving the house right before the boys landed so that they returned to an empty house instead of a full one where we were supposed to be waiting to welcome them home after a long stretch apart.

I don't mind. I've got a full belly, I'm wearing a kick-ass pair of scarlet, heeled booties, and I look fine as fuck in these jeans, my waves spilling down my back. I can't wait to see Garrett's reaction.

When they eventually locate us, that is.

The other part of Cara's plan involved sending them video clues in our group chat as we made our way around the city. They've been chasing after us, and it's been significantly entertaining reading their excited texts when they realize where we are, only to have it followed by a fuckton of swearing when they find we've already moved on. We've been at least two steps ahead of them the entire night.

Now I'm in the middle of the dance floor at Sapphire, sweaty as fuck as I spin around it, a tiny pregnant woman dancing more than I've ever seen—she's riding a *wild* sugar high from dessert—and Cara's double-fisting her martinis.

Even with all the noise, it's impossible to miss the chatter that starts, the small frenzy that suddenly ensues, and when a wicked smirk breaks across Cara's face, I know: they're here.

She shoves her martinis into Olivia's hands and points at a handsome, dark-haired man. "You. Dance with me."

His eyes double in size. "O-okay."

She snuggles into his chest and slides his hands over her hips as they start swaying together, and the poor guy looks like he's in heaven.

He might be in thirty seconds. Emmett looks like he's gonna put him through the floor.

The broad teddy bear of a man comes to a stop in front of them, staring down at his smiling wife. His fists clench and he flicks his gaze toward the man holding Cara. "Hands off my wife. *Now.*"

He drops Cara like she's on fire, sprinting off the dance floor, and I snicker-snort as Emmett scoops her up, tosses her over his shoulder, and carts her off toward the private booths in the back.

Hot breath kisses my neck, a shiver of anticipation dancing down my spine. "You're about to be next, somewhere a fuckload more private, and with my handprint tattooed on your ass. So if I were you, I'd quit laughing." There's a quick, sharp slap to my left ass cheek before Garrett struts by me, turns around, and calls out, "Found 'em!"

"Ollie!" Carter skids onto the dance floor, breathless. He looks down at Olivia, his gaze heating by the moment. "Ollie," he murmurs. "Baby, you look fucking—"

"You fuckers." Adam wraps me in a hug, smothering a compliment I don't need to hear. "You had us all over the city."

"It was Cara's idea," I say, hugging Jaxon next. "We're just the innocent bystanders."

Jaxon unbuttons his collar, eyes coasting over the club. "And I appreciate it." He grins down at me. "I need to blow off some steam tonight."

"Assuming that's code for get laid?"

That grin keeps growing, and he holds his hand out. "Wanna dance?"

I meet Garrett's narrowed gaze over his shoulder. "Love to."

Tattooed, my big guy mouths before I disappear with Jaxon.

I've grown to like Jaxon, and it hasn't taken much. Is he still a bit of an egotistical ass? Yes. Is he exceptionally horny? Who isn't? But he's friendly and easy, and there's something quiet about him that keeps me talking to him. Maybe it's because I've always felt a bit like the outsider within this group, and when he came along, he felt it too. He was accepted without hesitation, the same way I was, but sometimes I wonder if he questions his place here, the same as me.

"Does Andersen look pissed to you? He looks pissed to me."

Garrett has one elbow on the bar as he sips a sparkling lemon water, stare set on us. But does he look pissed? He looks like he's going to take what he wants as many times as he wants tonight before he finally gives me what *I* want; that's how he looks. Either way, sounds like a great night. Can't wait.

"You know what else I've noticed about that guy?" Jaxon brings my attention back to him. "He drinks when we're on road trips and stuff, or if the guys go out together, but whenever you're around, he only drinks sparkling water."

I've noticed, too, though we've not once talked about it since that night we shared our first kiss. Garrett never touches a drop when we're together, even if we're out with everyone else. He used to have a six-pack stowed in his fridge, but now it's hot chocolate or bust. Come to think of it, I can't remember the last time I've seen a beer bottle there.

"He's a supportive friend," is what I tell Jaxon.

"Yeah, he's a pretty good guy." The song ends, and Jaxon takes my hand, leading me off the dance floor. "Even if he does look like he wants to murder me. Maybe Cara was right."

"Right about what?"

"That he's got a crush on you. She said so on New Year's Eve."

I stumble over my own two feet, and a large hand lands on my lower back, catching me. Garrett steadies me, then guides me into our private booth, sliding in behind me.

Jaxon arches a brow, looking between us.

"There's something seriously wrong with you if you believe everything that woman says," Garrett finally says. He nods in the direction of the woman in question, who happens to be in her husband's lap, hands in his hair, tongue in his mouth. "C'mon, Riley."

Jaxon chuckles, shaking his head as he takes a seat across from us. "Fuck, yeah, you're right. Cara can't be trusted."

Cara flashes her middle finger over her shoulder.

Carter, Adam, and Olivia join us a moment later, Carter with a tray of various drinks and a food menu—priorities—and Adam half supporting a quickly failing Olivia. She looks to be both coming down from her sugar high and regretting her decision to wear heels.

An hour later, I haven't moved from my spot, and I'm having the time of my life. It's perhaps partly due to the unholy amount of sexual frustration rolling off the man next to me as he reads each text I send him without being able to outwardly react.

> **Me:** *Should I ride Indiana Bones tonight, or your face?*
> **Me:** *God, I can't stop thinking about your tongue on my pussy. I love when you make me your meal.*
> **Me:** *Maybe we can try that little glass plug tonight while I suck your cock.*
> **Me:** *If you slipped your hand between my legs right now, you'd find out how wet I am.*

Garrett's fist clenches so hard around his glass, I'm worried it might shatter. He sets it down and furiously types out a response.

> **Bear:** *How wet are you, sunshine? Don't leave out any details and I'll go easy on you tonight.*
> **Me:** *What if I don't want you to go easy on me, big guy?*
> **Bear:** *How. Wet. Are. You?*
> **Me:** *So drenched, you'd be able to slide right in.*

Garrett leaps to his feet, accidentally shoving Adam out of the booth. "Bathroom!" he shouts. "Gotta go. Pee. Bye. See ya."

I suppress my laugh as he dashes off, and the rest of the guys follow to grab more drinks. They're not gone more than thirty seconds when a tall, lean man with dark curls approaches, his deep brown eyes friendly and set on me. Nerves pull at my skin, and I cross one leg over the other, busying myself with my drink.

"Hi there," he says, stopping at the edge of the booth. "I'm—"

"Oh my God!" Olivia comes alive, clapping her hands. "You're Alejandro Perez!" She squeals, fists shaking beneath her chin. "Jennie, he's the—"

"Midfielder from the Vancouver Whitecaps," Alejandro finishes, laughing.

"So sorry. I'm fangirling a bit. I played soccer growing up and—"

"Soccer?" Cara sips her drink. "Thank God. You said midfielder and I was like, 'I haven't heard of that hockey position before. Which one of our guys plays it?'"

Alejandro's still grinning. He's got a great one, wide and toothy, but it's not goofy and lopsided like Garrett's. He holds his hand out, and I slip mine in simply because I don't know what else to do. "And who are you?"

"Jennie," I answer quietly, meeting Garrett's curious gaze as he approaches.

"Excuse me." He steps between me and Alejandro, sliding in next to me, extra close.

"Oh." Alejandro examines the proximity of our bodies. "Are you two…?"

I look at Garrett. He looks at me. It's Cara who answers the question.

"No, our Jennie here is single as a Pringle. Isn't that right, Gare-Bear?"

Garrett's gaze lingers before he drops it, sipping his water, and I don't know why, but when he murmurs, "Right," my stomach dips, heavy with disappointment.

"Cool." Alejandro extends his hand. "Hey, you're Garrett Andersen, right? Right-winger for the Vipers? I'm a big fan."

Garrett shakes his hand, giving him a smile that seems a little tight to me. "Right back 'atcha. The guys and I already have tickets for your home opener."

"Right on. We should grab some drinks afterward." Before Garrett can respond, Alejandro turns his attention back to me. I shift in my seat, not wanting it, not used to it. "And I was hoping to buy you a drink right now, Jennie."

"Oh…" Uncomfortable heat prickles my neck. "I don't drink."

"Water counts just fine."

"Yeah, Jennie," Cara pipes up. "Water counts just fine."

I flash her a warning look, and she folds her lips into her mouth. Olivia's watching me with an indecipherable expression, gaze flickering to Garrett, who feels like ice beside me. I don't want him to feel like ice; I like when he's warm like sunshine.

I clear my throat, steel my spine, and smile up at Alejandro. "Thank you for the offer, but I'm not interested."

"Not interested in general, or not interested in me?"

My eyes coast the bar for something to say to shut this down quickly. I catch sight of the boys returning with drinks, my brother leading the way with what looks like an extremely ostentatious helping of blue and pink cotton candy sitting atop a glass of champagne, and I can guess that's the only reason he ordered it. "Truth be told, I'm not really looking to expand my pool of professional athletes. I've already got an over-protective one on retainer as my big brother."

"Ollie, look! This drink came with cotton candy!" Carter shoves said cotton candy in her face, then rips a piece off and eats it. His eyes widen when he sees Alejandro. "Oh hey! Perez!"

Alejandro looks from Carter to me. "Jesus, you two are nearly identical. How did I miss that?"

Carter sits with a chuckle. "Yeah, Jennie gets her strikingly good looks from me."

I may not want Alejandro's attention, but when he pulls up a chair next to Carter and everyone becomes quick friends, a strange sense of disappointment washes over me, mixed with déjà vu.

I had his attention, and now Carter does, and that's just the way life goes when your brother is the captain of an NHL team.

Forcing my drink to my lips, I take a sip, the fingers of my free hand playing with my soggy napkin in my lap. A big hand covers mine, pulling the napkin free and setting it on the table. A second later, Garrett tucks his pinky carefully around mine, and something inside me settles.

I've got the only attention I want.

Forty-five minutes, several dirty texts, one dance with Adam, two with Cara, and a virgin cotton candy drink later, I'm hiding out in the bathroom. It's becoming impossible not to look at Garrett, and his pinky hooked around mine below the table isn't enough anymore. I'm hot and hungry, dying to get out of here and go home, where we can finally say a proper hello.

I pat my neck with a cool, damp cloth and sigh before heading out into the dark hallway.

Strong fingers wrap around my wrist, tugging me into a hidden alcove. My pulse thunders, a fiery heat spreading through my lower belly as my back is pressed to a hard, broad chest. A warm hand dips below the hem of my shirt, gliding over my torso. Soft lips touch my exposed shoulder.

"You have goose bumps," Garrett whispers.

"Because you scared the crap out of me, you dink." The words end in a moan when his mouth opens on my neck. When his name slips out of my mouth on a whimper, his hand covers it.

"Shh, sunshine. Make any more noise and I won't be able to get what I came over here for, and I gotta tell ya, I can't wait another minute." He captures my jaw in his hand, turning my face to his, showing me the hungry darkness that glints in his eyes.

And then his mouth takes mine.

It's everything I want it to be: starved, possessive, wet, *hot*. God, it's so hot. But more than that, it's…wistful. Yearning. *Reverent.*

He missed me. Maybe as much as I missed him.

As if to prove my point, he pulls back, resting his forehead against mine with a gentle sigh. "I miss you." Present tense, not past.

I thread our fingers together. "I'm right here."

"I know, but I've been busy with hockey, and you with dance and smelly Simon. I'm just grumpy 'cause I feel like I'm on time-out."

"Well then, you must've been a bad boy."

"So bad," he murmurs, mouth taking mine again with a low growl. He pushes me against the wall and casts a glance over his shoulder before his fingers dance up my front, wrapping lightly around my throat. "I'm gonna take you home and fuck your soaking wet pussy with Indiana Bones. Then I'm gonna lick you clean and make you come all over again, this time on my tongue."

Oh, *Jesus.*

"Got it?"

I swallow, nodding, and a deep ache settles between my legs as Garrett trails his nose down my neck, then back up to my ear.

"Use your words, sunshine. I know you have them."

My tongue drags across my lips, desperate to taste him again. "Yes."

"Good girl." He presses himself against me, letting me feel the weight of his own need. "Now, let's go back to the table and you can pretend like you hate me still."

"You like when I pretend to hate you."

"Yeah." He pops a quick kiss to my cheek, then stuffs his hand down his pants to adjust that glorious lump, hissing. "It turns me on when you're sassy to me."

I giggle, but it doesn't last.

In fact, it dies quickly when my eyes meet those wide hazel ones watching us.

Jaxon stands before us, gaze pinballing between Garrett and me, jaw getting closer and closer to the ground. He grins suddenly, but it's one of those terrified, awkward ones, all bright, clenched teeth.

"Uh..." He clears his throat and claps his fist into his opposite hand. "So, um, I heard that..."

"Oh no." I cover my trembling mouth with my hands. "*No.*" Tears fill my eyes, ready to spill. "Carter's going to kill me."

"Oh. Oh fuck. No." Jaxon waves his hands erratically. "Fuck, no, please don't cry. I won't—I won't tell him. I promise. Please don't cry." He looks to Garrett for help before squeezing both my shoulders. "Hey, it's okay. Your secret's safe with me, Jennie, really. And, uh..." His gaze falls to Garrett's crotch. "I won't tell everyone you named your junk after Indiana Jones. I haven't heard that one before. It's...new."

I sniffle, wiping at my eyes. "Thanks, Jaxon. You're a good friend."

We watch him leave, and when he disappears, Garrett raises his fist.

"Good call on the tears."

I bump my fist off his. "Gets 'em every time."

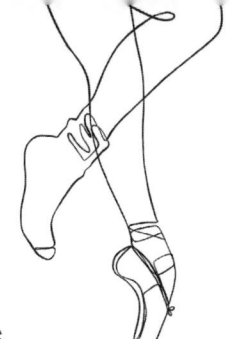

TWENTY-SEVEN
DISNEYLAND VS. INDIANA BONES

Jennie

"WHAT DID I SAY?"

My back hits the wall with a thud, Garrett's hazy eyes tracking mine. They're more blue than green tonight, dark and a little daunting, like an angry sea, turning my breath shallow, setting my body ablaze.

I let my tongue glide slowly across my bottom lip, enjoying the way Garrett's pulse drums in his neck as he watches. "That you missed me."

He growls, taking another step toward me. "No."

"You did," I argue, pushing him a little bit further. I want to see how far I can take him without making him snap. Or maybe I *do* want him to snap. Either way it's going to be fun. "It was rather sweet, Garrett." I stroke my fingers down the side of his face and kiss his jaw, smiling against the light layer of scruff when his chest rumbles. "You're just a soft, gooey cinnamon roll."

Garrett shoves me harder against the wall, takes both my wrists in one hand, and pins them over my head, his other hand at my throat, fingers pressing. I've done it. I've unlocked him.

"You like pissing me off."

"Don't be ridiculous, Garrett. *I love it.*"

He releases my throat and trails one broad fingertip across the waist of my jeans. "I fucking hate these jeans."

"I might, too, if my name was on the credit card that paid for them. They were expensive after all, and I bought three pairs."

A throaty, dark chuckle leaves his lips. "Then I have two pairs to destroy."

"Don't you dare," I warn lowly. My ass looks divine in these jeans; the way both Garrett and Jaxon can't ever take their eyes off it when I wear them around those two tells me so.

With his gaze fixed on mine, Garrett slips his hand below the waist of the tight denim and jerks my hips forward. "Then they need to be on the fucking floor, because that's the only way I like them."

My fingertips dance up his biceps, over his broad chest, sinking into his hair as I brush my lips over his. "Then I guess you better get to work, Andersen."

I leave him in my entryway as I saunter down the hall, stripping my shirt off on the way, casting a lingering glance over my shoulder when I ditch it behind me. The jeans are next, and I hang them off the tip of my pointer finger before dropping them outside my bedroom door. Finally, Garrett kicks his ass into high gear, but not fast enough to catch me before I disappear into the attached bathroom.

I'm not doing a thing in here other than admiring the way my body looks in my matching bra and panty set, satin and lace the color of emeralds. I've gained a little weight in the time I've spent with Garrett, something that would've sent me on a three-week spiral years ago. But today, I palm my boobs, enjoying the heaviness to them, peek at myself in the mirror, loving the cheeky fit of my ass in these panties.

I run my fingers through my braid, breaking up the thick waves until my hair is a fluffy mess around my shoulders, and I can't wait for Garrett to worship me.

I've said it before and I'll say it again: the man's got the most incredible hockey ass. He stands so casually as he waits for me, the sleeves of his button-down folded nearly up to his elbows, tapered pants snug around his lean waist, perfect butt, and thick thighs.

He turns toward me, pupils dilating, throat working as I close the space between us.

"So handsome," I murmur, wrapping his tie around my fist, giving it a tug. He comes tumbling forward, gripping my biceps for balance. I drop the silk tie to our feet and work the buttons of his shirt. "Will you fuck me in your suit one day?"

His eyes widen, fingertips digging into my skin. I like when we do this flip-flop thing, trading off on the bold and the shy. We do it so effort-lessly, like we were always meant to complement each other.

"Garrett?" My palms glide over his chest and shoulders, slipping his shirt off until it dissolves to a puddle on the ground. "I asked you a question."

"I'll do whatever the fuck you want me to do, Jennie."

I smile, loosening his belt buckle, pulling his zipper down. When my palm closes around his cock through his boxers and he groans, my chest surges with pride.

"Good boy," I murmur, letting his pants pool around his ankles. I push my hands down the back of his boxers, feeling the way his ass flexes under my touch before I drop them, too, to the ground. "Garrett?"

"Yeah?"

"I want you to sit down."

"I—"

Palm on his collarbone, I shove him to the edge of the bed. His lips part, tongue running across, eyes fixed on me as I stand between his legs. I take his hand, grazing my belly with his fingers.

"Want to touch? Or watch?"

He swallows. "Can the answer be both?"

I giggle quietly. "No. It can't."

I open my bedside drawer, fingers fluttering over my favorite rainbow before wrapping around the one I'm looking for. Garrett said he wanted to fuck me with this, but I want to show him how I can fuck myself with it.

His breath stutters when I turn back to him. "Jennie, I—*ho-ly fuck.*" He drags his hands down his face in slow motion when I slap the suction cup base to the floor, right between his legs. "Are you gonna—you're not gonna—right there? Oh my—I-I-I-I—I think I'm broken. Short-circuiting. Put me in rice. Is it a good time or a bad time to tell you I love you?" He laughs anxiously. "Holy-fuck-shit I think I really love you right now."

My God, he's the most endearing, adorable, and lovable human I've ever encountered. Nobody makes me smile like he does.

The bra goes first, satin straps slipping off my shoulders, dropping to Garrett's lap before I hook my thumbs in my panties and shimmy them over my hips.

He clutches my underwear to his chest as I guide his legs wider, and when I hit the power on Indiana Bones, making him dance, Garrett's hand closes around mine, stopping me.

"Do you need lube or something?"

I guide his hand between my legs, swiping his fingers through my center, where I'm absolutely drenched. He groans, and when I lift his glistening fingers, I ask, "What do you think, Garrett?" Based on the strangled sob that leaves his lips when I slowly suck his fingers into my mouth, I think he might be dying. "Do I need lube?"

"No," he croaks.

"No," I agree, collecting my wetness on the tips of my fingers, stroking slowly over my toy, coating it.

On my knees between Garrett's legs, I guide the head of the cock to where I want this man before me most. Every thought leaves my brain as I ease myself down the length of it, moaning as it stretches me.

"Jesus fucking fuckballs." Garrett's fingernails bite into the flesh of his thighs. "I-I-I—I'm in heaven. I'm dead. Am I dead?"

God, it's so deep, and when it pulses inside me, hitting that spot, I fall toward his lap, gripping his thighs, crying out. "*Garrett.*"

"Oh my God. I'm not dead." He fists my hair, eyes wild as I pick myself up and drop, again and again, slowly, enjoying every aching second of it. "How the fuck are you real?"

Finding my rhythm, I wrap my fist around Garrett's eager cock. Gazes locked, I drag my tongue along the underside of his rock-hard length before I swallow the tip, and my mouth slides down, down, until his cock hits the back of my throat.

Garrett's head lolls back as he whimpers, and when he rights it again, large hands bracket my face as he stares down at me, watching. "You are a goddamn masterpiece."

I'm not sure I've ever wanted something as much as I want to give myself to Garrett. I've given him pieces; now I want him to have the rest.

It's been on my mind for a while. But I've never been sure I was ready, and that told me I wasn't. *And that was okay.* He didn't need anything else from me, only what I was willing to give. For once in my life, I was enough.

I've never been enough for anyone except myself. Garrett changes all of that. I never knew how much I needed someone like him until I found him, and I don't think he realizes how grateful I am to have him.

So I'm going to show him.

My fingers find my clit, circling slowly as I ride the cock below me. Cupping Garrett's balls in my free hand, I massage them lightly, and with a hiss, he jerks his hips forward. His cock slides down the back of my throat, making me gag, and I smile up at him.

Garrett groans, fingers plowing through my hair, gripping it in his fists. "Don't you fucking look at me like that while you've got my cock in your mouth."

I release him with a pop, and lick the corner of my wet mouth. "Or what?"

"Or I'll show you exactly what it feels like to be fucked by me when you're being a fucking brat."

Gripping the base of his cock, I pump slowly, holding his gaze as I lick a languid stroke along it, swirling around the tip as he hisses above me. My hips rock back and forward, grinding. I feel like I'm glowing from the inside out. "Is that supposed to be a threat, big guy?"

Oh hello, angry Garrett. I've hit the jackpot.

One second I'm between his legs with his cock in my mouth, and the next he's behind me, one hand digging into my waist, the other grasping my wrists tightly behind my back.

He holds me still, keeping me full but stopping me from chasing my high. I whimper, squirming, desperate for relief.

His teeth graze my ear, warm breath sending a shiver of desire down my spine. "What's the matter, sunshine? You wanna come?"

"I can make myself come."

"You sure can. But when I'm here, I make you come." A rough hand squeezes my breast, thumb scraping across my nipple before his fingers dance down my stomach, finding that tight nub that always wants Garrett's attention. Soft lips touch my shoulder. "The day we fuck is going to be like lightning, Jennie. I'm gonna light up your entire sky, the same way you do mine."

There's that tightness in my chest again, the one that's been there for nearly a month now. It squeezes a little harder every time I'm with Garrett. I don't know what to do about it. I want to tell him how I feel, to ask him where we go from here. Because I don't know. This is all so new to me, and I feel inexperienced, overwhelmed. The truth is I'm fucking scared.

Scared the sex won't satisfy him. Scared he'll get bored. Scared it won't work and we won't be able to stay friends. Scared it *will* work, but somebody won't like it.

I'm tired of being scared. I just want to be happy.

Garrett's chin comes to rest gently on my shoulder, his hand on my jaw as he turns my face to his. He smiles, so handsome I think my chest might break wide open.

"Hi," he whispers against my lips. "I hope you know you're beautiful." He kisses the tip of my nose, the apple of my cheek, down my neck, and along my jaw. He stops at my ear, and my nerve endings dance when he grips my chin, holding me there. "But I'm still gonna show you what it feels like to piss me off."

With a punishing hold on my hips, he slams me down on the rubber cock. I fall forward with a scream, clawing at the floor, and his chest vibrates with a sinister growl. Then his open palm hits my ass, and when I come, I scream all over again.

"That's a good fucking girl," he murmurs darkly as he maneuvers my body, pushing and pulling, taking and giving. Jesus Christ, does the man ever give. Fingers wrap around my throat, yanking me up to him, holding me against his solid chest as he works me over, thrusting, plunging, driving. "I can't wait to see how perfectly you fit my cock. Can't wait to see your beautiful face the first time I come inside you."

A tingle starts low in my belly, spreading like wildfire through every fiber as my vision blurs. I writhe in his grasp as a second orgasm barrels toward me head-on, and when he whispers "Come for me" in my ear, he does exactly what he promised to do: makes my sky explode.

Fluorescent colors streak across my field of vision, lighting my world. My words dissolve until they're nothing but garbled, nonsense sobs, and I collapse against Garrett's body.

He sweeps me into his arms and stands, carrying me to the shower where he washes me tenderly beneath the warm spray. I can't find it in me to speak a single word until we're wrapped in blankets on my living room couch twenty minutes later, eating bowls of Corn Pops with my back against his chest.

"I got my ticket for your recital."

I spin, nearly knocking his bowl onto my own head. "You did?"

"Mhmm. Can't wait."

I'm excited too. All my favorite people will be there, watching from the audience, and Garrett's my favorite of all.

"I know we're going for dinner afterward to celebrate with everyone—"

"For Carter's birthday," I clarify.

Garrett rolls his eyes. "He says to celebrate you; you say to celebrate him. I think we can celebrate you both."

"Beckett's don't share center stage, Garrett."

He chuckles softly and takes my bowl after he sets his down, draining the milk. "Well, I was thinking maybe we could do something afterward. Just the two of us."

"We always do something with just the two of us."

"Right. But this would be different." His gaze bounces away, then back.

"Different how?"

"I donno." He lifts a shoulder. "Special."

"Special how?"

His throat works and his eyes track the lock of my hair that he twirls around his finger.

"Special how, Garrett?"

"Like a date, maybe. For Valentine's Day. If you want."

"If I want?" My heart gallops, a grin blooming. "Do *you* want?"

He licks his lips, tentative gaze meeting mine, and nods. "Yeah. I want." He clears his throat and goes for it: *word vomit*, my favorite of his specialties. "I know it's two weeks away, but I leave in two days for another road trip, and then I'm only home for one night, and we fly home again the day before the recital, so there's not much time beforehand, and I know I said something special but we can't really go anywhere because it's a secret and all that but I thought maybe we could just make it special, like if we both don't order dessert at the restaurant we could have it together instead and set up a picnic or something, maybe with candles and pillows and I donno, and you don't have to get me a gift or anything, but I thought maybe it would be nice to, like…" He inhales a shaky breath and lets it go. "Have a real date." He scratches his temple and winces. "That was rough, wasn't it?"

"It was terrible," I confirm. "But I think I can squeeze you in."

His eyes flit down to mine, face flush with color, and he smiles. "Yeah?"

I smile too. "Yeah."

"Grool." He cringes. "Holy fuck. I did the *Mean Girls* thing. I started to say great but finished with cool."

Snickering, I turn, slinging my arms around his neck. "You're tired. You need to sleep."

He sighs, squeezing my ass. "You're right."

I roll off him, taking the bowls to the kitchen. I find Garrett at the door, slipping his shoes on and doing up his pants.

"You're going?"

He looks up, halting. "I thought..."

"No, that's cool. Just asking."

"'Cause you said I should sleep," he explains.

"Right. I did."

"So I should probably—"

"Do you maybe wanna—"

"Oh." Garrett's brows lift. "Were you saying something?"

"No. No, definitely not." I wave my hands around, extra flail-y to distract from the fact that I have no idea what I'm doing. "You're leaving."

"I mean..." He rubs the back of his neck. "Unless you were gonna say...?"

"Who, me?" I point at myself. Yep, definitely turning into Garrett. "I wasn't gonna say anything."

Garrett's head bobs slowly. "Great. Cool. Guess I'll...leave then."

I grin. "Grool."

His laugh is my favorite, a hearty, warm sound, and when he tows me into him with a fistful of my shirt, the wave of emotions that hits me is truly staggering.

"Grool," he whispers against my lips. "So grool."

TWENTY-EIGHT
RULES? WHAT RULES?

Garrett

"THAT'S GAME, BOYS." I sweep my hand over the table, gathering the cards.

Carter flips his upside down and crosses his arms, scowling. "It's fucking bullshit is what it is."

"You know what they say," I murmur. "You have to learn to lose before you can—"

"If you tell me I need to learn how to lose in order to appreciate winning, I'll toss you off this fucking airplane."

"Oh, so Olivia can say it, but I can't? Double fucking standards."

"Olivia can say anything she wants! She's growing my baby and sucking my dick!"

"Carter," Adam mumbles around his sandwich, not looking up from the book in his other hand. "Stop being a sore loser."

"I'm not a sore loser," he grumbles, slumping in his seat.

"You are." Jaxon and I just smoked Carter and Emmett in euchre three times in a row. It was only supposed to be one game, and then two, and, well…you know Carter. "You can't be the best at everything."

Carter toes at the bottom of my seat. "Emmett's playing like shit."

"Hey!" Emmett glances up from his phone. This might be the first time he's realized the game has ended. "I haven't seen my wife in five days and she's sending me very detailed texts about how she's going to welcome me home tonight." His phone dings, his eyes turn feral, and he stands abruptly. "I, uh...I gotta...go. Take a leak."

Carter stands next, stretching his arms overhead with a yawn. "I'm gonna go too. Wanna sext Ollie before I crash for the rest of this flight. Need some energy so I can rock her world when I get home. Pregnancy's making her super horny. She's hard to keep up with some days." He chuckles quietly, a far-off look in his eyes. "The other day she woke me up by s—"

"Stop." Adam holds his sandwich up like a shield. "For fuck's sake, Carter, just stop. We don't wanna know, and Olivia doesn't want us to know; trust me on that."

Carter pulls a face, gathering up the wrappers from his stress-eating when he was losing. He jabs Adam's book. "You need to get laid. If you need some tips—"

"I don't."

"You sure? Word on the street is I know how to talk to the ladies."

Adam flips a page in his book. "And how Ollie got so lucky, we'll never know."

"What book you reading today?" I ask as Carter disappears.

Adam flashes me the cover, and Jaxon and I laugh. *The Subtle Art of Not Giving a F*ck.*

"What do you wanna not give a fuck about anymore?"

"I donno. Nothing. Everything. I donno." He drops the book to his chest and sighs. "Should I say fuck it to dating? Should I just take what all the girls seem to be offering?"

I shake my head, shuffling the cards. "Nah, you don't wanna do that. It's not you."

"Maybe it should be. I'm not looking to fuck around and hurt anyone's feelings. But none of them give a fuck about me, so why do I give so many?"

"'Cause you're a good guy," Jaxon says. "And you're not the no-strings-attached-fucking kinda guy. That's me, and while I do enjoy it and normally highly recommend it, I don't think it'd be your scene."

Adam's fingers plunge into his curls. "I don't really think it is either."

I chuckle. "Then why are you considering it?"

He pulls his dark-framed reading glasses off and rubs his eyes. "I guess I'm not really. Maybe I'm just giving up the dating fight. All it's doing is making me feel lonelier."

"So take a break. You're filling your spare time with the kids at the home, and you're enjoying that, right?"

His smile is instantaneous. "I really am. It's so cool to be part of the reason some of these kids are coming out of their shells."

"Then focus on that for a while. Spend time doing what makes you happy. I know you want to meet someone, but you're not having fun doing it right now. Revisit in a couple months."

Adam rolls his bottom lip, then nods. "When did you get so wise?"

The truth is, talking to Jennie helps. I'm always trying to show her that I understand, and I like helping her find her way through to the other side of her problems. But I can't tell Adam that, so I tell him the other truth.

"I have three highly emotional little sisters who fight over everything. Sometimes I need to be wise." And sometimes I'm clueless when I should be wise, like last week when *I think* Jennie was trying to ask me to stay over.

Thinking about her lately has been hard. Between hockey and recital rehearsals, our schedules have been clashing. Late-night chats aren't an option with Adam as my roommate. I'm lucky to get five minutes to see her face or hear her voice.

She's the only person I want to spend my one night home with, so I shoot off a quick text.

Me: *Home in an hour. Come over?*
Sunshine: *Because you miss me?*
Me: *Because I want a blowjob.*
Sunshine: *Tell the truth, Gare-Bear. I don't hang with liars. I only hang with grool boys.*

She's not letting that whole *grool* incident go, but the joke's on her. My favorite jokes are the ones we share together.

Me: *Fine. I miss u & I want a blowjob. Please come over.*
Sunshine: *And?*
Me: *And I'd like to hug u because it's been 5 days. Please come over.*

Me: *And I'll tickle ur back. Please come over.*
Me: *And I'll feed u. Please come over.*
Me: *Please. Please. Please.*
Sunshine: *OMG no need to be so desperate. I'm already here anyway.*

I'm about to ask her what she means, when a photo of her snuggled in my bed comes through. She's got a Pop-Tart between her teeth and she's making the peace sign with her free hand, chestnut hair splayed over my pillow. I can't wait to join her there, and if I'm really lucky, I'll get to keep her all night long.

Sunshine: *Your sheets are magical and you've got better snacks. I came to eat and nap. Was gonna surprise you at your door wearing nothing but my hair ribbon tied around my neck like the gift I am.*

Jesus Christ, I'm never letting her go.

"Who are you texting?"

"J—" My fingers halt. My gaze slowly rises, finding Adam with one brow arched while he waits for me to finish that *J* name. "—axon. Jaxon." I clear my throat. "Riley. Jaxon Riley." *Shut. Up. Garrett.*

"You're texting Jaxon while he's sitting across from you?"

My gaze slides to Jaxon. He waits, hands folded on the table between us, phone nowhere in sight. Fuck it, it's worth a shot. "Yes?"

"Garrett," Adam warns under his breath. "I swear to God, if that's Jennie—"

"She just—she just—she-she-she…no, she just needs a ride to…I'm not…it's not…" I give up, raking my hands up and down my face. "Aaah."

"Aw, c'mon!" Adam tosses his book to the seat next to him, burying his face in his hands. "Garrett, no! You promised it was only the one time!"

"Well, Adam, I lied!"

He gasps, expression holding all the betrayal I expected.

"I'm sorry. I didn't want to lie to you, but I couldn't tell you. You would've made me stop."

"Because I don't want to lose my best friends!" he whisper-yells, checking that no one is listening other than Jaxon, who's snickering like a fucking donkey. "You'd be six feet deep, and Carter would be in jail for putting you there!"

"Stop yelling at me!" I shout back under my breath. "I don't like it!"

"Fuck me. I don't even know what to...to...*fuck*." He gestures at Jaxon. "You knew about this?"

Jaxon holds his hands up. "Hey, I accidentally saw something I never wanted to see. And then she cried and—"

"Oh c'mon," Adam scoffs. "She cried? No, she played you like a damn fiddle, that's what she did. She's a goddamn Beckett, Riley. Get your head in the game."

"Damn, he's harsh when he's mad. But I *think* I know when a girl is fake crying." When I grin, he balks. "Fuck, she's good."

"You can't tell Carter," I plead with them. "Please."

"Tell him what?" Jaxon glances over his shoulder. Carter's eight rows ahead of us, seat reclined, headphones on, Olivia's face on his iPad screen. "That you're fucking his baby sister?"

"No, it's not like that anymore. I mean, it was." I squeeze my eyes shut, head wagging. "No, we're...we haven't, uh..."

Jaxon's brows skyrocket. "You haven't fucked her?"

"We do...other stuff." *What am I doing?* This doesn't feel right.

"Right. For fun?"

Adam's jaw drops. "Friends with benefits? No. Not with her of all people, Garrett."

"No. I mean, yes. I mean, I donno?" I rub the back of my neck. "It started that way, just fun, with rules so it didn't get serious..."

Jaxon hums. "And now you wanna fuck the rules."

I don't want what I wanted before. The limited time, the lack of strings, the freedom to leave whenever it suited either of us, *the fucking rules*. And I hate that I'm telling someone else before I tell Jennie.

"I really like her," I whisper. The words taste funny, not because it's a new revelation, because it's not. But because it's the first time I'm saying them out loud, getting to be honest with somebody other than myself. Out of fear of losing what we have, I've had to swallow the words day after day, bury them right along with my intentions, all my hopes.

But now it doesn't feel so hopeless.

"I asked her out on a proper date after her show on the fourteenth. She said yes, so...I think she likes me too. Plus, she's..." My eyes drift to

Adam's. The hardness wanes, compassion returning. "She's my best friend."

Adam stares for a long moment. I know why the fear is there. The same reason it's there for me. He sighs, scrubbing his face. "I want you to be happy. So long as you know Carter's going to lose his shit."

The last thing I ever want to do is hurt Jennie. I'm just not sure that will be enough for Carter.

Jaxon must sense my defeat, because he interjects. "Well, you said you haven't had a real date yet. See how that goes first. You know, make sure you're on the same page and everything. When you know it's going somewhere, then you can talk to Carter. Is he really going to hold it against you if you make his sister happy?"

I can't say I ever saw myself getting advice from Jaxon, or better yet, *liking* it, but it does make sense. I don't feel like I need to wait and see if things between us will work, but I do need to make sure it's a step she's ready for. Plus, it gives me a little more time, rather than trying to get Carter's permission to date his sister in the next week.

After all, I'd like to *see* Jennie's recital, not livestream it from a hospital bed.

～

The door's not even closed behind me and Jennie's already dancing down the hallway, bounding into my arms.

"You clearly missed me way more than I missed you," I mumble into her hair. She's soft and warm as she clings to me, smelling like cinnamon and coffee, and a little like my laundry. She's all my favorite things rolled into one.

"Pfft. That's not even possible. You're obsessed with me." She slides down my body and spins, popping a hip. "Besides, I'm too grool to miss you that much."

"Not gonna let that go, huh," I murmur, watching as she sashays into my kitchen. "What are you wearing?"

She glances over her shoulder. "Are you having trouble with your vision?"

"I'm having trouble wrapping my head around the idea of you lounging around my apartment in just your panties and my T-shirt while I'm not here to enjoy it." She presents a pizza box. "And you ordered dinner?"

"You're always hungry when you get home. It got here ten minutes ago, so it's still hot, and—" her lids flutter closed as she inhales, "—it smells *so* good."

I *am* hungry. But not for the pizza.

I amble toward Jennie as she drops a bite into her mouth, humming happily. She swallows, smiles, and I grip her hips.

"Hi," I whisper, touching a kiss to her lips. "I missed you. Way more than you missed me."

She sets the slice down, draping her arms over my shoulders as I start walking us down the hall. Her smile is so happy tonight, eyes so light, tiny flecks of gold swimming in a pool of blue.

"I did miss you. The back tickler you got me for Christmas is great, but nothing beats your fingers."

"Mmm. You do like my fingers."

I pull her shirt—*my shirt*—off, ditching it on my bedroom floor. She's not wearing a bra, and her nipples pebble under the heat of my gaze.

Her fingertips dance up my tie, finding the knot at my neck, playing with it as she peers at me from beneath dark, sinful lashes. "This thing is never straight, Garrett," she murmurs, slowly pulling the red silk free. She winds both ends around her fists and guides my face down to hers. "Kiss me."

Caging her in against the wall, I bracket her chin with my fingers, tipping her face to mine. Her cheeks are alive with color, warm brown waves framing her face.

Pretty bowed lips part, breathless. "What are you waiting for?"

I drag my thumb across her lower lip. "Just looking at you. Sometimes I can't believe you exist."

Right before our lips can meet, I spot something blue on my bed.

"What the fuck is that?" I turn her head toward the sleek dildo, the piece that juts out near the base that does to her clit what my mouth likes to do. "Where you masturbating in my bed?"

Her lashes flutter, dimples pulling in a cheeky grin as she tugs on the tie wrapped around her fists. "What are you gonna do about it, big guy?"

I answer her with that kiss she was begging for a moment ago, then gently pry her fingers from the tie, letting the silk slip through her hand as I pull it away.

Taking her hands in one of mine, I wind the silk around her wrists. "Do you trust me, Jennie?"

"Yes," she answers without hesitation.

"Good." I yank on the ends of the tie, instantly tightening it around her wrists, bringing them together between us. She gasps.

"What are you doing?" The words are thick with wonder, desire. She wants this—her, helpless; me, in control—as much as I do.

"At the moment? Nothing." I force her to the bed and spread her legs wide. She takes her bottom lip between her teeth as I loop the silk through the headboard, securing her hands above her head. "In a minute? Fucking your pussy however I please, until you scream my name loud enough for the neighbors to hear."

Her skin dots with goose bumps as she quivers, my name barely a breath when it leaves her mouth.

"Mmm, something like that." I drag the pad of my thumb up the seam of her legs, where a dark, wet spot decorates the pale pink cotton. Heat pours out, and she lifts her hips off the bed, desperate for more. "But a whole fuckload louder."

A gasp pierces the air when I dip my hand inside, swiping my fingers through her slit. Jennie jerks forward, struggling against the tie.

"Does it hurt?" I ask. She shakes her head, panting as I drag her panties down her legs. I bend her knee, trailing kisses up the inside of her thigh. "Are you okay? With this? Or would you feel more comfortable if I stopped?"

"*Oh*," she cries, back arching when I nip at the junction of her thigh. "More, please."

I flick the tip of my tongue over her swollen clit and tug it gently between my teeth. "Answer the question, Jennie."

"God, please don't stop, Garrett," she begs when I pull away. "*Please.*"

Slowly, I push two fingers inside her, reveling in the way she squeezes around me. I suck my fingers into my mouth, and Jennie's eyes hood as she squirms, searching for my touch, begging for it without words.

"Fuckin' delicious, sunshine."

I reach across the rumpled sheets, wrapping my fingers around my replacement. The little wand whirs to life when I hit the power button. Jennie once told me this was one of her favorites, right up there with Indiana Bones. *Dual stimulation*, she said; *you can't beat it.*

"How many times did you use this?" I ask, dragging the head of the toy up her slit, swirling it around her clit, watching her shake.

"Once."

I pull it away.

"Three times," she cries desperately, and when I push it slowly inside her, she moans, tossing her head back in the pillows. "It wasn't enough. Nothing's ever enough when it's not you."

I like those words more than I care to admit, and when I push the toy a little farther, when that curved head hits that spot she likes, she gasps, yanking at the tie. My thumb covers the small addition to the toy, feeling the power of the suction. When I fix it over her clit, Jennie's eyes roll, words lost in a garbled cry.

She writhes and moans, rocking with the toy, pushing herself into me as I pull one rosy nipple into my mouth.

"What were you thinking about? While you were fucking yourself?"

"You," she sobs, hips bucking, back arching. She pulls on the headboard, trying to free herself. "Oh God, Garrett."

"What about me?"

Her head falls backward, eyes closing as a sound rips up her throat when I slowly remove the toy, then plunge it back inside. "I was thinking about...you fucking me."

"With my tongue? Or my fingers?"

Her teeth clamp down on her lower lip as she rocks herself into the toy.

"Be specific, Jennie."

"With your cock," she yelps. "I wished it was you inside me."

Angling my body over hers, I wrap my fingers around her throat, watching her face as she climbs toward that peak. It's getting harder to be gentle with her. Lately, all I want to do is bend her over, fuck her so hard she forgets her own name. Rip her to pieces then put her back together. I want her to scream that she's mine, and I want her to mean it.

But I want to be hers too.

"How do you think you'll like it?" My mouth hovers above hers as I thrust harder, hitting that spot that leaves her breathless. "When I take you, do you want me to do it slowly? Do you want me to be gentle?

Sweet?" I press my lips to the corner of her mouth as she pants. "Or do you want me to fuck you hard? Rough? Do you want me to show you how badly I want you? How I've wanted you for fucking *ages*? How I've dreamt about it every fucking night?"

My gaze coasts her face, all the soft edges I love, and when I follow the line of her arms up to her wrists above her head, I find her hands reaching for me.

"Garrett," she whimpers, trembling when I release her throat and lace my fingers through hers, watching as she teeters along the edge.

"Don't worry. We can take our time, do it all. I have no plans of letting you walk out that door once I have you."

I pull the toy from between her legs before driving it back inside her, and when her toes curl and her back arches, I take her mouth with mine, swallowing my name as she screams it.

With a swift tug of the tie, I free her from the headboard and flip her over, jerking her hips off the bed, her perfect, round ass in the air.

"I'm so fucking far from done with you, sunshine."

I've had this body wrapped around mine too many times to count. Watched her thick lashes rest against her cheekbones, her chest rise and fall steadily as she sleeps. I've felt the way her hold on me tightens when I shift, and I've smiled at the frown that pulls at the corners of her mouth when she's dreaming, the way it quirks upward when I brush the pad of my thumb across the swell of her bottom lip, stroke a finger down the side of her face, or touch my lips to her forehead.

And still, I have no idea what it's like to fall asleep with her in my arms. To sleep soundly with her legs tangled with mine. To wake in the morning with her warm body still tucked into mine and see the way the sunshine makes her face glow as it bathes her from the window.

I'm tired of not knowing what it's like. I don't want to dream about it anymore; I want to live it.

I turn the TV off and tuck the remote away. Jennie stirs, lashes fluttering, blue eyes peering up at me. Heat rushes to her cheeks when she finds me watching her.

"What are you looking at?"

I brush her hair off her forehead, tucking it behind her ear. "You."

"Why?"

Why? Why the fuck not? She's beautiful, my best friend. She makes me smile when she's not even doing a damn thing, and she lives rent-free in my head twenty-four seven. Who had any right making her this magnificent?

When I look at her, a thousand emotions swirl inside me, and it's hard to choose just one to focus on. I wish I could put it into words, but I don't know how.

But there's one thing I can do.

I cup her face, coaxing her gaze back to mine. She's nervous, more nervous than me. But I don't want her to be nervous; I want her to be sure.

"Stay," I whisper. "Right here, with me. Please, Jennie. Stay with me."

Her wide eyes move cautiously between mine. That fear begins to dissipate, leaving me with a devastating smile that shatters her face, ignites a fire inside my chest, and warms me from the inside out.

"Okay," Jennie says. "I'll stay."

TWENTY-NINE
DID I JUST MAKE A FRIEND?

Jennie

"No hair gel," I murmur, rifling through the drawer. "Seriously? It looks that good all on its own? Un-fucking-believable."

It's surprisingly tidy in here for a bachelor's bathroom. I'd be impressed, except I can't find what I'm looking for, so annoyance is winning by a landslide.

So far, his vanity has yielded an unholy amount of Q-tips, those flossing sticks instead of the thread, which immediately ups Garrett a few notches, and an array of hair trimmers. They're all different, but I can't fathom why he needs so many. I shouldn't complain; whatever he's doing with his facial hair is working for me. I quite enjoy the way it tickles between my thighs.

I examine a bottle of cologne before spritzing it on my T-shirt. It's technically Garrett's, so it already smells like him, but a little more won't hurt.

"Oooh." I pull the cotton to my nose, inhaling. He smells like heaven always, fresh like citrus from his shower, but the cologne adds an earthy smell, the kind that has me picturing him out in the woods in a plaid flannel, wielding an axe. "So good."

"Snooping?"

Yelping, I slam the drawer shut, turning to find Garrett in the doorway. He's naked, which is distracting. Lieutenant Johnson is super rock hard and massive, waving hello, which is *extremely* fucking distracting.

"Snooping? No. Me? No." My arm flails in the direction of the countertop, where his things are spread, and I accidentally swipe his cologne clear off it. It's in a pretty glass bottle, and I can't pronounce the name, so I likely can't afford to replace it if it smashes at our feet.

Probably why I fling myself forward, arms outstretched.

Garrett simply holds out his hand and catches the bottle, cradling it into his chest, and I go crashing into him.

"Are you all right?" He's not asking if I'm physically intact and pain-free. He's questioning my sanity, and his tone indicates he finds it humorous.

"I was looking for a toothbrush." I bury the words against his collar-bone. "I can't kiss you with morning breath. That's disgusting."

His blue-green eyes are hazy, heavy with sleep as he stares down at me. If his sleep was anything like mine, it was glorious. I haven't slept so deep in ages as I did with Garrett's warm body locked around mine all night, his hand splayed over my stomach, face buried in my neck. He's really the biggest snuggle bear ever, and I think I might be too.

He releases me and moves to the counter, tucking his cologne away and producing a small woven basket. Inside is a packaged pink tooth-brush, hair ties, deodorant, lip balm, makeup remover wipes, and a small box of tampons.

A knot clenches in my stomach like an angry fist. My attempt to tamp down the surge of jealousy moving through me is unsuccessful. I swallow and plant a forced smile on my lips. "You keep feminine products here for the girls you have over?"

Two lines appear between his eyebrows when they quirk. Garrett leans over me, pulling out his toothpaste and depositing it in my hand.

"No." He hooks his thumb under my chin and lifts my mouth to his, kissing me deeply. "I keep feminine products here for you." He claps a hand to my ass before sauntering back into the bedroom, unbelievable hockey butt swinging back and forth as he goes.

"Ugh," he groans, snagging his sweatpants from the floor. He peeks over his shoulder, teasing smile playing at his lips. "Your morning breath is gross."

Dancing has been my life for as long as I've known, but when I lost my dad, it became my savior. It was the only way I could get lost, step outside of my life, my nightmares, and rise above it, even if only for as long as the song lasts. It doesn't matter where I am or who I'm with; I close my eyes and the music takes me wherever I want to be.

Two hands wrap around my waist before I'm in the air, wind fluttering at my face as Simon spins the both of us. When my feet touch the ground, I dash across the stage, the lyrics to my favorite song chasing at my heels. My body soars as I leap through the air as James Arthur sings about two people falling in love the way stars fall from the sky, and Garrett's face floods my mind. I'm caught off guard by the vision, and a shiver of apprehension rockets through me at the meaning behind it.

I've never been in love. I thought I was, and when Kevin broke my heart, I thought love was the reason it hurt so much. But over the years, I've realized that's not what it was. I was just a girl, someone who longed for acceptance, intimacy, and I latched onto what he gave me. It wasn't love; it was a lesson learned.

What I have with Garrett feels…different. Unique and fleeting, something you don't let go of. But I'm only one-half of a whole; I can't control when someone else wants to let go. Quite frankly, walking into something with that logic is frightening.

I'm learning to keep my shoulders back, to take the steps even when I'm uncertain.

Thing is, though, as shaky as the steps may be, they don't feel all that uncertain when that man is the one waiting at the destination.

A hand clasps mine, and Simon smiles at me when my eyes snap open. He spins me into him, pulling me against his chest, and his eyes drop to my lips as his face hovers above mine, inching closer as the song drifts to an end. My pulse thunders as silence encases us, though I know he won't close the gap. When applause echoes through the auditorium, we break apart, both of us breathless and sweaty.

Mikhail wipes at nonexistent tears. "Beautiful. Absolutely *stunning*." He climbs the steps at side stage. "Simon, the emotion is on point. You look absolutely enthralled with Miss Beckett. Jennie, you look a teensy bit scared of Simon, but it works, like your love for each other is daunting."

"Yeah, daunting." I swipe my hair off my damp neck. "That's definitely it."

"My diamond dazzlers," he murmurs, chin resting on his fist as he stares at us. "And Jennie, you're still not feeling the kiss at the end?"

"Still not feeling it."

He raises his hands in defeat. "Well, okay. I think you two have got this thing nailed down anyway. You'd never know you aren't a real couple." He checks his watch. "Okay, I've got a meeting in ten and a lunch date later at Rapscallion. You two should head home for some rest. You've earned it. Let's not stretch ourselves."

"Thanks, Mik." I grab my yoga pants and wiggle them over my ass. "Make sure you get the oysters. They're—" I bring the tips of my fingers to my lips, kissing them, "—chef's kiss."

Simon snakes his arm around my shoulders when I'm finished dressing. "Wanna grab some lunch? Mexican? Italian? Oooh, what about Thai?"

My stomach grumbles. "I could absolutely fuck with some Thai, but I'm heading to Hank's with Carter."

"Dinner?'

"Can't." I've got a large and extremely sexy hockey player at home who flies out later tonight. I plan to make use of our fleeting hours.

Simon puts his hand over his heart. "You're killing me, Beckett."

There's an easiness to my laugh. Things have been smooth sailing with Simon since his apology. Our upcoming show means lots of late nights together practicing and finishing on the floor of the studio with a box of takeout. Things have been perfectly platonic, and it feels nice to have a friend.

"We can do Thai tomorrow," I tell him.

"Deal." With a hug, he sends me through the front door, where Carter is waiting by the curb.

"Jennie," Carter calls rather loudly, arms waving. "Jennie! I'm right here!" His legs eat the distance between us as he scowls at Simon. "Jennie," he scolds, tucking me beneath his arm. "What have I told you about hanging out with douchebags?"

"Don't?"

"That's fucking right." He opens my door and gives Simon a dazzling smile. "Bye, Steve!"

Carter's overprotective dad-bro stints—especially the ones where he's intent on embarrassing me via shouting my names and waving like one of those wacky inflatable flailing arm things you see at car dealerships—are beyond irritating, but I'm too happy to care right now.

He's been especially suffocating since the movie theater shitstorm with Kevin. He blames himself, which is absurd, but Carter's always been one to think he could've somehow been better. He thinks he should've dropped everything to be with me when Garrett mentioned I had a bad day. The only good thing to come out of this is Carter not questioning me and Garrett getting closer as friends.

Anyway, Carter's been extra attentive, which means by the time we're at Hank's, I'm unwrapping my breakfast sandwich from McDonald's while sipping my apple crisp macchiato from Starbucks, because Carter went through two different drive-thrus for me.

"How come she got Starbucks and I'm drinking McDonald's coffee?" Hank grumbles.

"You *like* McDonald's coffee! You said you prefer it!"

"I think you're making things up," Hank argues, nudging me with his elbow when Carter sighs loudly. "Riling him up is so much fun."

"I totally agree." I slip Dublin a bite of my hash brown. "That's why you and I are such great friends."

"So how come Carter picked you up today? Didn't he lend you one of his cars?"

"It's snowy today. I get anxious driving in the snow." *And sometimes I accidentally run into stop signs in my brother's hundred-thousand-dollar Benz; sue me.*

Hank's hand searches for mine. He squeezes, and so does my heart. "That's okay, sweetheart. You drive when you feel comfortable."

"In the spring, I think."

"Well, how you gonna get to school then?" Carter asks, huffing.

"The same way I did before. On the bus." I watch as he peels apart his breakfast sandwiches and proceeds to stack all three sausage patties together. He's acting grumbly, but he's actually in a good mood because he and Olivia went for an ultrasound this morning. So I try my luck. "Garrett gave me a ride this morning."

Two rides, technically. One to school, and before that, one on his face. Both were enjoyable, but the latter more so, for obvious reasons.

Carter's head whips. "Huh?"

I take an extra-large gulp of my coffee, nodding. "I ran into him this morning. He offered to drop me off."

"Oh." Carter blinks. Three times. Then he lifts his triple-decker sandwich to his mouth and takes a gigantic bite. "O-tay. Dat nice ub him."

"You're nearly twenty-nine years old. Would it kill you to swallow before you speak?"

Hank pats my hand. "You can't teach an old dog new tricks. Carter can't be changed."

Maybe, but a year ago I would've never expected him to be sitting here playing the audio of his unborn baby's heartbeat on repeat.

"Doc said his heart's beating at a hundred-and-sixty-two beats per minute. Faster than the rest already."

"Only you would be competitive about fetal heart rates," I murmur. Hank grins. "Guess you never heard the old wives' tale that a high heartbeat is a sign of a girl?"

Carter snorts. "Yeah, okay, Hank. Whatever."

"Ireland and I always wanted a little girl," Hank says wistfully. "Tried for years, and it shattered her when it didn't work. My heart broke because I couldn't give her what she wanted, and I wanted to give her the whole world." He pats the corner of his eye and smiles, clasping both our hands. "Might've taken a lot longer than I thought, but eventually I got my girl *and* my boy. Maybe a little more arrogant than I'd imagined, but I love you both all the same, and I know Ireland brought you into my life."

My nose tingles and wrinkles. "I don't come here to cry, Hank. Stop making me feel things."

"Someone's got to. You two Beckett's tend to be pretty closed off until someone comes knocking on your walls." His gaze wanders, and he manages to make me feel like he's staring right into my soul when it finally stops, pinpointing me. "Carter's already let someone knock down his walls. When are you going to let someone do the same for you?"

"Jennie!"

I glance over my shoulder in my strut across the lobby. The strut would be more impressive if I hadn't settled on my moccasin slippers when leaving this morning. To be fair, I was in a rush. Garrett got me naked, then he got me dressed. Then *I* accidentally got *him* naked, and then we accidentally tumbled into the shower, and I'm betting the imprint of the shower tiles is still lingering on my knees. My point is I had exactly one minute to change into fresh clothes and slip on a pair of shoes.

Emily dashes toward me from the concierge desk. "Oh, you're here. Thank God."

I press the call button for the elevator. "I live here. Where else would I be?"

"I've been waiting for an hour already."

"Waiting for what? Waiting for me? Why?"

She follows me into the elevator, slumping against the wall. "I lost my keys."

"Sucks to suck."

She levels me with an unimpressed look, sticking her tongue out at me. I stick mine right back. "They're having a new set made for me, but they won't be ready until tonight, so I need somewhere to go."

"Where are you going to go?" I ask as I exit the elevator. Looking over my shoulder, I find her waiting behind me, hands clasped under her chin, eyes as bright as her hopeful smile. "Oh come on. *Me*?"

"Please," she begs as I unlock my door. "Garrett's the only other person I know here. I didn't think you'd appreciate me and him alone in his apartment, even though I wouldn't try anything."

"Garrett can do whatever he wants." It's not a lie, I guess, but it feels like one, simply because I don't like it.

Emily rolls her eyes. "Oh please."

"We aren't dating."

"Okay, Jennie. You're not dating and you wouldn't care if he and I were alone for a couple hours in his apartment because you're totally not jealous because you're just fucking so it's no big deal."

Pinning my arms across my chest, I arch a brow. "Is this any way to get yourself invited into my apartment?"

She folds her hands together again, pouting.

"You know I don't have any wine."

"*Yes*, Jennie, *I know*." There go her eyes again. I think she might roll them as much as I do. "I don't care. We don't need liquor to have fun."

The corner of my mouth quirks when I realize I said nearly the exact words to Krissy just days ago.

"Please?" She grips my shoulders, giving them a shake. "Please, please, *please*."

I groan, and she cheers, whooping a fist through the air as she pushes by me and makes herself at home in my apartment.

Literally right at home. She kicks off her shoes, tosses her purse and coat to the couch, and starts snooping through all my shit. It only takes her five minutes to make it to the last stop in my apartment, which is my bedroom, and I haven't been able to stop her from going through a single thing. She's highly entitled and nosy, and kinda reminds me of Carter.

Emily does a slow spin, humming her approval. Her eyes land on the small stand beside my bed, the drawer half-open, and I all but throw myself on it, nearly putting it through the wall and tackling Emily to the floor. My giggle is high-pitched and anxious as fuck. "Yeah, so, maybe don't open that."

"Why not?"

"Because. It's private."

Realization dawns, her smirk slow, irritating, and arrogant. "You have a sex toy in there, don't you?"

Heat rockets up my chest, into my face, right to the tips of my ears as my shrill giggle pierces the air. "No. What? No. Ha. That's...ridiculous." I hang my head. "It's more like a collection."

"Well, well, well," she murmurs. "Jennie's a dirty little girl."

"I'm not at *all* surprised Garrett sees your toys as allies, not enemies. We love a man who knows how and when to incorporate some battery-powered boyfriends to increase his lady's pleasure. Garrett can be such a sweetheart, and he's head over heels for you, so."

"He is not," I mumble, using my teeth to tug my scarf higher. Emily goaded me into a late lunch, so now we're walking through downtown Vancouver, braving the fierce weather conditions.

Okay, it's light flurries, but still.

"So you're telling me the man—who can get virtually any woman he wants, by the way—has willingly gone without sex for the last two-plus months to fool around exclusively with you, and he has no feelings for you?"

"Correct."

"You can't seriously believe that."

"Well, maybe not, but he hasn't come right out and said it. I don't want to assume anything."

"But you guys broke the rules last night. You slept over."

"So?"

"*Jennie.*" She grips my arms, shaking me. "Guys don't break rules! That means he likes you!"

Heat rushes into my cheeks despite the cold wind that slaps at them. "I've been thinking of making a move," I admit as she ushers me inside a warm café. "He asked me on a date, sort of. At first I thought he was just being nice because it's Valentine's Day, so he felt like he should do something special, but he seemed nervous about it..." My mind wanders to the way Garrett blushed and fumbled over his words. "He was so cute."

"That sounds positive to me. I think you should go for it."

"Yeah?" I pull off my mitts as my body starts to thaw. "I guess I'm nervous. This is all new to me, and he's Carter's friend, so I'm worried about messing things up." My eyes drift over the small café, all the happy people warming up with something hot. Everything smells so good, and as my gaze coasts over a lean man with a Toronto Maple Leaf baseball cap on, over to the menu, I'm considering ordering one of everything.

My head swivels fast enough to give me whiplash.

"Oh my God," I mutter from behind the hand I clap over my face, turning my back on the man in the blue and white hat. "You've got to be fucking kidding me."

"What?" Emily glances over my shoulder. "Ex?"

"How do I manage to avoid him for six years and somehow run into him twice in the last week?"

"No offense, Jen, but he looks like a dipshit."

"He *is* a dipshit. But I still don't want to see him. Mind if we go somewhere else?"

She's already marching toward the exit.

It'd be nice to get out of here unseen, but I haven't ever been that lucky. So I'm not surprised when a hand wraps around my elbow, whirling me around as I step outside.

In what world does he think it's acceptable to ever lay a hand on me again, and all while grinning?

"Twice in one week? C'mon, Jennie. This has gotta be a sign."

"Get your hand off me, Kevin," I bite through gritted teeth. "Right the fuck now."

"Aw, c'mon. Don't be like that."

Emily steps between us. "My friend asked you to take your hand off her, *Kevin*. Do you have a hearing problem or a comprehension problem?"

"Whoa." He pulls his hand back, raising both in surrender. "Calm down." His eyes glide over me, and I hate the way they heat when they do. Most of all, though? I hate how they light with intrigue, humor, like this is all some fun joke to him. "You've gotta get over it, Jennie. It's been years." He lifts a shoulder, like having someone make and leak a sex tape of you without your consent is no big deal. "You looked hot."

A bitter, disbelieving chuckle leaves Emily's lips and she places her hand on my shoulder, angling me away from Kevin. Her mouth dips to my ear. "On a scale of one to ten—"

"Twenty."

"And are you opposed to violence?"

"Not at all."

"Great." She spins back to Kevin, her grin so expansive, so conniving as she steps into him. "Hey, Kevin?" she asks, syrupy sweet.

His eyes bounce between us. "Yeah?"

Her fist connects with his nose with a crack that echoes in the chilled air, along with the collective gasp from onlookers passing by.

She wipes the blood off her knuckles. "Go fuck yourself."

As Emily loops her arm through mine, towing me away from the man clutching his face, the most startling revelation comes to light.

Despite that she's slept with the man I'm falling for, I actually...*like* Emily.

THIRTY
FALLING

Garrett

Jennie's Valentine's present is about to be a goddamn Apple Watch so she can't ignore my text messages anymore.

I've never been an impatient or needy kind of guy, and yet here I am, knocking on her door even though she hasn't responded to a single text with whether I can come over yet. But I leave in two hours and fuck me, I'm coming over.

Though I'm a little shocked to see a smiling blonde greet me on the other side of the door. In fact, I turn all the way around to see if that concussion from November has royally fucked me and I've forgotten which side of the hall Jennie lives on.

"You're in the right place, Casanova."

"Then you're in the wrong place," I blurt, then promptly fold my lips into my mouth. I like Emily, but she's about as scary as Jennie, and maybe a touch more violent. She could definitely take me if she wanted to. "Why are you here?" *Not much better, Garrett. You'll get 'em next time.*

She steps aside, waving me in. "We went for lunch."

I pause inside the door, midway through kicking off my shoes. *"You're* the friend?"

Her grin is triumphant. "I'm the motherfucking friend." She gathers her things. "I'm taking off. Thanks for hanging with me, Jen!"

Jen?

"Bye, Em!" Jennie calls from the kitchen, humming to the music drifting through the warm space. She smiles over her shoulder. "Hey, big guy. Sorry I didn't reply earlier. I wanted to make you dinner before you left." She pops up on her toes and kisses my lips, and I catch sight of the sizzling pan. "Coconut chicken curry over rice."

"And she cooks too," I murmur, tasting the spoon she offers. "Mmm, spicy."

"I always make you food."

"You always make me bowls of cereal."

"You like cereal."

"I like you."

Jennie's blush is electric, a rosy flush that climbs her neck like a vine, painting her creamy skin. She pulls her bottom lip into her mouth, focusing on the pan. "You also like Flamin' hot Funyuns, so your judgment is flawed."

Spying the dishes stacked on the edge of the small dining table, I ask, "Are we being fancy and sitting at the table for dinner?"

Cheeks still aflame, she lifts a lazy shoulder and lets it fall. She peeks sideways as I watch her, then sighs excessively, rolling her eyes. "Stop grinning like a jackass and go set the table."

"Yes, ma'am."

I do as I'm told, even set the utensils up the way my gran taught me when I was a kid. Then I crack a fancy bottle of sparkling water, pouring it into champagne flutes and garnishing with lemon wedges.

Hands on my hips, chest puffed with pride, I step back and inspect my table setup. "Nailed it."

Jennie giggles, shifting the pan to a back burner and turning off the stovetop. The music changes, her favorite song spilling out of the speakers, and she tucks her hair behind her ear before hitting me with a brilliant smile that nearly knocks the breath clean from my lungs.

She shimmies her way across the room and tugs on the pocket of my hoodie, mischief dancing in those overcast eyes. "C'mon, Gare-Bear. Dance with me."

I hold my hand out, grinning when she slips hers into mine and starts pulling me around the living room. I let her, because, quite frankly, I'd do anything for this woman.

"I think I made a friend today," she whispers as we sway.

I hug her tight. "I'm happy for you, Jennie."

"I'm happy for me too."

I drop my forehead to her shoulder, burying my face in her neck. "Hey, by the way, speaking of friends...there's something I forgot to mention last night." I press my lips to her silky skin, either to muffle the words or butter her up with a kiss; one of the two. "Adam knows."

She pushes back to look at me. "Adam knows what?"

I'd rather not elaborate, so I just give her a look, real wide-eyed and innocent, hoping she'll go easy on me.

"*Garrett.*"

"I'm sorry." I nuzzle her neck. "It was an accident."

"How did you accidentally let it slip that you like to fuck my mouth on days that end with *Y*?"

"When you put it that way it sounds a lot more difficult."

"You're terrible at keeping secrets," she scolds but lays her cheek on my chest, snuggling close.

I stroke a hand down her braid. "Jennie?"

"Mmm?"

"You're my favorite secret."

She graces me with a detonating grin before pulling my face down to hers. "And you're mine."

I thread our fingers together and lift our clasped hands above her head. Jennie spins out, then twirls back into me. I catch her against my chest, chuckling at the unsteady way we sway for a moment before regaining our balance. The hearty sound catches in my throat at the way she peers up at me from beneath her lashes, her smile soft, sheepish.

She's stunning, a beautiful soul, my best friend even though I wasn't looking. And as we sway together, the music telling us how quickly we're falling, how hard, the future that could lie before us if we let it, I realize how difficult the words on the tip of my tongue are becoming to swallow down.

Is she ready?

The look in her eyes tells me she's afraid, but her fingers tangled in mine tell me she wants to jump, so long as I'll be here to catch her.

I'll always be here. Doesn't she know that?

I sweep her braid over her shoulder and press a kiss right there, feeling her skin heat below my lingering lips. Brushing the pad of my thumb over the swell of her bottom lip, I make her a promise.

"You're safe with me."

Something in her eyes shifts, softening, opening. She places her hand over mine, sinking into my touch. "I know."

~

Sunshine: *If my vagina were a car, what kind of car would it be?*

I pull up the search bar and type in the words I'm looking for. When I find an appropriate picture, I forward it to Jennie with the words *after I'm done with it.*

Her response comes exactly four seconds later.

Sunshine: *Did you seriously send me a picture of a wrecked car?*

It takes me a solid minute to type out my reply. I'm snickering so much I'm shaking.

Me: *Get it? If ur vagina was a car, it'd be WRECKED after I was done with it *crying laughing emoji**
Sunshine: *How old are you????*
Me: *Old enough to know how to wreck ur pussy and then make it feel better.*
Sunshine: **eye roll emoji* Get over yourself, you're not even that good.*
Me: *I rock ur world, sunshine. Admit it.*
Sunshine: *Whatever.*

Before I can reply, she starts typing again. Over and over those dots wiggle, endlessly for two entire minutes. Then they stop.

I've just about given up when a text finally rolls through.

Sunshine: *I can't wait to see you today.*

This is my favorite part of my day, lounging in my hotel room, spending these fleeting moments texting with Jennie about nothing before I have to drag myself out of my snug cocoon and start my day, before she heads off to rehearsal.

This past stretch has felt like the longest road trip of my life. Maybe because I know what's waiting for me, because tomorrow I'm finally going to open my damn mouth and tell Jennie exactly what I want and hope to God it's what she wants too. I know things are complicated with her brother and her looming job offer, but I'd rather take the leap and commit to figuring it out together than never try. I'm not reckless enough to let her slip through my fingers.

So when our plane takes off forty-five minutes later and I'm munching on my breakfast, all I'm doing is counting the hours until we land, until Jennie's done with her final rehearsal, and I can watch her bound over to the car when she finds me waiting out front.

"You're coming," Carter grumbles the order.

Jaxon groans, pushing his empty tray away. "Dance isn't even a real sport."

"The fuck it's not. Try telling that to my sister and then see if you can backtrack fast enough to avoid getting your ass kicked by a girl. She works out just as much as I do, and I promise you, she can take you."

"What if I have a date tomorrow night? It's Valentine's Day."

"Nobody wants to go on a date with you," I quip, and immediately regret it.

Jaxon's eyes spark. "What about you, Andersen? You got a date tomorrow?"

"Uh, no. I'll be at the recital, like everyone else."

"The night is long. Nobody you're hanging out with later?"

I frown so hard it hurts, and scratch at my temple, squinting. "Nope. Can't think of anyone."

"Really? Not a single person? Wow." Jaxon's drawl is as irritating as his smirk, and I flip him the bird when Carter glances down at his phone. "Hey, Beckett. I heard your sister is close with her dance partner. They a thing?"

"*Ha.*" Carter sticks his hand in his box of Oreo O's. "Jennie wouldn't touch him with a ten-foot pole."

"It's inevitable they'd give it a go at least once, no? Dancing's so intimate, and they've been together for years.

There's a twitch in my left eye, and my pulse thunders in my neck.

Carter crushes his cereal in his fist before shoveling it in his mouth. "Abso-fucking-lutely not. I'd let her date you before I'd let her date him."

"You don't get to pick who she dates," Adam reminds him. "Jennie's an adult."

"Wouldn't the main thing be her happiness?" I add as casually as I can manage. "No matter who she's with? Even if it's Simon." Simon's face is gonna meet my fist if he ever tries to touch her without her consent again.

Carter looks out the window. "She's not interested in a relationship, so this conversation is pointless."

My nape prickles. "What?"

"She's not ready." His eyes meet mine, conveying without words what he's referring to. But I also think he's wrong.

"Maybe she is now."

"She's not."

"Did she say that?" Emmett asks. "Or are you assuming? Sometimes sisters prefer to not tell their excessively overprotective brothers about their sex lives."

"I'm not assuming anything. She said it just a couple days ago when we were at Hank's. He asked her when she was going to be ready to let someone in, and she said she didn't feel like committing to anything or anyone right now. Didn't want to be tied down, and didn't see a reason to make any changes when she's happy as is. We don't lie to each other."

The heat of Adam and Jaxon's stares burn into my face. Both hold sympathy, but I don't need it. I'm right about Jennie.

That's what I tell myself for the next four hours, but each mile we fly closer to Vancouver has me more uncertain than the last, and I hate that I've gone from confident to second-guessing in the same morning. We lose Wi-Fi halfway through the flight, so even if Jennie wasn't busy with Simon, I still wouldn't be able to get a response.

Adam claps my shoulder as I walk through the parking lot, head down, waiting for service to return as I bury my face in my phone.

"Don't let what Carter said back there bother you. Just talk to her. I'm sure you're both on the same page."

"Right." I nod. "Yeah, I'm sure we are."

Cranking both the ignition and heat, I wait for my phone to connect to my car, fingers tapping on the heated steering wheel. When it finally connects, it buzzes and dings, over and over, and a knot clenches between my shoulders at the notifications waiting for me.

Eight missed calls and twelve texts. All from my sisters.

I hit the most recent call, Gabby's soft sniffles quickly filling my car, the fear in her voice thick and shaky, making me want to jump right back on a plane.

"Garrett," she whimpers. "I'm scared. I want you to come home."

"What's wrong, Gabs?"

"Mom and Dad got in a fight."

"A fight? Is everyone okay?"

"They were screaming and Alexa made me and Stephie come into her room."

"Is everyone okay?" I repeat.

"I don't know, Garrett!" Her sobs pierce the air and my heart squeezes in my chest.

"Where's Alexa? Let me talk to her."

I pinch the bridge of my nose while I wait. My parents fought a lot when I was a kid, but the source was always my dad's drinking. Since the girls have come along and my dad's been sober, things are different. I can't pretend to know all that happens from across the country, but every time I'm home, they're a happy family, and I feel a little bit left on the outside.

"Garrett?"

"Lex. What's going on?"

"Can you come home? Please?"

"I can't come home. Not right now. You know that."

"Hockey's always more important to you than we are!" Alexa's voice trembles with each ragged breath, her telltale sign she's trying not to cry, barely hanging on.

"Alexa," I coax gently. "You're upset and overwhelmed right now; I can hear that. I'm tied to a contract with my job. That means I can't jump on a plane and fly home whenever I want to. That doesn't mean I don't love you, or that you aren't important to me. I do love you, and you guys are the most important things in my life."

"That's not true. If it was, you wouldn't always leave us."

"Lex—"

"No! You're never here when we need you! I...I..." The dam breaks, and through Alexa's sobs, I still hear the way she chokes out her next words before she hangs up on me. "I hate you!"

"For fuck's sake." I scrub my hand over my face, then my chest, right where it fucking hurts. I tap on my mom's contact, and the call connects on the first ring. "Mom? What's going on? The girls are upset, and they said you and Dad had a fight."

"Garrett," Mom cries softly. "He left."

"Left? What do you mean he left?"

"We had a fight, and he just…he…walked out."

My mind races to process her words, but before I truly can, she adds on a whisper, "He took a bottle of whiskey with him."

As I pace my living room, I try my dad's number over and over, each time hoping for a different outcome. It's always the same: straight to voice mail. I leave one each time, until it tells me his mailbox is full.

I try the only other person I want to talk to. She's always been the one that's needed me, but right now, I think I need her. To talk me down, to tell me my dad won't relapse, that he's stronger than that, that he's not going to put my sisters through the same thing he put me through, that he isn't going to drag my mom—and himself—through this all over again.

Except she can't make those promises. None of those choices are hers to make, and the only person who gets to decide how this plays out is my dad.

I just need her here, need her hand in mine to remember that good things happen, that it doesn't always need to be so fucking rainy when you've got a sun that shines so bright.

But Jennie's phone goes straight to voice mail too.

THIRTY-ONE
STAY

Jennie

"*Fuck yes!*"

Simon claps both hands to mine, and I can't stop grinning, euphoria coasting through me.

"That felt fucking awesome," he rasps out, hands on his waist as he catches his breath.

"We fucking nailed it!" I feel so good about it, I can't help tossing my arms around his neck, hugging him tightly. He lifts me in the air, spinning me.

"I feel the love," Mikhail exclaims, hands clasped beneath his chin. "It's breathtaking and awe inspiring and you two are going to be the hit of the show."

God, I hope so. I'm beyond exhausted, teetering on the edge of delirium. Every inch of my body aches from nonstop rehearsals, my brain demolished from lack of sleep. I'm eager for tomorrow, ready to give it my all on stage and then leave it right there for a little while, take a well-deserved break before we plow full steam ahead into choreography for our year-end performance.

"We're always the hit of the show," Simon says. "Think it's impossible not to be when I've got this beautiful woman up there with me." He winks, poking my waist. "I'm lucky to be your partner."

"You're damn right you are." Sure, I was thinking it, but it's Mikhail who speaks it. "I can't wait for the day I'm paying to see you on Broadway, Jennie."

Yuck, sounds terrifying. Do I like being center stage? Obviously; *let me shine, baby*. But also, let's keep the shining to a time-limited and controlled atmosphere. Broadway comes with publicity, being stuck in the on position for far too long, things I'd rather avoid.

Mikhail prattles on about how fantastic we are, and I'm extra pleased when he remarks that kiss he suggested months ago isn't needed between our chemistry and talent. He sends us home to rest, and Simon and I hit the sauna first for a quick steam. It's amazing how quickly the knots begin to unfurl, but by the time I'm toweling off after my shower, I can barely keep my eyes open. I'm worried I'm going to curl up in Garrett's lap and fall asleep when all I want to do is talk to him.

I pull a set of fresh clothes from my locker and dig my phone from my bag. Missed calls from Garrett sprinkled throughout the afternoon litter my screen, which is mostly how our days look lately. We almost never manage to catch each other, and I've found myself spending the majority of our fleeting video chats reacquainting myself with the way the skin around his eyes crinkles when he laughs, or how his mouth tilts, tugging up on the right side first before giving way to a full explosion, his striking blue-green eyes always so beautifully vulnerable and breathtaking, like a robin's egg in the spring.

As I pull my sweater on, that bear emoji dances across my screen once more. I'm about to answer when I hear that awful, patronizing laugh, the one that makes me want to drag my nails down a chalkboard.

I tuck my phone in my pocket and sweep my hair over my shoulders before securing it in a knot. I smile forcefully at Krissy and the Ashleys.

"I spotted those UGGs and knew it must be you. You're the only person I know who still wears those."

"It's snowing." I yank the zipper of my bag closed and hook the strap over my shoulder. "They're warm and comfy."

"Ugly too." She must think her giggle softens the blow, but it only pisses me off. She props her hip against the door frame, blocking my exit, and her friends look about as uncomfortable as I do. "Everyone's going out tomorrow night after the show. Wanna come?"

"Really?" I can't stop the eager way the word flies from my mouth, my fist tightening around the strap of my bag. A hopeful smile tugs at my lips, and my heart thuds with excitement.

304 | BECKA MACK

"Of course. You never come out with us."

"You've never asked me," I remind her.

She dismisses me with a wave. "We've asked you plenty of times."

They haven't, actually, but—"Oh shit. Tomorrow? I can't. It's my brother's birthday. We're going to dinner after the show."

"So come later. Meet us at the club."

"I…" have a date. A real one. And though I'm sure he'd tell me to go, to make friends and have fun, I'd rather be with him. "I can't. I'm sorry."

Krissy's eyes narrow. She's really a beautiful girl. Shame she has the personality of a slimy, evil snail. "You can't, or you won't?"

"I have plans that I'm not going to reschedule." I'm not in the mood to take her bait. I want to go home and spend the rest of the night with my best friend. So I give her a smile as I squeeze through the door and into the hall. "I'm free the rest of the weekend if you want to go out again. I'd love to celebrate with you guys."

"When are you going to stop living in your brother's shadow?"

The question stops me in my tracks, fingernails biting into my palm. There's an angry tic in my jaw and a hard, fast gallop in my ears. Slowly, I spin back to Krissy and her lackeys. They look just as stunned at what she's said. "What did you say?"

"You heard me." Krissy lifts a brow, pinning her arms across her chest. "But then why would you ever want to stop living in his shadow? Being Carter Beckett's sister has afforded you so many luxuries. A fancy apartment, an expensive car, a scholarship to an exclusive program, and a job offer most people could only dream of." She's got an inch on me, such a minuscule difference, but one that feels humongous when she looks down her nose at me as if I'm the smallest, most insignificant thing she's ever encountered. "Becoming your own person would require you to work for something for once in your life. And that's something I'm not sure you know how to do."

My jaw clenches, the air in my lungs rattling against my rib cage. When her mouth tugs into that self-righteous smirk, a match lights inside me, igniting a fire so fierce there won't be any survivors.

"Look at you," she continues, soft and condescending. "You don't even know how to think for yourself, do you?"

I used to want to disappear for Krissy. Hide all the special parts that made me me, yearning for acceptance. But I've come to realize I'm tired of hiding; nobody is worth disappearing for. Tough shit if she doesn't want me the way I am; that's exactly what I'm about to give her.

"I'm sorry, Krissy," I murmur, closing the distance between us. "But I don't speak dipshit."

Her eyes blaze. "What did you say?"

"You heard me," I parrot back. When I take a step forward, she takes one back. "I cannot believe I ever wanted to be a part of your group. What would ever entice me to be friends with you? I am *nothing* like you. I used to think it was my fault, that I didn't know how to make friends, that there must be something wrong with me. Now I know I just have fucking standards." My gaze flicks to Ashley and Ashlee as they step away from Krissy like they want nothing to do with this. "You girls should think about getting some."

"You're a bitch," Krissy spits. "The only reason anybody ever wants to be your friend is because of your brother."

I used to think so, too, but I'm slowly learning there are people in my life who love me for exactly who I am and what I have to offer.

"My brother is funny as fuck, compassionate, and loves harder than anybody I know. I don't blame people if they see what he has to offer and want to add another Beckett to their lives. Quite frankly, we kick fucking ass. But you..." I lift a brow, looking her over. "You know what you are, Krissy? You're the type of girl who peaked in high school. Pretty enough, popular enough, with a cute enough boyfriend. You thought it could only go up from there. Then you stepped into the real world and realized you were only one of many. That you didn't stand out the way you wanted to. That your version of enough wasn't *enough* anymore. Everybody else grew up, but you're stuck wishing for a life that doesn't exist."

Stalking toward her, I revel in the way she stumbles as she frantically tries to match each step, and I continue.

"You're mean, nasty, miserable, and quite frankly, a solid six out of ten at best when it comes to dance."

Krissy gasps. "Fuck you."

"I used to wonder why you hated me, kept myself awake wondering how I could make myself better so you'd want to be my friend. But that's impossible, isn't it? You hate me because you're nothing like me, but you wish you were. You're jealous. You have the friends, the popularity, the army that follows you so recklessly, but you're still miserable. My group may be small, but my people love me for exactly who I am, and who I am is something I refuse to change, not for you, and not for anyone.

"So, walk in my brother's shadow? I don't fucking think so. The only people who walk in shadows are those who follow you so blindly, who have no idea there's a life out there that you're not a part of, one that's happier, with friendships so much more fulfilling than the ugly way you dictate yours."

Krissy's shallow breathing fills the hallway. "I hate you."

"Guess what? I don't give a fuck. Not anymore."

She trips over her feet when she spins, catching herself before she can fall, and as she storms away, she orders her friends to follow.

Ashlee lingers, eyes bouncing between Krissy's quickly retreating form and me. "You didn't just take her down a peg or two; you demolished her entire ship." Her head swivels when Krissy screams her name, and when she looks back at me, she grins. "Glad I got to see it. See ya later, Jennie. Can't wait to watch you kick ass tomorrow."

She turns her back on Krissy and heads for the exit behind me, throwing her middle finger up over her shoulder when Krissy shrieks once more.

A slow clap fills the hallway, and Simon emerges from the doorway of the gym, whistling lowly. "Dang, Jennie. Look at you go."

"That was long overdue." I roll my neck over my shoulders, sighing as it cracks. I've released an unholy amount of tension, but it's only made me aware just how much I was carrying. "I can't wait to never see them again."

"Don't worry about them." Simon grips my shoulders, fingers digging into my tight, sore muscles. "They're not all that fun."

"Says the guy who's slept with all three of them." I shrug out of Simon's grasp, though the massage feels heavenly. "They must have been fun enough to fuck."

"If they were fun, I'd still be sleeping with them." His mouth dips to my ear. "If they were *really* fun, I'd be sleeping with all three of them at the same time."

I swat him away. "You're gross."

Simon chuckles. "Truly disgusting. Wanna come back to my place? We can soak in the jacuzzi, let our muscles rest."

"I can't. Garrett's picking me up soon."

"Your boyfriend?"

"He's not my boyfriend."

"He picks you up all the time."

"He does not pick me up all the time." *Sometimes he's out of the country.* "We live in the same building. It's purely convenience. There's abso-lutely nothing romantic between us."

Simon's eyes glide over my face, examining the authenticity of my words, I'd guess, but I've gotten fairly good at lying about this. "Really?"

"Just friends."

"All right," he whispers, palm curving around my nape as he tows me closer. "Well, your *friend* is here, looking ultra jealous, which is odd since you're...*just* friends."

My head snaps, finding Garrett hovering in the doorway, keys dangling from the tip of his pointer finger, other hand tucked into the front pocket of his hoodie as he watches us. Deep crease in his forehead, full lips turned down in a frown, and a highly noticeable tic in his jaw, Garrett Andersen looks nothing like the goofy, sweet man I've come to know over the past months. The sight alone is enough to make my stomach twist and knot.

"I'll see you tomorrow," I toss out, dashing toward Garrett, my smile brightening as I go. "Hey, big guy."

The crease between his brows doesn't diminish as he stares down at me, and when he finally whispers, "Hi," I know well enough that something's not right.

I grab his elbow and tug him toward his waiting car, desperate for privacy. "I missed you. How was your flight?"

"Fine," he mumbles, and before I can ask him what's wrong, he whisks me into my seat and closes the door. It's not my imagination that he stalls getting in, pretending to look for the keys he had in his hands a moment ago. When he finally climbs in, the chill of the outdoors returns, stealing the warmth of his heated car.

The first thing I notice is the empty cupholders. Without asking, Garrett consistently shows up with a cinnamon bun cappuccino. He presses it into my hands, warming them on contact, and touches his lips to mine before he shifts into drive and asks how my day was.

It's not the lack of coffee that bothers me, but the lack of everything else. Physical contact, fucking *eye* contact, conversation as we drive in silence, and I don't know why.

"Is everything okay, Garrett?" I'm dying to hold his hand, but he keeps his glued to the steering wheel, and I miss his fingertip trailing over my thigh. "You seem upset."

"Fine." The single word is so low, I barely hear it.

My mind races, searching for something I've done wrong in the hours since we've talked. Garrett's never been upset with me before, and the disconnection is heavy and staggering. We're strangers all over again, tiptoeing around what we really want to say.

Until he opens his mouth.

"You gonna tell him to keep his hands off you, or should I?"

My heart skitters to a stop. "What?"

Garrett's grip on the steering wheel tightens as he keeps his eyes on the road. "I don't like the way he touches you."

"Garrett...Simon's my dance partner. He has to touch me."

"You know as well as I do he wants to be more than that. I can handle the way he touches you when you're dancing, but I won't tolerate him putting his hands all over you the rest of the time, like he thinks you're his."

"Okay, back up." I swivel in my seat, hands braced in front of me. "What are you talking about? I'm not Simon's. I'm not anybody's."

"Right," Garrett agrees, clipped. "You're happy being single."

"Can you fucking look at me?" I snap. "Why are you upset with me?"

"I'm not upset with you," he lies. "I'm reiterating a point you've made a couple of times now."

"A point I'm not aware of, clearly, so why don't you enlighten me." I fold my arms over my chest and wait as he pulls into the parking garage, finding his spot.

"You don't want to date an athlete. You don't want to be in a relationship. You're happy being single and on your own." He throws each sentence out like it's etched in stone, tendons flexing in his clenched fists. "You've said it three times now."

"Three times?"

"When Gabby called you my girlfriend at Christmas, when we were at that club the other week, and a couple days ago when you told Carter you didn't want to be tied down to anyone, that you were happy being on your own."

My thoughts drift to my last visit with Carter and Hank, where Hank pestered me about letting someone in, finding my person the way Carter found his. But I'd already found my person; I just couldn't tell them that.

"They were only words," I promise softly, anger dimming. "I can't very well say I'm sleeping with my brother's best friend, can I? Nobody's supposed to know about us."

"And when you said to Simon that we were just friends, that our relationship was just convenient…were those only words too?" Though the words are harsh, there's a vulnerability to him that simmers below the surface, like he's about to crack wide open. I don't want him to break, but I do want him to let me in.

"Garrett," I coax gently, laying my hand on his cheek. My heart aches when his gaze finds mine, sad, angry, and lost. "Are you jealous?"

His eyes flicker, and there's that damn bob in his throat again as he looks away.

"I know sometimes you struggle to give your feelings words. I need you to talk to me right now. I'm listening."

"I-I…I can't…" His knee starts bouncing, fingers stretching over them before curling back into his palms. He shoves a hand through his hair, knocking his hat off and tugging on those golden waves. "I can't think. I can't talk. Fuck. I hate this."

I take his hand in mine, squeezing gently. "Take a breath. I'm right here. I'll wait."

He blinks at me, once, twice, and then the words come rushing out. "My sisters hate me. They need me, and I'm here, and I'm failing them, just like my dad failed me. And I can't…I can't get a hold of him. And no one is answering their phone, and you…" His beautiful eyes swim with pain as he looks at me. "I called you because I-I…I needed you. And you weren't there." The words are jagged, broken fractures that let me peek into this man's big heart.

I take his face in my hands. "I'm sorry I missed your calls. I'm here now. Your sisters love you, Garrett. I promise." I push his hair off his forehead. "It must be hard when you're so far apart. You'll fix it."

His eyes bore into mine. "What if it can't be fixed?"

"Everything can be fixed."

He hangs his head. "I'm not so sure about that." His voice drops, so low I barely hear his next words. "Especially when you're not on the same page." He blows out a defeated breath, running his fingers through his hair. "Or even reading the same damn book."

Why do I get the distinct feeling this is about more than his sisters?

Before I can ask, he shifts out of my grasp and steps out of the car. Without a word, he takes my hand, swallowing it in his big one as he pulls me from my seat and leads me to the elevator. Everything feels hazy and big, confusing and overwhelming. He's too quiet, and I don't know the right words to fill the space, to take away his pain and make everything better and safe.

But I'll figure it out, and I'll start by making him a big mug of hot chocolate, like he always does for me.

Except when I prop my door open with my hip and kick my shoes off, Garrett doesn't follow. He stands in the hallway, hands tucked in his pockets, looking at the floor.

"I'm not going to come in, Jennie."

"What? Why? I'll make hot chocolate. We can order in. Or I can...I think I have the stuff to make spaghetti. I can make spaghetti for dinner. Just tell me what you want." I hate everything about the desperation dripping from my tone, the way it tastes, the way it hurts, makes me feel weak, like I need him.

But I think I do, because I didn't really find myself until I found him.

His eyes lift to mine, exhaustion stealing their sparkle. "I think...I think I want space." The soft way he speaks the words, laced with guilt and regret, has my heart hammering against my chest, looking for a way out.

"Space?" My shoulders hunch as I curl into myself. "From me?"

"From this. It's...I'm..." He rubs his neck, searching for his words. "I can't think straight right now. I'm overwhelmed, I'm confused, and I'm tired. Fuck, I'm so fucking tired."

"We can just relax." I take his hand, tugging him forward. "We can curl up on the couch and—"

"Jennie, no." Garrett shakes his hand free. His eyes are bloodshot, defeated, and mine begin to sting. "I don't know if I can keep doing this. Things are...they're different. I need some time to think, that's all."

A burning sensation crawls up my throat, one I can't swallow down. "That's what people always say when it's easier than good-bye."

The uncertain way he licks his lips contradicts his shaking head. "I'm not saying that word."

"I don't understand." My chest rises sharply, eyes prickling. "You're my best friend."

His gaze holds mine, like he's searching for any hint of duplicity. There is none. In a couple of short months, this man has become my best friend, my cheerleader, my rock. I don't know how to handle losing him.

But I can see it, the anguish he wears, the heartache etched in his eyes, making it waver. Only I'm not sure why it's there.

Until he swallows, thick and slow, and finally speaks his next words.

"It's not enough for me anymore."

I stagger backward as the words sink in.

Not enough? But...I've always been enough for him.

Tears well in my eyes, ready to spill. My fingers close around my tightening throat, trying to claw away the anxious thoughts, the fear that he'll leave and take all of me with him even though I'll be left standing right here, all alone, like I've been all my life.

I've shown him all of me, and he doesn't want me.

Garrett's hands close around my wrists, bringing me into his chest. He dips his face, his chest heaving in time with mine. "You are nothing short of perfect, Jennie."

"If that were true, you wouldn't be leaving."

His lips part, eyes running over me, even as the elevator dings and springs open. Emily steps off, smiling brightly at us.

"Hey, lovebirds."

Garrett's mouth opens, but before he can say anything, his phone rings. He digs it out of his pocket, and his sister's name, Alexa, shines on the screen. He curses under his breath, and when he looks back at me, his eyes swim with so much pain, confusion, heartache, I can't separate it all. I don't want to be the cause of any of it. I want to help him through this.

"Garrett, I—"

His phone rings again, and he swallows. "I have to go. I'm sorry, Jennie."

I don't want him to apologize. I want him to stay.

He hesitates before cupping my jaw, thumb sweeping over my lower lip. He brings his mouth to mine in a kiss that feels so much like good-bye, one I'm not ready for, one I don't want.

His warm hands fall away, leaving me feeling cold and exposed, his stare flooded with regret as it touches my face, like he's memorizing the way I look. Garrett brushes a fallen wave off my neck, kisses the tip of my nose, and with one last look, leaves me standing there as he brings his phone to his ear.

When the elevator door closes behind him, I meet Emily's gaze.

"Hey," she whispers. "You okay?"

My throat burns and I lick my lips, staring up at the ceiling.

And then it happens. My vision clouds. My nose tingles. No amount of blinking helps. My mouth opens to answer, chin trembling, but instead that first tear falls, followed by the second, and the third, all of them cascading down my cheeks, and Emily soars across the hallway.

She holds my quivering body tight to hers, and my words finally come, broken and shattered, just like me.

"You said he wanted me too."

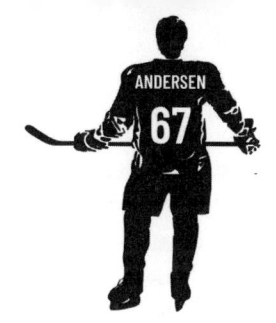

THIRTY-TWO
SECOND CHANCES

Garrett

I'VE SPENT twelve hours on an airplane today.

Twelve fucking hours, Denver to Vancouver, Vancouver to Halifax.

Nova Scotia isn't at all where I expected to find myself this morning when I woke up, but here I am. It's just after eleven p.m., my time, when I touchdown in Halifax, but here on the east coast, it's three in the morning.

Three in the fucking morning, and instead of home, where it should be, I find my dad's car exactly where I knew it would be: the only twenty-four-hour diner around. He's the only customer here, aside from the same old man who's been sitting at the counter every morning at the ass crack of dawn for the last twenty years.

"Alycia," I greet the woman behind the counter, the one who smiles brightly when I walk in, despite the hint of remorse. She's been working here since we were sixteen. I used to drop her off for her shift, then drive back an hour before it ended, sit at the counter and dip my free French fries in my free shake while I waited for my girlfriend to get off work so we could make out in the backseat of my car. "What are you doing still working here? You said you were going to quit."

"Garrett." She pushes through the swinging door and engulfs me in a hug, familiar and warm. "Just a couple extra shifts here and there. Kids are so damn expensive." She pulls back, her eyes soft and kind like they always were. Once upon a time we said we were going to get married.

But she wanted me to stay here, and I wanted to leave. Things weren't meant to be, and that's okay. "I tried calling you, but your number's different now. I was going to stop by your place on the way home this morning, let your mom know he was here."

"How long's he been here?"

"Two hours, give or take. Figure he came by when the bar closed." Her gaze lands on my dad, slumped over in a booth. "Hasn't had a thing to eat or drink since he's been here."

"What about before?"

She shrugs. "Not sure. He doesn't want to talk, so I've let him be."

"Thanks for keeping an eye on him."

She catches my elbow as I turn away. "Will you be around for a couple days?"

I shake my head. "My flight is at noon."

She squeezes gently. "Take care of yourself."

My dad is tucked away in the back corner, head in his hands, eyes downcast. For a moment, sympathy takes over, and I feel for the man. But then I think about the wife and daughters he left at home, afraid and without answers, and I remember being in that position too many times to count. And anger wins.

"What the hell are you doing?"

Dad's head snaps up as I stand above him, eyes bloodshot, face tear streaked. Just like that, every bit of anger wavers, ebbing when—for once—I want it to flow. I've never been good at holding onto it. It makes me feel sick, miserable, tired. But I need an outlet, and I thought for sure this would be it, because making Jennie my outlet several hours ago sure as fuck wasn't it.

"Garrett." He swipes furiously beneath his eyes. "What are you... What are you doing here?"

"What are *you* doing here? You have a family who depends on you to come home, to be present. Instead you're out all night getting drunk."

"I'm...no." His head shakes rapidly, and while his eyes are tired and red rimmed, they don't have that sluggish, glazed look to them, the one that told me his mood when I was younger, whether I could talk to him, or if I should hide out in my bedroom for the rest of the night.

He reaches under his coat, showing me the neck on a bottle of whiskey, the seal still intact, before he quickly covers it back up. "I didn't."

"What about before this? At the bar?"

"I wanted to. Fuck, I wanted to." He drags his fingers through his hair, tugging. "I ordered it. Whiskey neat. Double. Stared at it for five fucking hours. Wouldn't let the bartender take it away but couldn't bring myself to drink it either." He scrubs a hand over his eyes before choking out his next words. "I'm a fucking failure."

"No, you're not," I argue without thinking.

"I am. Here's my son, saving my ass like he's done a hundred times before. Only difference is he's not a kid anymore. My problems never should have been yours."

"No, they shouldn't have," I agree quietly, sliding in across from him. "But I loved you then, and I love you now. Standing beside you is where I'll be while you solve your problems." I touch the back of his hand, and his tentative gaze meets mine. "But I can't help you if I don't know what's going on."

"I don't know where to start," he admits.

"From the beginning would be a good spot."

He nods, silence stretching between us as he looks for his beginning.

"Back in December, right around Christmas, they announced at work that they'd sold the factory. There was talk the new owners were going to lay everybody off, clean house and start fresh. I started looking for another job right away, but they showed up after the holidays and everything was business as usual. We thought we were safe. And then yesterday..." His chest heaves, voice cracking. "Yesterday they came in. Laid everyone off. *Everyone.* Just walked in, told us all to go home, to not bother coming back."

He chuckles, a low, exasperated sound. "Three months' salary. I've given them twenty-five years, they lay me off with zero notice, and all I get is three months' fucking salary. How am I supposed to support my family on that? I can't, Garrett. I just can't."

The reminder is on the tip of my tongue, that I can support them just fine, help out as much as they need. Hell, I've been trying to get them to relocate to Vancouver for years. But I know it's not the solution he's looking for.

"And you haven't talked to Mom," I guess.

Dad shakes his head. "She knew I was worried about it when you came home at Christmas, but then everything seemed fine. I stopped looking for work and we both stopped worrying. Now I...I don't know how to tell her. There's nothing for me out there, Garrett. I don't have a college degree."

"Because you took a steady job that paid well so you could provide for your girlfriend and your new baby," I remind him. It's never been lost on me that my dad gave up on a lot of things to become a father at the age of eighteen. The only thing he did for himself was finish high school. Being thrust into such a heavy role of responsibility at a young age only perpetuated his habits, and I spent many years feeling guilty for being born, telling myself he never would have struggled if they hadn't had me. Logically, I know my dad's struggle isn't my fault, but when you're a kid who's responsible for your father more than he is for you, it's hard to remind yourself of that.

"How am I supposed to send three girls to college? I don't know how to be the husband my wife deserves, the father the girls deserve, that *you* deserve."

I lay my hand on his. "We don't need you to be anybody other than who you are, Dad. We just need you to show up."

His gaze falls to our clasped hands, and his callused thumb glides over mine. "I didn't show up for you." His words are laced with remorse, but more than that, recognition. He's not looking for me to convince him he was there; he needs me to know he realizes his faults, the places he went wrong.

"Not for a little while," I admit. "But maybe sometimes we need to hit rock bottom to gain a new perspective. You put the work in and came back stronger than ever. You became the dad I always wanted, and I'm grateful to know that man, that that's the man my sisters know. That you struggled, that you still struggle sometimes, it doesn't make you a failure. It makes you human."

Tears gather in his eyes and start a slow roll down his cheek. "You and your sisters are the only thing I got right. I'm so proud of you."

"And I'm proud of you."

The house is dark when I pull into the driveway, save for the faint glow of the light over the stove, the one I can see from the window above the kitchen sink. Mom leaves it on in case someone wakes in the middle of the night.

My dad's leg bounces in the passenger seat, gaze trained on the front door as he spins his sobriety chip between his fingers. "What if she leaves me again?"

"I think she's forgiven you for worse things than being part of a major layoff. Mom has a big heart. She doesn't give up without a fight."

The look on his face tells me he knows, but the fear in his eyes says he let her down enough once before, and he can't live without her a second time.

"If that happens, we'll work through it together. But you need to believe that your relationship is strong enough to withstand this together."

Silence fills the car while he holds my gaze, and when he nods, I turn off the engine. Outside the car, he embraces me, a hug I didn't know I needed.

"Thank you for believing in me. For giving me so many more chances than I ever deserved."

I hope one day he realizes he's always been worth every second chance.

Light illuminates the living room the second I step inside, briefly blinding me as my mom leaps from the couch.

Confusion mars her grief-stricken face. "Garrett? What are you doing here?"

I step aside and my dad takes one tentative step forward, then another.

"Lucas," Mom gasps quietly, clapping a hand to her mouth as tears pool in her eyes.

"I'm so sorry," he says softly, and I watch as tears slide down both their cheeks before my mom throws herself in his arms.

I steal away down the dark hallway, creeping up the staircase. Every bedroom door is open, every bed empty, except Alexa's. When the door opens with a creak, I find all three of my sisters snuggled together. Moonlight streaks across their faces from the bay window, illuminating Gabby's eyelids as they flutter.

She sits up, blinking. "Hello? Who's there?"

The bedside lamp flicks on, and Alexa scrambles to sitting, rubbing her eyes with her fists. "Garrett?"

"*Garrett!*" Gabby scrambles from bed, rushing over to me in her kitten pajamas.

"Shhh." I wrap my arms around her as she buries her head against my torso. "Don't wake Stephie."

"You came home?" Alexa asks, watching as I carry Gabby back to bed.

"You said you needed me."

Her bottom lip wobbles. "So you came back for us?"

I bend, pressing a kiss to the crown of her head. Alexa likes to play tough, but she's got the softest heart, like Jennie. "I'll always be here when you need me. Now get back to sleep. I just wanted to check in on you."

Gabby grins up at me, pulling back the covers, patting the mattress. "Will you sleep with us?"

I chuckle. "There's no room."

She pouts, scooting closer to Stephie in the middle. "We can make room."

I glance at Alexa, the uncertainty that dances across her face. Slowly, her brows smooth, and she lays her head back down on her pillow, eyes flitting to the empty spot next to Gabby.

"Do any of you snore?" I ask.

"Lex does," Gabby states. "Like a trucker, Dad says."

"Shut. *Up*. Gabby."

Laughing, I peel my hoodie off and toss it in the corner of the room, leaving me in a T-shirt and sweats as I climb into my sister's double bed, content in knowing I'll be falling off this at some point in the night.

Gabby takes my arm, draping it across her as Alexa turns off the lamp, blanketing the room in darkness. Her breathing grows shallow and steady within minutes, but my mind is racing too fast to sleep.

The past twenty-four hours have been a giant clusterfuck of problems and emotions, things I wasn't prepared to handle. It feels like I handled this issue right, but my gut tells me I fucked my other one straight into the ground, because the only thing I see every time I close my eyes is Jennie's face, the way her eyes clouded with rejection when I told her I needed space.

I know I wasn't thinking straight, but Jesus Christ, what was I fucking thinking? Was that the solution to my jealousy, to my uncertainty when it came to how she felt for me, whether we were growing together or separately? To feeling helpless with my family?

"Garrett?"

Through the darkness, I find Alexa peering at me from her pillow. "Hmm?"

"I'm sorry I said I hated you. I don't hate you."

I smile. "I know, Lex."

"I was just really scared, and Stephie and Gabby were scared, and I felt like I had to be brave for them. But I didn't know how. I wanted you to come home and be brave for us."

"It's okay to be scared. But for what it's worth, I think you were plenty brave for all of us." I stretch my arm across the space between us, and when Alexa reaches for my hand, I hook my pointer finger around hers. "I love you."

"I love you too."

"Next time you're scared, it's important for us to communicate, okay? Nearly everything can be fixed with a little communication."

The irony isn't lost on me that communicating is not on the list of things I did well with Jennie hours ago. I grew up straddling a thin line, too afraid to speak my mind out of fear of upsetting my dad whenever he was teetering on the edge, but that's exactly what I did to Jennie. I was scared, so I talked *at* her. She put her trust in me, trust I fought tooth and nail to earn, and in the matter of a half hour, I threw it all away because I was too afraid to swallow my pride and tell her what I was scared of: losing her, losing my dad, failing my family.

"Are you taking your girlfriend on a date for Valentine's Day?" Alexa asks, as if she knows exactly what's going on in my head.

"Jennie's not my girlfriend," I grumble.

"Then how come you knew who I was talking about?" she tosses back, all snarky.

"Three siblings," I mutter, "and not a single one is a boy."

"I listened to you talk to her on the phone after her dance recital."

"*Alexa.*"

She snickers. "What? It was cute. You called her your best friend and you said you made snowman ornaments with your handprints. I know I'm only twelve, but I'm pretty sure that means she's your girlfriend."

"Maybe she was, kinda, or at least I wanted her to be," I confess. "I wanted her to be more than just a friend. But I'm pretty sure I messed it up." I close my eyes and sigh. "No, I *know* I messed it up."

"Why? Did she break up with you?"

"No. I think I did."

"Ew. Why would you do that? Jennie's cool and nice and she makes fun of you but keeps you around anyway even though you're annoyin'."

I chuckle quietly. "You're right. She's all of those things and more. I guess I was scared."

"I thought it was okay to be scared," Alexa whispers back to me.

I sigh. "It is."

"Are you going to talk to her?"

"Should I?"

She snorts. "Are all boys this clueless? Don't you like her?"

"I'm not sure *like* is a strong enough word."

"Doesn't that answer your question? Why would you want to be away from her and sad when you can be with her and happy?" She laces her fingers through mine, squeezing. "I bet if you ask her for another chance, she'll give it to you."

"You think so?"

"You're worth a second chance, Garrett."

The theater is dark, the atmosphere humming as the audience buzzes excitedly.

I check my ticket for the seventeenth time, which is super unnecessary; I've memorized it.

"Excuse me," I whisper, indicating to the empty seat halfway down the row before I start inching toward it. "Pardon me. Sorry. So sorry. Excuse me."

Unbuttoning my suit jacket, I plop down with a sigh, and Adam, Jaxon, and Cara all arch a brow.

Carter leans around everyone, exhaling heavily. "Oh thank fuck. I was worried you were bailing. Jennie woulda kicked you right in the balls."

I think she might anyway, but instead of saying that, I laugh. It's a lot shriller and more panicked than I'd like.

Adam clears his throat, eyes on the empty stage. "Everything okay?"

"With my dad? Yes. He's going to start his counseling sessions again, and my mom was helping him with his resume before I left."

"Good. I'm glad. And with her?" He doesn't say her name. He doesn't have to. "She called me this morning. Asked if I knew where you were because you had a fight, and she went to your place to try to talk to you, but you weren't there. It wasn't my place to tell her, Garrett, so I didn't, but you need to. She's either part of your life, or she's not. You don't get to ask her to let you in and then not do the same for her, especially when it affects your relationship. You have every right to be upset about everything, what happened with your dad, what she said, even though I doubt she meant it...but you don't shut her out. You're smarter than that." His eyes shift sideways, meeting mine. "You're here, so I assume that means you're going to be honest with her."

"Yes, Dad," I grumble.

His mouth quirks. "Make me proud, son."

The theater goes quiet, a single spotlight shining on the stage.

Carter leans forward, glaring down the row at everyone. "*Shhh!*"

"Nobody said any—" Jaxon clamps his mouth shut, then pretends to button it, eyes wide at the fierce expression Carter wears.

My eyes fall to the tall object sitting on the floor between him and Olivia, and I bury my face in my hand. "Does he have a fucking tripod stand and a video recorder? Does he not know cellphones come equipped with video function now?"

Adam chuckles. "He's a proud brother."

Proud he is. He spends the entire show half-assed clapping at the end of each performance before he examines the program and announces how many songs there are until Jennie's. It's the very last song, so by the time we get there and Carter leans forward and opens his big mouth, our entire row and the one behind us all drone in unison, "*It's Jennie's turn.*"

But I don't blame him for being proud. When those curtains open, Jennie's automatically the most magnificent person who's taken this stage tonight.

Draped in crimson, silk ribbons and chiffon, her chocolate waves flowing around her shoulders, every inch of her glows.

Her head lifts, revealing the deep shade of lipstick that matches her dress, and the sadness etched in her eyes rocks me to my core as she stares out at the audience.

Those pale blue eyes sweep slowly through the crowd, up and down the rows, like they're cataloging each attendee.

Or looking for someone.

Because when they stop on me, everything changes. The lines in her face ease, her shoulders drop, and she stands a little taller. The grief in her eyes fades as the music starts, the familiar chords of her favorite song making me grin. A smile starts in the corner of her mouth, a slow beginning that gives way to an earth-shattering explosion, igniting her face with the most devastating happiness, making her shine.

She always fucking shines.

She's a masterpiece as she comes to life, letting the music carry her across the stage. Simon fades into the background compared to her, not worthy to be any part of her whole. The show belongs to her, and in this moment, the world does too. If she wants to be a star, they're waiting. If she wants her own studio, she can have it. There's nothing this woman can't do; I'm sure of it.

I'm so enthralled in her I barely notice that Carter's got the camera off the tripod, that he's standing in the aisle with the video camera as he tapes the entire performance, head bobbing along.

I'm so in awe of her that I don't spare a second thought to the arm Simon wraps around her waist before dipping her, his hand running a slow path up her side as the music begins to drift to a close.

I'm so mind-blowingly obsessed with her that I almost miss the look in Simon's eyes as he draws her into his chest, the way his hand slides along her jaw as the music stops, the way he takes her chin between his fingers and tilts her face up.

I almost miss the way his mouth covers hers as he sears her with a kiss for their grand finale.

But I don't.

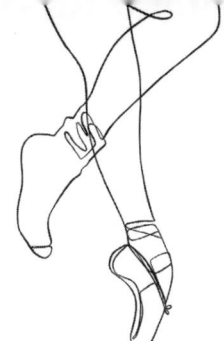

THIRTY-THREE
IS THIS THE WAY IT GOES?

Jennie

THE ROAR of the crowd rings in my ears, but it's my anger that's thundering.

Dangerous. Explosive. *Lethal.*

My heart thrashes, throwing itself at my rib cage like it might burst as I wait for the curtains to close.

"Jennie," Simon starts once we're encased in darkness, eager, excited as he releases me. "That was so—"

I twirl so fast I no longer feel the ground beneath my bare feet. The sound of my palm striking his cheek echoes behind the stage, stunning the crew to silence, leaving only the cheers of the audience.

Simon covers the red handprint on his cheek. The dumbfounded expression he wears only spurs me on.

"How dare you," I seethe. "How fucking *dare* you."

"Dazzling! That. Was. *Dazzling*!" Mikhail rushes toward us but stops short, his grin falling. "Jennie? Is everything okay?"

"No. Everything is not okay." I stalk toward Simon, every inch of my body hot, right up to the tips of my ears. "No." I shove my finger in his chest. "I. Said. No. Do you know what no means?"

His hands rise in surrender, or defense, as he nods rapidly.

"That's funny. Because I've said it once." *Another jab to the chest.* "I've said it twice." *Another.* "I've lost count of how many fucking times I've said that two-letter word to you, yet you still—" *jab,* "—don't—" *jab,*

"—get it." One more jab, extra fucking hard, just for good fucking measure. "How fucking flawed is my judgment that I could never truly see you for who you are? That I gave you chance after chance, believed there was anything decent about you?"

"It was an accident," he pleads on a whisper, eyes pinballing. "Keep your voice down."

My brows fly up my forehead. "An accident? You *accidentally* kissed me without my consent? For the second time?"

There's the gasp I was waiting for, Mikhail right on cue. "*Simon.*"

"I-I...I got caught up. It felt right. With acting like we're in love for the show and everything...It just felt right, Jennie."

The laugh that leaves my lips is nothing short of menacing. "I don't need to pretend like there's anything more going on between us for the sake of the show. I'm a damn hard worker and my dancing will do all the talking, like it always does, like it has my entire life."

I storm past the watching dance cast, finding my cubby, my bag, my outfit for dinner tonight, and I sling it all over my shoulder. The faster I get the hell out of here, the better.

I pause at the exit, meeting Simon's worried gaze. "That was the last time we'll ever dance together. I'm done with pairs, and I'm done with you." I look to Mikhail. "Understood?"

He gives me a curt nod and a salute. "Yes, ma'am."

I keep my head up as I push through the crowd filtering out of the auditorium, heading for the spot where Carter promised to be waiting.

He's there. They're all there. Except for one.

I try not to notice, but the same way his presence shifted my entire mood, brought me to life on stage, Garrett's sudden absence leaves my body aching, tired, and I'm reminded that welcoming that man into my life brought me a whole lot of happiness I never knew I was missing.

It's so staggeringly silent and gray without him, and I hate it.

The fury Carter is feeling is as palpable as my own as I march toward him. He opens his mouth, and I shove my finger in his face.

"Don't even start. I don't want to hear his fucking name. Not today, not tomorrow, and if you bring it up anyway, yours will be the next face I slap tonight, got it?"

Carter's lips mash together, eyes wide. "Got it. I'll go get the car."

I'm wrapped in hold after hold, passed between family and friends as they praise my performance, and when I take a step back for some air, a hand wraps around my elbow, tugging me around the corner.

Garrett takes my face in his strong hands, thumbs sweeping over my cheekbones as his gaze touches every inch of me. His eyes are hard, reeling with a fury so deep it makes his grasp tremble. But there's something else there. Something tangible. Something strong and profound and genuine that throws me for a loop, because I used to believe I saw it, but I spent last night convincing myself it was never there.

"Are you okay, Jennie?"

"I'm…" Not. I'm not okay. Simon took something that didn't belong to him. Kevin took something that didn't belong to him. The only person I've willingly and eagerly given any pieces of myself to is this man right here. I didn't do it blindly or unknowingly. I did it slowly, cautiously, sometimes while I stared fear right in the face, dared it to prove me wrong about Garrett. It never did. Every time I gave him another piece, he took it carefully in his hands, like each piece was delicate glass, something to be admired.

But now what? Where do we stand? Have I given all my pieces to someone who no longer wants them? Have I lost the only person who's ever accepted all of me?

"No," I finally whisper. "I'm not okay."

The hardness in his eyes fades, giving way to the softness I've come to know, the tenderness I love.

Before he can say anything, Adam appears.

"Sorry to interrupt. Carter just pulled up out front, Jennie. He's calling for you."

I want Garrett to say no. I want him to take me home and tell me he didn't mean anything he said yesterday. I want everything to go back to the way it was.

But he nods, and Adam places his hand on my lower back, guiding me away.

Something catches my pinky, and I look back, watching as Garrett's own squeezes mine before slipping away, and somewhere deep inside me, my heart restarts.

∾

It's a quiet ride to the restaurant, Mom, Olivia, and Hank discussing how beautiful I was on stage. Carter keeps opening his mouth before second-guessing, which is probably for the best. Ninety-nine percent of the words that come out of his mouth are the wrong ones anyway.

When everyone exits the car, I slip one dress off in favor of another, right here in the front seat while Carter hands his keys over to the valet.

He takes my hand, helping me out and pulling me into his side for a hug. "You look beautiful, Jennie." He kisses my temple. "And you kicked ass on stage. I'm proud of you."

A sassy eight-year-old attaches herself to my torso as the hostess leads us to our table. "You rock, like, *so hard*, Auntie J." Alannah's not really my niece; she's Carter and Olivia's. But I love being Auntie J, and I think she's the coolest kid out there. "If I wasn't already a kick-ass hockey player, I'd be a dancer."

"You could do both," I suggest weakly. "Maybe you can be my first dancer when I open my studio."

Her nose wrinkles. "Uncle Carter says you're moving to Toronto to be a dancer."

"I don't know what I'm do...ing..." My train of thought derails when I spy the blond-haired giant of a man already seated at our table, anxiously drumming his fingers on the white tablecloth, and I trip over my own feet, bouncing off Olivia's small frame.

Olivia's gaze moves between me and Garrett as we stare at each other. She doesn't say a word, but I her face softens before she pulls out the seat next to him, gesturing for me to sit.

"Oh, I...I should—"

Cara grips my shoulder, shoving me down. "You should sit."

"Hold on." Jaxon hauls me back up. "You didn't take your coat off." He slips it over my shoulders, fingertips trailing down my arms as he peels off my coat. He looks directly at Garrett, smirking as he does it. "Stunning," he murmurs with a whistle. "Right, Andersen?"

Carter's face appears between us. "Did you just whistle at my sister?"

Jaxon's face drains of color. He shoves my coat into Carter's chest. "No."

"Great." Carter takes the seat beside me, and now I'm stuck between my brother and the man I...I...I truly don't know how to finish that sentence.

Well, that's a lie. I know how to finish it. I just refuse to, now that I…
we…now that we…

"You look like you're gonna cry."

"Huh?" My head snaps, finding Carter examining me. "No." Oh
fuck. I'm totally gonna cry. "I'm not feeling very well."

"That happens to me sometimes when I play too hard on the ice,
Auntie J," Alannah pipes up. "It usually goes away with food, but sometimes I need a long nap."

I struggle to smile back from across the table while feeling the weight
of Garrett's gaze on me, or rather, the hand I lay in my lap, face up. It's
bright red and still stinging with pain from the force of my slap. I prod
at the pads below each finger, each one slightly swollen. While Alannah
continues, I briefly consider submerging my entire hand in the bucket of
ice the bottles of champagne and sparkling water sit in.

"Uncle Carter probably needs a big meal and a nap too. He looked
pretty angry when that guy kissed you, and he's always happier after he
eats and naps with Auntie Ollie. He gave me twenty dollars after he was
done with the video camera though."

Jeremy, Alannah's dad and Olivia's brother, barks a laugh. "I'm
pretty sure Uncle Carter crushed the video camera between his hands."

"I didn't crush it, per se," Carter argues weakly.

"Oh, my apologies. You shouted out a string of expletives and then
finished with, 'God-fucking-damnit, I broke the camera.'"

"So I'll edit that last bit out. No big deal."

"Do you know anything about editing video footage, Carter?" Adam
asks.

He props his cheek against his fist and frowns. "I'll pay someone.
Might be able to edit *S-T-E-V-E* right out."

"I'm not a dog, Carter," I finally interject. "You can't spell his name
and expect me not to be able to string the letters together, the way you
do with Dublin and the word *walk*."

Carter mutters something about Dublin being more pleasant than
me, and as everyone breaks into conversation, I tune it all out, con-
centrating instead on the loneliness that's come roaring back into my life.

I thought I was alone before, but it was Garrett who showed me I
wasn't, that I was surrounded by people who loved me, who wanted to
share a space with me.

But as I look around the table, all I see is a space I don't belong in.

Couples in love. Friends with more connections. Where do I fit in? I thought this was the one place I did belong, here with these people, but now I'm just not sure.

My heart begs me to argue with my brain, but I don't have the energy. Not today, not anymore, and every inch of my body aches as it curls in on itself, begging for solitude, which is ironic; I don't want to be alone anymore. But I don't want to be lost either.

A clinking sound draws my attention, and I watch curiously as Garrett scoops his ice from his unused glass, wrapping it in the cloth napkin from his lap. Turquoise eyes meet mine, and he takes my hand in his beneath the table, pressing the covered ice to it, curling my fingers around it.

My sore skin is instantly soothed, and for a moment, Garrett squeezes a bit harder, his palm warm on the back of my hand before he releases me. He reaches for a bottle of sparkling water, filling my glass and his before passing it around the table.

I watch as he brings his glass to his plush lips before laying both hands back in his lap, and God, I want to touch him. So badly, I want his hands on me. I want that full, safe feeling that comes with having my fingers laced through his.

I'm not ready to give up; I don't care if that makes me naïve. What we have, it's not something you simply let go. I don't have much experience with relationships, but this feels like one of those once-in-a-lifetime things.

How many times can I tell myself I'm tired of being scared? That all I want to do is close my eyes and jump? Except I don't need to close my eyes with Garrett. I've always been sure of who he is, what he means to me.

My hand moves on its own accord, inching toward his below the tablecloth. He spreads his fingers a little wider, like his pinky is reaching for mine, and I know that whatever has happened, we can work through it together.

"Excuse me. Garrett, right?"

My eyes lift to the raven-haired beauty hovering at the edge of the table, grinning at Garrett. I pull my hand back as the table quiets, every head turning in their direction.

The woman lays a hand at the base of her throat. "Susie. I was the—"

"Oh!" Carter snaps his fingers. "You're the photographer! From the photoshoot for the suits. The hockey butts!" He cocks a smug brow. "My name is Carter Beckett, and I have a hockey butt."

Susie giggles. "Yeah, that's me. You guys were the most fun I've ever had at work before." Her eyes move over me and widen. "And oh my gosh, hey! You're that dancer! I just photographed your show! You were amazing! I got tons of great shots, and that kiss at the end?" She lays her hands over her heart. "Total swoon. You could really feel the love between you two." With a shy smile, she turns to Garrett, and my stomach flip-flops, making me nauseous. "I was kinda bummed out not to hear from you."

"Oh, I..." Garrett's cheeks flame, eyes bouncing around the table. The only face he avoids is mine.

"He's seeing someone," Carter pipes up. "Or not anymore?" He scratches his head, frowning. "You haven't mentioned her in a while."

"I was," Garrett replies slowly, and I watch his fists ball as my throat closes.

"I'm sorry it didn't work out," Susie says. "Maybe we could go out one night?"

It feels like all my blood rushes to my head as I wait for his reply, but it's not him who speaks next.

"C'mon, Gare. It's Valentine's Day. Gotta jump headfirst into any chance at love."

I guess there's a first time for everything. Like me, right now, being upset with Hank.

Garrett hesitates before standing. With a delicate touch to Susie's shoulder, he gestures toward the lobby. "Why don't we go somewhere private to talk?"

My napkin slips, landing on the ground below Garrett's chair, ice scattering. "Oh shit." I bend to retrieve it, rolling too far forward, landing on the floor between Garrett's chair and mine. "Oh fuckballs." I laugh, super anxious. Reaching under his seat, I grab the melting ice cubes and hammer my head off the edge of the chair on my way back up. "Oh motherfucker." I grip my head with one hand, holding the ice up with the other, and grin, extra shaky. "Got it."

I'm going to vomit. And cry. And hyperventilate. Right here at the table. At the same fucking time. I'm about to have a crisis, and the only person I want to hold me while I have it is the one currently guiding another woman out of the restaurant.

"Jennie," Cara calls, eyes holding the remorse of someone who's just watched a good old-fashioned heart-stomping. "I need to use the bathroom. Will you come with me?"

"Yes. No." My hands tremble and my throat squeezes. Everything hurts. Is this the way it goes? Why does it feel like my entire body is breaking? My face feels hot, and I don't know how to get enough air into my lungs. "I really don't feel well." I place my hand on my cheek. It's clammy and warm. "I think I'm going to be sick."

Olivia digs in her purse and pulls out a set of keys. "I'll take you home."

"What?" Carter looks from me to her. "You can't drive. I'll take her."

"It's your birthday. You stay. Her apartment is down the road. I'll be back before the appetizers get here."

"I'll be fine. Really." I stand quickly, knocking over Garrett's water. I pick up the glass and swipe the sweat from my forehead. "Just need to get some air. I'll be right back."

I weave through the restaurant before anyone can argue, and step into the frigid night air, the wind slapping at my damp skin.

A hand lands on my lower back as I watch Garrett and Susie talk in the parking lot.

"Come on," Olivia says, my bag and coat tucked under her arm. "Let's get you home."

But when the valet brings the car around and I climb in, watching through the blowing snow as Garrett embraces Susie, all I want is for me to be the one in his arms.

～

Five minutes. A five-minute drive home, and I can't keep it in check.

I tell myself I'm just fine, that I'm holding it together, that I was fine on my own before Garrett, and I'll be fine on my own after Garrett.

But we're thirty seconds from the restaurant when the first tear rolls down my cheek as I stare out the window. And with the first one comes the second, then the third, and the fourth.

Olivia doesn't say a single word as we drive in silence, and I must be some kind of stupid to think she's going to let me out of this car just like that when we get home.

Her hand wraps around my elbow, stopping me when I reach for the door handle. Her big brown eyes soften when she turns me to face her, and she takes my hands in hers.

"For the sake of my marriage, Jennie, we're not going to use names right now. When your brother inevitably finds out, I need to be able to say I did not know *who* it was you were seeing."

Tears slide down my face faster, and I've never felt so weak before. I hate it. "You would do that for me?"

"I would do anything for you, Jennie. I love you."

"Everything was fine," I cry softly. "Everything was fine until yesterday when he got home. He picked me up from school and we had a fight, but I don't even know what for. I think I hurt his feelings, but I didn't mean to. He's my-he's my…" I pull in a sniffle, wiping at my eyes, the tips of my fingers coming away smeared with black. "He's my best friend and I…He means so much to me. I would never want to hurt him."

Olivia's gaze holds all the compassion of a woman who's going to make the most amazing mother, and I'm so thankful my brother has her.

"It sounds like there's been a big miscommunication somewhere along the way. Sometimes we do silly things when we're jealous and scared, when we're hurting, or when someone we love is hurting. You two need to be honest with each other, lay it all out. You Becketts are good at that. Don't be afraid to show him how you feel."

She brushes my hair off my damp face, tucking it behind my ear. "Your brother once told me we miss out on the best things in life when we're scared. I was scared for a long time, and when I finally jumped, I couldn't even remember why I'd been so scared."

"That's because Carter's obsessed with you," I choke out.

"If I were to have seen anything tonight, it would have been a man who had his eyes on you every single time you looked away, someone who's as equally obsessed as my husband. If you jump, Jennie, I think he's going to be waiting there to catch you."

So badly, I want her to be right.

For once in my life, I just want to be loved. Loved for who I am, for what I have to give. I want someone to see everything I bring to the table and eagerly sit down with me.

I've spent way too many years coming up with excuses, making myself smaller for people who didn't know how to handle everything I was. I've never had to hide with Garrett. There were times when I've moved slower, tested the water before diving in, but Garrett's always been there, waiting with open arms.

He takes every bit of me, the shattered trust, the deep, never-ending grief, the bold and loud, the soft and quiet, both the confident and the timid, and he makes a space for all of it, for all of me in his big heart, and he never asks for anything more.

Is this what love feels like? Is this what it's like to be loved by someone with no obligation to be anything other than myself?

Warm and fuzzy, like curling up on the couch on a cold, snowy night in my favorite of his hoodies and a mug of hot chocolate after a long day. Like my favorite person smiling down at me, pressing his lips to mine before he lifts the blankets and slides in beside me, pulling me into his warmth, the safety net he casts around me every time he's near.

Because with him, I'm safe. Safe to be myself, safe to feel, safe to want, safe to *be*.

If this is love, I'm in it.

If this is love, I never want to let go.

Upstairs, I stare at each carefully wrapped Valentine gift, pretty packages finished with red silk ribbons.

I ditched the dress the second I walked in, sitting here now in his hoodie and a pair of sleep shorts. My face has been scrubbed clean, and despite the overwhelming exhaustion that runs rampant, adrenaline keeps me moving while I watch the clock.

I don't know how this night will end, but I can't wait any longer. Bottling up these emotions is wreaking havoc on my brain; I need to let them free.

So I slip my feet into my slippers, shuffle over to my door, and throw it open.

"Garrett," I gasp softly, coming alive as I stare up at the only love I've ever craved.

The gift bag he's holding lands at my feet, his gaze searing and intent as he sweeps into my apartment, locking the door behind him.

"I'm so fucking tired of pretending."

"Pretending what?" It's nothing but a breathy whisper as he prowls toward me, matching each of my steps backward.

His strong hands cup my face, piercing gaze locked on mine as he looms above me. My heart slams in my chest as his thumb sweeps across my lower lip, and his eyes dip, watching as my lips part on a jagged inhale, before flipping back up to mine.

"I'm so fucking tired of pretending I'm not in love with you."

THIRTY-FOUR
LIKE THE STARS

Jennie

SOMETHING'S SHORT-CIRCUITING, and I think it's my brain.

"I think you said…no, because you…Garrett, I think you accidentally just said—"

"I'm in love with you," he finishes for me, which is great. Pretty sure we're about to do that thing where we switch spots, where he becomes the confident one and me the mindless rambler.

I don't know how it's possible for my heart to beat as fast as it is, but there it goes, galloping away. My throat keeps squeezing, and I don't know how to get my words out.

"Are you…Are you sure?"

"I've never been surer of anything." His words are tender, like the fingers he presses to my jaw, forbidding me from looking away. "I love you, Jennie."

Nobody's ever loved me before, not like this. And to be loved by the only person I want to love me…I can't wrap my head around it.

"Maybe you could, like…" I draw in a sniffle, rubbing furiously at my eye while gripping Garrett's forearm so I don't do something ridiculous, like fall straight to my ass. "Say it again."

There's that smile, breathtaking, goofy, just the right amount of arrogance. With my face in his hands, he sweeps the tears from below my eyes and whispers, "I love you."

No. Nope. *Now's not the time for strange, choking sounds, Jennie. Be cool.*

"Again?"

"I love you." He presses a kiss to my cheek. "I love you." The other cheek. "And once more, Jennie, for good measure. I fucking love you."

"I'm not crying," I cry. "Just in case you were wondering." I choke out a pathetic sob. "It's allergy season."

"It's February."

"Shut up."

Garrett laughs, pulling me into his embrace. He's warm and solid, and I can't wrap my head around how ferociously I missed him when he wasn't even gone long.

"But what about Susie?"

He shifts back, holding my stare. "I took Susie outside, told her I was in love with the brunette who fell off her chair and then whacked her head off mine, but that I hadn't even told her yet because I'm a dumbass. Then I said you'd call me a twat-waffle, not a dumbass." Broad fingertips sweep over my cheekbone, brushing away wisps of hair. "There's nobody else, Jennie. There never has been and never will be."

"But why?"

He frowns. "Why do I love you?"

I nod. What does he see that no one else ever saw? What does he love that everyone else thought was too complicated, too time-consuming?

"Hmm." He scoops me up and carries me to the kitchen island, setting me on top. He steps between my legs, bracketing my body with his hands on the countertop. "The short and simple answer is why not? There's nothing I don't love. But I think you need to know all the reasons, and I came prepared." He winks, tapping his temple. "Got 'em locked up here in my Jennie bank."

"Jennie bank?"

"Like spank bank, except all things Jennie."

Giggling, I swipe the remainder of my allergies from my cheeks before slinging my arms over his shoulders. "Okay, have at it."

"I love your toys."

I shove him away. "Not a good start, you donkey."

Laughing, he reclaims his spot between my legs, draping my arms around him again. "You didn't let me finish. So impatient. I love that you took your satisfaction into your own hands. That you created boundaries for yourself and explored within them. I think it's sexy, not because of what's in your drawer, but because you're not afraid to be the person who makes yourself feel good."

"Good save, big guy."

"Circling back to your impatience…I love that too. It's not selfish or tiring, but the opposite. You're so genuinely hyped up about so many things that you want to take them into your hands right away. It makes me want to experience everything with you. Your happiness is addicting."

My face heats, teeth tugging at my lower lip. "Go on."

"I wanted you to let me in so long ago." He cups my cheek when my face falls at his quiet words. "Because I wanted to know everything, Jennie. Why you sometimes shut down on me, why you were against things like sex, and didn't have many friends. But I realize now that's not what I really wanted. You made me practice patience, and in doing so I learned to trust you, to trust myself a little more. Your walls were there for a reason, and you didn't let me push you into tearing them down on my own schedule."

He smiles. "I like that your walls were there. You committed to knowing yourself better than anyone before letting someone else in, and I admire that. So many people have shallow, empty relationships because they don't really know themselves. But I only know you so well because *you* do, because you're able to be unapologetically yourself."

Hooking my legs around his hips, I tug him closer. "You think you know me?"

"Mhmm. You scream when you're angry and cry when you're sad. But you also *cry* when you're *angry* and *scream* when you're *sad.* You're embarrassed when you cry because you think it makes you weak, but I think showing your soft side is strong and brave, and I wish more people did it, me included. You're quiet when you're overwhelmed or scared, and you hold my hand the most then too. You're honest and loud and you're your own biggest fan when it comes to dance, but I wish you were your biggest fan about all the other stuff too. Your favorite way to snuggle is with your cheek on my chest and your leg shoved between mine, and I think sharing Dunkaroos with you on the couch or getting my ass kicked on repeat to *Just Dance* is my favorite thing in the world. You make me laugh more than anyone ever has, and you have the oddest insults in the world and you—"

"Garrett?" I lay my hand on his cheek, guiding his gaze back to mine.

"Yeah?"

"How many more reasons do you have?"

He scratches his head. "Uh, I donno. I was going through all of them on the plane ride home today. It was six hours long, and I ran out of time."

I snicker, because I believe it. Garrett's painfully honest, if only because he's the world's shittiest liar. I don't think he has the heart for it.

"Why were you on an airplane today? Where were you?"

He sets me on my feet and takes my hand, leading me to the couch where we sit together. He runs his fingers through his hair, looking lost, his expression pained, heavy, exhausted.

I rest my hand on his thigh. "Is everything okay?"

"Yeah, now it is. I think so, at least. I guess it started yesterday morning, on the flight home from Colorado. You came up in conversation, and Carter said you weren't ready to date. Normally I blow off everything he says, but he said you told him you were happy alone, that you didn't want anything to change or to be tied down to anyone. And you're allowed to say that and feel it. We hadn't talked about being anything else, but I guess with the date we were supposed to have tonight, I just thought that maybe...maybe you were ready.

"Then I lost Wi-Fi on the plane and I couldn't text you, and by the time we landed, I had a bunch of missed calls from my sisters. My parents were fighting and my dad walked out with a bottle of booze. My sisters were scared and wanted me to come home, and the only person I wanted to talk to was you." He peers at me from beneath his lashes. "I needed you, and you weren't there."

My chest tightens at the heartache in his voice. "I'm so sorry, Garrett."

He shakes his head quickly. "Please don't apologize. It's not your fault, and I knew you were busy. But I let my fears get the best of me. I let myself think what we had meant more to me than it did to you."

"That's not true." I lay my hand on his cheek, turning his face back to mine. "That's not true," I repeat. "What we have means everything to me. I'm sorry I wasn't there when you needed me. I'm here now."

"When I saw Simon with his hands on you, when I heard you repeating everything I was afraid of, that we were nothing more than friends, that our relationship was just convenient...It tipped me over the edge. It felt like I was barely hanging on with my family stuff, and then…"

"And then you said you needed space." It makes sense, but it doesn't stop the pain from roaring back, and I clutch at my chest, right where it hurts.

Garrett places his hand on top of mine, pressing my palm to my heart. "I'm so sorry, Jennie. I was hurting and overwhelmed, and the longer I sat there by myself, the more I questioned everything. And I just…I don't know. I fell, I think. My head was a mess, and I pushed you away because I couldn't sort through my thoughts."

I sit with his words for a moment before threading my fingers through his. "I forgive you."

"You do?"

"That's what friends do when they love each other, when they make mistakes and apologize. You forgave me for getting angry and running out on you the night we saw Kevin."

Garrett's gaze steals down to our clasped hands before lifting back to me. "You're my best friend, Jennie, but I don't want to be just friends anymore. I don't want some of the benefits, I want all of them. I want all of you."

"I'm already yours, Garrett, because of the friendship we built."

"I like that." He sweeps a kiss across my knuckles, then tells me about his short trip home. He tells me about finding his dad at the diner, how he was so angry for only a moment, until he saw how broken he was. He tells me why his dad was on the verge of relapsing, how they talked through it together, how he brought him home to his mom and curled up with his sisters.

"I've been asking them for years to move out here. This feels like the perfect opportunity for a fresh start. He said he'll consider it, but who knows." He shrugs. "I don't want my sisters to have to call me when they need me. I want to be there all the time for them, and I don't want to watch them grow up over FaceTime."

"You're a good big brother."

His smiles softly before looking away, swallowing.

"Garrett? What else?"

He hesitates, licks his lips. "My dad's made a lot of mistakes, more than I could ever keep count of. But what's mattered to me is that he's tried so hard to come out on the other side. He always tries to be better.

I'm glad he was able to give my sisters the life he couldn't give me, and I love him for that. But...do you hate him?"

I shift back, surprised. "Hate him? Why would I hate him?"

"Because...it could have easily been him behind the wheel." He doesn't need to clarify, to tell me *what* wheel, the one that killed my dad. "Somebody just like my dad took your dad away from you. I don't know how to ask you to support him."

My nose tingles, and I scrunch it in an effort to stave off the ache building in my chest. It manages to slip out the way it normally does, a single tear sneaking down the side of my face. When I reach for the locket that used to hang around my neck, finding nothing but skin, a second and a third tear fall too.

"Nobody can take him from me. I'll always keep him with me. And you don't need to ask me to support your dad. I support you and anyone you love, anyone who tries to be better than they were. Isn't that life? Aren't we all trying to be better than the version of ourselves we were yesterday?"

"Thank you." His arms come around me, hugging me tightly to him. "I'm sorry I didn't communicate better with you about how I was feeling and where I wanted things to go with us. Sometimes I don't know how to put my feelings into words. I've always been better with actions, so I kinda..." He gestures at the gift bag he dropped at the door earlier. "I had this plan to let you know how much you mean to me."

My hands clasp together at my chest and a squeal slips out. I like presents; sue me. "You can still show me." I leap to my feet, dashing to the door. "And I got you something too."

He groans and I roll my eyes, setting the gifts on the coffee table.

"It's silly, really. Nothing special." I shove the first box in his hands. "This one's edible."

"Better be edible underwear," he grumbles, then grins as he slips off the ribbon and lifts the lid on the box of custom sugar cookies. Twelve hearts, twelve penises, and a whole lot of *I heart your dick*'s written all over them. He picks up one tiny penis cookie, examining it. "Not made to size, I see."

"No, that was the smallest cookie cutter they had."

Garrett snorts a laugh.

I thrust the next package into his chest, clapping eagerly. "Next!"

He pulls out the underwear inside, lips moving as he reads, and promptly falls forward with a burst of laughter.

I point at the bright yellow caution sign on the crotch, the words that read *CAUTION: CHOKING HAZARD.* "That's you, big guy!"

"You are unbelievable." He kisses my cheek, then reaches for the last box.

I elbow him out of the way, nabbing the box and hugging it to my chest. "You don't have to open this one. It's actually…it's…it's not for you. It got mixed in. It's for Dublin."

"You got the dog a Valentine's gift?"

I press my lips together. "Mhmm."

"I don't believe you." He snatches the gift away.

"Garrett!" I lunge at him, but he holds his palm against my collarbone, keeping me at bay. Then he twists, squishing me into the couch cushions with his back, essentially lying on top of me as he opens the small box. My ears burn when he pulls out the keychain, the small silver charm attached, a bear etched into the metal, standing on its hind legs, right below the sun. "It's stupid," I mumble. "Just, like…" I wave a hand around as he looks over his shoulder at me. "I don't even know why I got it."

He rolls off me and pulls me onto his lap. "I love it." He hauls me forward by my nape, but pauses, mouth hovering above mine in question.

"Kiss me," I whisper. "Please."

The moment his lips touch mine, my sky explodes, fireworks that make the night glow. I sink into his touch, lips parting with a sigh, and his tongue sweeps inside, tentative, tender. He pulls back, kissing me once, twice more, then rests his forehead against mine, smiling.

"My turn." Shifting me off his lap, he hands me the pink gift bag, dotted with gold foil hearts, the matching tissue paper, and chuckles, anxious and so utterly Garrett as he scratches his jaw. "I hope you like it."

I pull out the first thing my fingers find below the tissue, a long, slim box, blushing velvet. The box creaks when I open it, and I trace the gold sunflower set on a dainty chain. "It's beautiful, Garrett."

"Open it," he urges gently.

I pull the necklace from the box, turning the small flower between my fingers until I find the seam and coax it open. *You are my sunshine* is etched into one side, making me smile, but it's the other side that brings out my gasp, has my heart leaping to my throat. Because my dad's face and mine smile up at me.

"I know it's not the same locket your dad got you. I tried to find it. I contacted the company, but they don't make the same one anymore. So I got you this one because you're my sunshine, and I think you were your dad's too."

I throw myself in his lap, knocking him to his back as tears blur my vision. "Thank you, Garrett. So much. This is the best gift ever."

He chuckles. "Well, there's one more, and you might love it more."

"I doubt that." I stick my hand into the tissue paper, feeling the softness of the object below. It's plush but a little coarse at the same time, kind of cozy, like something that's been well-loved. "I don't think anything could top the—" My words fizzle, dying in my throat as I pull the stuffed animal from the bag. Its pink fur, once so bright, is pale and muted, just the way I remember, the white patch on its chest a little gray from years of dragging it everywhere, the black button eye on the left hanging loose.

I clutch my favorite bunny to my chest, inhaling the smell, the familiarity, welcoming the memories that flood my mind, and tears spill down my cheeks.

"Princess Bubblegum," I weep into her fur. "You found her."

"I thought maybe she fell out in the moving truck. I called the company and they let me go through the lost and found bin, but it wasn't there. I went by the house one day and looked everywhere. Up and down the street, in the garden...I found her in the bushes by the road, half-buried in a pile of snow. She was all muddy, so I washed her up for you, and I hope—"

I crush my mouth to his, sinking my fingers in his hair, smooshing my stuffie between us. When I pull away, his cheeks glisten with my tears, lips red, hair a mess from my assault.

"This is the kindest, most thoughtful thing anyone has ever done for me."

"Yeah, well..." He rubs the back of his neck. "I'd do anything for you, Jennie."

"'Cause I'm your sunshine?"

He nods. "The brightest."

"And you love me?"

"I do. Wild, huh?"

I don't answer him. Not with words anyway. Instead, I stand, pressing a kiss to Princess Bubblegum's head before I tuck her on my bookshelf, right next to a picture of me and Dad. Then I take Garrett's hand in mine and tow him down the hallway.

His palm grows damp, fingers clutching tightly at mine, a telltale sign of the nerves that grow with each step closer to my bedroom.

"We don't have to do anything, Jennie. It's not...I'm not, like...We don't have to do anything." The way he fumbles over his words when he's anxious is one of my favorites of his traits. "I'm cool to just snuggle. And plus," he chuckles, running his fingers through his hair when I yank him through the door, "I don't have a condom."

"That's okay."

"Okay." His body deflates with a whooshing sigh. He sinks to the edge of the bed. "Grool." He shakes his head, cringing. "Fuck. *Cool.* Cool."

"I've been on the pill for a month and a half now."

Aw, he's so cute when he looks like he's going to be sick.

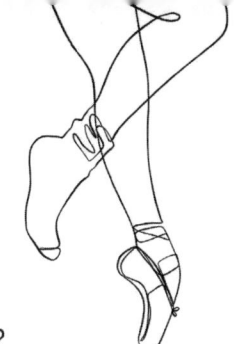

THIRTY-FIVE
HOW DO YOU LIKE YOUR EGGS?

Jennie

"You want to—but I—" Garrett's face pales, jaw hanging. He snaps it shut and shakes his head. "No."

"No? You don't want me?"

"No, I—" He drags his hands down his face, groaning. "I didn't tell you I love you so you would have sex with me. If you want to wait longer, we can wait longer."

He's so sweet, so gentle sometimes it makes my heart ache. He's never wanted to take anything that didn't belong to him, but I think this part of me was always meant for him.

I step between his legs, draping my arms around his neck. His hands move up the backs of my thighs, squeezing my ass before he lifts me onto his lap. He wraps his arms around me, burying his face in my neck.

"I love when you wear my sweater," he murmurs. "Everything in me screams *mine* when you do."

"I am yours." I kiss the edge of his jaw, working down his throat as I tug his tie free. The silk slips through my fingers as I drop it to the ground. Guiding him backward, I work the buttons of his shirt. My hands skim across his broad chest as I sweep his shirt down his arms, and when it finds its way to the floor, I admire the spectacular body below.

Garrett is solid and warm, skin kissed golden, even in the winter. The light patch of hair on his chest is soft as I run my fingers through it, and the muscles carved into his torso beg to be tasted. Before I can do that, his hands slip below his hoodie, sliding up the curve of my back, making it arch beneath his touch. When I lift my arms, he guides the thick material over my head, letting it fall behind me.

"One more thing I love about you." The pad of his thumb scrapes over my nipple, making it harden. "You never wear a fucking bra at home."

"It's not good to restrict the girls." A whimper trembles in my throat as his hot tongue rolls over the tight bud. "Gotta let 'em breathe."

Garrett grips my hips, grinding me gently over him. A moan falls from my lips as my lower belly tightens with desire. Pushing a hand between us, I step down from his lap. He follows, and when I reach for his belt, he puts his hand over mine.

"I'm serious, Jennie. We don't have to do anything you're not ready to do."

"I know what I want, Garrett, and I know my limits. Okay?"

His eyes search mine for a moment before he nods, letting me work his pants and boxers off him, his erection springing free. When I reach for my sleep shorts, he stops me, spinning me so that my back presses into his chest. His hand moves over my torso, fingertips dancing up until he finds my throat. He holds me tenderly, his breath heavy in my ear as he slips his free hand into my shorts. His chest rumbles when he finds me hot and wet, and when he skims my clit, I shudder. My shorts fall to my ankles, and he nudges my legs apart with his knee.

"You wanna know something?" he asks, stroking that bundle of nerves at the cleft of my thighs. His fingers dip, gliding through my wetness, and when he pushes one broad finger inside, I gasp. "You're a fucking dream come true."

Gentle fingers press into my throat, holding me to him as he brings me higher up my mountain, climbing toward my peak. His cock hardens at his breathless, whimpered name, pushing into my back, and when he adds a second finger, when his thumb finds my clit, I cry out again.

"Dreamt about my name on your lips for so long before you finally said it. Dreamt about the way you'd feel below me, the way you'd taste...but I never could've dreamed I'd find my best friend. That in finding you, I'd find more of myself."

He holds my gaze over my shoulder as he works me faster, and when his fingers curl, my knees buckle. The corner of his mouth lifts as he watches me fall apart around him, and when I sob out his name, he swallows it with a kiss.

"I love you, Jennie. And I'm so fucking glad I caught you masturbating to me that one night."

I wheeze a laugh, and he guides me down to the bed, crawling overtop of me.

"What do you want, Jennie? Tell me, please."

"Everything, as long as it's with you."

"All mine?" he asks on a whisper.

"All yours."

His forehead drops to my shoulder, and he pulls in a deep breath.

With my hand on his jaw, I coax his gaze back to mine. "Are you nervous?"

Color dots his cheek. He swallows slowly and nods. "Are you?"

"No," I tell him honestly. "I have no reason to be. You've always given me everything I need, and I've always felt safe with you. This is no different. Your patience with me gave me all the time I needed to know this is something I want to share with only you, to trust you, to fall in love with you. I've never been more certain, and I'm so happy to do this with you."

His lips cover my collarbone with kisses. "You're right. It'll be—" His head snaps up. "No, but you-you said...you said—"

"I love you, too, Garrett."

His eyes come alive, brilliant and electric. "You do? Really?"

"I do, really."

His grin is detonating, laugh eager as he crushes me to him, falling to his back, dragging me on top. "Thank fuck. I mean, obviously. Who can resist all this? About time you admitted it."

"Garrett?"

"Yeah?"

"Shut up."

"Yes, ma'am." He sinks his fingers into the hair at the nape of my neck as his mouth takes mine. Winding an arm around my waist, he lays me down, hooking my legs around his hips. "To be fair, though, you taught me to be loud and proud about my thoughts, about what I want. You're who I think about and all I want. So maybe I don't wanna shut up about that."

My head falls back with a soft cry as he rocks into me, and when I right myself again, he runs the tip of his nose against mine.

"Can I ask you something, Jennie? How did you picture your first time? Did you want music? Candles? Maybe this can be your do-over."

Honestly, I'd never put much stock into the aesthetics of my first time. I'd always wanted it to be special, but special hadn't meant fancy things or putting on a show. It meant feeling loved, accepted, wanted. It meant feeling safe to share all my parts with someone else, not having any doubts about being enough, and knowing I'd still be enough afterward. Special meant unhurried, taking our time, appreciating each other for who we were and how we made each other better.

I hadn't had that experience, and I'd always felt robbed. But right now? Garrett is giving me the experience I always craved, the one I deserved.

"This," I finally answer. "Right here with you is how I pictured it. Being with someone I love, someone who reminds me I'm already enough."

"You are enough, Jennie. I used to be scared of how enough you were, unattainable almost. I wasn't sure I could stack up. But I know now. Everything I was missing was something you brought with you, evening me out. I realized I was never not enough; I was waiting for you so we could be whole together."

His words touch a deep part of me, branding my heart. Because only with Garrett do I embrace all of me.

I stroke a hand down the side of his face. "Look at you, putting your feelings into words. Proud of you."

"See what you do to me? I'm so in love with you I can't even think straight.

"To be fair, you've never been able to think straight."

He huffs a laugh, rocking his hips against mine. "I'm not afraid to shut you up with my cock down your throat."

"You wouldn't."

"In a heartbeat. Not tonight, though. Tonight, sunshine, I love you soft and slow."

I take a deep breath. "I'm ready."

He brushes a tender kiss to my lips. "Thank you for trusting me, Jennie."

Fisting his cock, he runs it through my slit, watching as I soak him. Our eyes lock, and slowly, *so damn slowly*, he pushes inside.

"*Fuck*," he groans. "Fucking...heaven."

My back arches off the bed as I gasp, feeling the way I stretch to accommodate him, molding around him. He's heavy and thick and takes up every bit of space, making me feel fuller than I ever have.

Hand bracketing my jaw, he keeps our eyes locked. "You okay?"

"It's just...full. So full."

"Fuck you, Indiana Bones," he mutters, coaxing a giggle from me. His thumb brushes beneath my eye, bringing my gaze back to him. "Hey, stay with me. We're gonna do this at your pace, okay?"

My palms glide over his back as I get used to his size. "I love when you ramble."

His mouth quirks. "What?"

"You're adorable when you do. And you think you have trouble speaking honestly, but that says more about how you feel than most people can communicate with words." I hold onto his shoulders as my hips lift, bringing him a little bit deeper, drawing another gasp from my lips as I find friction. "You're so kind, and I don't even think you realize it most of the time. You do things for others without thinking, like bringing me coffee after school, or dancing with me in your kitchen to cheer me up, flying home to help your dad even though you were angry with him, and to be with your sisters. You're not afraid to be gentle, and I love your tenderness. I think everyone deserves a Garrett in their lives, but selfishly, I'm glad it's me who gets to keep you. I'm so lucky."

I bring his mouth down to mine, and his hips rock slowly as our tongues meet. Squeezing me closer, we start to move together. He eases his length out before sinking back in, each slow thrust drawing another whimper, another moan as my body comes to life, wanting more, *needing* more.

I see it there in his eyes as he watches me. The hesitancy, the compassion. He's trying so hard, holding back just for me, waiting for my cue. I want it all, everything he'll give me, but mostly, I just want him.

My fingernails bite into his shoulders as he plunges a little deeper, a little harder. When his cock hits that hard-to-find spot, my eyes roll back and my head falls to the pillows.

"Oh fuck," I cry, raking my nails down his biceps.

"Christ, Jennie." He drives himself forward. "You're killing me."

My heels dig into his ass as he lifts my hips off the bed, and my fingers plow through his hair, hanging on for dear life as he takes me higher than I've ever been.

Garrett drags hot, wet kisses across my chest, his jagged breath lashing at each one. His lips sweep up my throat and he sinks his fingers in my hair, peering down at me as his skin slaps against mine.

"Unbelievable. So fucking beautiful it's unbelievable."

"*Garrett.*" His name is choked and garbled, a nearly unrecognizable sound as my spine quivers, a fire sparking deep in my belly, and he moves faster, thrusts deeper. His hips roll against mine, giving me that friction I didn't know I needed, and my entire world starts to crumble. "Oh my *God*, Garrett, *please.*"

Fingertips press into my jaw, holding me captive. "I can't believe how in love with you I am. It's fucking mind-blowing."

I can't think straight when he watches me like that, like he's seeing in color for the first time. My mind is a wonderful mess, where all I know is every single part of me lights up with his touch, lets me know that right here with him is exactly where I was always meant to be.

My eyes prickle with tears of relief. I've never felt more me than I do with him, and I can't explain how freeing it feels to not have to hide. After all this time, all this heartache, I've finally found my person, my place in this world. Every shroud of pain falls away until it's nothing more than a sliver that's shaped who I am, brought me to this point where I wouldn't change a thing.

With a fistful of his hair, I bring his forehead to mine as he drives us closer to that finish line. Everything tingles and tightens, squeezing him deeper, like I don't want this to end. But I don't think I can hold on any longer.

Garrett's eyes move between mine, reading my thoughts. "Me, too, baby," he promises.

His mouth crashes down on mine as he pistons inside me, swallowing the cry ripping up my throat. When we come together, all I see is the stars, the ones he so effortlessly hung in my sky.

Strong arms tug me into a broad chest, and Garrett rolls us onto our sides, whispering how much he loves me as he holds me.

For so long, I'd convinced myself I was better off on my own. I'd grown so accustomed to my independence, told myself I needed it to be strong, I hadn't realized how alone I felt.

Then Garrett gave me my best friend, a partner to stand by my side and hold my hand. And the world feels a lot less scary when we face it together rather than separately. I don't ever want to go without this feeling again.

Garrett's lips dot my shoulder, marking a path up my neck with his whispered promise. "I'm not going anywhere."

And he doesn't. I wake in the morning to an empty, rumpled bed, but I hear him. Hear music humming softly from the kitchen, his feet padding around, pans clanging.

I slip his shirt on, rolling the sleeves up to my wrists, buttoning just enough, and pad down the hallway. I find him cooking at the stove in only his boxers, drowning in the sunshine pouring through the windows, like he belongs exactly right here.

He smiles at me over his shoulder, a breathtaking sight.

"Morning, sunshine." Tugging me close, he kisses my lips, tracing the edge of my jaw, the columns of my throat. He finishes with a loud smack on my cheek and the clap of his palm over my ass. "How do you like your eggs?"

I must be some kind of stupid to consider answering *fertilized*.

Instead, I clear my throat, tuck my hair behind my ear, and ask the real question.

"Is *in a cake* an option?"

THIRTY-SIX
DON'T GO BACON HIS FACE

Garrett

I CANNOT BELIEVE Jennie grew up with this.

I've underestimated her strength, her resilience. What a grueling life she's led. It's as sad as it is admirable.

"Time for another classic, this one by Elton John and Kiki Dee." Carter whirls around, cocking one ridiculous eyebrow as he stares out at his six-person audience, microphone at his mouth. "With a one-of-a-kind Carter Beckett twist that, arguably, makes it better than the original." Music roars from the speakers, lyrics starting to roll across the TV, and Carter stares Olivia dead in the eye. "Don't Go Bacon My Heart." He points at his wife. *This one's for you, Ollie girl!*"

"Jesus Christ," I mutter from behind the palm I've buried my face in as Carter explodes into song and dance. It's not so much dance as it is… gyrating? I don't fucking know, but Olivia looks like she's gonna cry. I give her knee a shake. "You okay?"

"Of course she's not okay," Emmett retorts. "She's about to bring a baby into this world that's gonna be a carbon copy of her husband."

Adam jogs over, handing her a frosty pint of beer. "Here. It's nonalcoholic." Olivia pulls an unimpressed face, and Adam offers her a pity-ing, gritty grin. "I know. I'm sorry."

"The worst part is it's supposed to be a duet," Cara murmurs, watching Carter spin around, "but he's singing both parts."

"So, *oooh, oooh!*" He twirls, stopping in front of his wife—who looks oddly unfazed—and points at her. "Don't go bacon my heart!"

"I'm so in love with him it's unbelievable," is I think what Olivia mutters beside me.

"What?"

"Oh nothing." She smiles like she forgot I was here, then pats my thigh. "So, Garrett. How's...everything?"

"Everything? G-good. Really good." *Why is she grinning like that, all devious and shit?* Short, pregnant women shouldn't be allowed to be devious. They're scary enough as it is. "Yeah, everything is...so good."

"I haven't seen you since the restaurant on Valentine's Day. You took off in a hurry."

"Well, we've been traveling for the last three days," I remind her.

"Uh-huh, and you were holed up the entire five-day home stretch before that."

"Yeah, I..." I run a hand through my hair. "Busy."

She cocks her head. "I busy?"

"Is that a hickey?" It's Carter this time, breathless as he collapses between us. He prods my collarbone. "Yeah, it is."

I slap his hand away. "No, it's not." *It totally fucking is.* I told Jennie not to, but does she ever listen to me? No, of fucking course she doesn't. She's so difficult to rein in, and I don't really want to anyway.

Carter wags his brows. "Things goin' good with Susie, eh?"

Cara snorts. Adam promptly leaps to his feet, heading into the kitchen. Olivia turns away, and Jaxon busies himself in his phone. Carter and Emmett are...oblivious.

It's Emmett I'm most surprised about. Cara promised not to tell, but I guess I wasn't expecting her to be this loyal to us. I think it's Jennie she's being loyal to, really.

And Olivia? She's just perceptive, I guess. Plus, she came back from dropping Jennie off on Valentine's Day and "accidentally" elbowed me really fucking hard in the shoulder when she sat down, so I was pretty sure she knew before Jennie even told me she knew.

Cara stands. "I've gotta jet. I have to meet with some clients about a charity event."

I pull out my phone to distract from the fierce battle of tonsil hockey her and Emmett start right here in the living room.

"Is Jennie coming over?" Olivia asks.

"No," I answer on autopilot, scrolling through the sports updates on my phone. My fingers pause for only a second before I force them to keep moving, while I tell myself to act cool. "'Cause she's got classes, right? Hey, Jaxon, Nashville's one and four out of their last five games. Looks like they need you back there guarding their goalie."

The name of the game is deflection, and Jaxon plays along just fine, engaging me in a mindless conversation about hockey stats, but Carter's not paying us any attention anyway.

No, he's got his face pressed to Olivia's belly, his hands cupped around his mouth as he makes these weird, deep, staticky breathing noises.

"What the fuck are you doing, dude?" Jaxon finally asks.

"Luke," Carter speaks into Olivia's stomach. Two more raspy noises. "I am your father."

"Holy fuck." I scrub my tired eyes. "Not Darth Vader."

Olivia pushes Carter off her lap and stands. "Garrett, the things I deal with on a regular basis would bring you to tears." Taking Carter's frowning face in her hands, she kisses him. "I couldn't love you more." She starts hobbling away, one hand on her lower back. "But if Jennie's not coming over, mama's gonna go take a bath." Her footsteps sound on the staircase before she calls, "Carter! Can you make sure they make the kung pao chicken extra spicy?"

"Yes, pumpkin!"

"I thought we were getting dinner from Amy's Wok?" Adam asks, taking Olivia's spot on the couch. Along with his tea, he's returned with an entire box of Oreos. "Amy's Wok doesn't have kung pao chicken."

"I know. Gotta order separately from Golden Village."

"Why don't you just tell Ollie they don't have it instead of ordering from two places?"

Carter pulls a face, setting up the Xbox. "Have you met her? She's scary as fuck right now."

"She's five feet tall!"

Carter jabs his shoulder. "Five foot *one*."

I snicker, tossing a cookie into my mouth. "I agwee. Aw-wie is pwetty scawy wight now." I take the controller passed to me and swallow. "I wouldn't wanna mess with her."

"She's got these wild cravings, and nothing is ever exactly what she wants. I'll gladly order from two different places if it means keeping her happy."

We flip-flop between *Call of Duty* and *NHL* for an hour, and I suppress a groan when I realize I still have another ninety minutes to go before picking up Jennie from school. I haven't seen her in three days, which isn't a whole lot and definitely not the longest we've gone, but when you spent the five days before that fucking like wild animals, it feels like a goddamn eternity.

I'm not surprised Jennie's got her kinks, given the variety and quantity of her toy collection, but I was a little surprised she was ready to jump right into the rough, wild stuff the next day. Blame my unbelievably good looks and adorable ramblings. Jennie says I'm endearing.

Plus, every time we fuck like animals, we follow it up with a round of soft and sweet. I think that might be my favorite. While I love pulling her hair and slapping her ass, I really love looking into her eyes when I tell her I love her, kissing her while we come together. Holding her is my second favorite thing to do, right after loving her.

I glance at Carter before pulling out my phone to text Jennie, but I've already got one waiting for me.

Sunshine: *Can't wait to see you, big guy *tongue emoji* *eggplant emoji* *water droplets emoji**

The second one rolls in before I can acknowledge how truly alike the Beckett siblings are, which is for the best.

Sunshine: *Missed you *heart emoji**

"*Carterrr*," Olivia's voice calls from upstairs.

"Yeah, pumpkin?" he hollers back.

"I'm hungry!"

He pulls his phone out, frantically tapping at his screen. "Ordering right now!"

"I want something sweet! Can you make me an ice cream sundae?"

Carter looks up, blinking. "Ice cream sun—" He jogs to the bottom of the staircase, and I lean over the back of the couch, watching him. "With Oreo ice cream?"

"And brownies, please!"

"Brownies," he murmurs, hands on his hips. "What kinda brownies, Ollie girl?"

"The ones you make with the brownie batter and the Oreos and the cookie dough!"

"Oooh." I rub my belly. "I could fuck with those."

Carter glances at me, frowning. "We don't—we don't have any. I can go get the ingredients."

"It'll take too long," Olivia wails. "I want it now!"

He runs an agitated hand through his hair. "Babe, we don't have them right now! Let me go to the store!"

"No!"

"Ruh-roh," I murmur in my best Scooby-Doo, snickering, picking another cookie out.

Adam smacks it out of my hand. "Don't eat all of Ollie's cookies. I'm scared."

"We have regular Oreos and birthday cake Oreos," Carter calls. "I can make you a sundae with those!"

"It's not the same," Olivia cries.

Carter drags two hands down his face. "I don't know what to do! What do you want me to do?" His arms flail above his head. "Tell me what you want me to do!"

"Just forget it! I'll *starve*!"

Emmett's face pales. "Oh fuck. If Olivia is this scary, what's Cara gonna be like when she's pregnant?" He wipes his damp forehead. "I don't know if I can handle it if she ups the scare factor."

Jaxon shakes his head. "Fuck that. I'll be on a nine-month Cara fast. Nope. That woman terrifies me in a way I never thought possible."

I laugh as I pull my vibrating phone from my pocket. It's Jennie, and when I'm with Carter, she only calls if something is wrong. For instance, sometimes she accidentally hits stop signs. So I race to the bathroom and greet her with a breathless noise.

"Can you pick me up early, please?"

"Sure, sunshine. Everything okay?"

There's the hesitation I was looking for, the one that tells me no, not really, without outwardly admitting it.

"I'm leaving now," I tell her. "But don't forget: you kick ass and take names. Don't let anyone walk all over you."

I'm out the door two minutes later without a word from Carter. He was too busy ripping apart his pantry and having a breakdown about ice cream sundaes and brownies to care.

When I pull up out front of SFU, Jennie comes flying out, Simon hot on her heels as he yells after her. She whips open the door and slides in, and I really wanna kiss her, but I also want to keep my balls attached to my body.

"Hey." I tap her thigh, drawing her gaze to mine, then tug her into me, pressing a kiss to her forehead. "Hang on a sec, 'kay, sunshine?"

"Where are you going?"

"I'll be right back," I promise, shutting the door behind me.

It's cold as balls and I can't wait for winter to end. I have this vision of spending my summer by a pool where Jennie is scantily clad the entire time.

"Mmm, mmm," I hum to myself as I stalk toward Simon, that damn song stuck in my head. "Don't go bacon my heart."

His eyes zero in on me, angry, confused, before an infuriating smile spreads across his face.

"She really sent you over here to yell at me? Pathetic. I'm not scared of you. Jennie's so fucking dramatic. If she wasn't flirting with me all the time, I wouldn't have kissed her."

When I stop in front of him, he flinches back, just an inch, before quickly recovering.

Chuckling lowly, he looks me over. "Fucking her brother's friend and teammate. Classic. Is Jennie as boring in bed as she is the rest of the time? Vanilla sex to go with her vanilla pers—"

The sound of my fist slamming into the flesh of his cheek ends his words prematurely, and *fuck*, that felt good.

Simon brings a trembling hand to his shocked face. "You—"

My fist connects with his nose this time, blood spattering my knuckles. I grip the collar of his coat and yank him into me.

"Say her name one more time," I whisper. "I fucking dare you."

Blood seeps from his nose, gathering on his top lip. His arms come up in surrender.

"I told you not to touch her again without her consent. What does *no* mean, Simon?"

His lips part, but all that comes out is a croak.

"What does *no* mean?" I urge again.

"No," he sputters. "No means no."

"That's fucking right, Simon. No means no." I release his collar and wipe my knuckles on my hoodie. I liked this one, and I especially liked watching Jennie wander around my apartment wearing nothing but it and her panties. Now I have to replace it. "Speak to her again and I'll put you through the pavement."

I'm oddly calm as I head to the car, hands tucked in my pockets. I should probably formulate some sort of apology to Jennie for punching Simon on school property or something.

"Hey, so, about that…" I meet her gaze when I slide into my seat. She's just staring at me, mouth gaped, hazy blue eyes dazed. I slip my fingers beneath my toque, scratching my head. "Are you mad at me? Because I—"

"I didn't think I was attracted to caveman," she murmurs, "but I am. I'm attracted to caveman."

I note the way she's inching toward me, bottom lip sliding between her teeth, and Lieutenant Johnson stirs in my pants, letting me know he's ready for duty.

"You want me to take you home and go caveman on you?"

"Yes, I want you to take me home and exert all force necessary."

"Mmm…" My hand slides along her jaw, angling her face toward mine. "Show you how much stronger I am than you?"

Her fingers glide up my forearms, gripping my biceps. "*So* strong."

My lips skim hers. "You want me to tie you up?"

"I want you to strip me down, render me powerless, and fuck me so hard, until I can't walk and the shape of your cock is imprinted inside me."

I stare at her, unblinking, for a solid twenty seconds, before finally muttering, "Jesus fucking Christ."

She grins, giggles, then pops a kiss on my mouth. "I love you. Oh, one sec." She hits the power button on the window, letting the cold air in as she leans out. "Fuck you, Steve," she screams at Simon, flipping him the double bird. She turns back around, sinking into her seat with a happy sigh.

"I am so ready to get fucked straight to heaven. Let's go home, Garrett."

THIRTY-SEVEN

LIEUTENANT JOHNSON VS. DISNEYLAND: SURVIVAL OF THE FITTEST

Garrett

"JENNIE—"

"No, I changed my mind." She tosses her braid over her shoulder—it's tied off with an emerald velvet ribbon today, cute as fuck—and struts away, leaving me staring after her ass while I follow her into the elevator.

"Like fuck you did."

"Well, believe it, buddy." She hammers *21* three times and pins her arms across her chest. "You're in the penalty box tonight."

Jennie's so funny and sassy, I don't know what to do with her sometimes. She likes to play this game, pretend she's mad at me, drag it out until one of us is begging. She likes both outcomes, and so the fuck do I.

Why is she pretending to be mad at me right now? We went through the Starbucks drive-thru and they didn't have any ginger molasses cookies. They offered her an oatmeal raisin quinoa cookie and I was afraid she was going to leap through the window. I think the barista was too.

It's not my fault, but for the sake of getting us both riled up, she's pretending it is.

"You're being a brat."

"I'm not *being* one, Garrett. I *am* one."

"Yeah, tell me about it." The doors pop open and I scoop her bag up before stalking ahead of her. "Bigger brat than all three of my sisters combined."

Jennie gasps, hand pressed to her throat. I'm gonna squeeze that later.

"Keep your mouth open like that and I'll shove my cock down your throat, sunshine."

There's that sparkle, right there in those electric violet-blue eyes. "You wouldn't."

I prowl toward her, excitement stirring as she backs herself into her apartment and right against the wall. "Oh, I would."

She licks her lips, watching me pull my bloodstained hoodie over my head. "No," she murmurs, slinging her arms around my neck, fingers creeping into my hair as she kisses my jaw. "You're just my sweet, gentle giant. That's why everyone calls you Gare-Bear."

With a snarl, I sink my hand into the base of her braid, fisting it tightly. I press her chest to the wall and her ass juts, grinding against my cock. Dipping beneath her top, my fingertips dance over her stomach, feeling her muscles jump. I open my mouth on her neck, and her head drops over my shoulder with a moan.

I skim the waistband of her leggings. "You want me to touch you?" My lips glide over her skin. "Taste you?" I drag the tip of one finger up the seam of her legs. "Fuck you?"

"God, *yes*."

"Beg for it."

"Garrett," she whimpers, trembling.

"Yeah," I murmur. "That's a good fucking start."

She whirls around, hands on my chest as she pushes me into the wall. She kicks off her shoes, rips her shirt over her head, and yanks her leggings down. I follow suit, until we're left in nothing but our underwear.

Jennie holds me to the wall with her palm on my collarbone, free hand gliding down my torso. Sneaking below the band of my boxers, she wraps her fist around my cock. I hiss at the surge of pleasure, and a triumphant grin ignites across her face.

"I don't beg," Jennie whispers against my lips. "You do." She releases my cock, pats my stomach, and…walks away.

I sure don't mind the view, all black lace and long, golden limbs. I let her get halfway down the hall before I ditch my boxers, eat the distance between us, and cage her in against the wall, my chest against her back.

"Not today, sunshine. Today I want you on your knees."

I dip my hand into her panties and bury my groan in her neck at what's waiting for me.

"Jesus, Jennie. You're fucking drenched."

"Thinking about mounting Indiana Bones," she chokes out, gasping as I sink one finger inside her. "He always fucks me so good."

I pump my finger at a pace I know drives her wild, waiting until she's arching into my palm, writhing below me. "Take it back."

"So big," she rasps, hips rocking. "So good."

That emerald ribbon is taunting me with feigned innocence, so I wind one end around my middle finger and tug. Her silky hair frees itself from the braid, cascading down her back, and the scent of vanilla and cinnamon encases me, suffocating me in the best way.

Her thick waves slip through my fingers. "So fucking gorgeous."

She hits me with a cheeky smirk over her shoulder, dimples pulled in. "I know."

She thinks she's won.

Slowly, I remove my finger, taking great pleasure in her falling smile, eyes storming as she spins around.

"What the fuck are you doing?"

"Tasting."

Her gaze ignites as she watches my finger disappear inside my mouth. She takes a small step forward, reaching for me. I circle her wrists, stopping her. Her body hums with anticipation when I wind the ribbon around her wrists, finishing with a bow.

Taking her chin between my thumb and index finger, I bring her gaze to mine. The eagerness that swims there, the trust, the love, it shatters me. I love her so much, but it's not going to stop my next words.

"Get on your knees."

Her eyes gleam as she licks her lips. "Make me."

I stride forward, staring down at her. She holds my gaze and matches each one of my steps with her own backward, until we're beside her bed. Wide, blue eyes peer up at me, waiting for instruction but ready to fight it too.

She's not going to fight it, though.

"Get on your fucking knees," I repeat lowly, and she falls to them without another protest. "Good fucking girl."

This endearing mixture of sassy, take-no-shit confidence, sweet innocence, and her desire for praise is what makes things so explosive between us, the way we can switch off, both take control and wield it as we please, always giving and getting what we need.

That and she just makes everything better. I was whole without her but unbalanced, like things weren't quite right, everything slightly off center. With her, everything is brighter and clearer, stoking the passion that vibrates so intensely between us.

I brush my thumb over her bottom lip. "This mouth gets you into a lot of trouble, huh?"

"You call it trouble; I call it fun."

"The best fucking fun. Now open your mouth, sunshine."

My fingers plow through her hair as I sink inside her hot, wet mouth. She takes me eagerly, moaning greedily around me.

"Fuck." Holding her in place, I pull back, then thrust forward.

Her bound wrists lift, and she cups my balls, massaging them gently. My cock hits the back of her throat, over and over, and Jennie starts writhing, rocking, searching for friction. Her hands fall and a satisfied moan vibrates around me as she dips into her panties and works that pink bud at the cleft of her thighs. Her eyes roll toward the ceiling and her throat opens as she takes me farther, like she's trying to swallow me.

"Jesus, Jennie. Fuck. Just like that."

I'm gonna come, and I can tell by the desperation in her eyes, the way she's grinding down on her hand, the garbled sounds my cock muffles, that she is too.

But she's supposed to be begging.

I yank her hands off herself, holding onto that green ribbon, and she cries out, looking damn near on the verge of tears as I thrust forward once more, spilling down her throat.

"You're a—"

"On the bed," I direct gruffly, winding an arm around her and tossing her exactly there. Her chest heaves, swollen lips parted as I fist my cock. "Open your legs."

She doesn't hesitate, feet flat on the mattress, showing me her soaked panties, the wetness coating the inside of her thighs. I lie between her legs, and she shudders as my mouth follows the slick line up her thighs, tasting, savoring.

"Garrett," she pleads, squirming as I shift her lace out of the way just a touch, nibbling, licking. "Take them off."

"Why?"

"Lick me," she begs. "*Please.*"

"I can lick you just fine with them on." My tongue does one languid pass up the center of her panties, pulling a full-body tremble from her. "Do you want to feel my tongue?"

"God, *yes.*"

I trail the tip of my finger up her seam, ghosting over her clit. "Ask nicely."

Her eyes blaze with her unwillingness to back down, so I flick my tongue over that needy, lace-covered clit, and watch how fast she folds.

"Oh *fuck.* Please, Garrett. *Please.*"

Hooking a finger in the crotch of her panties, I inch them down. She smells like paradise, a wildly intoxicating mix of earthy and sweet. If this were my last night on earth, I'd happily spend it buried between her thighs, devouring every last bit of her. She'd be my last meal, and I'd die a happy man.

"Please what?"

She throws her head back with a growl. "For fuck's sake, Garrett, bury your face between my goddamn legs and make me scream your name before I cry, *please.*"

I smother my chuckle against her thigh. "You're not being very nice right now. So these..." Lifting her wrists, I hook the ribbon onto the iron bed rail. "Go here. No touching." She arches into me as I pull one taut nipple between my teeth. "Got it, sunshine?"

She whimpers as I discard her panties, cupping her pussy in my hand.

"Use your words, Jennie. You didn't seem to have a problem with it thirty seconds ago."

"Yes." The single syllable is muddled and messy, thick with frustration, desire.

My mouth slides over the swell of her tits, loving on each rosy nipple before continuing my path down, watching as her stomach flexes.

I pause, peering at the ring that peeks up at me from her belly button. It's new, silver, with a tiny turquoise gem up top, a bigger one down below. I don't know how I didn't notice this earlier, but my best guess would be I was too preoccupied to notice much of anything other than the way her eyes were fixed on mine while she had a mouthful of my cock.

"You got a new belly button ring. I like it."

Jennie grins, lashes fluttering. "I thought you would. It's the same color as your eyes."

I groan, covering her body with the weight of mine before I sear her with a kiss. "You're the fucking best."

I reach over, slapping at the bedside table until I find the knob on the drawer. Inside, I pull out the first thing I find. It's small and black and mighty as fuck. We haven't used it together, but I've jerked it to her using it on FaceTime. If she amps it all the way up to ten, she can come in two minutes.

I drop it beside her and start my path back down her body, tugging that belly ring between my teeth, sucking on her hip bone, nibbling the inside of her thigh until she's whimpering, begging, barely breathing.

"*Garrett*," she cries when I lick a leisurely stroke up her swollen, glistening slit. She struggles against the bed rail, feet pressing into the mattress as she lifts, pushing herself closer. When I suck her clit into my mouth, her head falls back with a sharp gasp.

"I fucking love this pussy." Hooking my arms around her thighs, I yank her closer. "Tastes like fucking bliss."

She's already close, shaking, toes curling, and when I plunge two fingers inside her, she cries out. I'm obsessed with her, the way she's addicted to watching me get her off, like the sight itself is enough to take her there. Just looking at her as she slowly unravels is enough to take me there. As I pump my fingers, tongue flicking over her bud, I revel in the way she feels when she comes, clamping around me and calling my name.

Without missing a beat, I grab the tiny toy, power it to 50 percent and suction it over her clit, fingers still thrusting.

"Holy shhh—" Her words dissolve, a jagged inhale piercing the air when I kick the power straight up to ten. "Oh my God. Oh my *God*, yes. Holy fucking—" Her head rolls, as do her eyes, fixed on the ceiling as her fingers curl around the bed rail. "*F-f-f-fuuuck*. I-I…" Her head lolls forward, wide eyes landing on me as she pants. "I'm gonna…I'm gonna…"

"Come." I curl my fingers, and a fiery red heat crawls up her neck, painting her cheeks when I hit that spot she loves. Her hips buck as she comes a second time, leaving my hand drenched.

I unhook her from the rail, sling her bound wrists around my neck, position her over my lap, and promptly drop her on my rock-hard cock before I combust.

"Jesus Christ," I hiss as she buries her scream in my shoulder.

I grip her waist, lifting her off me before I drop her again and again, burying myself to the hilt, my fingernails biting into her skin as she rakes hers up my back. She yanks at the hair at the nape of my neck as she arches away from me, perfect tits bouncing in my face, and I lean forward, sucking her into my mouth.

I want to be deeper, until she can feel me again in her fucking throat. I want to memorize the way she feels around me, like we were always made to fit together, the final two pieces of a puzzle.

Pulling her off me, I tug the ribbon free. She wastes no time cupping my face in her hands, slamming her mouth to mine. When she pulls away, I flip her onto her hands and knees, swiftly painting her heart-shaped ass with my handprint.

"Mine," I tell her, pressing my lips to the bright red mark.

She wanted caveman; caveman is exactly what she's getting.

She fists the sheets as I sink back inside her. "Yours."

"Fuck, Jennie." I grip her hips and piston forward. "Sometimes I just wanna fucking...*destroy you*. Fuck you until you feel weightless, like you're floating and you can't feel anything else. Fuck you so hard you can feel me even when I'm gone." I haul her up to me, back pressed to my chest as I hold onto her throat. "You're perfection, flawless, and all I wanna do is mark you with reminders that you're mine and I'm yours, that we belong to each other."

Jennie squeezes around me, breath husky and fractured as she reaches back, her hand on the side of my neck as we ride together.

Releasing her throat, I drag her hand between her legs. Pressing her fingers to her clit, I move our hands together in a circle, making her rub herself as my orgasm starts barreling down my spine. My balls tighten, and when Jennie whimpers my name once, then twice, I clutch her hips and thrust forward as hard as I can, over and over, until we tumble over the edge of the cliff together, free-falling into the sky.

Breathless, I collapse onto my back, draping Jennie overtop of me, limp and lifeless, gasping for air. I clap a hand to her ass and kiss her lips.

"I love you," we say at the same time, followed by a laugh.

"Christ, I'm tired." I drag a hand through my damp hair. "You're wild."

"*Me*?"

"Yeah, you, sunshine. You got me all riled up on purpose."

"Starbucks didn't have my ginger molasses cookie. They offered me raisins and *quinoa*, Garrett."

My stomach grumbles, reminding me I skipped out on dinner so I could pick up Jennie early. "Chinese food," I murmur as seductively as I can manage, lips skimming her jaw.

Jennie laughs. "Let me clean myself up and get a menu."

I follow her to the bathroom, where we decide a quick shower would be best, and I spend 99 percent of it kissing her under the steady stream. While she retrieves the menu from the kitchen, I wipe down the toy and tuck it back in its home.

A shiny gem catches my eye, and I pull out the small, pink glass plug it's attached to. When Jennie strolls back into the bedroom, I give her a questioning look, brows raised. She likes adventure, and I like to be adventurous with her.

"Absolutely not, Garrett."

I cock my head, pouting.

She rolls her eyes and sighs. "Fine, maybe one day."

"It's a fucking maybe, ladies and gentlemen!" I slam the drawer, dive-bomb the bed, hugging her to me as she giggles, and I snuggle in as we read the menu together.

We eat in bed when the food gets here, and then we have one round of soft and sweet before she wraps herself around me like a koala, settling in for the night.

Without my permission, my mind wanders to Carter. Beyond being my captain, he's one of my best friends. He took me in the moment I stepped off that plane all those years ago, when I had nobody. He invited me into his home, his life beyond hockey, and he did it without a second thought.

It was fun at first, the secrecy, the sneaking around, when the plan was always for this to be temporary. But now, as I stare down at her face, noting the way every tiny line has faded with the peace sleep brings her, I know Jennie's someone I'm not willing to live without.

The longer we hide this from Carter, the worse the outcome will be.

The lies are getting harder to swallow, making my stomach churn and ache as my feelings for Jennie only grow impossibly deeper.

Beyond that, I'm tired of not being able to talk about her like she isn't the very best and brightest thing in my world. I'm tired of the short-lived moments, the lingering glances across crowded rooms, the forced distance and detachment.

Spending time with Jennie is like a Sunday you don't want to ever end. Every moment leading up to it is perfect, a weekend that goes by way too fast. Sunday comes sooner than you want it to, and you hold on to every fleeting moment, every single minute, not ready to put it down, to say good-bye. You think if you just don't close your eyes, you won't have to.

But then nighttime comes along, the good-bye inevitable, and you wake up on Monday morning alone, ready to start another tedious week. You tuck your weekend away and become the person you don't really want to be, pretending you aren't managing to get by without the person who matters most, the one that makes everything easier, just waiting for the weekend all over again, when you can finally be together.

I don't want to wait anymore, and I'm tired of hiding.

THIRTY-EIGHT
BUBBLE-WRAPPED

Jennie

I LOVE THIS BUBBLE.

Everything about it is warm and bright. I'm constantly basking in sunshine, wrapped in strong arms, pulled back against a solid chest, a steady stream of "I love you" whispered in my ear.

Worry doesn't live here. There's no place for fears or insecurities. Those things only exist outside the bubble, where we're forced to pretend there isn't an *us*, that we aren't two halves of an incredible whole.

This is my favorite place to be, right next to this man, surrounded by his love, his support, the way he constantly lifts me up.

I smooth my palm over his bare chest, feeling the heat of his skin, the gentle thrum of the heart that beats below. I wonder if he knows that I radiate happiness because he gave me the space to shine.

My lips touch his collarbone, and the body below me hums and comes to life, hugging me to his chest with one muscular arm while the other shoots up over his head with a stretch, long legs flexing.

"You're such a fuckin' bed hog," Garrett grumbles, right before I'm on my back, flattened by the weight of his body sprawled on mine.

His lids flutter, sleepy turquoise eyes peering down at me. The corner of his mouth lifts as he shifts, straddling my hips, fingers circling my wrists as he pins them on either side of my head.

"My bed," he murmurs, kissing my shoulder. "My Jennie." His lips move up my neck, my chin, until he's hovering above me, shaggy golden hair a mess. A grin blossoms on his face, so warm and inviting, intoxicating. "My fucking sunshine." His mouth covers mine, tongue sweeping inside as he releases my wrists to thread our fingers together, to light a fire of desire inside me as he skims my side.

Garrett grips my waist as he grinds down on me. I wind my legs around him and moan, hips lifting, silently begging, and I swallow his sigh as he sinks inside.

"How many times is too many?"

I gasp as he hikes my leg up, plunging deeper. "To have sex?"

"To tell you I love you."

"I like hearing it. No one's ever loved me the way you love me, and I've never loved anyone the way I love you."

He smiles down at me before resting his forehead on mine. As we move together, both of us taking and giving, when I come with him inside me and he follows me, I don't know where I end and he begins. We're just one; one body, one love, one heart.

"Are you excited for tonight?" he asks as I pull on a pair of panties and my sleep romper, the one he got me for Christmas with *angel* scrawled across the ass, finishing with a pair of his thick, woolly socks.

I crawl back onto the bed, sitting cross-legged. "Yes and no. I hate having to pretend we're only friends."

It's been like this for two weeks now, this on and off where I'm in a relationship one moment and single the next, having to hide every time we're around our friends. The glances from the people who know make it harder, but it's the person who doesn't know that makes it impossibly terrifying. Tonight will be no different, but still, I'm glad to have friends to spend my time with, to be enjoying a night out with them. Though I wish I was allowed to dance with my boyfriend.

Garrett picks up my hand, laying my palm up. He traces all the lines, the length of my fingers, and his throat bobs before he peeks up at me. "I want to tell Carter."

I can't say I didn't see this coming. He's been a ball of angst lately where Carter's involved.

It's taking a toll on him, though Garrett hasn't outwardly admitted it, other than saying he wishes he could have his hands on me all the time. Most of the time he finds a way, whether it's skimming my lower back as he moves past me, his pinky tucked around mine if we're lucky

368 | BECKA MACK

enough to sit next to each other on a couch or at a table. If we're especially lucky, I get a full-hand ass grab.

But what started out as fun and a simple lie has turned into a full-blown secret relationship behind my brother's back, one of Garrett's best friends. Carter might be self-absorbed, but his family and friends are his world, and lying to him for so long feels like the ultimate betrayal. He's my forever best friend, my protector, the shoulder that's always been there every time I needed one. That I've been lying to him for so long might break his heart, and I'm ashamed to be the reason behind it.

"I don't like lying to him anymore, Jennie. Not when I don't see an end in sight for us."

My heart pitter-patters. "You don't?"

"I really don't, sunshine."

"Oh good." My body sags with relief. "Neither do I, but I don't know how these things go."

"Would you be up for telling him tomorrow morning? Together? Maybe if we ask him and Olivia to come over for breakfast. Or, you ask him, so he doesn't have a heart attack before he even gets here." His laugh is forced and anxious, and he rubs at his chest with a grimace.

I squeeze his hand. "You're nervous."

In his anxious gaze, I see the unrelenting compassion that swims in it, all his soft, gentle bits that make him who he is, the man I love.

"I'm worried he won't think I'm good enough for you."

"You are *so* good for me, Garrett. But more than that, we're good for each other. You've helped me overcome things in a few months that I haven't been able to get over in several years. I think in the end that'll be what matters to Carter."

Garrett gnaws his lip. "Maybe I'll bring Oreos as a peace offering. I've been hanging on to a special edition flavor from the States for this occasion."

"You're joking. How long?"

"Adam's mom last sent me a box at Christmas, so…around then?"

"But—"

"But nothing. That's when I realized I had feelings for you, and would eventually need to bribe Carter into letting me date his sister."

"I might not have been interested," I toss back with a cheeky grin.

He crawls over me, pushing me back to the mattress. "Like hell you wouldn't have been. You're obsessed with me."

The alarm on his phone blares, and he drops his forehead to my chest with a groan.

I push his hair back off his face. "You've gotta get ready. There are some excited kids waiting to meet their hero."

"I can't believe I'm anyone's hero."

"I can." He's been mine before, even if I always wanted to be the only one who saved me. But sometimes you need to let someone else in so they can help save you.

With Adam spending so much time at the children's home, he's built some incredible connections with the kids there and turned them all into hockey fans. At their last early afternoon home game, he bought tickets for everyone, provided all the snacks, and organized a tour before the game. Today he's got the entire team paying them a visit.

"You gonna drive over to Carter and Ollie's this morning, or do you want me to drop you off on my way to Adam's?" Garrett calls from the bathroom as he cranks the shower.

It's only the first day of March, but spring is peeking its head out here on the west coast. I'm not complaining; I hate having to choose between my cute coat and my warm coat.

With the absence of snow, I've been getting back out on the road more with Carter's car. I haven't hit any stop signs, and in fact, I now stop about ten feet away. Garrett says that's not great, either, but Garrett can kiss my ass.

"Can you give me a ride?" I've been casually dropping to Carter that Garrett's been giving me rides to school on his way to grab his morning coffee. It should work in our favor, because it shows Carter our friendship is growing, that we've had time to get to know each other.

Or maybe I'm totally delusional and hoping for a miracle.

"Oh, that reminds me," I yell over the shower. "I had to get air in the tires yesterday. I got a great deal!"

Nothing but the sound of water raining down.

And then: "A deal? On air?"

"Yeah, I took it to that shop over on Renfrew, and they knocked the price down to four hundred dollars!"

The water stops, silence hanging heavy in the air as steam seeps from the bathroom. Slow as molasses, Garrett appears in the doorway, naked, soaking wet, not even bothering to cover his XL cock.

"Pardon?"

"A hundred bucks a tire! For premium air! Can you believe it?"

"P...Premium air?"

"They said they normally charge double!"

"Oh my God." His hands come up, head moving rapidly between them like he isn't sure what to do, before he finally drags them down his face. "Oh my God. Jennie, what the fuck? How-how-how...You got ripped off!"

"What are you talking about?"

"Air is—*oh my God*! Jennie, it costs, like, a dollar to put air in your tires!"

"What?"

His arms fly around his head. "You do it at the gas station! At those little pumps with the hose! Jesus fuck." He scrubs his face, and I think it's hilarious he's somehow managing to get an erection right now. "We're gonna have to skip breakfast. We'll stop at the shop on the way to Carter's. I'll get you your money back."

My chest rumbles. I bite my lip, trying to stop it, but when Garrett's flustered gaze meets mine, I can't help it. A snicker-snort comes out my nose, and I fold forward as the rest of my laugh comes barreling out.

"It's a TikTok trend," I choke out, rolling on the bed. "I can't believe you fell for it. You're so gullible!"

He picks up a balled-up pair of socks and tosses it at my head. "I'm gonna fuck your brains out later tonight just for that."

"*Oh no*," I mock. "*Anything but that.*" I hop off the bed and head into the bathroom, slipping my arms around his middle and hugging him from behind. "I love you."

"You Becketts and your fucking TokToks."

"*Tik*Toks." I give him another squeeze, Lieutenant Johnson one quick pump. "I'll go make us breakfast."

"Jennie?" he calls after me. "I love you too."

I know he does, that's why I make him a four-pancake stack, topped with Reese's spread and sliced bananas, dusted with icing sugar and drizzled with real maple syrup, with a side of Canadian bacon. I just finish plating it when he claps two hands firmly to my ass, making me gasp.

"Your ass looked lonely without my hands on it." He kisses my cheek and inhales. "Looks and smells incredible."

"Thank you. It's all natural."

He pinches my butt. "I was talking about breakfast, you turtle."

He spins me around, and I push him back a step, gaze coasting down his body. He's so ridiculously beautiful it hurts.

"What is this?" I ask, touching the collar of his jacket.

He looks down at himself. "A jean jacket."

"Hmm. I'm into it."

He grins and tugs on the denim lapels. "Yeah?"

"Yeah," I murmur, skimming the buttons as my teeth press into my bottom lip. Gripping the collar, I yank him down to me. "I'm into *you*."

Garrett laughs, hearty and rumbly, both hands on my butt, squeezing. The tip of his nose touches mine as he brushes a soft kiss to my lips. "I can't wait until I get to love you out in the open."

"I'm ready," I tell him honestly.

"Me too."

$\sim$

"This is the most incredible thing in the world."

"Isn't it?" Olivia's brown eyes shine as she smiles down at her stomach. "I wish you could feel it from the inside."

My palm glides over her firm, round belly, searching for my niece or nephew. Olivia takes my hand and places it on the right, near the bottom of her rib cage. She presses my hand into her skin and a moment later something pushes back.

I gasp, watching in wonder as her stomach jumps.

"Auntie J loves you so much already," I whisper to my niece or nephew, running my hand over the home that's kept him or her safe. "I can't wait to meet you."

The front door opens, and Dublin flies off the couch and down the hallway.

"Hi, Dubs," Carter coos. "Who's my handsome man? Did you miss Daddy? Daddy missed you. Yes, I did, Mr. Handsome." He strolls into the living room, carrying the seventy-pound dog in his arms before setting him down. "Saying hi to your nephew?"

"Or niece," I point out, then gasp when he essentially shoves me to the floor so he can press his hands to Olivia's belly. I slam my fist into his quad. "You asshole."

"Hi, baby," he speaks against her stomach. "How's my little man?"

372 | BECKA MACK

"Carter, for fuck's sake, help your sister up and stop assuming the sex of our baby."

"Okay, bossy pants." He hoists me back to the couch, then cups Olivia's face and presses a kiss to her lips. "But you're gonna feel awfully silly when that baby comes out all man."

"You're the one that didn't want to find out," I remind him.

"Because I just know." He taps his temple and winks. "Call it a father-son connection."

"Call it ignorance," Olivia mutters, then smiles brightly when Carter sets a treat-filled plate on the coffee table. "Mmm, come to mama."

"Weren't you on a no-junk-food kick?" I ask as they dig in.

"I've learned it's best to have no goals or expectations when pregnant. That way I don't get upset with myself when I accidentally go through the Taco Bell drive-thru, order three tacos, one Crunchwrap Supreme, and large chili cheese fries, then devour all four in ten minutes."

"Should we find out?" Carter asks suddenly. "The gender? We still have a month. We could find out. Do you wanna find out?" He holds up a hand. "No, don't answer that. I don't wanna find out."

He flops down in a chair, drumming his fingers. Is his eye twitching? His jaw definitely is. He sweeps his hand out and then second-guesses, bringing it back in, resting his chin on his fist.

"What if it's a girl? It won't be, right? No, because my mom had me first, and your mom had Jeremy first, so that means we'll have a boy first. It's just, like, science."

I open my mouth to tell him that's not how it works, but Olivia touches my hand and gives her head the tiniest shake, continuing to watch Carter. He's alternating between staring off into space and tugging at his hair, going off about genetics and DNA, both of which he's not qualified to talk about.

Suddenly, he leaps to his feet, eyes wild as he lays a hand on his chest. "If it's a girl, Olivia, I will die. I. Will. *Die*." He storms down the hallway, shoving his fingers through his hair and muttering to himself. Heavy footsteps pound up the stairs.

"What the hell was that? And did he just call you by your full name?" The only time I've heard it in conversation is when they said their vows. It's Ollie, Ol, Liv, princess, pumpkin, pumpkin pie, or Mrs. Beckett, but *never* Olivia unless he's singing that song he likes.

Olivia waves a dismissive hand through the air. "He's just made himself a girl dad in his head, and now he's thinking about the fact that one day somebody will try to take her from him. It really upsets him. He needs some time to cool off." She hooks her toes beneath the coffee table, dragging it closer, and snatches another cookie off the plate. "Happens about once a week." She looks down the hall. "You only have fifteen minutes to freak out, Carter! You need to be showered, dressed, and ready to go in a half hour!"

"*I'm not freaking out!*" Carter screeches back. "*You're freaking out!*"

She twists her cookie apart. "Six foot four, well over two hundred pounds, crushes people into the boards for a living, and the idea of a seven-pound baby girl terrifies the living hell out of him."

"I so hope it's a girl."

"You and me both, Jennie. You and me both."

"Carter, if you do the Darth Vader voice one more time, I'm leaving."

Olivia says it, but I'm 100 percent on board with her decision. The three of us are out for dinner before we meet everyone else at the club, and Carter's garnered so much attention talking to Olivia's bump.

"Fine, but when that baby is outta there, I won't be stopped." He sips his beer, eyes flitting to the three men at the table next to us as they holler at the TV, empty beer pitchers and glasses strewn across the table. He looks back to us. "Anyway, it was fun today, with all the kids. They were so psyched we were there. Adam's talking about hosting a couple extra fundraisers this year so they can upgrade the facilities, see if we can get these kids meeting some families, that kinda stuff. Cara's going to help plan them."

"That man is the sweetest human being on this planet," Olivia says. "I hope he finds the special person he's looking for." She grins mischievously at me. "Hey, Jennie, maybe—"

"No." Carter pats her head. "No, pumpkin."

I snort a laugh as my phone vibrates. If the idea of me dating Adam Lockwood, golden boy, is any indication, telling him about Garrett and I is going to be a dumpster fire.

Bear: *U gonna have an attitude later tonight?*

Me: *Already got one, big guy.*
Bear: *Perfect. Feel like pulling ur hair and fucking ur throat.*

The spot between my legs tingles with anticipation at the promise, and I shift in my seat.

"Garrett's friend was there too," Carter says. "Emma? Your neighbor."

"Emily," I correct.

"Apparently she does pro bono work there every now and then, works with the kids. Some of them really struggle." He snickers. "Garrett thought she was a cheerleader."

Bear: *PS. Did u know Emily is a child psychologist??? She was at the home today.*

A vague memory runs through my mind of her telling me her job was boring and unimportant, waving me off when I asked the question a half hour after she punched Kevin in the face.

I pull up her contact and type out a message.

Me: *Boring and unimportant job, huh?*
Emily: *Shut up.*
Me: *My little softie.*
Emily: *Don't ruin my bad bitch image, J.*

"I'm pretty sure her and Garrett are still fucking. 'Cause he says he's not dating that photographer girl, but he had scratches all down his back in the change room last week, and him and Emily were talking in the corner today."

Bear: *She pulled me aside and asked if I thought Jaxon and Adam were up for a threesome.*
Emily: *Can you talk your boyfriend into hooking me up with his sexy friends? He didn't think I was serious, but if I were to get pegged by two guys at a time, I'd at least want to be absolutely wrecked, you know? They looked capable.*
Me: *I don't think Adam's a threesome kinda guy, Em. Sorry.*

Emily: **sigh* Yeah, I got that vibe as well. I'd probably ruin him. Hey, wanna have a girls' night next weekend?*
Me: *A girls' night?*
Emily: *Yeah, you know, takeout, movies, nonalcoholic wine...*

Something blooms in my chest as Carter prattles on about having enough kids to build their own hockey team, and even though Olivia's sitting right in front of me, she texts in our group chat with Cara asking if we want to have a sleepover when the boys go away next. Emily starts listing off other things we can do if I don't want to stay in, like going for dinner or out dancing. Garrett sends me a picture of the small charm on the keychain I got him for Valentine's Day, the bear and the sunshine looking up at me from his palm, with a message telling me he loves me and he's already worked out a plan with Adam and Jaxon to get us sitting together at the club, and I feel so full it's nearly painful.

Where did all this love come from? This incredible family, the friendships I've been blessed with? Have they always been here and I've just been too hard on myself to believe they were really here for me?

As Carter pays the bill, the men next to us request another round.

"I'm sorry," the waitress says. "I can't serve you anymore."

"What the fuck does that mean?" one of them asks, climbing unsteadily to his feet. "We're watchin' the game, and we want another."

She shakes her head. "You boys have had enough. I can call you a cab once you've paid your bill."

"We don't need a fuckin' cab," he spits, tearing the bill from her hand.

A ball of unease settles low in my stomach, and Carter takes Olivia's hand in his, placing his other on my back as he guides us toward the door. I glance over my shoulder, watching as the men snatch their coats up, tossing bills down on the table. For some reason, my heart pounds a little harder, and my chest begins to tighten.

When we step into the cool night, I take a deep breath, exhaling slowly. The knot in my stomach slowly unfurls and I relax as we head for the car.

The restaurant door slams open, and the three men pour out.

"Fuckin' bitch," one says.

"Where we gonna go now?" the other slurs.

The third fishes a set of car keys from his pocket. "I know a place."

No. *No.* I grip my brother's arm.

"You better put those the fuck away," Carter growls, pointing at the keys. "You even so much as step toward a car in your state, I'll put you through the ground."

The man holding the keys sways, eyes glassy as he watches Carter. Then he laughs and takes a step forward. "Get outta my way, superstar."

Carter puts his hand on his chest, looming over him. "One more step. I'll fucking end you."

"In front of your pregnant wife? Nah, I don't think so. There are three of us and one of you. Who do you think will wind up hurt?"

"Carter," Olivia pleads quietly, reaching for him. "I'm scared."

"Hear that? Your wife is scared. Get in your car and take her home."

Carter squeezes her hand and guides her to me. "Jennie, get in the car and call the cops."

My chest rises sharply, eyes darting around the men as they close in around Carter. Olivia clutches my arm, one hand on her stomach.

"Jennie," she whimpers. "I don't feel good."

"Get in the car," Carter repeats. "*Now.*"

I'm trying, but my feet aren't moving. *Why aren't my feet moving? Why are those men walking toward him like that? Why isn't he coming with us?* I try to call for him, but something inside me is frozen in fear. When I close my eyes, all I see is my dad's unrecognizable car. All I smell is stale beer. All I feel is…terror.

One of the men looks at Olivia, then me, and grins. "This isn't gonna be fun for you two to watch."

Olivia's breath hitches as her eyes widen with panic, and I yank my phone out, dialing those three numbers.

"Nine-one-one, do you need fire, ambulance, or police?"

My response gets lost in my throat as all three men descend on Carter at once, a tangled mass of bodies rocking into a nearby car before falling to the ground.

Olivia's bloodcurdling scream drowns everything else out except my own voice when I choke out, "I think I'm having a panic attack."

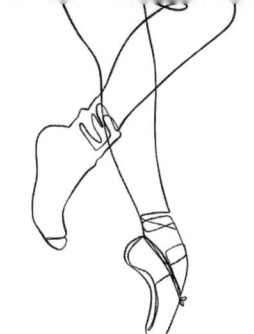

THIRTY-NINE
POPPING THE BUBBLE

Jennie

"Mom, stop. I'm fine, I promise."

She swipes at the tears beneath her bloodshot eyes, the ones she insists aren't really there. She folds her trembling hands together in her lap, and I cover them with mine.

"I was so scared," she whispers.

My heart plummets. I pull my mom into my arms, hugging her tight. Once is too many times to be on the receiving end of a phone call where a drunk driver has been involved.

"I'm safe. Olivia and the baby are safe, and Carter is safe. We're all safe."

Everyone other than Randall Duncan. Randall's got a broken nose. His mouth is busted up pretty good too.

The other two got off easy, deciding they'd rather not be on the receiving end of Carter's fist after they saw the damage he was doing to Randall. They scrambled away but didn't get far.

Randall blew a 0.23 BAC, nearly triple the legal limit. I've been sitting here for the last hour, thinking about what might have happened if he'd gotten behind that wheel, whose life might have been lost.

My mom kisses my forehead. "I'm going to find the vending machine."

"Okay." I pick at the needle in the back of my hand where my IV is attached. "This thing is itchy as fuck. Can I take it out?"

"Jennifer Beckett, don't touch it. Wait for the nurse to come back. You passed out, for heaven's sake."

"I had a panic attack." I roll my eyes to make it sound like anything other than the big deal it was while I try to forget that, in that moment, all I could think about was a drunk driver taking the life of another person I love. "I'm gonna go see Olivia."

Mom pushes me right back down to the bed when I stand. "You'll wait here until I get back."

I'm back on my feet when the door shuts behind her. My IV pole and I head out the door.

I find Olivia's room in thirty seconds; I can hear Carter arguing with the staff.

"Oh, she can't eat this. We'll see the premium food menu, please."

"Uh, we only have the one menu, Mr. Beckett."

I watch from the doorway as Carter holds up a triangle of grilled cheese between his thumb and forefinger, keeping it at a distance like a disease might jump out.

"This is way too soggy. What kind of cheese is this? Ollie likes her grilled cheese on pumpernickel rye with aged smoked gouda, bonus points if you add bacon."

"Right, well, we don't, uh…" The poor woman scratches at her throat, face red. "We don't have smoked gouda."

Carter sighs, tossing the sandwich back to the tray. "Okay."

Olivia smiles up at the woman. "It's perfect. Thank you so much." Her gaze finds mine in the doorway when the woman leaves. "Jennie! How are you feeling?"

Carter leaps out of his seat and flies across the room, guiding me across it by my elbow at the pace of a literal snail. "Easy," he murmurs.

"Carter." I shake off his grip, but if I'm being honest, it feels nice to be on the receiving end of his attention, even if it's selfish of me. Olivia and the baby are more important, and they're his life. They need him right now, not me. "I can walk all on my own."

"'I can walk all on my own,'" he mimics, leading me to his chair. His large hands swallow my entire head as he yanks me into him, plopping a kiss to my hair. When he sits on the other side of Olivia's bed, I notice his swollen, cracked knuckles, an angry shade of red. "Don't know how I got saddled with two snarky brunettes."

The chances that he's about to be saddled with a third in a few weeks are ridiculously high, but he looks incredibly strung out right now. I won't push him.

Olivia reaches for my hand, and I scoot closer, snuggling into her.

"I'm sorry," I murmur into her hair before I pull away.

"Sorry? What are you sorry for?"

"You were scared and sick and you needed me and I—"

"Absolutely not. None of this is your fault." She whips around, pointing a finger at Carter. "And it's not yours, either, so don't even *think* about going down that road again."

Carter's chin hits his fist as he frowns and mouths, *Meow.*

"So what's going on?" I lay my hand on her belly, giving it a little rub.

"The baby's fine. We saw him or her wiggling around on the ultrasound machine, and—" She holds up a hand, silencing Carter when he opens his mouth. "That was a goddamn arm, Carter, don't make me tell you again." His face falls, and I swallow my snicker. "Heart rate was good. Everything looks good."

"And what about you? How's Mama feeling?"

"I'm good," she replies, but her words are soft, careful. "The whole thing was just scary."

"The doctor said she's under too much stress," Carter grumbles. "Probably the kids at school, and then this..."

Yes, probably the kids at school...

"I've developed gestational hypertension, where your blood pressure is elevated," Olivia clarifies. "It's okay, but we'll need to do some monitoring. It can lead to more serious things, like preeclampsia."

I've never seen Carter look more scared than he does right now as he brings his wife's hand to his mouth, brushing a kiss across her knuckles, his other hand moving slowly over her belly.

"I'm going to take care of you," he promises. "Baths and foot rubs and every meal delivered right to you, and I'll carry you down the stairs and—"

"And I don't think I'll be allowed to do anything for myself until this baby decides to exit."

I laugh quietly. "I'll help with whatever you need."

Olivia's smile is grateful. "Thanks, Jennie."

"I was trying to figure out if there was a way to keep this from

Garrett," Carter starts, "but I'm pretty sure Cara already opened her big mouth."

I frown. "Why would you want to keep this from him?"

"Because I know how he is. He won't say anything, but he'll get this idea in his head that, once upon a time, it could've been his dad's fuckup. He'll wonder if it reminds us of Dad, and then he'll talk himself into believing that he means less to us because he loves someone that took advantage of the same thing that killed our dad, that put us all in danger today."

"Garrett has a big heart," Olivia says softly, gaze flitting my way. "I'm not surprised he takes on the guilt of others. But we'll make sure he knows how important he is to us."

I don't want him to second-guess, the way he did when his dad nearly relapsed. I don't want him to carry around the weight of someone else's decisions. I want to show him how loved he is, not only by me but by everyone.

"I better get back to my room before Mom returns from finding the vending machine. I'll check in on you tomorrow." I stand, and Carter loops his arm through mine, leading me into the hallway.

"How are you? You're good, right? You're okay?" His vibrant green eyes bounce between mine, the concern heavy and dark, like it's the only thing he's capable of feeling right now.

So how do I tell him the answer is no? That even though I'm physically fine, I feel like I'm walking on a tightrope, ready to plummet? That in the moment when he collided with those three drunk men, when they fell to the ground together, when Olivia screamed and it felt like my lungs were being crushed, I genuinely thought he was going to die?

I get it; it's extreme. But that's the way life works after you've lost someone to a tragedy. No matter how good things are going, you're constantly waiting for the other shoe to drop, for something horrific and life altering to happen, to have your happiness snatched from your hands no matter how tightly you cling to it.

But Carter doesn't have time to worry about me. I can't put this on him.

So I plaster on a smile and promise, "I feel fine, Carter."

He visibly deflates before pulling me into one of his suffocating holds.

We both tense when we hear Olivia's weak voice call his name, followed by the sound of retching. He kisses my temple and disappears, and I tuck myself back into my room.

"Where were you? I was worried sick."

With a pointed look at my mom, I take a seat on the edge of the bed. She's chowing down on a Snickers. "You really look it." Sighing, I start picking at the medical tape on my hand. I want to get the hell out of here. I'm growing antsier by the minute.

It's another half hour before Nurse Matt walks in, all smiles. "All right, Miss Jennie. You're good to go. Stay hydrated and get a good meal in you. Maybe relax with a movie tonight." He takes my hand in his, disconnecting the IV and removing the needle. He covers the small pinprick with a Wonder Woman bandage and winks. "Got you the special ones."

I giggle, reaching for my coat. "Thanks, Matt."

Matt glances away, then back. "So, there's not a great time to ask you this, and I know your mom is here, but I, uh…well, I think you're really funny and I was wondering if you might like to maybe…" He clears his throat into his fist. "Give me your number."

I wish it were my imagination, but my mom absolutely squeals, hitting me with two thumbs up.

"Thank you for asking, Matt, and I think you're funny too. But I'm not available."

"What?" Mom's wide eyes meet mine. "Wait. Really?"

"It's new, but I am confident about where it's going." I smile at Matt. "Thank you so much for your help tonight."

Mom pounces as soon as we step out, heading for the waiting room where our family waits. "You're seeing someone? Since when? Who is he? Why haven't I met him? Will you bring him for dinner?"

I rub my temple as if I can scrub away the pain. Everything is achy, and my brain feels so muddled. I want to crawl into bed and forget any of this happened. "Can we talk about this later?" I ask as the room comes into sight, Cara jumping to her feet. "I'm tired and I want —*Garrett.*"

The doors to the waiting room burst open, revealing the only man I want to see right now, his desperate gaze sweeping the space. His wild eyes land on me, and I don't know why my knees start quivering, why all the weight on my shoulders suddenly melts and my eyes well with tears, but the second he murmurs my name and starts moving across the room, I move too.

I throw my arms around his neck, and my legs circle his waist the moment he hoists me up. When his lips meet mine, a collective gasp moves through the room.

My mom is squealing again.

Garrett rests his forehead on mine. "Are you okay?"

With my hand on his cheek, I nod, and those fucking tears work their way out of my eyes and down my cheeks. I bury my face in his neck as he holds me tight.

"I was so scared," he whispers. "So fucking scared, Jennie."

"I didn't know," Cara whisper-yells at Emmett, arms in the air. "Okay, I knew, like, a little bit." She points at Adam and Jaxon, who followed Garrett in. "But they knew too!"

Emmett throws his arms overhead. "Oh, so everyone knew except me?"

"That's not true," Cara argues.

Adam scrubs a hand over his face. "Yeah, Carter also doesn't know."

"I didn't know!" Mom cries, hands clasped under her chin. "But I'm so happy!"

"What?" Hank asks, head whipping back and forth. "What am I missing? What's happening?"

Cara leans over, whispering in his ear, and a smile erupts on his face.

"Oh boy. Carter's not gonna like that now, is he? Mr. Nice Guy Adam might have been a safer bet, Jennie, but if you're going to go for it, go all the way, that's what I always say."

Garrett sighs. "I'm sorry. I acted without thinking. I saw you and I... I...I don't know, Jennie. I was terrified."

I press my whispered words to his lips. "I love you."

"Oh shoot. Fuck. Fuck." Mom's body collides with ours. She slaps at my arm, trying to fit her hands between us, then yanks on my shoulder. "Down. Get down!"

"Carter!" Cara calls, then dashes down the hall, out of sight.

I slip down Garrett's body, and he lifts my hand to his lips and gives me a sad smile before stepping away. Five seconds later, Cara and Carter appear, followed by a doctor.

"Everything's fine. Olivia's fine, and the baby is fine." Without Olivia by his side, he looks years older, utterly exhausted. The skin on his face

is ashy and muted, eyes lacking their usual playful sparkle. He looks...
broken. "They're gonna keep us overnight—"

"Uh." The doctor pushes her glasses up her nose. "We technically
only need to keep Mrs. Bec—" Her teeth clatter when she slams her jaw,
meeting Carter's menacing expression. "Both of you. We definitely need
to keep both of you."

"They're going do some monitoring before sending her home in the
morning. She's gotta go off work until the baby comes, take it easy and
hang out on the couch." Carter hangs his head. "I don't want her to be
alone."

"She won't be," Jeremy, Olivia's brother, says. He tugs Carter into his
arms, clapping a hand to his back. "We'll watch out for her when you're
on the road."

A camera flash goes off, and Cara pulls her phone back, sniffling.
"She'll never believe you two hugged if I don't have photographic
evidence." She pats at the raw skin below her eyes and slings her purse
over her shoulder. "Okay, I'm going to get her a twenty pack of spicy
nuggets and a large Oreo McFlurry. She can't eat this hospital slop." She
embraces me tightly. "So glad you're safe, Jennie. I'll come by in the
morning with some breakfast for you."

When she pulls back, I find Carter's gaze on me. He's shut down, I
think. I almost don't recognize him like this, and I don't know what's
changed so quickly, or if he simply can't handle any more.

He looks between Garrett and me. "Since you're here, Gare, do you
mind taking Jennie home? That way I can stay."

Garrett nods, his hand on my lower back as he gently guides me
forward, and as soon as we're through the doors, he threads his fingers
through mine and tells me how much he loves me.

~

There's something to be said about a man who drives with only one
hand on the wheel. Something so inherently sexy about the way he finds
a way to keep a hand on my thigh the entire time, squeezing, fingers
trailing, like he needs to feel me to know I'm there, I'm safe.

He doesn't let go until we're in my apartment, where he forces me to
the kitchen island to eat before disappearing down my hallway.

When I'm finished, I find Garrett in the main bathroom, sleeves rolled to his elbows as he kneels in front of the tub. He wipes his wrist across his face, and when he stands and turns to me, his right brow is covered in bubbles.

I giggle, swiping them away. "What are you doing?"

"I ran you a bubble bath. So you can relax."

"Thank you. That's sweet of you." I stand still as he undresses me. "Are you going to get in with me? It's a big tub."

"Do you want me to?"

I nod, reaching for the hem of his shirt, and he lets me peel it off him.

He turns on the music and helps me in, then steps in behind me, sinking into the bubbles. Fingers wrapping around my hips, he guides me down between his legs. When I sink with a sigh, he winds his arms around me and buries his face in my neck.

"Garrett?" I place my hand on his as it slides over my belly. "I love you, and I'm proud of you."

"Proud of me? For what?"

"For giving your dad the chance to change. For supporting him always, even if sometimes the journey has felt long and challenging." I turn my head when I feel his cheek on my shoulder, and he peers up at me. "I'm proud of your dad for choosing himself and his family, because I can't imagine how hard it is to fight your addiction every day. He's so strong, and I hope I'll get to meet him one day."

Garrett covers my mouth with his. "Thank you, Jennie. I know today isn't about me, but I think I really needed to hear that."

"What are we going to do about tomorrow? I don't want to stress Olivia out with all of this, but I'm tired of hiding."

"I don't know. Maybe we can get her advice, see what she thinks is best."

That sounds like a good idea, but if I'm being honest, there's more on my mind than just telling my brother about us without giving him a heart attack and sending Olivia into labor too early.

"Garrett?"

"Yeah?"

"You said you didn't see any end in sight, but...What about my interview? Maybe I should just cancel."

"You have to go," he insists quietly. "I know you aren't sure if it's what you want anymore, but you owe it to yourself to check it out, give it a chance. Go to Toronto and see how you feel."

"But what if I feel empty without you?"

"I don't think that's possible. You don't need me to make you feel full. You're already enough. It's okay to not want to be apart, but I don't want you to make any decisions because of me."

"I don't want to lose this." *Him.* I don't want to lose him.

"We won't. If you want this, even if you want to leave, we'll work it out. I promise."

A soft moan leaves my lips as he trails his fingers along the inside of my thigh in the warm water as he palms my breast. "It's hard to focus when you're doing that."

"That's the point," he murmurs against my neck. "I want you to forget, just for a few minutes. Forget about today, forget about tomorrow, forget about the job." He drags one finger up my slit, making me shudder. "Let me take care of you. Let me do something."

"You do everything." My head falls to his shoulder as he pushes inside me. "You *are* everything."

"You're *my* everything."

I've never been anyone's anything, but Garrett makes me feel like I haven't missed a thing, like all this time I was simply waiting for him so he could show me what it meant to be loved so wholly, to find your best friend, your partner, your soul mate, all in one. To find the person who knows just how you tick, how to help when you're too stubborn to ask for it, how to be patient and let you crawl out of your shadow at your own pace, all while being confident in knowing that he's there, he's waiting, and he'll keep waiting. The person who matches your rhythm, whose smooth edges soften your jagged ones.

I don't know how to put all that into words, to tell him exactly what he means to me, so as his fingers move inside me, each thrust purposeful and deep, as his thumb circles with precision, I reach back, fingers sinking through his locks, holding him close. And as he stares down at me, so much unbridled love shining in his eyes, as he brings me higher while the music drifts around us, encasing us in this perfect bubble of happiness, I press my mouth to his.

～

"Just a small cup," Garrett tells me sternly, watching me slip on his button-up shirt over my panties as he drains the tub. "Too much hot chocolate will keep you up." He pulls his boxer briefs on and claps a hand to my ass as we stumble into the hallway, and he calls for Google to turn the music off.

"What if I'm not tired?" I press him against the wall. "What if I wanna take you to Pound Town?"

He chuckles, hands sliding up the backs of my thighs, squeezing my ass. "If anyone's taking anyone to Pound Town, it's *me* taking *you*."

"Maybe you can take me first, and I'll take you second."

"Tomorrow, sunshine." The amused but firm look in his eyes tells me he's not going to relent, and when I sigh, he takes my chin and sears me with a kiss. "Don't be a brat."

"Sounds like a challenge to me, big guy."

Taking his hand in mine, I tow him toward the kitchen. The glow of the light above the stove throws shadows across the dark hall, and my chest tightens as one of those shadows steps out of the doorway, into the light.

"Carter," I breathe out, Garrett's body crashing into mine as I skid to a stop.

"Shit." Garrett wraps his hands around my waist, keeping me upright. The warm air from the vents nips at my bare legs, like the heat from his bare chest as he holds me to him.

"I knocked," Carter whispers, gaze ricocheting between us, barely dressed and still wet. With each moment that passes, his chest heaves faster, each breath shallower than the last. "But you didn't...I was worried you...I..."

"Hey, man, listen." Garrett takes a step forward, hands out in front of him like he's approaching a trapped animal.

Carter's eyes flash with anger, betrayal, and his fists ball as he stares at me. He steps back.

I shake my head, reaching for him. "No, it's not...it's not..." My heart leaps to my throat as he takes another step back, then another. "Carter."

I don't know what I expected, but it wasn't this, the silence. Rage, I think I could deal with. Screaming. But not this, not my brother who always has something to say just standing here staring at us, at *me*, like he's never felt so deceived.

I want him to fight with me, to get it all out. I want him to tell me he's angry we lied. I want to tell him that for the first time in my life, I'm in love with a man who treats me like the dream he always wanted.

Instead, he grips the doorhandle and turns away.

"Carter, please," I beg. "Don't go." The weight of the day returns all at once, crushing my chest. I lay my hand over it, clutching it as I struggle to breathe. Tears come without warning, streaming down my cheeks, and as Carter hesitates, head down, I whisper, "I'm sorry."

He looks to the ceiling, throat bobbing.

"No," he finally utters, the word barely audible. He tugs the door open, but before it slams behind him, he gives us two more words, and that bubble I was so content to stay in shatters around us like glass. "Fuck this."

FORTY
CLUSTERFUCK

Garrett

CARTER HASN'T ANSWERED his phone in six days.

Six fucking days.

On the fourth day, Jennie gave up. She cried and she got angry. She sat by herself on the couch and said she wanted to be alone, and she curled into my side and asked me not to let go.

Every time Jennie closed her eyes and drifted to sleep, I called him.

But if Carter Beckett isn't answering his sister's phone calls, he's sure as hell not answering the calls of the guy who's fucking her.

Because that's all Carter thinks this is. He thinks I see Jennie as an opportunity, easy access four floors below. He thinks I would lie, throw away years of friendship over a piece of ass.

He doesn't see the commitment, the love, the fucking endless, earth-shattering friendship we've built, poured all of ourselves into in order to build the trust, to overcome every obstacle, to help each other be better on our own so we can be better together. He doesn't see that I can't imagine my life with anyone other than Jennie by my side.

If he'd just pick up his goddamn phone and listen, he'd know.

I keep telling Jennie he just needs time, but I don't know how much more distance she can take. The longer he's silent, the more Jennie thinks he's never coming back.

We had a plan, but if life has taught me anything, it's that nothing ever goes to plan. Almost everything goes to shit.

I guess that's not entirely true. Because life gave me Jennie, and Jennie gave me life.

But I'm running out of ideas. I don't know how to get Carter to listen, to just give us a damn chance to explain that we never meant for any of this to happen. I sure as hell didn't imagine she'd sweep into my life and become my best friend, my favorite person, in such a short time. Only she did. She's mine, and I'm hers. I think that's the way it was always meant to be.

I'm not going to let her be just my Sunday night anymore. I want her to be my sleepy Monday morning, my thank-fuck-it's-Friday, my stay-in-bed Saturday, and all the other days too. I'm not going to force myself to live without the brightest spot in my world.

I pull into my parking space at the arena, then sigh down at my phone, the text message from Olivia that asks if Jennie's actually sick or if she just doesn't want to see her right now. When I tell her she's not, in fact, sick, she replies that she'll send Cara over to drag her out by her hair.

I appreciate the tenacity of those two, that they rarely let Jennie hide, not that she often tries. They're patient with her while also knowing when she needs a bit of a shove to get her ass in gear.

She's allowed to be upset. It's a testament to how passionately she loves her people. But I need her to remember that it's not her brother who fills her life with people who love her. It's her.

The halls are relatively quiet for a pregame, but I'm here early. Carter hasn't played all week, instead tending to Olivia after the accident. He can avoid my phone calls, but he can't avoid me here now that he's back.

I drop my things in the locker room and head off in search of Carter. I find him in our head coach's office, lounging in one of the chairs across from the desk, munching on an apple. When he stands, Coach's gaze flicks to me, and something about it makes my skin itch with uncertainty.

I've always been a good player. I'm not a troublemaker, I don't take stupid penalties, and I'm nice to everyone. I do what I'm told, because I don't see any reason not to, and I leave any personal shit in the change room and give it my all every night on the ice.

I tuck my hands into my pockets as Carter opens the door, his expression unfazed.

"Uh, hey," I start cautiously. "I was hoping we could—"

"Oh good. You're here. We need to talk."

"Yeah, talking would be great. That's what I was hoping for."

I make to head back to the change room, but Carter remains in the doorway. He gestures inside with the tilt of his head.

"Oh. Okay." I step inside, swallowing at the uneasy gaze Coach gives me, sparked with sympathy. It makes my hands clammy, and I wipe them on my pants before taking a seat. "What's going on?"

Coach taps his pen against his desk. "We're going to try you on the second line tonight."

"The second line?" I look to Carter, his eyes cool and distant. "But I… I always play with you and Em. On the first line."

"We think this would be for the best," Carter says simply.

Irritation squeezes my lungs. "We, or you?"

"You haven't been playing your best." *Bullshit.*

"We're trying to avoid any tension that might affect the rest of the team and the game," Coach explains.

"We'll re-evaluate next game, Andersen."

Anger sears through me. I give him a clipped nod before heading for the door. "Yes, *Captain.*"

I play like fucking shit. I'm a first-string player for a reason, and I've earned my spot on my team's starting lineup. Carter and Emmett and I have been playing together for years. We're in sync on the ice, fluid, like we can hear each other's thoughts. I'm too fast for the second line. Thinking too far ahead of them. We don't jive the way I do with Carter and Emmett, and by the time the buzzer sounds at the end of the third period, even though we've won, I'm negative three in points, my worst game of the season.

"Tough game," Carter says as he clomps by on his skates, whipping his helmet off. "Might need to keep you back for a while."

It's after ten p.m. when I climb into my car, and I drop my face to my hands as the heat blasts, warming the confined space.

This is such a fucking clusterfuck, the word itself doesn't feel cluster-fuckery enough. I don't know who's going to be more pissed about Carter shoving me down the line, me or Jennie. Or Olivia. For a tiny, pregnant woman, she can be scary as fuck, nearly as scary as Cara. And Jennie.

Fuck, I'm surrounded by so many scary, powerful women.

When I sync my phone to my car, a text message pops up from my dad, asking me to call. A month ago, it would've been unusual. I think my dad sort of thrived off our distance when I left Nova Scotia. Maybe he let go of some of the guilt he was carrying because I wasn't there as a constant reminder of his mistakes. But the physical distance made the emotional distance grow, and I was lucky to get a *good game* text.

Granted, it's only been three weeks, but he's been different since his near relapse. I can see the effort he's putting in, not only with me but with himself. There's a happiness radiating off him lately. Maybe, in a way, losing his job has been the best thing for him.

"Hey, Gare," he greets happily, even though it's after two in the morning on the east coast. "Tough game tonight, buddy. Take it Beckett's still not hot on you dating his sister?"

"You guessed right." I run a hand through my damp hair before fixing my toque back over my head. "What's up? Shouldn't you be asleep?"

"Probably. Guess I'm a little excited."

"'Bout what?"

"I heard there's a pretty great support program out your way. One of the best in the country, apparently."

"Oh yeah?"

"And they've got this big steel factory over by Fraser River, looking for a crane operator."

My heartbeat picks up. "What are you saying?"

There's a moment of hesitation, but when my dad speaks next, all I hear is the enthusiasm, the bliss. "I'm saying I got a job, Garrett. I start end of April."

"You're…You guys are moving to Vancouver?"

"We're doing it, Garrett. We're moving to Vancouver."

My condo is warm when I step inside, dimly lit by the glow above the stove.

Jennie does that. She notches the heat up a couple degrees before she goes to bed if she knows I'm getting in late so the floors will be warm on my feet when I come in from the cold and kick my shoes off. That way, I'm nice and toasty when I climb into bed and wrap my body around hers.

The light above the stove is her too. She doesn't want me to come home to darkness, and it reminds me of my mom, the way she started leaving the same light on when I started crawling out of bed in the middle of the night for a cup of water, continued to leave it on for those teenage years when I stumbled in well after curfew.

There's a note on the kitchen counter scribbled in pink pen on a puppy sticky note, letting me know there's dinner in the microwave, and I scarf it down faster than I've ever eaten, desperate to be with my person.

She's curled up on my side of the bed, one hand between her cheek and my pillow, the other curled beneath her chin, chocolate waves scattered over her shoulders. She's so beautiful it hurts to look at her, the sharp angle of her high cheekbones, the soft swell of her heart-shaped lips, the bottom one slightly fuller than the top. Her dark lashes rest against her flushed skin, and if you're lucky to get as close as I am on a regular basis, you'll be able to count the tiniest freckles that speckle the bridge of her nose.

My thumb traces the edge of her jaw, up her chin, following the curve of her mouth. When it swoops over her cheekbone, her lashes flutter, sleepy blue eyes blinking up at me.

"Hi, sunshine," I whisper, and my heart thuds at the dimply smile she gives me.

Jennie peels back the covers, and I don't think I'll ever get tired of her in my bed, wearing nothing but my T-shirt. Her arms come around my neck, legs around my waist, and I scoop her up before I roll into the newly vacant spot and settle her on top of me.

She presses her palm to my heart. "I'm sorry the game didn't go the way you wanted it to."

I cover her hand with mine. "That's okay. Did you at least have fun watching with Ollie and Cara?"

She doesn't answer, and I know she didn't go. I won't push her.

After a moment, she asks, "Did Carter move you there? To the second line?"

"Yes."

She tenses. "I'm sorry."

"Hey." Hooking a finger under her chin, I tip her face up. "It's not your fault. It's how he's dealing with it right now, but it won't be forever. Don't apologize for somebody else's decisions."

It's there, eating at her, the urge to argue with me, to say *she's* the reason for not only this decision but for all of his decisions this week. Instead, she snuggles closer.

I twine her hair around my fingers. "Can I tell you something good?"

She gives me a bright smile. "I love good things."

"My dad called after the game. He got a job."

"Garrett! That's amazing!"

"Mhmm. That's not all though." I trace the length of her nose with the tips of her hair, watching as it scrunches. "The job is here."

"Oh my God." She tears the blankets away and climbs to her knees, nearly hammering me in the junk in the process. "They're moving to Vancouver? I get to meet your parents? Your little sisters? Oh my God! They're gonna terrorize you on the daily, and I'm gonna help!"

Laughing, I reach around and give her butt a swift smack. "Give it a try and I'll tie you to this bedpost."

She rolls back into me, arms around my middle. "Note to self: help Garrett's sisters terrorize him." Her face nuzzles my chest as I turn off the lamp, the dark night settling around us. "I'm so happy for you, Garrett. You're going to have your family here."

Jennie drifts to sleep in my arms, and I know I already have my family right here.

But the feeling is short-lived, because when I wake up, my arms are alarmingly empty.

It's not even seven in the morning, the ass crack of dawn just beginning its creep into the sky, and without Jennie clinging to my body, I'm cold. I toss on a pair of sweats and a T-shirt, padding down the hallway, and stop short when I find her sitting beneath the window in the living room, clutching Princess Bubblegum, shoulders shaking with her quiet cries.

Jennie is a lot of things. She's bold and loud, confident and fierce, quiet and soft. She's strong and resilient, persistent. She's got a big, sensitive heart that feels everything. But she's not fragile. She fights for everything. She pushes herself and comes out on the other side, always, even if it takes time.

This version of her, so broken and lost, makes every inch of me ache for her. I don't know how to make this better, and I hate the incompetency.

I go to her, pulling her into my lap, and she curls into me, trembling as she sobs.

"I hate this," she weeps into my chest. "I hate this so much."

"I know, baby."

"I miss my brother. I miss—" Her mouth opens on a gasp that steals the breath from my own lungs. She clutches at her chest like the words hurt. "I miss my dad. I miss him so much, Garrett. Everything feels so heavy and dark."

"Your brother and your dad both love you, Jennie. Carter will always be here for you." I cover her heart with my hand. "And your dad will always be *here*. You're never alone."

"He's so mad at me. What if he never forgives me?"

"Hey, look at me." Cupping her face in my hands, I sweep at the tears that keep falling. "He's going to forgive us. He's going to see how much we love each other, and he'll understand."

"What if it's not enough? What if he holds onto this for so long? What if I lose Olivia? Cara?" Her blue eyes flit between mine, doused in agony. "What if I lose my niece or nephew?"

"That's not going to happen, Jennie. I promise you."

She shakes her head, climbing to her feet. "You-you can't promise that. You can't, Garrett."

"I absolutely can," I tell her with certainty, following her. "I can, Jennie, because Olivia and Cara love you."

She spins away, one hand on her forehead, the other on her hip, and her pink bunny falls to my rug. "They love me because of Carter. Because it's convenient. That's what I am, Garrett. Convenient." She gestures toward the door. "Four floors below you, how much more convenient could I get."

Darkness curls inside me. "Don't you fucking say that. I love you for who you are, not because of your brother, and sure as shit not because you live four floors below me. You could take that job in Toronto and I'd still love you, and I'd keep loving you for the rest of my life. Because I love *you*, Jennie."

"Do you even know who I am? You love the confident me. The snarky comebacks and the bold girl who says everything that comes to her mind. But what if this is me? What if this broken, shattered version is what's real?"

"You're allowed to feel things, Jennie. You're allowed to grieve. You're allowed to be uncertain instead of confident. Those things don't make you broken; they make you you."

"None of you would have ever found me if it weren't for Carter."

My heart squeezes for her, the way she's convincing herself that she's losing more than just Carter, that without him, she has nothing to offer. How someone as self-assured as Jennie can, at times, be so unsure of what she brings to the table is gut-wrenching. I wish for five minutes she could see herself from everybody else's eyes, see that even on her darkest days, she's always been enough, not just for us, but for herself.

Jennie's always been like the sun rising after a black but starless night spent driving alone. You're a little lost, a little off track, but you keep going, searching for that light, and when you find it, it shines so bright, guiding you home. But when she stops herself from shining, everything is bleak and gray, dull, like a foggy, misty morning in the middle of nowhere. When she stops herself from rising, I can't find my way home. Not without her.

"So what?" I finally say. "Maybe we found you because of Carter. That doesn't mean you're not the reason we stay."

Her gaze stays on mine for a quiet moment, like she's weighing the truth behind my words. When I stop in front of her, her mouth opens, hanging there like she's not sure if the next sentence is the right one to speak.

"Maybe I belong in Toronto."

Panic knots in my stomach at the thought of losing her, but before I can say anything, she continues, broken.

"Maybe I have been standing in Carter's shadow."

"You shine way too fucking bright to stand in anyone's shadow, Jennie."

She blinks once, slowly, and tears cascade down her beautiful, heart-broken face. "I can start fresh. Maybe I'll...Maybe I'll learn to stand on my own. And you...You get your friends back, your team. You play the position you earned, the one you deserve, because I'm gone, and your family comes, too, and..." She sniffles, wiping the back of her wrist across her nose. "And everything is better."

Fury climbs my chest like a vine, and I step into Jennie, gripping her jaw, keeping her gaze locked on mine.

"If you stay in Toronto, you do it for the right fucking reasons. You stay because you love it, because the job is your dream, more than owning your own studio, than teaching kids to love dance the same way you do. You stay because you feel at home there, and you fall in love with the city, and it feels wrong to be anywhere else. You don't stay because you're standing in someone's shadow; you don't even stand in your own. You don't stay because your friends came from your brother. Those friends are the family that chose you, that keep choosing you, day in and day out. And you sure as shit don't stay to learn to stand on your own, because you already fucking soar without anyone's help."

My pulse drums in my ears as she quivers, her fingers circling my wrists where I hold her. The depth in her eyes begs for understanding, for leniency, for fucking *help*.

"This thing you're doing right here, trying to convince yourself that you don't belong with the people who love you, it feels a whole fuck-load like good-bye, Jennie, and I hate that. I *won't* say good-bye to you."

Her lips part on a cry as my mouth crashes down on hers, and she sinks against my chest as I haul her closer, where I think we both belong.

But her brain is muddled and her heart is tired, the same way mine were when I walked away from her three weeks ago, when I didn't know which way to turn.

That's why a half hour later, she promises she'll be back, that it's not good-bye when she presses her mouth to mine.

Yet *good-bye* is the last word that falls from her lips as she disappears with her bag over her shoulder and my heart on the floor.

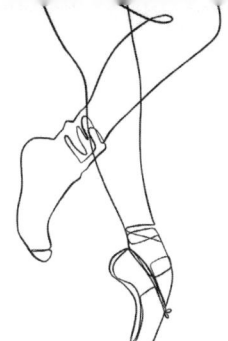

FORTY-ONE
STRIKE 13: COLD AS FUCKBALLS

Jennie

IT'S COLDER HERE. Harsh and biting, a bitter, frigid wind that slaps every inch of exposed skin until you feel like you're both numb and on fire. It's a prickly, uncomfortable feeling, and with a sound of distaste, I bring my phone to my face and pull up my *Toronto Pros & Cons* list, adding *cold as fuckballs* to the con side.

It's alarmingly full for someone who's only been in the city for an hour.

- No Garrett
- No Mom, Carter, Olivia, Hank, Cara
- No baby smooches
- No Dublin
- No dance studio
- Work for someone else & follow rules, ugh
- No karaoke with Carter
- No hot chocolate with Garrett
- No dance battles with Garrett
- No slow dancing in the kitchen with Garrett
- No back tickles with Garrett
- No cuddles with Garrett
- Cold as fuckballs

Not a whole lot of reasons for me to do anything other than stay in Vancouver.

My eyes flit to the pros.

- Nobody knows me here.

But an alluring reason for me to leave, even if a little scary.

A lump grows in the back of my throat at the thought of not being able to drive to my mom's, snuggle up with her on the couch, and watch a movie whenever I want to.

My phone buzzes, and my heart patters like it hopes it might be Garrett, even though I asked for some space.

Emily: *Red or white nonalcoholic wine? Already got some bubbly.*
Me: *What?*
Emily: *Girls' night?*
Me: *Oh shit. I'm so sorry. I forgot. I'm in Toronto for that interview.*
Emily: *Ew.*
Emily: *I mean, cool, follow your heart and all that. But does Toronto have this?*

A photo pops up, and Emily's scrunched nose, folded lips, and crossed eyes fill my screen.

Me: *Is that a cheerleading outfit?*
Emily: *Yeah, about to have some company/get railed *winking emoji**

Snickering, I navigate back to my list.

- No Emily

…

- No Garrett. No Garrett. No. Fucking. Garrett.

A painful burst of air leaves my lips as I clutch my phone to my chest, the weight of what I could lose making me sink deeper into the cushions of the loveseat I'm curled up in.

I peer out the window of my hotel room as if the answer is waiting for me in all the skyscrapers, the busy streets where the city races below. It's frantic and captivating, like watching a fast-paced dance where everyone moves in sync, despite the panicked way they move, this game of give and take.

Except there's no answer there, no sign telling me which path to choose. Just a whole lot of chaos, which is exactly reflective of the current state of my brain: *chaotic*.

I've always liked the city, the bright lights, the way everything comes to life at nighttime. But there's something to be said about a quiet morning overlooking the mountains, the sea of pine trees painting the skyline, the way they dance in the ripple of the water they frame.

Here in Toronto, it's so loud you can barely think. In the northern end of Vancouver, your mind is yours. I'm just not sure which is worse. When you're someone who fluctuates between overanalyzing and needing an escape, both have their perks.

With a sigh, I slip out of the chair to get ready for my interview.

I spent three hours trying on outfits for Garrett, only for him to deem that each one was inappropriate and should come off immediately. They all did, which is *why* it took three hours to choose the outfit. In the end, he picked the first one I'd tried on—little shit—so I slip on my flared pants and my white blouse, tucking it into the high waist, and finish with my favorite pair of black booties. I tug the elastic from my braid and run my fingers through my hair until my waves hang free, and finish with a couple quick swipes of mascara and a pinch of color on my lips. Garrett helped me pick that too.

At least I think he did. I tested each color by pressing a lipstick kiss to his abs. All his responses were garbled, but he choked the most when I placed this particular kiss to his heated skin, so I knew it was the right choice.

It had nothing to do with the placement being so low on his torso, right above the waistband of his underwear, and *definitely* nothing to do with those lips being wrapped around his cock ten seconds later.

I wish I'd listened to him about my coat, too, because when I step outside, I find myself cursing myself for brushing off his warning. He insisted that I should pack my warm coat, just in case, and yet here I stand in my pretty lilac trench coat, made for west coast springs.

"I'm a doorknob," I mutter as I climb into my waiting Uber.

It should only take ten minutes to get there, but it takes us thirty. Luckily, I planned for this; Toronto traffic is a shit show.

"Thank you so much, Manny," I say to my driver as I climb out.

"Good luck on your interview, Jennie!" he shouts through his open window.

The building before me isn't all that tall, but as I stare up at it, it feels massive, like the decision that's weighing on me, pulling my future in every direction like a rag doll. Indecision swirls in my stomach, making it ache, and my gaze roams the space for a place to sit, to catch my breath.

"I don't know what I'm doing," I ramble, pacing the walkway. Apprehension claws at my chest and my heartbeat runs rampant. I press my hand there as if I can still the frantic racing. "I can't do this. What am I doing here?"

My phone pings once, then twice, and the world skids to a stop at the tiny bear lighting my screen.

Bear: *I know you need space to make this decision on your own, but I couldn't let you go in there without saying something first.*
Bear: *You can do this. You deserve this. You've earned it. If you want it, all you have to do is reach out and take it. I'm proud of you, Jennie, and no matter what, you'll always be my best friend, and I'll always be your safe place to land.*

A sneaky tear leaks out of my sneaky tear duct, trailing a sneaky path down my not-so-sneaky cheek. I quickly swipe at it, sniffling as I reread his message once, twice, and then a third time, just for good measure.

With a steadying inhale, I tuck my phone away, march up the front steps, and throw the doors open.

∼

"Jennifer?"

"Hmm?" My gaze falls from space, searching for the person who spoke my name. Monica, Leah's friend, gives me a soft smile and looks to her right, where Annalise is watching me. "I'm so sorry. Adjusting to the time change." Also, she keeps calling me Jennifer, even though I've requested several times now to be called Jennie.

"You'd think you'd have more energy, since we're, what? Four hours ahead here?"

"Three." It's 6:30 p.m. here, which means it's 3:30 p.m. at home. Garrett would be picking me up from school and we'd be going home for a quick nap. Nap time is one of my favorite times.

Annalise smiles. There's a hint of tightness behind it, seen in the firm way she presses her lips together, but then again, I haven't seen her teeth once all afternoon. She's in her sixties, and something tells me she hasn't gotten laid in at least twenty years.

"Nevertheless, we were just saying that we think you'd fit right in with us here."

I'm not sure about that. Earlier today I watched half of them bark orders at ballerinas who looked on the verge of passing out, or crying, which is exactly why I left ballet in the first place. Still, that they want *me* is exciting all the same, and my shoulders fall back as I sit taller and beam.

"Really?"

"Of course. We've been watching you for years. You're a beautiful dancer."

"And Leah always has the most wonderful things to say about you," Monica adds.

I like Monica. Like Leah, she's younger and still, I don't know...full of life? Not beaten down by the dictators of the professional dance world? A nice human being? She's friendly and personable, and she spent most of the tour whispering in my ear about Annalise every time that woman turned her back. At one point, I had to pretend I was coughing to hide my laughter.

Before I can respond, a young man stops at our table. "Are we ready to order?"

Annalise gestures at me. "Why don't you start us off?"

"Hmmm..." My eyes sweep the menu. *Six-ounce teriyaki sirloin.* Sold. My stomach sings with glee, and I tap on the option. "I'll have the sirloin, medium rare, with a twice-baked potato, fully loaded, and—"

"Oh, Jennifer, sweetheart." Annalise's patronizing gaze rises above her frameless glasses. "Wouldn't you prefer something lighter?"

"Um..." *Not fucking really?*

"It's a very rigorous program, so we of course expect our instructors to be as dedicated as our students when it comes to training. That includes nutrition."

"Of course." I plaster on a smile, slipping a protective hand over my belly beneath the table, chasing away the ashamed thoughts that try to enter, reminding me I'm not as slim as I was just a handful of months ago. "I'll have the grilled chicken caprese salad, please."

"An excellent choice, ma'am," the waiter replies, but the amusement dancing in his eyes tells me he knows as well as I do that that's fucking bullshit. At my narrowed gaze, he dips his head to hide his grin as he takes my menu. "And to drink?"

"She'll have a vodka soda water with a lemon." Annalise winks. "Sugar-free."

"Actually, I don't drink. A root beer would be great."

I wonder if the horror and disbelief in her expression are due to my self-inflicted sobriety or the sugar-laden soda. Before she can tear me down for either, I tell her, "My dad passed when I was sixteen after his car was struck by a drunk driver. I haven't had root beer in ages, up until very recently, because it was my dad's favorite drink. We loved that kind that came in the brown glass bottles, Dad's Old Fashioned Root Beer, it was called." I laugh. "My dad used to tell me that he made it, that's why it had his name on it. He came home from work every Friday with a six-pack, and we all drank one while we had our family pizza and movie night."

"That's...well—"

"I'll have a root beer, too, please," Monica interrupts. "Haven't had one since I was a kid." She looks to Annalise. "You were bragging about Jennie's dancing?"

She hesitates before nodding. "Yes, as I was saying, you'd be a lovely addition here." She sweeps her hands out and then clasps them below her chin, and I finally get a toothy grin from her. It's oddly reminiscent of Chandler Bing's famous engagement picture smile from *Friends*. "So, what do you think? Is it a yes?"

My brows fly up my forehead. "Is it a yes? You're offering me the job?"

"Yes!"

"Oh. Oh my God. Wow. I...really?"

"Of course really! You're our first choice, so we've put all other prospects on hold."

A strange tightness stretches across my shoulders, and my stomach erupts with butterflies, but they don't really feel like the good kind. "Do I have to make a decision right now? I wasn't expecting this. I thought I'd have some time."

Her smile wavers, and I quickly backtrack.

"My family is in Vancouver. I'm so grateful for this opportunity, really. It's a dream come true. I'm just not sure I'm ready to—"

"Stand on your own? Have your own life?"

Beneath the table, my fingers dig into my thighs. Stand on my own? Have my own life? Do I really need to move halfway across the country and leave my family behind to do those things?

"I'm not sure I'm ready to be so far away from them," I finish quietly, and when the rest of the table agrees it's a big decision, that I can decide before I fly home, I spend the rest of dinner thinking about it, a life without them.

"Fucking…goddamn…eastern Canadian…winter…"

I yank my leather boots off, and the snow that fell this evening and covered them flings into the air, lands on the carpet, and quickly melts.

I want to go home, where spring has already begun to show its spectacular face.

I change out of my clothes and into my warmest pajama pants and Garrett's hoodie, snuggling into the coziness, the smell, like I'm wrapped in one of his hugs.

When I'm ready for bed, I slip beneath the covers and stare out the window. There isn't a single star glowing in the sky. The city is wide awake below it, and the skyline is an uncomfortable shade of blue-gray, littered with the pollution all the lights bring.

The longer I lie here, waiting for a revelation, the more scrambled my brain gets. Everything aches. It's this tension I can't explain, knotting so tightly in my stomach, creeping up my back. A vast emptiness that tastes like poison, a silence so utterly thunderous. It's heavy and dark, daunting and heart wrenching, and all I want to do is put it down.

But I don't know how, and when my eyelids fall shut, like I can close out the fears, tears leak out the corners, stealing away across my temples. I curl onto my side, clutching Princess Bubblegum as my world begs me to help it right itself.

My phone rings, Hank on video call, right on time, as usual. Don't ask me why he insists on video calling when he can't see. We mostly let him do what he wants. He's persistent.

"You look beautiful," he says, a broad beam covering his face.

I snicker, sitting up and pulling my knees to my chest, grateful he can't see the tears I'm swatting away. "Do you like my outfit?"

"Oh yes. Just stunning. Did you wear that to your interview?"

"No, I'm not sure they would've appreciated me showing up in my pajamas."

Hank laughs, the skin around his eyes crinkling. "Good thing they're after your talent, not your fashion sense. So do you wanna talk about your interview first or the reason why you're crying? Or are the two related?"

A throaty gurgle of laughter bubbles. I run the back of my wrist across my nose, sniffling. "I hate how perceptive you are." I sigh. "The interview was okay. It was fine. Good, really. I just...I don't know. I'm not sure it's where I want to be."

"Why's that?"

"I'd be leaving a lot behind. A lot of people I love."

"Hmm. So why do you *want* the job?"

It's not something I even need to contemplate.

"For the first time in my life, I'm confident I've been chosen not because of my brother but because of what I bring to the table."

"And is that enough of a reason to take this job?"

The truth is, I don't know. Up until a week ago, I had no intention of taking it. I was excited to watch things between Garrett and I continue to grow. I was over the moon to become an auntie, and I was eager, if a little scared, to tell my brother I'd fallen in love.

"I guess I just...don't know where I belong."

"You belong wherever you want to belong, Jennie."

"That's easy enough to say, but Carter's been the only person I could rely on my entire life. He's always been in my corner, and now he's not, and I don't know what to do with that, or who to be without him here. So much of me is tied into him."

Hank's quiet for a moment as he considers my words. "Well, it may be true that you two are tied together, but it's simply not true that you don't know who to be without him. You're your own person, Jennie. Always have been."

"Then why is he the catalyst that brings every single person I care about to me? How do I know whether these people genuinely like me for me, or if I'm just a convenience because I'm always there?" The questions escape before I can swallow them back down.

"Have some of the most important people in your life found you through your brother? Yes. But so what? I believe life puts us in the path of those people we need, that we're going to stumble across each other one way or another. Let's not put stock in how it happens and just be grateful that it does, that our lives are filled with the love of the people who bring us happiness and comfort, the ones who make us laugh, who can change our entire day with a smile or a hug."

Damnit. There go those sneaky, leaky tear ducts again.

"Are you crying again?"

"No," I cry, drying my face with the neck of Garrett's hoodie. "I don't cry. Ever."

"Right. You Becketts are all very stoic, emotionless people. It's what makes you all so cold and detached." Hank hesitates. "Let me ask you something, Jennie. How did you and Garrett fall in love? It surely wasn't love at first sight; you met him years ago."

I smile as I think back on the last few months. The countless awkward encounters, the shameless flirting, the first kiss I was never expecting. The quiet nights spent on the couch, wrapped in each other. The hot chocolate, the dancing, the handprint ornaments. The hushed conversations late at night beneath the covers, the envy I'd never felt before, the desire to make something mine. The struggles and the tears, mixed in with all the laughter and the smiles. Crossing boundaries and pushing limits one step at a time. Two strangers who became best friends and then more, so much more.

Slowly, and yet suddenly, there he was.

One day Garrett was a stranger, a man who blushed every time I spoke to him, who couldn't string a handful of words together to form a response. And then suddenly, he was everywhere, everything, opening up to me, showing me the man beneath the shy exterior, the incredible friend, the compassionate brother and son. He drew me in, and with each bit he gave me, he showed me a place he had to hold parts of me too.

406 | BECKA MACK

So I tell Hank exactly that.

"Sounds like Garrett being in your life has everything to do with all the pieces of you that made him want to stay, Jennie. Not the person who brought him to you."

Hank is right. Garrett didn't fall in love with me because of Carter. He didn't choose me out of convenience. Carter put him in my life, and Garrett embraced me.

"You are worthy of every single thing you desire, Jennie. Don't you ever, ever give up your dream, whatever that dream may be."

My dream? I don't think this is it, not here.

My dream is at home. It's letting myself be loved by the people who want to love me, the ones who make me feel so full and beautiful and spectacular that I feel like I'm bursting.

I once read that there are different types of love. The ones where you learn, where you grow, realize what you need. That you'll fall in love over and over, until finally, you arrive at your destination. You find the one you've been searching for and everything just…fits.

But I can't imagine a better love than Garrett. Together, we've done it all. We've learned, grown, realized our needs and expressed them. He gives me everything I could have ever imagined needing, and I think I do the same for him too.

And a better fit? How could I possibly find someone whose edges so perfectly melt into mine, taking all our small, shattered pieces and making us one?

I've spent my time looking for my place in this world, but the more I see, the more I realize everything has been right under my nose this entire time.

Why would I keep looking? All I'd be doing is wandering farther away from the very people, the place that fills me with happiness.

I've given too much of myself to feeling stuck. Wedged between the desire to fulfill my craving for acceptance, for genuine connection, and the desire to hide. To hold onto all my special pieces, afraid that if I gave them to the wrong people, they'd take them, crush them so effortlessly in their fists, and I'd be left a shell of who I am, insignificant and un-recognizable. But if I keep them all to myself, I'm still me when they leave.

And now I'm standing here wondering about the only question I should have ever cared to ask myself: *Why is loving myself less important than the idea of other people loving me?*

Garrett once told me I wasn't made to fit in, that it wasn't possible for me to hide in the shadows. So why was I constantly trying? Why had I become an impostor in my own life? I never doubted my talents. I had all the confidence in the world when it came to dance, my ability to wow. And yet, so often I've been ready to fold myself in half to fit somebody else's idea of who I should be, to be someone that everybody else deemed worthy.

Just to be somebody that *I* deemed worthy. Worthy of love, acceptance.

I've lived too much of my life under pressure. But maybe all that pressure was coming from…me. The people who mattered never asked me for more, or different. They saw all of me, and they opened their arms and embraced all the pieces, the stories, the fears, the nuances that made me who I was.

Maybe I'd grown accustomed to being alone. To the thought that I wasn't *just right* for anyone, any relationship, friendship or otherwise. Maybe I convinced myself I was okay with that. The solitude had become a peaceful reprieve for me. It was my quiet place to rest, to take off all my masks, and let myself be without fear of rejection.

But what if falling in love is when being with that person is better than the comfort of the solitude? What if love is when you embrace it together, the chaos of your mind, and make it better than you ever thought it could be?

Because in the middle of my storm, the center of all my chaos, Garrett waits with open arms, ready to shatter me with a love so unconditional, one I didn't know existed before him.

And suddenly it clicks.

I can stand on my own, but I don't have to. I'm allowed to be one part of a whole.

I'm allowed to choose love.

FORTY-TWO
POUND TOWN

Garrett

"Should I call her? I should call her, right? Yeah, I'll call."

I pick up my phone, thumb hovering over that sunshine.

"No," I groan, chucking my phone on my bed. "I shouldn't call."

"I'm scared," Jaxon whispers from the doorway.

"Me too," Adam whispers back. "I've never seen him talk to himself before."

"I'm not talking to myself, you fucking turkeys." I stuff my sweatpants and hoodie inside my carry-on bag. "I'm talking to you two donkeys."

"It's one or the other, Andersen," Jaxon says, an irritating smirk on his face as he watches me pack for our flight later tonight. "Turkeys or donkeys. We can't be both."

"You'll be whatever the fuck I tell you to be."

Adam's eyes sparkle with amusement. "Gare-Bear's a prickly bear this morning."

"Thanks," I grumble, snatching the granola bar he hands me as I strut by.

"For fuck's sake, Garrett, just call her."

"I can't. She needed space to do this on her own." Yanking open the fridge, I pull out the orange juice, guzzling straight from the jug. "I don't wanna bug her."

"I don't think checking in and saying hi would be bugging her. You'd be letting her know you're thinking of her."

I can't *stop* thinking of her. My mind hasn't shut off since Jennie walked out of here twenty-four hours ago. The problem is not one single thought is coherent. Everything is a jumbled mess of *what if's*, one fear that leads to another, until I'm wandering down a dark road wondering what life looks like with her in Toronto. I can't see much, other than it being a cold, bleak future I don't want.

"What if she leaves?" I blurt. "What if she takes the job and moves to Toronto?"

Adam and Jaxon watch me carefully.

"What if she does?" Adam finally tosses back. "You can't follow her. Not right now, at least. And your family is moving here."

My throat squeezes. "I don't want to say good-bye to her."

"Long distance is hard," Jaxon says. "It's hard on any normal relationship, and yours isn't normal. You play professional hockey. When you're not traveling, you're bound to Vancouver. You'd see her in the off-season. Is that what you want?"

What I want is Jennie, any way I can have her. If I have to jizz on my hotel room carpet to her on FaceTime for eight-to-ten months of the year, I'll do it.

"Maybe you could ask her to stay," Jaxon suggests.

"I can't."

I want to. I want to be selfish. But I can't. Jennie deserves this opportunity. More than wanting her to stay, I want her to follow her dreams.

And I'd never ask her to pick me over her dreams.

"Are you worried it's not enough of a reason for her to stay?"

I'm not worried about not being enough for Jennie. Never has that woman asked me to be anything other than myself. Everything I've had to give has always been just right, exactly what she's needed. The same can be said for what she gives to me. I don't know how many ways exist to explain how two people fit together so perfectly, but I'm willing to spend the rest of my life stringing together sentences if that's what it takes to get her to believe that this right here is enough. That she's so goddamn *enough*.

"I think love is a good enough reason to do most things, but I don't need her to stay in Vancouver for me to love her. I'm going to love her wherever she is, and I'm going to make sure she feels it."

Because that, I think, is Jennie's greatest struggle: not understanding that she doesn't have to sacrifice a single piece of herself to have all the love she deserves.

Real love isn't conditional. It's seeing somebody for everything they are and accepting all of them. It's knowing you're friends first and lovers second, understanding that arguments are opportunities to know each other deeper. It's dinner waiting in the microwave, lights left on to welcome you home safely. It's showering together so you can kiss a little longer. It's two a.m. secrets spilled while you're wrapped up in each other, dancing in the kitchen, Disney movies on the couch while crying your heart out. It's supporting dreams, growing together, and growing separately. Because when you can stand strong on your own, you can stand strong together.

If I have to love Jennie from across the country, that's exactly what I'm going to do. And if distance isn't going to stop me, Carter Beckett sure as hell isn't.

He's not going to stop me, but he's sure as shit trying to, and he's pissing me the fuck off while he does it.

"Andersen, you're looking pretty good on the second line." He circles me on his skates, stick across his hips.

"Then I should move back to first. Since, you know, that's my spot."

"But then where would Kyle play?"

"In his spot," I reply through gritted teeth. "On the second line."

"I agree," Coach interjects. "We need Andersen back up on first with you and Emmett. You three are our star lineup for a reason." He cuts Carter off as soon as he opens his mouth. "Beckett, look me in the eyes and tell me where Andersen belongs on this team."

Carter's jaw tightens. "On the first line."

"And why?"

His gaze flicks to me, and beyond all the anger, I see something else. Something vulnerable and soft. For a moment, despite his shit attitude this past week, I feel for him. "Because he's a valuable player and an irreplaceable leader."

"Exactly. So sort your shit and let's play some real hockey tonight. Andersen, you're back on first."

"Atta boy!" Emmett claps his gloved hand to my ass. "Welcome back, baby. We missed ya."

"Speak for yourself," Carter grumbles, and that empathy I was hanging onto a moment ago vanishes. Jennie's tear-streaked face floats through my mind, and something inside me snaps.

"Grow the fuck up, Beckett."

Carter glides closer. "You got a problem, Andersen?"

"Yeah, I got a fucking problem." I skate forward until my chest touches his. "My problem is you're twenty-nine years old, but you're acting like a fucking toddler who got his goddamn birthday candles blown out."

I don't know which one of us drops our stick and throws our gloves to the ice first.

Carter grips a fistful of my jersey, missing my face and getting my shoulder when he swings. "You're fucking my sister!"

"No, I'm not!" I yank him into me, knocking his helmet off. "It's more—"

"You said you were gonna take her to Pound Town!"

Our legs tangle as he wraps an arm around my head, and my helmet pops off as we go tumbling to the ice.

"She said it first!"

"Yeah, well now *I'm* gonna take *you* to Pound Town, and not in the fun way!"

"Too bad you're already there," I grunt, rolling on top of him, pinning his flailing body to the ice. My fist barely connects with his mouth as his hand covers my face. "Because I just...fucking...took you!"

"Jesus fuck," someone mutters.

"Fucking embarrassing," another voice adds.

"Let them work it out. They've gotta play together tonight."

"I've got a hundred on Beckett. He's in it for blood. Andersen fucked his sister."

"I'll take that bet. You gotta be fucked up to test Beckett like that. I think Andersen's got it in him."

Carter's eyes darken, his battle cry echoing across the ice as he rolls on top of me. "You're fucking my sister!"

"I fucking love her!"

His mouth pops open as his grip on my jersey loosens. "What?"

I karate chop his wrists, gulping down air. "I said I fucking love her, okay?"

He sits up but doesn't get off me. "But I thought—"

"Because you don't fucking listen!" I scoop up a glove and chuck it at his face. "It's not about you, Carter! This was about me and her finding each other!"

"But she's my *sister*. You can't—"

"Why not? You don't think I'm good enough for her?"

"What? No, I—" His eyes shine with guilt. He shakes his head. "I didn't say that."

"Then what is it? Because all you wanted was for Olivia to give you a chance, and now you're not giving me one."

"You might...you might..." His chest rises and falls rapidly, a speckle of blood pooling in the center of his bottom lip. "You might hurt her!"

Another damn glove to the face. "You're the one hurting her right now, Carter! She can't handle you cutting her out like this. And why should she have to? You're her brother. Hasn't she lost enough in her life?"

Carter's throat bobs, and that guilt in his eyes starts to drown them.

"She's spent her life feeling overshadowed by you, thinking all she had to offer anyone was being Carter Beckett's little sister. She was finally realizing she had people in her life who wanted to be there for her, not for you. She found love, after everything she's gone through, all the fucking heartache, and what do you do? You leave her. You tell her she can't have it."

His head wags. "No, I...I would never say that."

"But that's what your silence sounds like. Don't you get that? You're allowed to be mad, but you're acting like a child. Jennie doesn't need you to protect her. She needs you to stand by and be her friend and her brother and watch her lead her own life because she kicks ass all on her own. You should want her to be happy no matter where she finds that happiness."

"I do want her to be happy," he whispers, finally climbing off me, sprawling out on the ice beside me. "Jennie deserves the world."

"And I want to give her it."

His head flops so he can stare at me."Ollie said I wasn't being fair. Made me sleep on the couch."

"You have, like, three spare bedrooms."

"Four. She said I didn't deserve a bed."

I sigh, running a hand through my soaked hair. "I haven't talked to my best friend in almost two fucking days."

Carter watches me carefully. "Best friend?"

"Jennie's my best friend, Carter."

"What if she takes the job in Toronto?"

"Then we'll figure it out. But to be honest, I don't even think she wants that job. I think the only reason she's considering taking it is because she thinks you don't want her here now, and that without you, she'll lose everyone else she loves."

"Shit. I fucked up."

"That's putting it lightly, yeah."

"*Beckett*," Coach calls from across the ice. "Get off the ice! You're done!"

Carter rockets up to sitting. "What? No, we were just—"

"Coach, it's all good. We won't—"

He stops in front of us, spraying Carter with ice, grinning. "You're needed at the hospital."

Carter's spine straightens. "What?"

"You're about to be a daddy."

"Holy shit!" Carter rolls over, throwing himself on top of me in some sort of hug before he scrambles to his feet, throws his arms out wide, and screeches, "*I'm gonna be a dad!*"

Adam hoists me to my feet as Carter flies across the ice.

"*Olivia! I'm coming, baby!*"

"Is this your first?"

The receptionist at the desk watches Carter with a smile. It's one of those humoring kinds, probably because he's pacing the hallway, flapping at his face. Cara's been recording to show Olivia later. Right now isn't the time to shove it in her face that her husband is falling apart.

"Baby? No." He lays a hand on his chest. "Dog dad."

Holly narrows her eyes. "Carter."

"What?" He looks at her. "Oh, human baby? Yeah, this is our first human baby. And our last." He laughs anxiously. "Just kidding. We're gonna have three, probably. Maybe five." Another shrill laugh. "Five human babies." He runs a shaky palm over his mouth, his skin exceptionally pale. "Hey, you got any buckets around here?"

The receptionist's brows pinch. "Buckets?"

Carter points across the room to a trash can, striding toward it. "Oh, that'll do." He grips the rim and promptly empties the entire contents of his stomach into the bin.

Alannah, Carter and Olivia's niece, nudges me. "About time, huh? I thought Uncle Carter was gonna puke an hour ago. He's so dramatic, and he's got a weak tummy when he's scared."

"I'm not scared!" Carter yells, then heaves into the bin once more. "It's the oatmeal I had for breakfast!" Another lurch of his stomach. "It must've been bad!"

Alannah lifts her brows in a *told ya so* kind of way. "Scaredy cat."

Carter's been here four hours, the rest of us two. He's been in and out of that room thirteen times, and each time his pitch has gone up an entire octave. His face is red, forehead drenched with sweat, and his hair is pointing in a thousand different directions. The man isn't scared; he's fucking terrified.

"I knew this was going to happen," Holly mutters, digging through her purse. She produces a packaged toothbrush and a tiny tube of toothpaste, shoving them into Carter's chest. "Here. Go brush your teeth and don't leave your wife's side again."

"Maybe I should go in there," Cara suggests, rising. "Do we really trust Carter? Plus, when they're both upset, they feed off each other's energy. Have you seen those two fight? It is *not* pretty."

Emmett tugs her down. "Carter's gonna put on his big boy undies and be strong for his wife."

Carter agrees, I think, with a lot of silent head bobbing before finally wandering down the hallway, toothbrush and paste squeezed in his fists.

I slump in my seat, drumming my fingers on my thighs. "Has anyone, uh...called Jennie? You know...to let her know."

Holly smiles at me. "Her flight left earlier this morning. She should be here soon."

I sit up. "Her flight? But I thought she was staying another day? She was supposed to come home tomorrow."

Holly just winks. I don't get it. If her flight left this morning, she didn't know Olivia was in labor. So why is she coming home early?

"What did she...does she...is she...ahhh." I bury my face in my hands and drop my elbows to my knees. "Just forget it."

The next hour and a half is spent wandering back and forth from the vending machine and the Tim Hortons downstairs in the cafeteria. I've eaten an entire twenty-pack of Timbits, and when Adam reaches into the empty box, he scowls.

"Sowwy," I mumble, swallowing the birthday cake–flavored Timbit. "I eat when I'm nervous."

A door bangs somewhere, followed by the fast, hard slap of foot-steps. Carter skids into the room, clothed in blue hospital scrubs, one of those little caps on his head.

"*It's a girl,*" he sobs, choking on the tears streaming down his face. "*I'm fucking terrified!*"

He disappears as quickly as he arrived, and we explode with cheers, embracing, and I wish Jennie was here.

"I fuckin' told you," I say, holding my palm out. With a collective groan, Emmett, Adam, Jaxon, and Olivia's brother, Jeremy, stuff a bill into my waiting hand. I tuck my winnings into my pocket. "Hank, you knew better, eh buddy?"

"Knew it would be a girl the moment Carter said it'd be a boy. My sweet Ireland always wanted a little girl, and do I ever wish I could've given her one. I dreamt of her too. A miniature version of the kindest woman I'd ever known, with the same big heart." He smiles up at the ceiling, eyes glassy. "Bet she's here now, making sure that little lady arrived safe and sound to her family."

Holly pats his hand. "I think you're right, Hank. Your Ireland has always been with us."

An hour later, Olivia's midwife greets us with a smile. "Mom and Dad would love for you to come meet their little girl."

I hang back as everyone climbs to their feet.

"Gare?" Adam glances back at me. "You coming?"

"Oh." I wave a hand around. "No. Probably not me."

"Carter specifically said everyone," the midwife clarifies

"Oh. Okay." I scrub my clammy palms down my thighs and stand. "Cool."

The room is massive, even with all of us in here, lining up to greet the brave mom.

I wrap one arm around Olivia and kiss her cheek. Exhausted as she looks, she's still beautiful. "Hi, little mama. You kicked ass, and you're brave as hell for letting us all in here at once."

She laughs, hugging me tighter. "We had to have our family here." Her eyes coast over the room, and she frowns when she sees the person who's missing.

"How are you feeling?"

"Would you believe me if I said the pain was forgotten as soon as I heard her cry?"

"My mom said the same when Alexa was born." I give her hand a squeeze. "You did it, Ol."

"She's going to be the luckiest little girl with an uncle like you. I'll even forgive you for giving Carter a split lip today of all days, only because he deserved it."

I chuckle, but it dies quickly at the voice screaming from the hallway.

"*I'm here*! I'm here. Fuck, I'm here."

Jennie slides into the room, breathless, hair in a knot on top of her head, drowning in my hoodie. Her gaze meets mine from across the room, and when she smiles, I think I've died and gone to heaven.

"Auntie J, that's one dollar for the swear j—"

Jeremy clamps his hand over Alannah's mouth. "Not today, dude."

Carter slowly rounds Olivia's bed with their daughter in his arms, swaddled in sage green. "Hank, we want you to hold her first."

Hank's white brows jump. "Me? Really?"

"Really."

His hands come up on either side of his head, shaking and flustered. "Well, okay then. Somebody find me a chair. It's been a long time since I've held a baby, and this one's extra precious."

Adam helps Hank down to a seat, and Carter places his brand-new daughter in his arms, all seven pounds and eleven ounces of perfection.

Nothing but pride and love shine in Carter's eyes as he brushes her cheek and murmurs, "Meet your pseudo-grandpa, sweet Ireland."

Hank's head whips up, Holly chokes on a sob, and Jennie swipes furiously at her cheeks.

Tears brew in Hank's blue eyes as he whispers, "Ireland?"

"Ollie and I couldn't imagine a more perfect name for our little miracle."

Hank's hand trembles as he skims it up the tiny bundle. The tip of his pointer finger stops at her tiny chin, and he cups her round cheek in his weathered hand. His chin quivers, and a tear drips from his lashes, landing on her blanket.

"You, sweet Ireland, are going to be the strongest, fiercest, most passionate and loved little girl." He runs his palm down her, and her hand shoots up, the tiniest fingers wrapping around one of his. Another tear falls, then another, and Hank lifts his captured finger, laying her tiny palm on his cheek and closing his eyes.

I'm captivated when Jennie holds her niece, like she's the most precious thing in the world. I think she just might be, rosy cheeks, a thick head of dark hair and matching lashes, a heart-shaped pout that Carter keeps leaning over and kissing every two minutes on the dot. I can't look away, and I don't want to.

"I hate to do this," Emmett starts, "but we gotta head out. We've gotta get to the arena." He lays his hand on Ireland's belly. "I'm gonna hold the shit out of you in two days when we get home."

Adam and Jaxon say their good-byes, but my feet don't move as I watch Jennie.

"We gotta go, Gare."

"Yeah, but I—"

"Garrett.

"Okay, I just wanna—"

"*Now.*"

A sound of frustration gurgles in my throat and I toss my head back, ball my fists, and definitely don't stomp a foot.

Adam lifts an amused brow. "Did you really just stomp?"

"No," I grumble, and with one last look in Jennie's direction, I follow Adam, Emmett, and Jaxon into the hall.

"Stop being grouchy." Jaxon flicks my temple. "She's here, a whole day earlier than she was supposed to be, and she was smiling at you."

"I just wanted to hug her," I mumble.

"What?"

"*I said I just wanted to hug her.* She was right there and all I wanted to do was—*oof!*" A body collides with mine from behind, and heat sparks, spreading through me like fire as two arms wrap around my middle, holding me tight.

Jennie moves in front of me, covering my heart with one hand, the other cupping my face. "I wanted to hug you too." She presses up on her toes and touches her lips to my cheek. "I missed you," she whispers against my skin, and when she tries to pull back, I clutch her to my chest, burying my face in her hair. She smells the same, like warm vanilla sugar, cinnamon, and coffee, and I'm never letting go.

"Break it up, lovebirds," Emmett calls. "We've gotta be at the arena in fifteen, and we're twenty minutes away."

Jennie smiles. "Good luck, big guy." When she kisses my cheek once more, I know I've *definitely* died and gone to heaven.

We take our home game by two goals, one of them mine, and when we board the plane to San Jose, it's nearly eleven at night.

An hour in, the plane is quiet and dark, aside from the glow of a few tablets and phones. Most of the team is sleeping, but through all my exhaustion, I'm wide awake.

Jennie's home early, and I want to be home with her. I want to ask her about her interview. I want to know everything that's going through her mind. I want to tell her I love her and support her, that I'm going to continue doing so no matter what she chooses.

I have to know. My thumbs have typed out the question over and over, only to delete it. I don't want to pressure her, and I don't know how much space she still needs, even if she hugged me like part of her was missing while she was away. Part of me was, anyway.

A light shines from my lap, drawing my attention away from the window, and my heart thuds at the sunshine on my screen.

Sunshine: *Wanna play a game?*
Me: *What's the game?*
Sunshine: *Toronto vs. Vancouver*

An attachment follows.

Toronto:

- Interesting sex shop on Cumberland St. Spent $$$
- 3 Sweet Jesus ice cream locations. Why did we close our only one?

Vancouver:

- Garrett makes the best hot chocolate.
- Garrett tickles my back in bed & when we watch movies on the couch.
- Dance battles with Garrett.
- Slow dancing in the kitchen with Garrett.
- Garrett does crafts with me.
- Garrett brings me snacks in bed.
- Cuddling with Garrett.
- Spending an entire shower just kissing Garrett.
- Garrett gives the best bear hugs.
- Garrett took me on my first date here & promised more.
- Garrett knows how to fix dented bumpers (very resourceful).
- Garrett sees my toys as friends, not competition.
- Nobody makes me laugh like Garrett.
- Garrett is patient & kind & accepts all of me.
- Garrett looks at me like I'm the best thing in his world. He's the best thing in mine.
- Garrett.
- Garrett.
- Garrett.

Sunshine: *C'mon, Garrett. Play with me.*

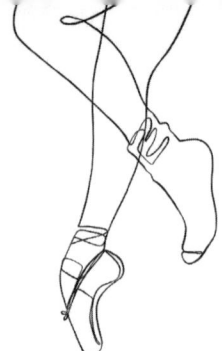

FORTY-THREE
SUNSHINE & CHAOS

Jennie

HAVE you ever seen a six-foot-four hulk of a man cradle his tiny, newborn baby girl in his arms while singing "You Are My Sunshine?"

"Damnit," I mutter. "They're cute."

"I'm wearing an adult diaper and I tore in places no women should ever tear, all because he has no self-control and couldn't pull out one fucking time, but I'm so goddamn in love with those two, it's absolutely unbelievable." Olivia gazes at Carter and Ireland as they slowly sway together. I swear I see the hint of tears before she scrunches her nose and shakes them away. "He's so far from perfect, Jennie, but he's got so much love in his heart. He loves you very much."

"He has a funny way of showing it sometimes." I watch as he smiles down at Ireland, then lowers his lips to hers. "He's the one who taught me how to communicate, how important it was to speak my mind, and then he disappeared on me."

"I know. You have every right to be upset with him. He made some mistakes, and now he needs to correct them." She rubs her eyes and sighs. "The night of your interview, Cara and Em were here doing karaoke. He did your song, the one you two always sing together."

I smile, thinking about the way we trade off so perfectly on our favorite *Frozen* song, "Love Is an Open Door."

"He wouldn't let anyone else sing with him, but he wouldn't sing your lines either. He was miserable, letting the microphone hang at his side." She shakes her head. "I don't know why in the world he didn't just...*not* do the song."

Her guess is as good as mine.

Olivia leans into me, laying her head on my shoulder. "Can I be honest with you, Jennie?"

"Always."

"I'm glad you decided Toronto wasn't for you. If you decided it was, I would've been happy for you but...sad for us. I love you so much, but I really wanted to keep loving you right here. I know it's selfish of me, but—"

I wrap her in my arms, heart squeezing. "Thank you."

"I'm so grateful for you, Jennie." She swipes discreetly at her eyes. "Okay, Carter. Time to let Auntie J have some baby loving."

"What? But I'm not done! She's just—" He hugs Ireland to his chest and frowns at Olivia, twisting away when she tries to take their daughter. "You can't have her!"

"Carter, give me the baby."

"No."

"*Carter.*"

His brows knit so tightly with his scowl, scrunching his forehead. With a huff, he turns toward me. "You have to be careful."

"I've already held her," I remind him.

"Well, don't forget."

"I won't forget."

"Sit on the couch. I don't want you trying to sit down when she's already in your arms."

I fight an eye roll and take a seat, reaching for her.

"Ah-ah," he tsks. "I will put her in your arms." He bends, then pulls back. "Tuck your necklace in your shirt so she doesn't try to eat it."

I tuck my necklace in my shirt in case my forty-eight-hour-old niece tries to eat it.

He leans in, then back again. "And don't forget to support her head."

"I will support her head." I slowly slide my hand between his palm and the back of her head.

"And don't—"

"For fuck's sake, Carter, I know how to hold a damn baby!"

"Geez," he mutters, gently shifting Ireland into my arms. "Someone's testy."

"I swear to God I will rip your balls off and you'll never father another child again. Now shut up, sit down, or get out of my face."

He sinks down beside me without another word, cowering from my stare like a scared little boy.

The warm bundle in my arms wiggles and coos, and I gaze down at the most perfect face in the entire universe. Big, hazy, gray-blue eyes stare back at me, framed by dark lashes, and hidden inside, barely noticeable, are tiny flecks of green. She's going to have her daddy's eyes.

I trace the bow of her little pink pout, the shape of her tiny nose, before laying my hand on her round, rosy cheek. "She's perfect."

Carter's chin hits my shoulder. "Right?"

"You're all Mama. Aren't you, baby girl?"

Carter snorts. "Whatever. Watch this." He strokes his finger down the side of her face. The corner of her mouth lifts, pulling a deep dimple into her cheek.

I gasp. "You've got your auntie's dimples."

"*Our* dimples."

"Yes, you look so cute with your auntie's dimples, don't you, sweet Ireland?"

She blinks up at me, slow and unsure, and when her tiny fingers wrap around one of mine, I lose it. I lift her to my chest, cradling her against me as I close my eyes, breathing in her innocence.

"I love you so much, sweet girl. I'll always be here for you; I promise."

Carter's heavy gaze watches me for a moment before he tentatively lays his hand on top of mine on Ireland's back, the pressure gentle but firm, comforting.

An alarm sounds, and Olivia starts whipping her shirt off.

"Lunch time! You can get Mama undressed faster than I can, little pumpkin," Carter coos, tapping her nose. "That's impressive as fuck, baby girl."

Olivia lets her shirt fall back into place. "You know what? I think we'll go upstairs to eat. You two can have some alone time."

I head into the kitchen when Olivia leaves me and Carter alone for the first time in over a week. I'm not hungry, but I open the pantry, pull out the birthday cake Oreos, twist three apart, layer the icing together until I've got one monster Oreo, and smash it between my teeth. I stare Carter directly in the eyes as I open the cupboard beneath the sink, step on the garbage pedal, and toss the remaining cookie pieces inside.

I've never seen him work so hard to control the twitch in his eye. There's a vein in his neck that looks like it might burst if I poke it just right.

He clears his throat, stuffs his hands in his pockets, and ambles over.

"So…" He clicks a beat out through his pursed lips, head bobbing. "Thinking of changing my TikTok handle."

"Oh yeah?" I check my nails. "To what?"

"*WorldsHottestDILF.*"

"But you're already so iconic as *TheTrophyHusband.*"

He sighs. "It's a tough choice."

"What does Ollie think?"

He rolls his eyes. "She thinks I should change it to my actual name."

"Ew. So unoriginal."

"Right? She wasn't made for the TikTok world." He stops at the edge of the counter, tracing aimless patterns on the marble. "I missed you."

I pin my arms over my chest. "You didn't have to miss me. I was right here."

"I was upset with you. Both of you."

"That's okay, but ghosting me for a week isn't. That's not how we solve problems in this family, Carter. Not you and me. We talk. We communicate."

He hangs his head. "I know."

"Do you, though? Because we've always had each other, and then suddenly you weren't there, and it made me feel so alone. You've always been my biggest supporter, but instead you shut us both out, me and Garrett, and I felt like I'd lost you.

"But the worst part of all? For a second there, I didn't know who I was without you by my side. I didn't know who to be if it wasn't your little sister. I told myself nobody would want me if we were no longer a package deal. I almost moved to Toronto because I convinced myself I was living in your shadow. But then I realized I'd never lived there. You're my brother, but I'm not just your sister. The only thing keeping me in your shadow…was me."

Carter's gaze holds all the remorse of someone who's had too much time to think about where he went wrong. "I'm sorry I shut you out. I'm sorry I made you feel alone. I'm sorry if I haven't given you enough space to shine. You always shine in my eyes."

"You do let me shine. And so does Garrett. He's so patient with me, and so kind. He makes me feel like I can be whoever I want to be. He talks and he listens. I feel safe with him, Carter."

"I feel like I've constantly failed you. I couldn't keep your heart safe when Dad died. I couldn't keep it safe in high school. I'm always…I'm always fucking worried, Jennie, that someone's going to hurt you. This time, because I let my ego get in the way, it was me." He takes my hand in his. "I'm supposed to protect you. I'm supposed to be the one you come to, the one you count on."

"And you are. That won't change. But I have to be able to take care of myself. Garrett helped me learn how to do that."

"But…" He nibbles his lower lip. "I thought I was your best friend."

"Oh, Carter." I clasp his hand tightly, stepping closer. "You are, and you always will be. But Garrett is, too, like Olivia is for you. When I found Garrett, *really* found him…I felt so lucky, like I finally found what you and Olivia had, something I thought was never meant for me. Don't you think I deserve to be loved the way you love Ollie?"

"You deserve the whole world, Jennie."

"I feel like I have it with Garrett."

He stares at me for a long moment. "He says he loves you."

"He does."

"Do you love him too?"

"So much." I grin. "He punched Simon for me."

His eyes light. "He did?"

"Twice."

His chest puffs. "I woulda done it three times."

"It's not a competition," I remind him gently.

He looks away, murmuring his next words. "I'm afraid you won't need me anymore."

My eyes sting, and I blink rapidly, trying to stop the tears before they can start. It's no use. Damnit. Stupid fucking tears. I hate this.

Carter's eyes widen, hands coming up in front of his face as he rocks and swivels in place, like he has no clue what to do. "Oh no. No, I didn't mean to—no. *Olivia!* I made her cry!"

"For fuck's sake," she yells back down. "Put on your big boy panties and fix it, Carter! I've got a tiny human gnawing on my nipple! I don't have time for your drama!"

I throw my arms around Carter's neck, and he holds me as I cry. "I'll always need you. That will never, ever change."

"Promise?" he asks on a whisper.

"Promise."

Garrett

I'm hit with a weird sense of déjà vu as I hesitate outside Jennie's door with my hockey bag slung over my shoulder, sticks in my hand, like the first time I was here to check on her, pre–exploding box of dildos in my face.

It's not that I'm afraid to knock; it's just that I'm…

I'm a little afraid. Jennie's so strong and confident. She's certain about so many things in her life, and the only thing I've ever been so sure about, well…it's her.

I've been dying to hold her, kiss her, but I don't know how to take what I want right now. Do we need time? Do we have to ease back into it? I've never felt like there was much easing into anything in our relationship. Sure, some of the pieces came with time. But for the most part, Jennie opened her heart right away and asked for what she wanted, and I gave it to her without hesitation: friendship. I got to have all of her, even the parts I didn't know I wanted. Now that I've had them, I don't know how to slow down. All I want to do is barrel forward, but I don't want to push her.

Clearing my throat, I knock. Music filters from inside, and after a few more knocks, I try the handle, stoked to find it unlocked.

The music coming from her bedroom is so loud it's no wonder she can't hear anything. I drop my equipment by the door, kick off my shoes, and head down the hall.

"Jennie?" I call softly, sticking my head into her room. Her bedside table is open, blankets mussed on the bed, and I plod toward the bathroom, where I hear her humming, calling my name.

I'm not sure what I expected, but it sure as hell wasn't a bright array of dildos and vibrators covering nearly every inch of the sparkly white quartz counter.

I also didn't expect to find Jennie naked and leaning against the wall, eyes closed while she moans, one hand moving between her legs, the other wrapped tightly around Indiana Bones, like she needs something to hang on to.

"Holy fuck."

Jennie's eyes flip open, and she leaps into the air, one of her blood-curdling shrieks leaving her mouth. Haven't heard one of those in a while. Forgot how much they spike my blood pressure.

She twists in every direction like she's looking for a place to hide, and when she doesn't find one, she accidentally swipes every single toy clear off the counter, until they're buzzing and jumping at her feet. Indiana Bones flings from her grasp, and a scream rips up my throat as that meaty fucker soars through the air, coming right for my face in slow motion.

"*Ah!*" I shriek, clapping a hand over the right side of my face as he strikes me and clatters to my feet. "*My eye!*"

"*Garrett!*" Jennie screeches, two hands on my chest as she shoves me out of the bathroom. "*Out! Get out!*"

The door slams in my face before I have time to comprehend what's happening, and when it opens again eight seconds later, Jennie's covered in one of my T-shirts, cheeks flushed red, music dialed down to a quiet hum. She doesn't look any less angry, and I haven't had time to process, so I'm still on edge.

"*What the hell are you doing here?*" she yells at me.

My arms come up, waving wildly through the air. Maybe if I make myself look bigger, she'll be less scary. "*Your door was unlocked! I-I-I...I heard my name!*"

"*I leave my door unlocked and say your name all the time!*"

"*Why would you leave your door unlocked if you had all your fuck toys out?*"

"*I do what I want!*"

"*Why are you masturbating with your door unlocked?*"

"I do what I want!" is all she shrieks again. *"You weren't supposed to be home 'til midnight, you dink!"*

"I flew home early to be with you, you turtle!"

She blinks up at me, the rise and fall of her chest slowing, our jagged breaths heavy in the air. "Oh. That's..." She scratches her scrunching nose. "Sweet."

We stare at each other for a long moment, and when she launches herself at my chest, I clutch her so tight.

"I fucking missed you so much," I whisper. She's so warm, so soft, this perfect body that wraps around mine and makes everything feel so incredibly *right.*

With her chin on my chest, she gives me a goofy, dimply smile, and when she tells me, "I love you so much," I cover her mouth with mine.

Jennie's fingers sink into my hair, tugging me closer as her tongue glides against mine. My hands creep beneath her shirt, skimming the arch low in her back, pressing into her smooth skin and holding her to me.

"You're really staying?"

"This is where I belong, Garrett."

"Together?"

"Nowhere else."

"What about your dream?"

"I want my own studio. I want to teach dance in a way that doesn't encourage obsessive-compulsive tendencies. I want to teach kids how to love something so much and still have healthy boundaries around it instead of letting it consume them. My dream is to have all the love I want, the love I need, and the love I deserve. And this, Garrett, is where I have that."

I lift her into my arms, winding her legs around my waist before I sit on the edge of her bed. "I'm proud of you for recognizing what you need and deserve. And selfishly, I'm happy you're staying."

"I was worried if I stayed, it would be because I was too comfortable here, because I didn't know how to stand on my own," she admits. "I didn't want to go for the wrong reasons, but I didn't want to stay for them either."

"Standing on your own doesn't mean without love, Jennie. It doesn't mean you have to do everything alone, that you won't grow unless you're doing it by yourself. Because you can already do all that. You're fierce and independent. You can grow on your own, and you can stand on your own. But the most important piece is knowing that you don't have to."

"It's okay to be one part of a whole." She speaks the words gently, like a realization that's already dawned, the final pieces coming together, taking it from a fantasy to a truth. Her soft blue eyes lift to mine, and the gratitude shining there, the love, it's enough to knock the breath from my lungs. "I think you're the biggest part, Garrett."

My lips crash down on hers, and suddenly we're nothing but grazing hands, sliding tongues, slow, wet kisses, like we have all the time in the world to be together. I think we do.

When we break apart, Jennie rests her forehead against mine. "Did you ever worry we'd never make sense? That we were too different to make this work?"

"Sometimes opposites attract. But for what it's worth, I don't think we're all that different, and there hasn't ever been a part of me that thought we couldn't be exactly what the other needed."

I take her face in my hands, studying those violet-blue eyes that hold all my favorite pieces, the humor, the relentless teasing, the confidence, the uncertainty, the compassion, *the love.*

"Every bit of you fits every piece of me, and that's how I know. We bring out the parts of each other we've spent so much of our lives being too scared to show. You're my best friend, and we found everything we needed when we found each other. Falling in love with you is like checking the very last thing off my bucket list."

She snuggles into me, her head on my shoulder. "You know, I'm not sure we ever really fell in love. I think we built it from the ground up. We made each other a priority, made our friendship a safe place to be together and learn together. We wanted honesty and trust, and we worked every day to get it. We planted the seeds, and when I bloomed, it was because you took my hand and made sure all of me got space to shine, even the parts I was content to leave inside the shadows."

Sometimes I can't believe she's a real, like she's a figment of my imagination, something my brain dreamed up and said, *Here's everything you could ever want, all rolled into one single person.* I don't know how I convinced her to be mine, but I do know I'm never going to let her go.

"I want to keep you forever. Please don't leave."

~

We spend the next hour wrapped up in each other, my fingers trailing up and down her spine as she tells me about the twat-waffle in Toronto who wouldn't let her order steak. She's still traumatized about her salad dinner, so I'm taking her on our second date, and we're getting steak.

"Let me finish putting my things away, then I'll get dressed," Jennie says.

I follow her into the bathroom, helping pick up her collection of toys, and I'm reminded that Jennie was masturbating when I walked in here.

"What were you doing with these all?"

"I was giving them a thorough cleaning and I got a little horny while I was waiting for you to get home." She taps Indiana Bones against my shoulder. "Sue a girl for touching herself while she thinks about her boyfriend."

"Hit me with that one more time and I get to use this on you tonight," I roll the pink glass plug between my fingers, "while you're tied up with this," I skim the edge of my tie, "while I make you fuck this." I flick the head of Indiana Bones and lean forward, kissing my way to Jennie's ear. "And you'll be on your knees, with my cock down your throat."

Heat floods her face, her bottom lip sliding between her teeth. The little devil reaches forward with her toy and smacks me once more.

With a growl, I clap a hand to her ass. "Get moving, or else we're staying here and you're not getting steak tonight."

She snickers and salutes me, then produces the labeled box those wonderful toys came from all those months ago, the day Indiana Bones and I met. "I thought these could find a new home at your place."

"My place? You movin' in?"

"No." She laughs. "That would be crazy. Right?"

"So crazy," I agree.

"We've only been officially dating for, like, four weeks."

"I've loved you a lot longer than four weeks, though, sunshine."

Her beam is bright and warm, just like her nickname. "You have? Me too."

Linking my fingers through hers, I tug her into me, and we start swaying to the music still drifting quietly through the speaker. My lips touch her shoulder, trailing the slope of her neck. She trembles when I pause at her ear.

"Can I tell you something?"

"Of course."

"I like crazy."

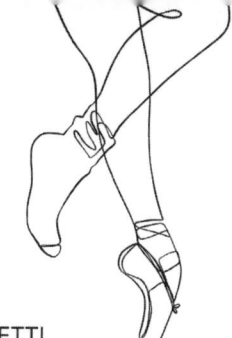

FORTY-FOUR
THROW DICKS AROUND LIKE CONFETTI

Jennie

"Do you think you'll get married? What about babies? Are you gonna have 'em? That would make us aunties, right? Oh, and can we be bridesmaids at the wedding? I wanna wear a—"

Alexa twists in her seat, trying to slap at Gabby in the back. "*Gabby*! Shut. Up. Jennie doesn't want you as a bridesmaid." She turns back around. "Sorry about her. *Cool* isn't in her dictionary."

A bloodcurdling shriek roars through the car as Gabby pinches Alexa, and I shove my arm between them, pushing them apart.

"All right, enough! Holy crap, I thought Carter and I were bad." I exhale loudly and meet Stephie's gaze in the rearview mirror. She shrugs. "You're lucky the car was already in park. I have a terrible track record with stop signs."

"But how?" Alexa asks. "Stop signs don't move."

"Yes, Alexa. I'm aware. Your brother likes to remind me at least weekly." Climbing out of the car, I glance back at Garrett's sisters. "Okay, ladies. Let's go."

Gabby's the fastest to escape, quickly linking her arm through mine, Stephie next. Alexa ambles beside us, watching our joined arms like she's feeling a little left out, even if she won't say it. She's in that grumpy preteen phase where cool and detached is the the only way to act. Mostly, she doesn't want to have to ask for the attention she's longing for. She pretends to be annoyed every time Garrett yanks her down beside him on the couch for movie night, but she's as much of a snuggle bear as he is. That's why she stays tucked into his side until the end credits roll.

"Hey, Lex," I call. "Will you sit next to me at lunch later?"

"Really?" Her hazel eyes glow before she schools her expression, lifts a shoulder. "If you want."

I give her a wink, making her flush. She's so much like her brother.

I don't think I truly realized the weight and depth of my love for Garrett until I saw him with his sisters. Watching him sway back and forth with Ireland in his arms while he babbles away to her really does it for me too.

Garrett and I aren't *technically* living together, but his family moved out here at the beginning of April. Garrett's dad doesn't start his job until the end of the month, and we're only halfway through it now, but it's given everyone a chance to get settled into their new city. They've been staying in my condo, and I've been staying with Garrett.

Today, his parents are signing the papers for their new home, the one they take possession of in four weeks. I don't know how to tell Garrett that I really just...don't want to leave.

Falling asleep wrapped in the heat of his body, waking with his lips on my skin, his murmured words in my ear...it's my favorite thing in the world. Even when he's on the road, there's something comforting about being in his space, something that feels like home.

"Wow," Stephie murmurs, coaxing me from my thoughts as we step through the front doors of SFU. Her eyes are wide with wonder as she looks around the expansive foyer. "It's so different in the daytime without all the people here."

"Recital nights are packed," I agree. We sold out two weekends in a row, and I'm proud to say an entire row was filled with my friends and family. I felt like I was dancing just for them. "But the semester is over now. Everyone's finishing up exams, so the school is quiet."

I sweep the girls into the dance studio. They *ooh* and *ahh* as they spin around the space, then follow me to the back where my cubby is.

As luck would have it, Simon has also chosen today to empty his cubby.

"Jennie." He drops a textbook to his feet. "I didn't know you were coming in today." He looks to the girls. "Who are they?"

"Garrett's sisters," I reply with disinterest, packing my things into my bag.

"Right. So you two are…?"

"Dating."

"Oh."

"Yeah, that's right," Gabby's voice snaps from behind me. I glance over my shoulder to find her scowling at Simon, arms pinned, hip popped. "My big brother's her boyfriend. And who are you, you frickin' turkey?"

Simon fumbles for a response before giving up and hovering at my shoulder. "Uh, hey, Jennie." He clears his throat into his fist. "Could we maybe…talk?"

"I don't see what the point would be." I yank the zipper, closing my bag. "You don't really know how to listen, do you, Simon?"

"Yeah, *Simon*." Gabby snaps her fingers through the air in the shape of a Z. "So back the heck up, *buddy*."

There's a tiny angel on my shoulder telling me I should reel her in, but the devil on my shoulder urges me to set her loose.

The angel wins. *Damnit.*

"All right, tiger. Rein it in." I turn away from Simon, gesturing for the girls to go ahead of me.

"You're really just gonna walk away?" Simon hollers. "After five years of friendship? Don't you think you're being a little dramatic? How many times do I have to tell you I'm sorry?"

My sneakers squeak as I skid to a stop, and rage thuds in my ears, in line with the beating of my heart.

His expression tells me everything I need to know: he's not sorry. He wasn't before and he's sure as hell not now. What he wants is forgiveness he doesn't deserve. He wants to walk away without the guilt of what he's done.

"Sometimes an apology isn't enough."

When he opens his mouth, I beat him to it.

"Sometimes it's not enough," I repeat. "People like you throw out apologies like greetings, empty and meaningless, something you feel required to say. And people like me, people who like to believe there's good in everyone, that we deserve second chances because we all make mistakes…people like me forgive you. We forgive you once, then twice. We

434 | BECKA MACK

forgive you again and again until somebody walks into our lives and shows us it's not hard to keep promises. To apologize and mean it. To commit to being better. Until somebody shows us there's no room in our lives for people who don't care about boundaries. For people like *you*, Simon."

Alexa slips her hand into mine, squeezing gently before she urges her younger sisters forward, and we head toward the exit, together.

I'm halfway out the door when I remember an item at the bottom of my backpack. I stowed it there at the beginning of the year. It was meant for an unsuspecting Krissy, but it wouldn't be wasted on Simon.

I dig the hefty item out of my bag, walk back to Simon, and place it in his hand. "Here. I got you this before everything. You might as well have it."

The smarmy grin that crawls up his face lets me know that, despite literally everything I've just said, he thinks this means I still care. So I stand there and wait for him to open the black cylinder.

Simon makes a triumphant noise as the object spring opens, and my grin grows as his dies.

Shiny confetti dicks in every shade of pink rain down around him, covering his hair, sticking to his cheeks, his clothing. They fall inside his open backpack, and a particularly large fucker catches on his top lip, clinging there as his eyes blaze.

For the life of me, I can't get my grin to stop growing. "Let's go, girls."

"Um," Stephie starts cautiously. "Were those...penises?"

"Yes. Don't tell your mother."

"Can we tell Daddy?"

"No. Wait. Yes." That man loves me. So does Garrett's mom, but she has a way of laying on the guilt with only the look in her eyes. I try to avoid being on the receiving end of that stare. Sometimes I just look anywhere but at her and she says she knows I'm avoiding her.

When we're loaded in the car, I face the girls.

"Don't ever let anyone walk all over you, ladies. Know your worth, set your boundaries, and don't let anyone disrespect either of those things. If they do, knee 'em in the nuts and hit 'em with an exploding confetti dick bomb straight to the face. Understood?"

"Yes, Jennie," they respond in unison.

"I wanna be strong like you when I grow up," Alexa says quietly.

"You already are strong. But it's okay to have days where you don't feel strong too."

"I wanna be a dancer and a cheerleader when I grow up," Gabby pipes up. "Like you and Emily."

"Oh, honey. Emily's not a real cheerleader."

"Then how come she was wearing a cheerleading outfit when she was saying good-bye to her friend yesterday? Me and Stephie were riding our scooters in the hallway and we saw her."

"You know what? That's a great question. You should definitely ask her at lunch."

I crank the ignition, connect my phone to the car with the adapter, then quickly yank the cord right back out at the message that lights the screen.

Bear: *Dreamt about fucking ur soaking wet pussy all night long until ur throat was raw from screaming my name.*
Bear: *Oops, autocorrect. That was supposed to say good morning, sunshine.*

"Is that Garrett?" Gabby asks, leaning around the seat to peek at my phone.

I tug it into my chest. "No."

Alexa squints at me. "You're lying."

"I have to admit, Jennie, you do look guilty." Stephie pokes my cheek. "Your face got super red when you read the message. Alexa was always like that when she was texting Jacob Daniels."

"My face did *not* get super red." *Her brother just lit my insides on fire with a simple text message.* "He was just being sweet. Super sweet." *I'm gonna let him tie me up tonight.*

"What did he say that was so sweet?" Stephie frowns. "Did he say he wants to braid your hair? 'Cause last week I caught him with one of the ribbons you use in your hair. When I asked him what he was doing, he said he was going to braid your hair for you. His face got really red, too, and he was kinda yelling." She shrugs. "I guess he really likes when you use those ribbons."

"Yes," I say slowly. "That's definitely why he had my ribbon."

"Maybe one day I'll have a boyfriend who wants to tie my hair with a ribbon too," Gabby says brightly.

Garrett's gonna kill me.

∽

It's been a long week without Garrett.

All right, it's only been four days.

It's been a long four days without Garrett. They've been on the road a lot the past few weeks as the regular season finished up. They nabbed second place in their division, and they get one day off tomorrow before jumping into the first round of the play-offs here at home.

School is done, which means I have unlimited free time until I either get a job or open my own studio. I really want the studio, but with it comes a lot of work, so I'm thinking of taking a business course to help me get there. In the meantime, I've been spending all my free time with the girls—Olivia, Ireland, Cara, Emily, and Garrett's sisters.

Watching my niece grow is truly the most incredible thing. She's changed so much in just five weeks, and Cara and I sleep there most nights when the boys are away. Carter is on FaceTime with Olivia every single minute he's not on the ice because he doesn't want to miss a thing with Ireland.

I've been busy, but it doesn't stop me from missing Garrett when he's gone. With play-offs here, I can't help but think about what lies on the other side: months with him all to myself.

Silver moonlight slices through the cracks in the blinds in Garrett's bedroom, bouncing off the oversized mirror that hangs on the wall. Garrett hung it just for me when I temporarily moved in because I complained about not having somewhere to check out my ass and my outfits.

I strip down and turn on the lamp, standing in the reflection of the orange glow, admiring the body that's carried my dreams of dancing for years on end.

I've filled out more in my time with Garrett, the result of endless mugs of hot chocolate with extra marshmallows, special edition Pop-Tarts, hearty dinners, munching on the couch while we watch movies, sleeping in in favor of early morning workouts, and just...appreciating every inch of myself, letting someone else appreciate it too. Areas that I spent years nit-picking, pulling at, looking for ways to make smaller, have softened in the most beautiful way. I'm more confident and in love with my body than I've ever been.

But my favorite parts are the tiny marks that paint my skin, faded hues of purple and pink, where Garrett's taken his time loving on every inch of me with his mouth. My fingers flutter over every stain, igniting a spark deep in my belly, as if I can feel his mouth on me.

I smile as I touch the mark on my collarbone, the one Garrett left on purpose for Carter to see. He called it payback for being a dick but then shrieked at the top of his lungs as Carter chased him throughout the house.

My heart skitters at the sound of the dead bolt sliding, and when the door opens and closes, butterflies erupt in my belly. A heavy thud as a bag falls to the ground, then the quick padding of footsteps echoes in my ears, drumming along with my pulse. Garrett appears in the reflection of the mirror, pausing in the doorway, and a grin ignites across my face.

His eyes dance as he watches me admire all the ways he's claimed pieces of me, and he slowly crosses the room, tugging on his tie, popping the first few buttons of his shirt.

Broad fingers slide along my waist, palms gliding over my belly, singeing my skin. Garrett's chin hits my shoulder as he wraps his arms around me.

"Mine," he murmurs, right before he skims my jaw and forces my face to his. His mouth covers mine and I open without hesitation, a soft sigh escaping my lips.

I reach back, fingers running through his blond waves as he trails wet kisses down my neck. Our gazes lock in the mirror, and his hand glides down my torso. My belly tightens as I watch his fingers creep closer, and my back arches, urging him there faster. He smiles against my neck, and when he dips two fingers between my legs, gathering my wetness, desire unfurls, shooting through me like flames.

Slowly, he works the tight bundle of nerves at the cleft of my thighs, drawing out each whimper, my fingernails clawing at his arms where he holds me. He sinks two fingers inside me, gaze heavy and heady as he watches me climb higher. I squirm, panting, and when his fingers curl, I come on a gasp, all while he whispers, "Mine."

His palm lands between my shoulder blades as he pushes me forward, guiding my hands to the frame of the large mirror. I watch with rapt attention as his tie slides from around his neck, white shirt falling to the ground behind him, the rest of his clothes following.

Garrett urges my legs farther apart, cock pressing into my back as his hands roam my body, fingertips dancing over my belly, palms squeezing my breasts, thumbs scraping over my taut nipples. A lopsided smile blooms on his face before his lips press below my ear.

"I love you," he murmurs. When he sinks inside me with one unhurried, deep thrust, he grips my throat and softly growls, "Mine."

His eyes watch me carefully, hooded and heated, searing every place they touch as he moves inside me. His hips slap against my ass, hands gripping my hips as he moves faster, spurred on by each jagged breath, the moans, the whimpers.

I don't want to leave. I want to stay here, right here with him.

"Your parents sealed the deal for the house today," I manage, jolting forward with the weight of his plunge.

"Mhmm."

"They move in four weeks."

"Yup."

"That means I can move back home soon."

"You're already home."

"What?"

"This is your home." The words lick at the skin on my neck, hot and sweet. "I'm keeping you."

"Are you asking me to move in with you?"

"I'm *telling you* you're not going anywhere."

"Hmm. Feels very bossy of you."

"Guess you're rubbing off on me, sunshine."

My head lolls forward with a soft cry when he brushes my clit. "It's only going to get worse if I-I...mmm, if I stay."

"I know. I'm dealing with it. We're all dealing with. I've warned everyone to expect a new, growly Garrett."

"But I like old, gentle Garrett."

His pace slows to a torturous speed, fingers easing off my hips, out of where they've dug a home in my skin.

"Garrett," I whine, slamming my ass backward. "Harder."

"You said you prefer gentle."

"There's a time and a place for gentle, and right now isn't it. Fuck me like you mean it."

His tongue glides up my neck. "Say please."

"Fuck me, *please*."

"C'mon, sunshine. You can do better than that."

A shudder rolls down my spine as he removes himself completely, then sinks back inside achingly slow.

"Please," I whimper as his thumb circles my clit. "Fuck me, Garrett. I don't want to be able to stand when you're done with me."

His hips still, keeping me full of him, and I feel his smile against my neck before he pulls out and drives himself forward with a single punishing plow that makes me scream, catching myself against the mirror. He tangles his fingers in my hair, pulling my head taut, keeping my gaze on his reflection as he pistons inside me with a ferocity he reserves just for me, just for the bedroom.

He yanks me off him and spins me around, lifting me up, winding my legs around his waist, and slamming me back down. My nails rake across his shoulders as he presses me against the mirror and fucks me, and every single inch of me trembles as pressure builds low in my belly.

My walls tighten around him, pulling him deeper as his thrusts quicken. His blue-green eyes stare down at me, shining with so much love, so much wonder, and I take his mouth, forcing him to swallow his own name when I come, soaking his cock.

"Mine," Garrett whispers.

He sinks down to the ground, pulling me between his legs, holding me to him as I watch the reflection of his lips dot my jaw, my neck, my shoulder.

"Mine," he murmurs with every kiss.

"Your what?"

His smile is so tender as he gazes at me in the mirror, beautiful and special, like it's all for me. His nose nudges my jaw until I turn my face to his, and he presses his lips to mine.

"My best friend, my sunshine, and my whole heart."

Fireworks erupt and my heart takes flight as I settle into the love I always wanted, the love I craved. I couldn't have ever imagined it'd feel like this, so whole, so complete it makes my shoulders uncurl, makes me stand a little taller.

I might have been confident before, bold and self-aware, but the more I look back on it, the more of an act it feels like. Nobody took the time to get to know me, so I put up walls to keep everyone out, to avoid the heartache altogether.

In the end, all I did was lose bits of myself. I placed myself in a box and hid my most vulnerable parts, the pieces I was too scared to show, the parts that made me exactly who I was, because I was afraid people wouldn't love me for me.

But maybe what I was actually afraid of was that somebody *would* love me for me. That they'd see all of me, the sharp, jagged edges right along with the soft, frayed ones, and still choose me.

And that's what Garrett does.

He sees all of me, and he chooses me, day in and day out.

He says I'm his sunshine, but I think he's mine.

I shine a whole lot brighter with that man igniting my sky.

EPILOGUE
OOPS

Garrett

July

"Who the fuck's idea was this?"

My gaze slides to my girlfriend. She's wearing tiny spandex shorts the color of cranberries, showing off her long, golden legs. A matching sports bra covers her stellar rack, perfect tits bouncing with each stride she takes beside me, keeping my pace. The soft dips in her torso flex as she moves, glistening with sweat, and I mentally catalog our surroundings, trying to locate an alley in the general vicinity.

I've got an urge to yank her shorts down and plow inside her while she's pressed against a brick wall, cover her mouth with my palm so nobody hears her when she screams my name.

But it's Friday morning in downtown Vancouver. Patios overflow with people enjoying their breakfast beneath the early July sun, tourists on bikes here to see everything the city has to offer. A horny couple fucking in an alley is likely not the sightseeing they're after.

"It was your idea," I remind Jennie. "*Let's go for one last run in our neighborhood*," I mimic, then squeal when she lands a punch on my shoulder. "Hey! Aggressive hands get tied up."

"I'm well aware, Garrett." She twists my way and pouts, and I know what's coming. "One last iced coffee at our local Starbucks?"

She's been doing this for the last two weeks as an excuse to get whatever she wants. *One last ice cream cone, one last trip to Udupi Palace, one last stroll through Stanley Park.* She gives me that pouty face, bottom lip sticking way out, fists curled under her chin, and five minutes later we're riding the elevator down so we can go wherever she wants.

I slow to a walk and tug Jennie into me so I can steal her breath right from her mouth. "You know we're only moving twenty minutes away to North Vancouver, not leaving the country, right?"

Her tongue slides against mine, a slow lap as she sinks into me, hands buried in the hair at my nape. "One last caramel Frappuccino," she whispers against my lips.

I clap my palm to her ass, not at all caring that we're out in public, that I've heard my name whispered at least three times in the last five minutes, and Jennie's too. Everyone lost their minds the first time I walked up to Jennie after exiting the change room and kissed her in front of a horde of reporters, and her brother.

To be fair, we'd just won the first round of the play-offs. I deserved to kiss her. It was the same when we lost in the third round, when all I wanted to do was lay my head on her shoulder and hold her.

To be honest, though, I was happy to start my summer with Jennie. Carter was happy to be home with his wife and daughter.

Jennie and I stroll down the street with our frozen drinks, fingers tangled together, and I smile as she hums happily around her straw. I'm so fucking happy her box of dildos exploded in my face. If it weren't for all the sexual tension it brought, my nickname for her might still be nothing but ironic, instead of so utterly genuine.

If Jennie were a color, she'd be the most vibrant shade of yellow. She's literal sunshine in human form. I don't care if I've said it a thousand times; I'm going to say it for the rest of my life.

I tug on her hand when she tries to head right, pulling her straight instead. "This way."

"But the condo—"

"I wanna show you something." I press my lips to hers the second she opens her mouth to argue with me, to tell me that we need to be at our new place with the moving truck in an hour and a half. "We'll be quick." At the disbelieving expression she wears, the one that reminds me I'm never, ever quick, I laugh. "C'mon, Jennie. Humor me."

With a wary sigh, she tucks her hand back into mine.

Her suspicious gaze coasts my way twelve times over the remaining four minutes of our walk, and when we stop in front of a small storefront space with sprawling windows, her nose scrunches in confusion.

"What is this place?" she asks as I unlock the glass door. "And why do you have a key?"

I usher her inside, past the front desk and into the open space behind it, watching as she twirls around the room.

"It used to be a yoga studio," I tell her.

I move behind her as she stops in front of the floor-to-ceiling mirrors. Her eyes meet mine in the reflection, tongue gliding slowly across her lower lip before she swallows, as if she already knows the answer to the question she's about to ask.

"And now?"

"Now it's a dance studio."

"Garrett," she gasps. "You didn't."

"I did." My chin hits her shoulder as I hug her to me. "I love you, Jennie. You've worked your ass off your entire life, and now you're doing your business classes. You're determined to make your dream a reality. You deserve this, and I'd be honored to be a part of this next step in your life."

Her nose wrinkles as she fights off the tears I knew would come. I love her soft, vulnerable bits just as much as her bold and sassy ones. "You did this for me?"

"I'd do anything for you, sunshine."

A lone tear escapes, tracking a path down her cheek, and I press my lips to it.

"Thank you for making my second most important dream come true."

"What was your first?"

She turns and takes my face in her hands, eyes gleaming with tenderness. She sweeps a soft kiss across my lips.

"You."

~

"Mine's bigger."

"No it's not."

"Yeah it is."

"*No* it's *not.*"

"*Yeah* it *is*."

"Holy fuck." Adam pushes between me and Carter, a large box in his arms. "Are we comparing houses or dicks? Nobody gives a fuck. They're both mini-mansions."

Carter gasps. "*Mini*? My house?" He sweeps his arms out, gesturing around mine and Jennie's new house. "I mean, this. *This* is mini. Mine is *huge*. Huge like my—"

"Ego," I finish for him.

Olivia steps inside, fist bumping me. "It's beautiful. Even Carter said so last week after doing the final walk-through with you guys." She unstraps the carrier she's wearing and hoists Ireland off her chest. "Want your Uncle Garrett snuggles?"

"Yes, she does," I coo, scooping the most beautiful little lady into my arms. Her wide green eyes peer up at me as she giggles, then promptly stuffs her entire fist into her mouth, drool dribbling down her chin. I kiss her fluffy, dark curls. "How's my princess?"

She's got a pink barrette in her hair, a sparkling sunshine set on the end of it, and her onesie says *I'm cute, Mom's hot, Dad's lucky*. I know for a fact Carter bought this. Ninety-nine percent of her outfits have some form of the word *dad* on them. And he's been essentially rotating between his *DILF* shirt and another that says *Girl Dad*.

"Is your daddy driving you nuts?" I twist out of Carter's reach as we bounce around my kitchen. "Do you wanna have a sleepover with Auntie Jennie and Uncle Gare to get away from him?"

Carter scoffs. "Please. She's obsessed with me." He reaches toward us, making grabby hands. "Lemme take her."

"No. She likes me." My sweet girl grabs a fistful of hair at the nape of my neck, before laying her cheek on my shoulder, still munching away on her fingers. I smile triumphantly. "See? She doesn't want you."

Carter frowns. "But I'm her daddy."

"Are you? How do I know for sure? You're not wearing any of your *dad* shirts."

Jennie snickers, walking by with a box labeled *kitchen*. She sets it down and plants a smooch on Ireland's cheek and my lips.

"Ew." Carter gags. "Do you have to do that right in front of me?"

Jennie tosses a *yes* over her shoulder as she struts away, and Carter narrows his eyes at me, swiping nonexistent dust from my counter.

"You know, Andersen, I only live five minutes down the road. That means I'm only five minutes away if you need your ass kicked."

"Yeah, and I'm only five minutes away if you need *your* ass kicked."

"I said that first!"

"I said it second!"

"Fucking children," Emmett mutters. He steals Ireland away, kissing her nose. "Hi, baby girl."

"It was my turn next," Adam whines. "I haven't seen her in two days."

"It's been nine for me," Jaxon mumbles, eyes hidden behind sunglasses as he ambles in with a box.

"That's because you took off to Cabo with some chick you met at the gym," I remind him.

He grins, flexing his biceps. "Yeah, tan's on point, huh?" He presses a kiss to Ireland's forehead, and she giggles. "Hi, princess."

Adam reaches for Ireland, and Emmett turns away. He frowns. "C'mon. Me now."

"I'm not done."

"I don't care. Come here, baby girl. You wanna come see Uncle Adam?" He tickles her belly, and she explodes with laughter, thrashing in Emmett's arms. She reaches toward Adam, laying her tiny, pudgy hand on his cheek, and somehow, we all wind up huddled around Ireland and Emmett, cooing and babbling, vying for her attention.

Holly strolls through the door and rips her sunglasses off, arms out wide. "*Glamma's here!*"

"That's our cue." Emmett deposits Ireland in her grandma's arms. "Back to work, boys."

Between the five of us, we get the rest of the moving truck unloaded over the next hour while the girls work on unpacking boxes in the kitchen and living room.

"That's the last of 'em." I drop two boxes on top of a stack in the front foyer, swiping my forearm across my damp brow. "Fuck, I'm tired. Snack break?"

"Let's get all the boxes to their designated rooms first," Adam suggests, moving toward the stack. He reads the label, and my heart skids to a stop at the single word. "Toys?"

He picks at the tape like he's about to check out the contents, and my brain short-circuits.

"No. No." I shove him out of the way, throwing myself on top of the box, head wagging. "No, no, no."

He steps back, hands up in surrender, expression both suspicious and scared.

Carter strolls down the hallway, whistling. "Did somebody say snacks?" His gaze lights when it falls to the box I'm half lying on top of. "Oooh, toys. What kinda toys?"

"*Nothing!*" I shriek, jerking it out of his reach. My shoulders tighten as I clutch it to my chest. I spread my fingers wide, trying to distort the word from view, even though he's already seen it. "*Nothing!*"

Carter looks at the box, then me. Back to the box, then back to me again.

After everything we've been through, I thought I was safe. I genuinely thought I'd get to keep my balls. But the longer he watches me without blinking, the less sure I become.

It would have been nice to procreate with Jennie one day, but I guess some things are only meant to be dreams.

Carter finally blinks, just once, slowly. "What's in the box, Garrett?"

"Nothing." A bead of sweat rolls down my temple. Carter's gaze flicks to the droplet, watching it roll. When our eyes meet again, I repeat quietly, "Nothing."

He stares at me for five seconds, then ten. It's a full twenty seconds before his next word comes, a terrified breath barely heard. "No."

"I'm so sorry," I whisper.

He steps back, head shaking. "No."

"It's—it's not what you—we don't....*she had them before!*" I shout after him as he runs out the door. "*I didn't buy them!*"

Adam squeezes my shoulder. "You don't know when to shut up, do you?"

I hang my head in defeat. "No." The only good thing it's ever brought me is Jennie, but I think she outweighs all the bad. With a sigh, I start up the stairs. "Gonna take this to our bedroom."

The room is expansive and bright, with wide, gray plank flooring, a stone fireplace, and a wall of windows overlooking the pine trees skating up the mountains behind us. Jennie spent five minutes standing here, hands pressed to the glass as she stared silently at the view. That's how I knew this house was the one.

I secure the box in the closet before making my way to my dresser.

We picked out new bedroom furniture together, and it was delivered yesterday afternoon after we picked up our keys and officially became the owners of our new home. We spent the night putting away our clothes and eating Thai food off the kitchen floor before we went back to our condo for one last night.

Oh sorry. One more thing. While we waited for the food to come, Jennie told me she wanted to christen our new house. I was already pulling my pants off before she could finish the request.

But it was when she pulled that little pink glass plug from her bag that I really began to short-circuit. I stood there with one foot stuck in my pants, the other pantleg in my hand, my jaw hanging as she slowly undressed, hoisted herself up on our kitchen island, spread her legs, and showed me how wet she was. When she finished giving herself her first orgasm, she held out the glass plug and asked me to fuck her.

So I did. Bent over the counter, on her hands and knees on the staircase, up against the window in the bedroom, and again under the spray of the shower.

Needless to say, we're big fans of that little glass plug.

I listen carefully, checking that I'm alone. When all I'm met with is the sound of chatter and laughter from downstairs, I cautiously pull open the top drawer of my dresser. I reach toward the back, below piles of underwear, and wrap my fingers around the small object.

My heart thuds as I open the velvet box, revealing the oval sapphire inside, more teal than it is blue, the vintage gold band it's set on, the three small marquise diamonds framing each side of it like flower petals.

I've had this ring for three weeks now. I asked Carter and Holly to help me pick out some designs Jennie might like one day when she was out with the girls. Carter sat there with this dumbfounded expression while his mom squealed.

Don't you think it's a little soon? he'd asked. Holly had shoved him so hard he toppled out of his chair.

We never made it to the store. Holly slipped off her own engagement ring, looked down at it with tears in her eyes, and then pressed it into my palm.

I remember finding the letters *H+T* inside the band, Jennie's parents' initials etched right next to a heart, the way I held the ring and just knew their love was the forever kind, the type that doesn't end despite the distance. Now, on the other side of the heart, *J+G* lives.

I can't wait to love Jennie forever.

"Garrett, I'm going to pick up some pizza and—" Jennie stops in the doorway, mouth gaping as she watches me shove the box back into my drawer and slam it so fast I catch my finger in the process.

"Motherfucker," I gasp, clutching my throbbing finger before I drop my elbow to the dresser, my chin to my fist, swallowing down the pain. "Jennie. Hey. S'up?"

Her brows do a slow rise. "S'up?"

"Mhmm. S'up."

With every slow, calculated step Jennie takes in my direction, my pulse races faster. I resist the urge to pick up the dresser, run it across the room, and throw it out the fucking window.

"What was that?" she asks.

"Hmm? What was what?"

She points to the drawer. "That."

"That what?" I glance at the drawer. "Oh this? It's my underwear drawer. Just making sure everything was...in...order...in there?" My eyes narrow painfully as I try not to cringe.

"Mhmm. And the box you threw inside?"

"The—the box? Oh, *the box*. Yeah, why didn't you say so?"

Why is her eyebrow arched so high on her forehead? Why won't she let me get away with lying to her just once? What's so hard about that? Can't she be nice to me *for once in my fucking life*?

"Would you believe me if I said it was a new toy for us to play with?"

She pins her arms across her chest and pops a hip. "I would not."

I throw my arms up in mock surrender. "Ah, well. I tried." I lift her off her feet and tow her out of the bedroom. "Let's go. Tons to do. Can't be standing around chatting to you about nothing."

She kicks her legs through the air, wriggling until I'm forced to put her down.

"What are you doing?" I ask on a huff.

"What are *you* doing?"

"I asked you first."

Her gaze slants, and then she swivels, sprinting back toward the bedroom. I catch her around the waist and shove her against the wall.

"I don't fucking think so," I murmur.

"But I—"

"Drop it," I whisper, trailing my mouth down her throat.

She sighs. "Fine. How long am I dropping it for?"

"How long do you want to drop it for?"

There's that Beckett blush, rare as all hell as she starts nibbling on the tip of her thumbnail. She lifts a shoulder. "Not that long."

"No?"

She shakes her head slowly, teeth pressing into her bottom lip with her shy smile.

"Well, you're still young. There's no rush."

"Right, right, right," she hums, nodding. Another shrug. "Well, I'll be twenty-five in a few months. I'm not *that* young."

"Quarter of a century," I point out.

"Halfway to fifty," she adds, hand at her chin as she holds her elbow and looks me over. "And you're not getting any younger, big guy."

"There is that," I agree.

"Plus, you already know you wanna be with me forever."

"Mmm, that's true. I do."

"So there's no sense in waiting all that long." A devious smirk blooms, and her fingers walk up my chest. She sinks them into my hair and angles my mouth above hers. "Unless you're scared. Are you scared, Gare-Bear?"

"So scared. What if you say no? Worse, what if you say yes? A lifetime of you snoring? Crying to Disney movies and dancing through the house? Making you hot chocolate with extra marshmallows and tickling your back while you snuggle up to me in bed? Ugh." I shudder. "Sounds like the worst life."

"You accidentally swapped your words. You were supposed to say *best*. That sounds like the *best* life. But I suppose it's natural to fear greatness. If you don't think you can handle me—"

Her words die a gasp when I pin her to the wall with my hips, wrists locked in my hands on either side of her head. "I'll marry you right the fuck now. Don't test me, baby Beckett."

She squirms, hips lifting. "I'm not a baby."

"No, you're not." I release one wrist so I can grab a fistful of her stellar ass and hoist her up to me, long legs coming around my waist. I drop my lips to her soft ones. "You're my sunshine, and one day, you'll be my wife."

"Okay," she says on a soft sigh as my mouth trails her jaw. "That sounds nice."

"I can't wait to fuck you for the rest of my life."

"Hey, Jennie, are we gettin' that pizza or—" Carter's words end a shriek as he stops at the top of the staircase, horrified gaze glued to our intimate position. I can only assume he heard my last words too.

I sigh, more irritated than anything that now I'm going to have to hear about his new trauma for at least the next month.

Carter spins away from us. "*Ollie! I need help!*"

"Do your breathing exercises, babe!" she shouts back.

His footsteps thud so quickly down the stairs it's a wonder he doesn't faceplant. "*I don't remember how!*"

I look back at my sunshine, the smug smirk on her beautiful face. Her fingers thread through my hair, and she lifts one shoulder in an innocent shrug.

"Oops."

ACKNOWLEDGMENTS

To my husband, for pushing me to chase my dreams.

To my girls—Hannah, Jerry, and Ki—thanks for keeping me young, even though I'm older than all of you. I'm so thankful to have you.

Liz, my American soul sister, your friendship is priceless, and I don't know where I'd be without you.

Zahra, thank you for hyping up this book well before I even had a release date. Thank you for loving Jennie and Garrett, and for being such a positive light in my book world.

To Alana, for bringing all my hockey sticker visions to life. You're amazing.

To Paisley, my lifelong friend turned editor. I'm never letting you go, ever. You're stuck with me, and I wouldn't have it any other way.

To Miss Bizzarro, always, for being the kind of teacher who's impossible to forget.

To my readers, for going on these journeys with me, for loving my characters, no matter how ridiculous and ostentatious they may be, for dealing with the drama on the way to that happily ever after.

And to my older brother, for being by my side, even though I can't see him.

From the bottom of my heart, thank you.

ABOUT THE AUTHOR

Becka is a steamy romance author, self-proclaimed sarcasm queen, professional procrastinator, and a superfan of dragging her readers through hell and back on the way to a happy ending.

When she's not staring blankly at her computer screen or deleting close to two hundred occurrences of the word *just* from her manuscript, she can be found teaching kindergarten (*gasp!*) in Ontario, Canada, and mom-ing with her incredibly sweet and beautiful little boy (he takes after his mama) and her animals.

Though she's always been an avid reader and forever dreamt of becoming an author, Becka didn't begin writing books until after the loss of her brother. While she loves to include all the fun stuff like heat, humor, and alpha men who are secret teddy bears, her writing comes from a place of heavy emotions, and she often can't resist letting those emotions seep into her pages.

Becka is so excited to share this journey with you!

Want some bonus scenes? Exclusive sneak peeks at what's next? Dying for Adam's book, and maybe Jaxon's too?

Head to Becka's website and sign up for her newsletter, and keep in touch by joining her Facebook group, Becka's Book Babes!

www.beckamack.com